Mary Fi...

The Very Thought of You

arrow books

1 3 5 7 9 10 8 6 4 2

Arrow Books
20 Vauxhall Bridge Road
London SW1V 2SA

Arrow Books is part of the Penguin Random House group of companies
whose addresses can be found at global.penguinrandomhouse.com.

Penguin
Random House
UK

First published in paperback by Arrow Books in 2015

www.randomhouse.co.uk

A CIP catalogue record for this book is
available from the British Library.

ISBN 9780099585459

Typeset in Palatino Std (11/13.5pt) by SX Composing DTP, Rayleigh, Essex
Printed and bound by CPI Group (UK) Ltd, Croydon, CR0 4YY

MIX
Paper from
responsible sources
FSC
www.fsc.org   FSC® C018179

Penguin Random House is committed to a sustainable future
for our business, our readers and our planet. This book is
made from Forest Stewardship Council® certified paper.

Chapter 1

London, Spring 1944

She watched the boy as he cycled slowly up the street. He was looking at the numbers on the doors of the red-brick terrace; then, satisfied that they were properly running in order, he speeded up.

There was no hesitation in her movement away from the window because she knew. She'd been expecting it for two years, and when the knock came, Catherine opened the door and held out her hand.

'Are you…' the telegraph boy hesitated, studying the name on the brown envelope, 'Mrs Fletcher? Mrs Catherine Fletcher?'

'Yes,' she said. Strangely, she felt quite calm, but her mother, Honorine, who had come from the back kitchen with six-month-old Lili in her arms, whispered, '*Mon Dieu, mon Dieu,*' and sat down heavily on the second step of the flight of stairs.

'I'm sorry,' the telegraph boy said awkwardly, as he put the envelope in Catherine's upturned palm. He was fifteen, and this was his second week at work, but he knew what the telegram contained and he wouldn't look Catherine in the eye. But this woman was composed, quiet, almost normal and he was the one who felt unnerved and gripped the handlebars of his bike tightly as he climbed on it.

'Ta-ra,' he said, and didn't look back as he cycled rapidly down the street and round the corner.

Catherine turned the envelope over in her hands. I have to open it, she told herself. Now, this minute, but, oh God, if I do, it will become real. She closed the door and walked back into the small front room. It was a room she was proud of, clean and well furnished with two comfortable armchairs and an Afghan rug.

Fitted bookcases filled the gaps on either side of the fireplace, full of books, mostly unread now, but dusted every day. There were two photographs on the cream tiled mantelpiece. One was of her in a long dress standing in front of a microphone, while arranged behind her was the band Bobby Crewe's Melody Men. She'd been their singer and had been so good that other bands had started sniffing around, eager to poach her.

But it was the other photograph she lingered over. It was of her on her wedding day, and she stood for a moment, staring at it. What a lovely day it had been, and how happy and proud she'd felt in her neat suit, with her arm tucked securely in Christopher's. The photograph was in black and white, but she saw the scene in colour. Her sky-blue suit with its narrow belt and box pleats, and Christopher's khaki uniform and his maroon cap with the winged badge of the Parachute Regiment. Everyone said what a handsome couple they were. Catherine so pretty with her shiny dark hair and enigmatic brown eyes, and Christopher tall and strong with an athleticism that belied his peacetime job as a college lecturer. He looked as if nothing could ever hurt him. But now?

She swallowed and turned round to face her mother

and her baby daughter. Both were silent, but tears were beginning to spill from her mother's eyes.

'Open it, *chérie*,' her mother whispered. 'You have to know.'

A hundred miles away from that street in London, Frances Parnell groaned as she heaved a sack of potatoes into the larder. She'd just driven it from the Home Farm, where Seth, the old tenant, had told her it was the last he had. 'The rest's gone to the military,' he said, chewing on his empty pipe. 'The buggers have taken everything.'

'I hope they paid you,' Frances said. She was concerned because Seth and Bessie, his wife, were on their own now. Both their boys were in the services, and although they did have a farmhand, he was older than Seth and no real help at all.

'Gave me a chitty,' Seth grunted. 'I'll get the money, but it'll take a few weeks.'

They were in the farmhouse kitchen and Bessie put a pot of tea and a plate of scones on the table. 'Take one, lovey,' she smiled at Frances. 'I've got more in the pantry. And take a couple home for Johnny.'

'Thanks,' Frances said, and smiled back at this woman she'd known all her life. 'Have you heard from young Seth or Eddie?'

Bessie nodded happily. 'We had a note from Eddie. He's here in England, I think. And he's well.'

'Going on about some girl he's courting.' Seth snorted. 'No better than she should be, I dare say.'

Bessie frowned. 'You old fool,' she growled. 'Our Eddie wouldn't even look at someone like that.'

Frances could feel a row brewing. This was exactly

3

how her mother and father started one of their monumental arguments. 'And young Seth? Have you heard from him?'

The old couple shook their heads.

'He's overseas. Don't know where,' Bessie sighed.

'Well' – Frances got up – 'I must get moving.' She put half a crown on the table. 'This is for the spuds, Seth. See you soon.' And with a wave she went out into the yard and drove home with the potato sack lurching around in the bucket of the old tractor.

All the way home she thought about money. How the hell were they going to manage? The electricity bill was enormous, and somehow she'd have to find enough cash to pay Maggie, the housekeeper, and Janet, the youngster her mother had just employed to do the rough work. Once again, Frances wondered if her mother really understood that the family was close to being broke, that living in their great house cost a fortune and that having a title counted for nothing with the coal merchant.

'You'll have to tell her, Pa,' Frances said to her father, when she'd washed her hands and joined him in the library. He was sitting in his leather chair struggling to make sense of a mounting pile of bills. 'She's taken on a girl from the village and we'll have to find the money for her.'

'I know, darling, and I have had words with your mother.' John Parnell raised his hands in a gesture of desperation and ran them through his salt-and-pepper hair. 'But she doesn't understand. We should have got rid of this bloody house long before the war. It's nothing but a millstone hanging round all our necks.'

'We mustn't get rid of the house,' Frances said fiercely. 'Hugo had really workable plans to raise money. The farms could be run more efficiently, he was sure of that, and he was going to improve the shooting. It's ridiculous raising the birds for only our friends to shoot when wealthy people from the city would pay for the opportunity. And then he was going to turn the stables into mews houses and rent them out.' She drummed her fingers on the desk to emphasise the point. 'Other people with houses like ours have done this sort of thing. We can't go under, not now.'

Her father sighed and leant back in his chair. 'Hugo's plans will have to go on hold until the war is ended, and, God willing, that won't be long now. The air war is over, and Hitler is retreating from the East. Invasion must be the next step. With our troops fighting on French soil, surely the Germans won't hold out, and then we'll be able to concentrate on the Japs. Then the boy will come home.'

Frances said nothing. Her elder brother, Hugo, was a prisoner of war in the Far East; at least, he had been when they'd last heard of him, eight months ago. Awful stories were coming out about the treatment of prisoners in Burma. Her breath caught in her throat. Oh God, she prayed. Let him be alright.

Lord Parnell cleared his throat. He knew what Frances was thinking because that was what preyed on his mind too. 'Anyway,' he said, 'somehow we have to get our hands on extra money.' He gave her a sideways glance. 'Of course, we could do something about selling the paintings in the long gallery. I mean, they would raise—' He got no further.

'Absolutely not, Pa,' Frances said hotly. 'Hugo would be furious. They're his inheritance.'

The two, so alike in looks, glowered at each other until Frances broke the silence. 'Look, Pa,' she said, 'I've decided I'm going to get a job. Beau Bennett offered me something when he came down last weekend.'

'A job? With Beau Bennett? Rolly Bennett's youngest?' Lord Parnell looked up in astonishment. 'What sort of a job?' He furrowed his eyebrows. 'Isn't he connected to the theatre? Some sort of actor? My God, Frances, you can't be serious.'

'I am,' she said with a grin, crinkling up her hazel eyes and tossing her long red hair. 'We need the cash.'

Della Stafford sat in the steamy cafe opposite the theatre and ordered cheese on toast. She was on her own, by choice, having grown tired of the constant chatter of her fellow chorus girls.

'Tea?' the waitress asked, and Della nodded.

'Alright.' The girl walked to the next table to pick up some dirty cups. A newspaper had been left on the seat and she held it up. 'D'you want this?'

'Thanks,' said Della, and reached over to take it. She put it on the table while she searched in her bag for her cigarettes. Damn, they weren't there. She must have left the packet in the dressing room she shared with the other girls. That's the last she'd see of those. Oh hell, she sighed, this day had gone from bad to worse.

Arriving at the theatre for the matinee, she'd been called into the manager's office. 'Miss Stafford,' he'd said, not getting up, but spreading his pudgy hands on the desk in front of him and giving her one of his leering

6

stares. 'We're making changes. Changing the act. Something fresh for the punters. And I'm thinking of you, sugar, because you're not bad-looking and you got a cracking figure. I love that blonde hair, never mind that it comes out of a bottle.'

Della narrowed her eyes. She didn't trust him. 'What changes?'

He had the grace to look away from her, swivelling his chair round so that he could look out of the window onto the grimy roofs and chimney pots of Shaftesbury Avenue. 'Well,' he said, 'I was thinking of something along the lines of what they do at the Windmill…'

'What?' Della said, horrified. 'A nude show? Striptease? Here?'

Abe Carson swivelled back to face her. 'Calm down, ducky. I've already put it to some of the other girls and they don't mind. What's the matter with showing a bit of flesh? I expect you've shown it to one or two boyfriends, so what's the difference?'

Della had stared at him. He was utterly loathsome, but she'd known that already. 'You'll never do it,' she said, as she walked towards the door. 'You won't get permission.'

'But if I do,' he called after her, 'you could be my lead girl, and there'd be more pay for that.'

Not bothering to reply, Della slammed the door after her and walked away. Now, after the normal matinee performance, she was still furious. How dare he? How could he imagine that she would be prepared to strip? To be part of a tawdry show when she was a trained dancer and had worked in the business since she was a youngster? I'm better than that, she told herself. So much better, and I'll have a career in the theatre if it kills me.

Was it fate that the paper the waitress had passed to her was the *Stage*? And that the first advert she saw was for performers to join a new company that was being formed specially to entertain the troops? She read the advert three times before getting up and going down the street to the telephone box.

'Sid?' she enquired when the phone was answered.

'Who's this?' the old man's breathless voice answered.

'Della. Della Stafford. Listen, Sid, I'm thinking of leaving the show and joining another company. One of these ENSA sort of groups. What d'you think?'

There was a long silence and Della could imagine what was going on at the other end. He'd be shuffling papers around on his desk, a thin cigarette drooping from his lips and a glass of lemon tea steaming gently beside him. Sid Wiseman, her agent, was really well past it. He should have retired years ago. God knows he was already old when he'd taken Della on as a sixteen-year-old, dancing in a variety show. But he'd become a father figure and she clung to his opinion.

'I hear Abe Carson is thinking about a nudey show,' he gasped. 'Is that why?'

'Yes.'

'Mm. Not for you, darling.'

'I know, Sid. So if you've nothing for me, I'm going to this audition.'

Della heard the slurp as he took a gulp of tea. 'Nothing's come in, girl. Who's running this troupe?'

'I don't know,' she replied. 'It was only a small advert.'

'Well, then,' Sid grunted. 'My advice is to go for it. If

it works, you'll be seen by thousands, and I did hear that impresarios are on the lookout for new talent, now that the theatres are up and running again.'

'Thanks, Sid.' Della smiled at herself in the phone-box mirror. 'Take care.'

The auditions were held in a bleak church hall in a bombed-out street near the docks. This part of London had taken a battering a couple of years ago and many of the buildings, including the church, had been destroyed. But now, as weeds grew up through the ruined houses, people were going about their business and even a few shops were open. A man getting off the bus in front of Catherine shouted a cheeky greeting to a middle-aged woman who was, incongruously, among all the surrounding rubble, sweeping the pavement outside her shop. He got a cheeky reply and a grin. As Catherine alighted, she heaved a sigh. Life went on...for some.

It was cold in the church hall. The winter had been cold and wet, and early spring no better. Now, it was starting to rain again. It pattered through the holes in the roof and down onto the stone-flagged floor, where, mixed with bird lime dropped from the sparrows who were flying about the rafters, it formed a damp, slippery surface. Catherine looked at it in distaste and pulled her green coat closer. She was wearing a maroon shantung dress underneath the coat, one that she wore sometimes when she was on stage. And after all, this was an audition, wasn't it? But she did wonder if it was a bit showy. Looking around at the other performers who had drifted in, it seemed that nobody else had bothered to dress up.

They all stood close together in the only dry area.

Catherine counted twelve of them, eight women and four men. She recognised one of the men, Tommy Rudd, a piano player, who'd been an occasional member of Bobby Crewe's band. She smiled at him and he gave her a wave. Catherine tried to remember why he hadn't been called up. The band members were generally older men or had some disability, but Tommy Rudd was her age and looked perfectly healthy.

'Hello.' A tall blonde girl came to stand beside her. She wore a black suit with a fur tippet over her shoulders. 'It's bloody freezing in here,' she said. 'You'd never think it was nearly April.'

'Yes, it is cold,' Catherine agreed. 'I don't think the rain and the holes in the roof help.'

'I'm Della Stafford,' the girl said, and held out her hand.

'Catherine Fletcher. How d'you do?'

Della grinned. 'You've got an accent,' she said. 'What are you, French or something?'

'My mother is French, but I grew up here in London. Holidays with my grandparents at Amiens, though, so I suppose there's a trace of an accent. Most people don't hear it.'

'Oh, I did.' Della adjusted her tippet. 'There were lots of foreigners where I lived. By the docks, you know, in Liverpool. The whole place is buggered now. Like this place.' She looked at the other people waiting for the auditions to start. 'Let's see. Who's here? Oh look, the Miller sisters.'

'Who?' asked Catherine.

'The Miller sisters. Those over there.' Della jerked her head towards three middle-aged women who were standing close together. 'They do novelty songs. Getting a bit past it, I'd have said.' She gave a throaty laugh. 'D'you know anyone?'

Catherine pointed to Tommy Rudd. 'I know him. He's a pianist, plays sometimes with Bobby Crewe's band.'

'He's a bit of alright,' smiled Della, giving him the onceover. 'Wonder why he's not in the services?'

'I can't remember,' Catherine replied. 'I was told, I think.'

A man and a woman came from the door at the back of the hall. She was young, with red hair and wearing brown slacks and a corduroy jacket. Her companion looked a little older, and Catherine noticed that he walked with a stick, dragging one foot along the floor as though he'd lost the ability to lift it. Poor devil, she thought, he probably has.

The young woman jumped onto the little stage and clapped her hands. 'Hello, everybody. Thank you for coming. I'm Frances Parnell, assistant to Mr Bennett.' She pointed to her companion, who was standing beside the steps leading to the stage. He was in his late twenties, perhaps even thirty, Catherine decided, and good-looking with fair, brushed-back hair.

'I know him,' Della whispered. 'Beau Bennett. He was an actor before the war. I saw him in a Noël Coward.'

Frances held up her hand. 'I suppose you all read the advertisement, but I'll tell you a bit more. We're forming a troupe to entertain the military. Now, you've all heard of ENSA and we're going to be rather like them, but perhaps a little more adventurous. We hope to be going abroad, but we will entertain at home too, and not only soldiers. There are factory workers, dockers and miners who are all doing important war work and deserve attention and entertainment. We have government approval and the ability to pay a decent fee.'

She looked down at Beau, who gave her a nod, and then he turned to face the crowd.

'Listen,' he said. 'This won't be a cakewalk. We might go to places that are still war zones, and there won't be special facilities for changing or making up. That might have to be done in the back of a lorry. We'll probably have to sleep in tents and go behind a bush for the necessary. So anyone who isn't prepared for that, please leave now.'

There was the tip, tap of high heels on flagstones as the Miller sisters bustled out. 'Behind a bush,' one of them said in an indignant voice. 'I never heard the like. We're artistes.'

Frances watched them go. 'Oh dear,' she said. 'But never mind, let's get on. We've got a piano' – she indicated an ancient upright, which stood rather unsteadily on the floor beside the steps that led up to the stage – 'but sadly, no pianist. He's cried off. I don't suppose…'

Tommy Rudd held up his hand. 'I'm a piano player. And guitar, when necessary.'

'Oh jolly good.' Frances smiled and waved her hand towards the piano. 'If you don't mind, Mr…?'

'Rudd. Tommy Rudd.'

Beau Bennett leant against the piano. 'I'm looking for singers,' he said. 'Anyone?'

Catherine walked forward. 'I'm a singer,' she said. 'I've been appearing with Bobby Crewe's Melody Men. I'm Catherine Fletcher.'

'I've seen you,' Beau grinned. 'At the Kit Kat Club.

You were brilliant. But I thought you'd retired.'

'No, not really. I had a little girl and my husband was overseas. Now I'm looking for work again.'

Beau grinned and grasped her hand. 'We'll start off with you, then, Mrs Fletcher. Set the standard for us, eh?'

She took off her coat and gave her music to Tommy Rudd. There was a murmur of appreciation as he played the opening bars, and then when she sang 'The Very Thought of You' in her wonderfully melodic voice, the room fell silent. Even the birds, perched on the rafters, seemed to stop their twittering. Despite her steeling herself to remain professional, Christopher was foremost in her mind, and that gave an extra poignancy to her performance.

'Oh my God,' Beau said, when she'd finished. 'That was just perfect, and if you're prepared to join our little venture, we'd be honoured to have you.'

'Thank you.'

Catherine smiled and looked over to Della, who gave her a thumbs-up sign and then, pushing herself to the front of the group, shouted, 'I'm a singer too.'

'Come on up – let's see what you can do,' said Beau, and without a moment's hesitation Della handed Catherine her fur tippet and stepped out of her skirt. Underneath, she was wearing a pair of red taffeta shorts over fishnet tights. When she sang 'Ain't She Sweet?', it was clear that she hadn't much of a voice, but she tap-danced in between the second verse and the chorus, and ended with a twirl and the splits.

'Wow!' Beau laughed. 'That'll cheer up the boys. You're hired. Give your details to Frances.'

In the end, six of the performers were hired. Catherine

and Della, along with Tommy Rudd and a ventriloquist, a magician and an older man who had a fine tenor voice. The rafters of the old church throbbed when he sang 'On the Road to Mandalay'.

On the bus going home, Catherine smiled to herself. She had a new job and had made a new friend. Best of all, she had been able to say out loud to Frances that her husband had been posted missing in action without bursting into tears. This is what I need, she told herself. Then perhaps I'll be able to come to terms with it.

Della lit a cigarette as she sat on her bus back to her room in Soho. Thank Christ, she thought. I can go and tell Abe Carson where to stick his striptease show. I've joined a new company, and Beau Bennett has good theatre connections. This is a definite step towards stardom.

And Frances, driving the truck back to Beau's flat with him asleep in the passenger seat, grinned. She'd had her first ever pay, in cash, and half of it had gone in an envelope and been sent to her father. It wasn't much, but it would help. Somehow, she'd have to work out how to get more.

Chapter 2

'Where are we going?' Della asked, looking from one to the other of the Bennett Players, who were lurching around in the back of the truck. 'Anyone know?'

'Er...Frances said something about Kent. An airfield, I think,' Godfrey James, the tenor, said hesitantly. 'Don't take my word, though. It isn't gospel.'

He was always hesitant, although he often bellowed when he spoke. Della guessed that it was a nervous habit and that someone was regularly putting him down. His wife, obviously. She'd been with him at the meeting point at Victoria Station and Della had taken an immediate dislike to her. She was a gaunt woman with an over-powdered face, taller than Godfrey and evidently under the illusion that she was coming on the trip too.

'Sorry,' said Frances. 'Performers only.'

'But I always accompany Mr James to the theatre,' Gertrude James had said indignantly. 'He needs me.'

'I'm afraid that isn't possible.' Frances was checking off the members of the company on her clipboard as they drifted in and gathered on the pavement outside the station. The truck was pulled up ready for them, and Beau was sitting impatiently in the passenger seat and tapping his watch. Frances waved her arm. 'All aboard,' she called.

Mrs James opened her mouth to argue, but Frances

turned her head to look at her. 'Yes?' she enquired sharply. 'Was there something else?'

Della dug Catherine in the ribs. 'D'you see that?' she whispered. 'She sounds as if she's speaking to one of the servants.'

Catherine smiled and started to climb into the truck. She was excited. This would be the first time she'd sung in front of an audience for nearly a year, and although part of her felt that she might be letting down the memory of Christopher, she was looking forward to the show. Tommy Rudd had a feel for her style and the couple of rehearsals at the church hall they'd had between the auditions and this, the first performance, had gone well.

'You're singing better than ever,' Tommy had said admiringly from his seat at the piano. 'More depth, more emotion.'

'D'you think so?' Catherine had asked. She leant over him to pick up her music, but he was taller than she remembered and her breast brushed against his head. 'Sorry,' she said quickly.

'Don't worry,' he grinned. 'I liked it.'

Her face hardened. 'I didn't,' she said coldly, and grabbing her coat, walked to the door.

Della watched her go. 'You're out of luck there, Tommy,' she laughed, and moving up to the piano, handed him her music. 'She's still in mourning.'

'I thought he was only posted as missing.' Tommy took a quick drag on his Woodbine and put the music sheet on top of the battered piano. It had lost its stand.

'"Posted missing" is a nice way of saying he's dead but they can't find the body.' Della shrugged. 'He's probably been blown up.'

16

'Christ,' said Tommy, running a hand through his black hair, 'you're hard.'

'Am I?' she asked. 'Or perhaps I'm being realistic. I lost someone that way, right at the beginning. It's better to know straight away.'

Frances, who had been sitting on the edge of the stage, interrupted. 'Get a move on, you two. We've only got this hall for another half-hour: the Home Guard meets here most evenings. And, Della, Beau wants you to open the show with an upbeat number, perhaps the one you did for the audition. It'll get everyone in the mood. He hasn't entirely worked out the rest yet, but rehearse at least one more number, because you'll be on again.'

Della did her song, belting it out as she'd done before and making the birds in the rafters fly about in alarm. An old man in Home Guard uniform, who'd walked in just before she started, gave enthusiastic applause and Della gave him an exaggerated curtsey.

'What about us?' The fruity voice belonged to Captain Fortescue, the ventriloquist's dummy. It had a monocle and was dressed in uniform, and always spoke before Eric Baxter, his alter ego. 'We've been first on the bill, don't you know? Not used to being overlooked, old girl.'

Frances turned her head towards Eric, who was sitting on the stage steps with Captain Fortescue on his knee. She gave him one of her haughty glares. 'Mr Baxter, you will not be first on the bill in this company. Mr Bennett is thinking of putting you on third, after Signor Splendoso's magic act, and Mr James will follow you. Beau is determined that Mrs Fletcher will have top billing.'

Captain Fortescue's painted eyebrows jerked up and

down angrily, and he gave what sounded like a growl. 'I call that a poor show, young woman. A damn poor show indeed.'

Frances stood up. 'Mr Baxter, when the order of performance has been decided, we won't be changing it, and what's more, I'd be very grateful if when you speak to me, you'd use your own voice and not that of the doll.'

Tommy Rudd gave a low whistle. 'My God,' he whispered to Della, 'she's treading on dangerous ground. Eric Baxter is not someone to cross. I've heard that he can be a bastard if he takes against you.'

Eric Baxter's own voice, when he answered, had a sort of indeterminate northern inflection, almost as though he'd forgotten what it was supposed to sound like. 'It's called a dummy, Miss Parnell, not a doll, and I'd be grateful also if you could remember that.' He stood up then and, opening his large suitcase, carefully packed Captain Fortescue inside it with the dummy's head laid on a purple satin cushion. The suitcase was snapped shut, and picking it up and his grey trilby, Eric prepared to leave. 'Good afternoon, ladies and gentlemen,' he said, as he walked towards the door. He spoke in the captain's voice.

The rehearsal ended on that sour note as more members of the local Home Guard shuffled in. 'Hello,' said one old man. 'Who's going to give us a turn?'

'Sorry, darling,' Della grinned, 'I've got to get my bus.' She cocked her head at him. 'Besides, my turn would give you a stroke.'

The man who'd been in earlier listening to Della's song chuckled. 'You've missed a treat,' he said to his colleagues. 'This one's a real saucy minx.'

Outside, the sun had come out, promising a lovely

end to the day. 'Fancy a drink?' asked Tommy. 'There's not a bad pub on the corner.'

Della considered his offer. They'd be working together, so they ought to be pals; besides, he was a good accompanist and would be useful if she decided to take up singing full-time. 'Yes, why not?' she smiled. 'A quick one, though, and you can tell me why you aren't in the forces.'

She thought about what he'd told her as they sat in the rattling truck. 'Dicky heart,' he'd said. 'I forget exactly what the doc said, but it was enough to have me classified not fit for service.'

'Crikey!' she'd laughed, looking for something cheerful to say. 'I hope you're not going to peg out in the middle of my act.'

Tommy had taken a swig of his drink. 'Depends what you do,' he said. 'Start stripping and you might be in for a shock.'

He'd laughed it off as nothing important, but obviously it was, and when the truck slowed down at the guard barrier to the airfield, she noticed that he took a deep breath. Having to hang on as the truck lurched around the country lanes had not suited him.

They stopped in front of a large Nissen hut and a corporal came running out with a wooden block to help them step down. 'We've cleared an area in one of the hangars for the performance and cobbled together a sort of makeshift stage,' he said, when everyone had emerged from the truck. He looked at Beau. 'Are you Major Bennett, sir?'

Beau nodded and held out his hand. 'Civilian now, Corporal. Are we alright for the show to go on at six?'

'Yes, sir.' The corporal looked at Catherine and Della. 'The ladies could change in one of the empty rooms in the crew quarters, and the men in another, and,' the corporal continued with a grin, 'the Wing Commander wonders if you'd like a cup of tea in the mess before you start. I'll lead the way.'

'Thank you, Corporal. We'll be with you in a sec.' Beau turned to the group. 'Listen,' he said, 'there's some people from the Ministry coming to see us tonight. If we impress, they'll keep us funded and, after we've done this tour, might…possibly…send us overseas. Which is what we want, isn't it?'

There was a murmur of agreement and Beau nodded. 'Good,' he said. 'You're all professionals, so I know you'll be fine.' He jerked his head to Frances and she shepherded the rest of the company to follow the corporal into the wooden mess hall. Catherine walked with Della and was just about to go inside when she heard her name being called.

'Mrs Fletcher?' It was Beau. 'Can I have a moment?'

Della raised her eyebrows and said under her breath, 'What's this about?'

'I don't know,' Catherine said. 'Perhaps I'm getting the sack.'

'Not you,' Della laughed, but she looked back over her shoulder as she followed the corporal into the mess hall.

Catherine walked back to where Beau was standing beside the truck. 'Please call me "Catherine",' she said, 'and drop the "Mrs Fletcher". If we're going to be in close proximity for the next few months, it would be silly to be so formal.'

20

'I agree,' he smiled, 'and I'm Beau. I'll tell the others too.' A spasm of pain washed over his face and he leant heavily on his stick for a moment. 'Damn!' he gasped. 'This bloody leg gives me gyp sometimes.'

She gently put a hand on his arm. 'Can I do something?'

'No, thanks.' He bit his lip and stood up straighter. 'I'm alright. Now, Catherine, someone from the War Office wants to speak to you. He's here tonight, so before you go on, can you have a word with him?'

Catherine felt her stomach rising into her chest and for a moment thought she might faint. 'Is it about my husband?' she whispered.

Beau immediately looked embarrassed. 'Oh God, sorry. I forgot about your husband, and I didn't mean to upset you. Honestly, I don't know what he wants, but…if you could see him?'

She nodded, in control of herself now. 'Where is he?'

'In the Wing Co.'s office. I'll get Frances to go with you.'

Frances and Catherine waited in an outer office while a sergeant knocked on the Wing Commander's door and announced who they were. When they were shown in, Catherine was surprised to see only one man, not an RAF officer, as they'd expected, but a man in civilian clothes.

'Good evening,' he said, looking from one to the other. 'I'm Robert Lennox, and one of you two ladies must be Mrs Catherine Fletcher?'

'That's me,' said Catherine, looking up at him. He was tall, with brown eyes and reddish-brown hair. He wore tortoiseshell-rimmed glasses that made him look middle-aged, but glancing at him again, Catherine decided that he was, in fact, quite young, perhaps thirty but not much more. There was a snort and a giggle from beside her and Frances stepped forward.

'Robbie?' She stuck out her hand. 'Don't you remember me? Fran Parnell. Hugo's sister. You used to come to our house during the holidays.'

'Good God, yes.' He smiled and grasped her hand. 'You've grown up. But what are you doing here? Don't tell me that Beau's got you working for him?'

'Yes,' she laughed. 'Needs must, I'm afraid. The old pile is falling down, and what with Hugo—'

'I heard,' he said quickly. 'It's tough.'

'But what about you?' she asked. 'I thought you'd joined up.'

'Ah,' he coughed. 'Long story with which I won't bore you.' He turned to Catherine and took her hand. 'How d'you do, Mrs Fletcher? I wonder if we might have a little chat.'

'Is it about my husband?' she asked. 'Has he been found?'

'I'm afraid not,' he said, and gave her an odd smile. 'I don't suppose that you've heard from him and not told us?'

'No,' Catherine said, astonished, and glanced at Frances to see what she thought of Mr Lennox's suggestion. Frances was frowning. 'No, I haven't,' Catherine insisted. 'That is a ridiculous suggestion.'

Robert nodded. 'Yes, of course you would have let the authorities know. Sorry. But there is something else.' He glanced over to Frances. 'Fran, d'you mind? This is rather private.'

She looked surprised, but giving Catherine's arm a squeeze, turned and left, closing the door behind her.

'Now, Mrs Fletcher, shall we sit down?' He indicated the seat in front of the desk, and he took the wing commander's chair on the other side. 'I understand from Major Bennett that you are half French. Is that so?'

'Yes,' Catherine nodded. 'My mother is from Amiens.'

'And you are bilingual?'

Again she nodded.

He spoke rapidly to her in French, making a remark about her act and asking how she'd started singing. She answered him, a little hesitantly at first, and then more confidently, using the language that was as much used when she was growing up as English.

'Very good,' Mr Lennox smiled. 'I would say accentless.'

Catherine was bewildered. Did they want her to sing in French as part of her act? That was fine: she could do that. She knew quite a few ballads and had sung Rina Ketty's 'I Will Wait' often.

'The thing is, Mrs Fletcher, I work for a department in Whitehall that – how shall I put it? – er...gathers information.' He leant back in the chair and took off his glasses, then polished them on his tie. Without them, his face was younger, cleverer, not so owlish. 'Now, Catherine...May I call you that? When you go abroad with the Bennett Players, you could be very useful to us.'

'But how?' Catherine was alarmed. 'Surely we'll only be going to the places that have been liberated?'

'Yes, officially. But with your ability to speak the language, there's no reason why you couldn't do some work for us.'

She stared at him, confused. What on earth was he saying? Did he want her to go into occupied France and spy for him, putting her life in danger?

'I couldn't,' Catherine said. 'It's out of the question, Mr Lennox. I have a little girl. And with my husband missing…I couldn't possibly do anything like you're suggesting.'

Robert steepled his fingers under his chin. 'I know about your daughter, Lili,' he said. 'I know that your mother – Honorine, is it? – looks after her when you're away. Since Beau mentioned you, we've done some investigations and you seem to be perfect for our purposes. And the singing is excellent cover.'

Catherine gazed at him. He knew her mother's name and that of her little girl. He or someone else must have been watching her. Watching her home, and maybe even following when she went to the shops or on the bus to the church hall for rehearsals. Suddenly she felt angry. How dare he? Haven't I got enough to contend with?

Robert must have noticed the change in her expression because he replaced his glasses before saying slowly, 'But, of course, Mrs Fletcher, nobody intends to make you do something you aren't comfortable with.'

Catherine stood up. 'I'm sorry, Mr Lennox. This isn't something that I'm prepared to even think about. I'm a singer. Nothing else.'

'So I can't persuade you?'

'No.' Catherine shook her head.

'Even though I can assure you that it would be vital for the war effort?'

'No.'

'Then' – Robert stood up – 'this conversation is at an

end. You will, of course, say nothing to your friends or to your mother.' Suddenly his charm seemed to have evaporated, and his brown eyes drilled into her face. 'I mean it. Tell them that I wanted you to do some translation work when you go overseas.' He walked round the desk and put out his hand. 'But I am very sorry.' His charm had returned, and his face softened into a smile. 'Maybe we'll speak again when you've thought it over.' He ushered her to the door. 'Now, I shall stay to hear you sing.' He grinned. 'Beau tells me I'm in for a treat.'

The show went well and the aircraft hangar rang with cheers after each turn. Signor Splendoso's magic act was received with gasps of surprise and much applause, and even Eric Baxter and Captain Fortescue found an appreciative audience. His jokes were very near the knuckle, but, Catherine supposed, from where she was standing with Della and Frances at the side of the stage, suitable for the young airmen and their girlfriends.

'I don't like him,' Frances whispered. 'He gives me the creeps.'

'He's popular with the audience,' Della said, 'but he's a nasty piece of work. Take my advice – don't cross him.'

Catherine closed the first half of the show singing 'I'll Be Seeing You' and the audience went wild. She could see Beau grinning like an idiot and Robert Lennox nodding slowly. Two civilians sitting in the front row applauded vigorously, and looking back to Beau, she saw him jerk his head towards them. She guessed that they were the men from the Ministry.

'That was terrific,' muttered Tommy after they came off. 'It's "The Very Thought of You" for the second half, yes?'

'Perhaps not,' she said. 'Hang on a minute while I get my music case.' She always carried her old case containing sheet music, and she was sure that somewhere within the collection of scores was the one she wanted. 'Look,' she said, pulling it out. 'Can you play this?'

'Of course,' Tommy grinned. 'I can't pronounce it, but I can play it.'

'Good,' she said. 'I'll sing it first in French and then in English.'

'You've cleared it with Beau?'

She shrugged. 'He'll have to like it or lump it.'

Myriad emotions were running through her when she went onto the stage as the last act. She felt exhausted by the whole experience of performing, and then, on top of that, there was the conversation she'd had with Mr Lennox. I'm not a fool, she thought. I know what he wants me to do. And I won't.

Tommy played the opening bars and she could see Beau frowning. This wasn't what he'd put on the play sheet. She had a moment of panic, wondering if her decision was right. Turning her head to Tommy, she held up her hand to stop him playing and then faced the audience once more.

'I'm going to sing something that means a lot to me. My husband, Christopher, who is a lieutenant in the Parachute Regiment, has been posted missing. I know he'll come home to me, and this song conveys everything that I feel about him. In French, it is "*J'attendrai*", which means "I Will Wait".' She paused and took a deep breath before speaking again, her eyes searching every face she could see. 'Believe me, like wives and sweethearts every-where, I *will* wait for him.'

26

A ripple of applause sounded throughout the hangar as she turned and nodded to Tommy.

Her wonderfully melodic voice soared to the rafters and not a few men had a tear in their eye as she sang. For a heart-stopping few seconds after she finished, there was silence, and then the place erupted in cheers. 'Bravo,' they cried, and men rushed towards the makeshift stage to shake her hand.

'Well done,' Beau, who had moved with the general rush, whispered in her ear.

Catherine glanced across to Robert Lennox and noticed that he was blowing his nose furiously. When he saw her looking, he turned away and walked out of the door.

'That was bloody good,' said Della, when the show was over and the airmen and their girls had filtered away.

'Thanks.' Catherine had a quick look over her shoulder to Beau, who was talking to Frances. 'I thought he'd be angry with me for changing the agreed song.'

'He wouldn't dare. Just you see.'

Frances joined them. 'Beau wants you to keep that number in,' she said, 'and he'd like you to speak to the audience as you did just now.'

'Alright.' Catherine raised her eyebrows to Della, who gave a little 'I told you so' grin.

'And' – Frances put her hand on Catherine's arm – 'I thought your song was so right. It made me think of...' She gave herself a shake. 'Well, that doesn't matter. Now, we're off to Liverpool, so if you can get into the truck, I'll take you all to Euston Station. It's a lunchtime show in a factory, so you can sleep on the train.'

'Liverpool.' Della's eyes lit up. 'D'you think I'll have time to go and see my ma? I do hope so.'

Chapter 3

It was difficult for some of them to sleep on the train. Catherine, Della and Frances sat on one side of the compartment, with the men on the other. Eric Baxter and the captain were somewhere else on the train and Catherine wasn't sorry. In the truck on the way to the station, he'd sat too close to her and rested his hand on her thigh.

'Don't,' she'd said fiercely, and pushed his hand away.

'A million apologies, dear lady,' he'd said in the captain's voice, but at the same time he was giving her a furtive grin.

Della, who was sitting across from them, said, 'I'd watch that wandering hand if I were you.'

'Would you?' Eric transferred his sly look to Della. 'You'd know all about wandering hands, I don't doubt. Welcomed quite a few of them in your time, I dare say.'

'Shut up,' she snarled.

'Hey, hey,' Tommy butted in. 'Let's cool it.'

And now, on the train, Catherine was glad that she wouldn't have to put up with Eric's smirk and the captain's weird voice all the way to Liverpool. But even so, she didn't look forward to the long journey ahead in the company of people she barely knew. The performance earlier that evening had gelled them together a bit, and during the rehearsals she'd become friendly with Della, but apart from Tommy, the others were still strangers.

She leant her head back against the velour-covered bench and tried to sleep, but it was impossible and she soon gave it up. Instead, she thought about baby Lili and her mother. The baby would be fine, she knew that: her mother was as loving as could be. But she did miss her, missed her little face and her chubby arms, which reached up so lovingly when Catherine bent over her cot in the morning. How Christopher would love her. Then those thoughts became too painful to continue and she turned her mind to Robert Lennox and the suggestion he'd put to her. It was too ridiculous to contemplate, really. After all, the war was nearly over – everyone was saying that – and anyway, she had to wait for Christopher.

'What did that man want you for, before the show?' asked Della, uncannily breaking into Catherine's thoughts. The others all looked up, eager to hear.

'Mr Lennox?' Catherine was sure she was blushing, but she made an effort to sound casual. 'Oh, he wanted me to do some translating, if and when we go to France. Beau told him I was half French.'

Beau had the grace to look uncomfortable. 'Yes, I did, and I'm sorry if it was wrong of me. I met him the other day, quite by chance, and I was telling him about the new company we'd formed. He was very interested.' He looked into the distance, remembering. 'You know, we were all at school together, him and me and Frances's brother. "The Three Musketeers", we called ourselves.'

'And was there a d'Artagnan?' Godfrey joined in.

'Yes,' Beau sighed. 'Johnny Petersham. D'you remember him, Frances?' He shook his head. 'Poor Johnny. He was killed at Dunkirk.'

'Mm. I remember him.' Frances's voice was a little husky and Catherine had a quick look at her and then at Della, who gave a meaningful nod.

Signor Splendoso woke up suddenly, with a grunt. He'd been the only one who'd slept, his head jammed on Godfrey's shoulder since five minutes after getting on board. Now he jerked upright and looked around. 'We're nae moving,' he said in his Glasgow accent. He had close-cut grey hair, having removed the black wig he wore on stage. Without the wig and make-up, particularly the mascara-bedecked false eyelashes, he looked his age, which was the wrong side of fifty, Catherine thought.

'No,' said Godfrey, massaging his shoulder. 'The train's been halted for the last twenty minutes. God knows what it's waiting for.'

'Probably for an express to go through, and I wish I was on it,' Tommy groaned. 'This bloody train has stopped at every station so far.'

Frances stood up. 'I've got a picnic in that wicker case.' She pointed to the luggage rack. 'Just a couple of flasks of tea and a few sandwiches, if someone can get it down.'

'Frances, darling, you're a lifesaver. Signor, do you mind?' asked Beau.

'For the love of God,' the magician said, standing up and reaching for the wicker case, 'will you nae call me "Colin", my given name? You know fine well that "Splendoso" is a stage name.'

'So you're not Italian, then?' asked Godfrey.

'No. Not at all. Colin Brown from Glasgow. I took the name "Splendoso" long before the war and it's caused me no end of trouble. I was nearly bloody interned when the Ities joined in.'

He looked so aggrieved that they all laughed, and when he got a half-bottle of whisky out of his coat pocket and poured some into everyone's tea, the awkwardness of strangers began to dissipate. They were able to chat normally, comparing experiences and talking about theatres and people they knew in common. Catherine noticed that Frances seemed a little left out, but she kept smiling as she handed round the sandwiches.

After they'd finished, she cleared away the picnic and they all settled down again. Catherine finally dropped off to sleep and had wild, puzzling dreams, which she immediately forgot the moment that Della jogged her arm.

'It's Crewe,' she said. 'Come on, we have to get off.'

'Oh God,' Catherine groaned, and standing up, reached for her suitcase.

'I know,' said Della. 'I feel like hell too.'

Crewe Station was nearly deserted, apart from a few youthful porters, who refused to leave the fireplace in the ticket office, and the troupe wearily lugged their suitcases over the bridge to find the platform for Liverpool. It was four in the morning and cold in the early dawn mist. The acrid railway-station smell of steam and coal bit the air, causing Della to wrinkle up her nose and search in her pocket for her packet of cigarettes.

'I'm afraid our train doesn't come in until seven,' said Frances, consulting her clipboard, 'but' – she looked up and down the empty platform – 'I see that the waiting room is open and we can go in there.'

At six o'clock, the station cafe opened and they gladly went in for tea and toast. The girls sat together, yawning over the thick, white china cups, with Della resting her head on her hand and smoking copious cigarettes. Frances put her feet up on her leather suitcase. She was wearing laced-up brown shoes, the heels rather worn down and the toes scuffed, even though Catherine had seen her attempting to polish them when they were getting ready to perform last night. Those shoes looked as if they'd been worn daily and heavily. Despite her cut-crystal accent, she seemed to be as hard up as the rest of them. She was difficult to figure out, and the other day, at rehearsal, Della and Catherine had agreed that Frances was a bit of an enigma.

'I think she's a pal of Beau's,' Della had said. 'Although not in show business like he was. She's new at the game.'

She was a pal, Catherine now decided, taking a sip of the tannin-laden tea. Hadn't Beau said that he was at school with her brother? But what did she do? Where had she come from?

'D'you live in London?' she asked her.

'No,' Frances smiled. 'I'm a country girl. Wiltshire.'

'Why didn't you get called up?' Della gave her a calculating look. 'You're not married, and I'd have thought that you'd be officer material, any day.'

Frances laughed. 'Do you? I don't think so. No, I was deferred. I'm a farm worker.'

'A farm worker? You?' Della patently didn't believe her.

'Yes,' Frances insisted. 'I work on my father's farms. The men have been called up, so I had to do it. But I've organised a land girl to take over my duties.'

'Did you say "farms"?' Della was getting interested, but Frances looked at her watch and stood up.

'The train will be in any moment. Let's get going.'

The factory was in a bombed part of Liverpool. Like the destroyed areas of London, dandelion and rosebay willowherb grew up through the rubble, their yellow and pink flowers standing out defiantly among the mess of broken stone and bricks. In London, Catherine remembered, they called it 'bomb weed' because it survived in the most hopeless of conditions. Just like the people did, because surviving was the only thing that mattered. But as they walked into the factory, the members of the Bennett Players found that the Liverpudlians were doing more than just survive; they were full of beans.

This resourcefulness was displayed by the cheerful receptionist who met them at the factory entrance. She grinned broadly at them and then yelled through the intercom for 'Mr Jones'. 'He's the boss,' she confided, 'but he's alright.'

Soon a man in a tight brown suit came racing down the stairs and, with a jolly laugh, announced that he was Howard Jones, the factory manager, and that everyone was most welcome. After shaking hands with Beau, he beckoned the company to follow him back up the stairs.

'Come along, do,' he said eagerly. 'My girls are really looking forward to the show.'

'Girls?' asked Beau. 'Aren't there any men?'

'Well, there's me and the chief engineer, and five or six others. The workforce is all women.'

'What d'you make?'

'Ah.' The manager tapped his nose. 'Can't tell you that, sir. Official secret.'

Beau shrugged. Nearly five years into the war, they were all used to official secrets and no longer asked questions. 'Alright,' he said. 'Lead on.'

The show was to be held in the works canteen, a huge room on the first floor with large, dirty windows and an echoing wooden floor.

'We'll draw the blackout curtains for you, lad,' the manager said, 'and we borrowed those spotlights from the Playhouse.' He pointed to two portable lights, which were connected by long, fabric-covered leads to an electric socket. 'We've put some of the tables together to form a stage, as you can see.' He looked over to Catherine and Della, who were standing together. 'You young ladies will have to be careful. No high kicks.'

Della scowled at the mocked-up stage. 'Bloody hell,' she said to Beau. 'I hope you're not expecting me to do the splits on that.'

Mr Jones squawked with laughter, a sheen of sweat making his plump red face glow. 'The splits indeed! Ooh, I say. I like the sound of that.'

The receptionist, who had followed them up the stairs, said, 'The ladies can change in the locker room, Mr Jones; we've cleared a space for them. But the men will have to make do with the lavvy.'

Eric Baxter frowned and in the captain's voice said to Beau, 'Not good enough, old bean. Rather infra dig, don't you know.'

There was a slight pause and then Beau replied, 'I'm afraid there's no choice. You'll have to change in there. It'll be alright.'

That was odd, Catherine thought. He'd sounded almost nervous.

The show went wonderfully well and the canteen echoed with cheers. The factory workers, tired-looking women in grey boiler suits, with their hair covered, turban style, in flowered triangles, loved every minute of it. Even Eric and Captain Fortescue pulled out all the stops, daring to tell some quite filthy jokes, which the women in the audience didn't mind one bit, screaming with laughter behind pretend-modest hands. Then Signor Splendoso drew gasps of delighted surprise when he pulled paper flowers out of his top hat and coins from the ears of one of the factory girls. He did some tricks with cards and ended by pretending to slice off Howard Jones's finger in a miniature guillotine.

'Pity it wasn't his you-know-what,' yelled one of the workers, but it was in a good-humoured way and gales of laughter followed, with Mr Jones joining in. They all quietened down to hear Godfrey sing the 'Serenade' from *The Student Prince*. His tenor voice filled the room and had some of the women in tears. Catherine, standing beside the door, smiled congratulations to him when he stepped down from the stage.

Della was next, and with Tommy's lively accompaniment, his foot jammed on the loud pedal, she sang out her number and, having calculated the size of the stage, jumped off and continued her energetic dance in the aisle between the seats.

'Well, I never,' one of the factory women yelled above the noise of clapping. 'That's Ma Flanagan's girl. I'd know her anywhere, even with that hair.' She stood up and cheered. 'Well done, Delia, love. Well done!'

Howard Jones, who'd applauded vigorously throughout, now looked as though he was about to have a heart attack. His grinning face was scarlet, and he seemed very short of breath, but the cheerful receptionist was obviously used to it and hurried off to find him a glass of water.

'Is he alright?' Della asked her anxiously.

'Oh yes.'

The receptionist was unconcerned, but Beau was determined to calm the room and beckoned Catherine forward. Tommy started the introduction to her French song and the room fell silent.

The melody and her sweet voice found a home in everyone's heart. She sang to each corner of the room, looking into the women's eyes and finding similar longings to her own.

'Lovely,' the women called, when she'd finished, and, 'Give us another one, duck.' Beau gave her a nod and she went over to Tommy and pointed to a piece of music. The strains of 'As Time Goes By' were heard in near silence, broken only by the occasional sniff and the odd little groan of contentment. Catherine poured all her yearning for Christopher into the words, remembering their early days together, walking hand in hand in Regent's Park and sitting on a bench by the lake. It was there that he'd asked her to marry him. She remembered the rain pouring down and them sitting very close together under a large umbrella. Of course she'd said yes. And then he'd kissed her, in full view of the Londoners scurrying by, and the rain was forgotten.

Oh God, how she missed him.

When Catherine stepped down from the stage, several of the factory workers came up to her and touched her hands and shoulders, and one even gave her a hug. They were doing the same to Della, and the older one who'd shouted out about her mother had grabbed her arm and was deep in conversation with her.

'You were both brilliant,' said Frances, when the three

of them were in the locker room, changing into their day clothes. 'Beau is so pleased, and I loved every minute.' She smiled at them, showing white, even teeth in a generous mouth. The flecks of green in her hazel eyes sparkled and Catherine realised, for the first time, that Frances was rather pretty.

'Thanks,' said Della. 'It was fun today.'

'Yes,' Catherine nodded. 'But I'm looking forward to going home. What time's our train?'

Frances consulted her clipboard. 'I'm sorry,' she said. 'It doesn't go until seven twenty-one, and I'm afraid we've got another wait.' She looked at her watch, gold on a thin moiré band. 'It's just gone one now, so we'll have to find something to do for the next five hours. I think we can get a bus to the shops in the centre of Liverpool, maybe, or go to a cafe.'

'I'm going to visit my ma,' Della said. 'She lives not more than a couple of streets away from here, and it's been over a year since I was home. It'll be nice to see her and my brother and sister, if they're around.' She turned to Catherine. 'Why don't you come too? Ma would love to meet you.'

'Alright,' Catherine nodded. 'I'd like that.'

There was an awkward pause while Frances picked up her coat and walked towards the door. 'You've got to be at Lime Street Station at seven o'clock,' she said, as they all went out into the corridor. 'Please don't be late.'

Tommy and Colin Brown were leaning against the door beside the gents' lavatory and looked up when the girls arrived. 'We're waiting for Godfrey; then we're going to the pub,' Tommy said. 'Colin knows one by the docks that will be open. D'you want to come?'

37

Della shook her head. 'I'm going to see me ma, and Catherine's coming with me.'

'Oh,' said Tommy, 'are you?' and then cocked an eyebrow at Frances. 'Pub?'

Frances smiled. 'Thanks, but I'll give it a miss. I have to keep my wits about me.'

'Okey-dokey.' Tommy looked slightly relieved, Catherine thought. Frances was still a bit of an outsider compared with the others. But he gave them a grin and hammered on the gents' door, yelling, 'Come on, Godfrey. What the hell are you doing in there?'

The girls said goodbye and started to walk down the stairs. As they turned onto a half-landing, Catherine looked down and saw Beau and Eric standing close together in the reception hall. Eric was speaking quickly into Beau's ear, and as she watched, Beau reached into his inside pocket and pulled out his wallet. They saw him take out a five-pound note and push it into Eric's open palm.

Della gave her a dig in the arm. 'I didn't realise we were being paid today,' she whispered.

'We're not,' Frances murmured from behind them. 'The money will be in next week.'

Eric had gone through the door to the street by the time they reached Beau. He looked a little flustered and was leaning heavily on his walking stick. 'Look,' he said, 'I've got some things to do, so I'll see you at the station.'

'I need to ask you about the schedule.' Frances held up her clipboard. 'Shall I organise better transport for the—'

'Not now, Fran.' Beau brushed a shaky hand through his blond hair and then straightened his tie. 'See you all later. Bye.'

Frances stood, frowning and obviously puzzled, and Catherine realised that she had intended to spend the afternoon with Beau.

'Well, let's go,' said Della, picking up her case and walking to the door, but Catherine lingered.

'What are you going to do?' she asked Frances, who was standing rather uncertainly, her clipboard with its dangling pencil still clutched to her chest.

'Oh, I don't know,' she said, and then smiled brightly. 'Perhaps I'll find a cafe or the cinema.' She sounded cheerful, but Catherine could see that she wasn't.

Della looked back over her shoulder. 'Oh Lord,' she groaned. 'Go on, then – come with us to see me ma.' She gave Frances a hard stare. 'But I'm telling you now – we aren't what you're used to. I'm sure of that. Ma lives in the Courts, and it's a bit rough, so be warned. But she'll give us a cup of tea and a bit of cake.'

'No,' Frances shook her head. 'I'll be alright on my own. Don't worry.'

'Do come,' Catherine urged. 'It'll be fun to get to know each other, won't it, Della?'

Della heaved a sigh and then nodded. 'Yes. But come on, for God's sake. It'll be time to go to the station if we don't get a move on.' She pushed open the door and Catherine linked her arm in Frances's and the two of them followed Della out of the building.

Outside, looking up the street, Catherine could see Beau. He was walking as quickly as his limp would allow and, ahead of him, carrying the suitcase that contained Captain Fortescue, was the thin, sloping figure of Eric Baxter.

Frances looked too and frowned.

'I didn't know that they were friends,' Della said.

'Neither did I,' said Frances. 'He never mentioned it to me.'

'Well, it takes all sorts.' Della shrugged as they walked along the street in the opposite direction. 'Perhaps he doesn't find him as horrible as we do, but…'

Catherine had another glance over her shoulder. Beau had disappeared, but Eric had stopped to light a cigarette and was looking back at her and the other two. Why did he make her feel so uncomfortable?

At the corner of the street, Della paused. 'We go down here,' she said, and pointed to a narrow lane leading off to the left. Catherine could see a warren of alleyways where lines of washing hung from building to building and tough-looking women stood, arms akimbo, gossiping with their neighbours and yelling at their grubby children.

Della looked back at Frances. 'Still sure you want to come?'

'Of course,' Frances laughed. 'Lead on.'

Chapter 4

The Courts was an area of slum houses, no different from the slums in any big city, Catherine supposed. And she'd seen plenty of those in London. The row of terraced houses where she'd grown up, and where she and Christopher had made their home, was perfectly respectable, and their neighbours had jobs and steady incomes, but she'd gone to a school a few streets away that was surrounded by run-down housing and she was used to seeing children without shoes and men and women struggling with poverty.

So when Della led Catherine and Frances through an archway and they found that they were in a large, square courtyard closely surrounded by tall, grimy houses, the area was not a surprise, or in the least bit alarming to Catherine. Frances, used to farm cottages with dirt floors and where the smell of animals pervaded the air, wasn't shocked either. It was a different type of poverty, that was all.

Water leaked from a hydrant erected on the cobbles at the centre of the courtyard, and puddles trickled slowly away in dirty little streams. An elderly woman was filling a big enamel jug from the tap, and a couple of young girls, dressed in ragged dresses and wellington boots, kicked through the puddles, sending sprays of mud all about the square. They were giggling and having a wonderful time, and Catherine and Frances smiled at them, but when a spurt of dirty water landed close to Della's white shoes, she didn't find it in any way charming.

'You little devils,' she shouted at them. 'I'll tell yer mam and you'll get in trouble.'

'You don't know who our mam is,' said one of the girls, with a cheeky laugh.

'That's what you think,' Della growled, as the children, still laughing, skipped away through the archway that led to the next court. The old woman with the enamel jug stared at her, her head on one side, obviously trying to place her.

'Do you know those children?' asked Frances.

'No, of course I don't,' Della snorted, stepping carefully across the cobbles. 'But it did get rid of them.'

Catherine and Frances looked at each other and smiled.

'Ma lives in that house,' Della said, pointing to a building across the square. It looked in better condition than the rest: the windows were cleaner, and the front door appeared to have been recently painted. Catherine recognised the colour as 'battleship grey' and guessed that it was the actual paint that the navy used for ships and was probably pinched from the dockyard. That grey door was open, and as the three girls walked towards it, a young man came out, his cap perched on the back of his head and his lips pursed as he whistled a tune.

'Paddy!' Della called. 'Why aren't you at school?' She looked back to her friends. 'He's my brother,' she said.

The boy stopped and then grinned and ran over. He

gave Della a clumsy hug. 'Delia,' he said joyfully. 'Where the hell have you come from? Does Ma know?'

'London, and no,' Della said. 'And you haven't answered my question. Why aren't you at school, you little beggar? You'll end up a dunce if you don't go.'

'I've left,' Paddy protested. 'I'm working now.'

'But you're only thirteen.'

'Fourteen,' he corrected. 'I left at Easter and Jerry Costigan gave me a job.'

'Doing what?' Catherine noticed that Della was frowning.

'I run errands for him,' Paddy said defensively, but he wouldn't meet her eye.

'I'll see about that,' said Della angrily, and walked across the cobbles and through the door, yelling, 'Ma? Ma, where are you?'

Paddy followed her in.

Frances and Catherine waited outside, nervous in case there was going to be a family row and not wanting to be involved. 'Have you noticed that people call her "Delia" round here, not "Della"?' asked Frances. 'And that her mother is "Mrs Flanagan", not "Mrs Stafford"?'

'I have,' Catherine nodded. '"Della" will be her stage name.'

'And "Stafford"?'

Catherine shrugged. 'Who knows?'

Suddenly a large, handsome woman strode out of the door, followed by Della. 'Will you ever come inside?' she roared, holding out her hands. 'Is me house not good enough for you?'

'This is my mother,' Della muttered, unnecessarily, for although Ma Flanagan had grey-streaked dark red hair

43

and was much heavier, the two women had exactly the same striking face and blue eyes. 'And this is Catherine Fletcher' – Della pushed Catherine forward – 'and' – she nodded to Frances – 'Frances Parnell.'

Ma Flanagan took hold of Catherine and Frances's hands and gave them a hearty shake. 'Friends of Delia, would you be? At the theatre? Well, you're most kindly welcome. Come in, do,' and she drew them towards the door. There, she paused and looked over Catherine's shoulder to the old woman with the enamel jug.

'Good day to you, Mrs Button,' she called. 'I'll be round later with your tonic.'

There was a cackling laugh in response, but Catherine didn't have time to look back, because Ma Flanagan had ushered them into a dark, over-furnished room, where a red velvet-covered sofa vied for space with two matching armchairs and a large mahogany table. Six velvet-seated chairs were arranged round the table, and Frances noticed that the glass vase that sat in the centre of it was a match to the Waterford set that they had at home. And, to her astonishment, she saw other nice pieces on a shelf and on the window-sill that would have certainly graced the formal dining room at Parnell Hall.

Della sighed. 'Ma, I told you – I'm not at the theatre now. I've joined this company where we entertain the troops and factory workers. We've just come from the engineering works round the corner. We put on quite a show.'

'Did you, indeed?' her mother said. 'And why didn't you let me know so I could come to see you? That would have been grand.'

44

Della shrugged. 'I dare say you'll be told about it: I recognised lots of the workers.'

Her mother nodded. 'Oh yes, many of the women from the Courts work there. Rather them than me.' She crossed herself. 'Mary, Mother of God but the work is dangerous.'

Catherine and Frances looked at each other and then at Della. She was giving her mother a puzzled look.

'What the hell are they making?' she asked.

'Munitions, of course. Filling shells with TNT or something. Sure and I wouldn't know what, and neither do those poor women.'

'Goodness,' laughed Frances, looking at Della. 'And there was you dancing up and down the aisle. You could have blown us to kingdom come. No wonder that Mr Jones was sweating.'

'Him?' Ma Flanagan snorted. 'He's always sweating. Too much exercise in the trouser department with the girls at the factory.' A glimmer of a smile crossed her face. 'The old eejit will peg out soon.'

Paddy was leaning against the door, jiggling the coins in his pocket. He was a good-looking boy, with the same strong features as his mother and sister.

Della scowled at him and then at her mother. 'Why is he working for Jerry Costigan?' she asked. 'Your man's nothing but a crook.' Catherine noticed that Della had fallen into the same Irish accent as her mother.

Ma Flanagan grimaced. 'Don't I know that? But, Jesus and Mary, wasn't I exhausted trying to keep the boy at school? And besides, I've had words with Mr Costigan. He'll keep him out of trouble. He knows there'll be hell to pay if he don't.'

Paddy straightened up. 'See?' he said with a cocky grin, and then, 'I've got a message to run, Ma. See you later,' and he disappeared through the door.

Ma Flanagan shook her head, rather indulgently Catherine thought, and then said, 'Now, you girls sit down and I'll fetch the tea. But first, I'm going to bring Maria down. She'll be thrilled to see you.'

'I'll get her,' said Della, and, turning to Catherine and Frances, said, 'Won't be a sec.'

They sat, not talking but looking around, waiting to see what would happen next. Ma Flanagan had gone through a door into the next room, but soon reappeared with a tray of cups and saucers, and a big fruit cake on a heavily decorated plate. Catherine wondered where she'd found the sugar and the dried fruit to make such a huge cake, and said so.

Ma Flanagan tapped her nose and grinned. 'There are ways,' she said, 'if you can find the money.'

Frances was looking at the plate. She recognised the china pattern: they had pieces of that at home, in a cabinet in the long gallery.

'I love that plate,' she said, pointing to it.

'Do you, darlin'?' Ma Flanagan smiled. ''Tis Royal Worcester.'

'Mm,' Frances nodded. 'I know. My parents have some plates like that.'

Ma gave her an inquisitive stare. 'Delia said your name is Parnell?'

Frances nodded.

'D'you come from the old country?'

'No,' Frances smiled. 'But I think my father's family had land in Ireland once. It's long gone now, though.'

Ma sighed. 'Isn't that always the way.' She turned her attention to Catherine. 'And you, darlin', do I catch a bit of an accent in your voice?'

'I'm half French,' said Catherine. 'My mother comes from Amiens. I spent my holidays at my French grandparents' farm.'

'And now the Germans are there, I suppose,' Ma sighed. 'And you've not heard from them?'

Catherine shook her head. 'No, nothing, and my mother is dreadfully worried. We'd do anything to find out how they are.' As soon as the words were out of her mouth, she realised that what she'd just said was a lie. Robert Lennox had asked her to go beyond the Allied lines in France and she'd refused. I used Christopher and Lili as an excuse, she thought, but could it be that I'm simply a coward? She could feel her cheeks flushing.

There was a noise at the door and Della walked in carrying a girl who looked about ten years old. She was thin, with long white legs dangling from beneath a blue nightgown. Catherine and Frances stood up and moved forward almost instinctively to help as Della gently laid the girl on the velvet sofa.

'Hello!' cried the girl elatedly.

'This is my sister, Maria,' Della smiled. 'And these are my friends, Catherine and Frances.'

Frances was the first to put out her hand. 'Hello, Maria,' she said. 'How lovely to meet you. I'm Frances.'

'And I am Catherine.' She gave the girl a smile.

'This is wonderful, isn't it, Ma?' said Maria, her face bright with excitement as she grasped first Frances's hand and then Catherine's. 'I love to meet new people.'

Ma Flanagan planted a big kiss on Maria's cheek and

dragged a shawl from the back of the sofa to wrap round the girl's wasted legs. Della put cushions behind her head and soon Maria was sitting upright and regarding the girls with pleasure as they retook their seats at the table.

Just as Ma was about to pour the tea, there was a knock on the door and a quavering voice called, 'Mrs Flanagan? Are you there?'

'Tch!' Ma put down the teapot. ''Tis Mrs Button. She can't wait.'

'I'll get it.' Della stood up. 'Is it in the cellar?'

'It is,' said Ma, and Maria, from the sofa, called after her, 'Make sure you get the money. A shilling.'

Della opened a different door from the one to the kitchen and a blast of cool air came into the room. The girls heard her white shoes tapping down stone steps, and in a minute she was back, carrying a small brown ribbed bottle. It must be the tonic Ma had promised earlier, Catherine thought, and wondered what was in it.

When Della came back to the table, she put down a shilling piece beside the tray. 'Put it in the tin,' demanded Maria, 'and hand me the account book, please.' She smiled as Della put the shilling in an old Lipton tea canister that sat on a shelf beside the small fireplace and handed her the book that lay beneath it. 'I'm the book-keeper,' she said proudly, and opening the ledger, took the pencil that was lying between the pages and wrote down the transaction.

Three times there was a knock at the door during the tea party, and three times Della went down to the cellar.

'Your tonic is very popular,' said Catherine, sipping her tea.

Ma grinned. 'It is, darlin'. Everyone seems to find that a swig cheers them up.'

'You buy it from the chemist?'

'Chemist?' Ma laughed. 'Jesus, no. I make it. 'Tis an old family recipe. Me da showed it me when I was child, and didn't I bring it from home all those years ago?'

Frances gave a brief glance towards Della and smiled when she saw that her friend was looking embarrassed. You didn't have to be a genius to guess what was in it.

It was cosy in that dark room, where barely any light came in from the small window, and Ma had to turn up the flame on the gas mantle. They talked about the newly formed troupe and what they all did.

Frances explained that she didn't do a turn, but was Beau's assistant. 'I've known him for years,' she said. 'My father is friendly with his, and of course, he went to school with my brother.'

'Is your brother in the forces?' asked Paddy. He'd come in from running his message and cut himself a large slice of cake before gently pushing Maria's legs aside, to sit on the couch next to her.

After a moment, Frances cleared her throat and said, 'Well, yes, but he's a prisoner of war. In the Far East. I think he's alright, but...we haven't heard from him for about nine months.' This last came out in a rush and Catherine saw that there were tears in Frances's eyes. She reached over and gave her friend's hand a squeeze.

'Isn't that dreadful?' Ma Flanagan murmured. 'But don't you worry, darlin' – you know where he is and he'll come home.'

Catherine felt a lump of ice settling in her stomach. Ma Flanagan's kind words to Frances had somehow made her loss worse. It had been a month since she'd had the telegram about Christopher, and every day that passed made his absence greater. She put down her piece of cake, unable now to eat another morsel.

'Catherine's husband is missing in action.' It was Della, up again from the cellar with another bottle of tonic. The woman waiting for it had walked into the room and had put her shilling on the table. She was the factory worker who'd shouted out during the performance and seemed to be a special friend of Ma Flanagan. Now she shook her head sadly.

'Oh dear,' she said. 'And you with the voice of an angel.' She turned to Ma Flanagan. 'Your Delia puts on a show that you'd walk a couple of miles to see, but that girl sings like a bird. A bluebird. She had me and quite a few others in tears.'

Ma Flanagan got up from her chair and, squeezing past Frances, put her ample arms about Catherine and gave her a hug. 'Keep your chin up, darlin'. Strange things happen in war.'

'They do,' said the factory worker. 'D'you remember Jessie Kearney's husband? Declared drowned, he was, when his ship went down, but he was found in a life raft, ten days after she was told he was gone.' She paused, then mused, 'Mind you, by the end of the first week, she'd sold his clothes and was already going tally with Cyril Stevens. Gave her quite a turn when she got the telegram to say that he was rescued.'

An awkward silence filled the room after that remark, and Catherine felt Ma Flanagan's arms stiffen around her body. She was plainly horrified that someone could have been embarrassed in her house, but then there was a little bubbling sound from Della, and looking past Ma's large body, she saw that her friend was endeavouring not to giggle, but failing.

'Oh God,' said Della, 'sorry,' and then burst into gales of laughter, followed swiftly by her brother and then Frances.

'Delia!' Ma Flanagan was scandalised, but Catherine could see how funny it was and started to laugh too. Eventually everyone was grinning, even Ma, and although she reached over and gave Della a reproving tap on the hand, the situation was saved and more tea was poured.

'I'd have loved to have heard you sing,' said Maria, when everyone had calmed down. 'I miss everything.'

'You don't,' Ma Flanagan insisted. 'I take you out in the chair when I go to the shops and you talk to everyone. And Paddy sometimes wheels you down to the docks.'

'Huh!' the girl grumbled. 'We get there, he parks my chair, and he goes to do some dodgy deal. He's a right scally!'

'I'm not,' Paddy said, his face reddening. 'I might see a few of my pals, that's all. Anyway, I took you to the fairground last Christmas. I didn't hear you complain then.'

'I will sing for you, if you'd like me to,' said Catherine. 'I'll do the one I sang in the factory – then you won't have missed anything.'

'Isn't she the darlin?' Ma enthused, grinning widely.

'And I'll do my number as well,' Della added, 'but there isn't room in here to do my dance.'

'I'll tell you what,' Ma said. 'Let's go outside and you can do your turn there.'

The factory worker grabbed her tonic. 'Wait five minutes,' she said. 'My Joe would love to see this. I'll go and get him.'

By the time Paddy had manoeuvred Maria's wheel-chair through the doorway and Della had carefully carried her sister outside and settled her comfortably into it, quite a crowd had assembled. Obviously, the factory worker had not only told Joe but most of the other residents of the courtyard.

Things had taken on a festive air. Residents young and old had come out of their houses, and the late-afternoon sun had pierced a hole in the grey clouds and sent a golden beam, like a spotlight, onto the cobbles. Catherine thought that the whole scene looked like a stage set.

'This is so wonderful,' Maria breathed, and Ma put a fond hand on her cheek, then frowned as Paddy wandered off to the other side of the square to speak to a tall, brown-haired man. He looked different from the other people gathered. He had smarter clothes and a clever face, and as he reached up to brush his hair away from his forehead, Catherine, watching the byplay, caught a glimpse of not only a gold ring on his little finger but a gold wristwatch too. She knew, instinctively, that this was Jerry Costigan.

'What's he doing here?' Della grumbled to her mother.

'Leave it,' Ma Flanagan snapped. 'Don't make trouble.'

Della gave her mother a hard stare but said nothing.

Frances pushed Catherine forward. 'You'd better get on with it,' she whispered, looking at her watch. 'Remember, we have a train to catch. I'll do the introductions.

'Ladies and gentlemen,' she called out. 'We're part of a troupe set up to entertain the military and the workers, and we hope we're doing some good. We all know boys who are overseas, and some have been sadly lost, and we do remember them. Those of you working in the factories are doing jobs of equal importance, and we know that the government recognises your efforts. So' – she looked down at Maria – 'for the sake of those who missed us, we're going to perform a couple of the numbers we did this afternoon at the factory.'

She nodded to Catherine, who stepped into the centre of the square and stood beside the water hydrant. She loved to sing, so an impromptu performance didn't matter to her, and when she opened her mouth and sang the opening lines, the crowd fell silent. She thought of the many times she'd sung this while appearing at night-clubs and music halls with the Melody Men and how, before they'd started going out together, Christopher would sit at a table closest to the stage and watch her.

'Your professor is here again,' Bobby Crewe would whisper away from the microphone. 'He can't get enough of you. One of these days, he'll pluck up the courage to ask you out.'

'Why d'you call him "the professor"?' she'd murmured back.

'Don't you remember? The first time he came was with some students. They were joining up and he brought them here for a leaving party. He must be deferred.'

But he wasn't. Soon he was in uniform, and, somehow, that uniform gave him the courage to wait for her at the stage door. They married four months later, and then he went overseas.

The cheers and applause that echoed round the courtyard when she'd finished broke into Catherine's memories and she smiled, looking around and nodding her head in thanks.

'Oh, Catherine,' squealed Maria, 'that was beautiful. Will our Delia sing next?'

'Yes, she will,' Frances grinned. 'And hold on to your hat.'

Della blasted out 'I Wish I Were In Love Again', while throwing in a couple of high kicks and some daring twirls, which drew gasps of delight. She invited the audience to sing the chorus with her, which at first they were reluctant to do, but Catherine and even Frances joined in, encouraging first Maria and then Ma to try, and soon the whole square rang to the sound of a Broadway number.

'More!' shouted the audience, but Frances had one eye on her watch.

'We'll have to go soon,' she said.

Maria took her hand. 'Just one more,' she pleaded, and Frances looked at Della and Catherine.

'Who's going to do it?'

'Let's sing together,' suggested Della. 'You too, Frances. I heard you just now and you've not got a bad voice. We'll do one of the Andrews Sisters numbers... "I'll Be With You In Apple Blossom Time". D'you know it?'

Catherine nodded, and Frances said, 'I can remember some of it, but I'll hum what I don't know.'

They stood together, Catherine in the middle, and after Della beat them in with a 'One, two, three, four', they sang in harmony. It worked well, their three voices complementing each other, and after they'd finished, they looked at each other in amazement.

'Wow!' laughed Della. 'How did we do that? D'you know, with a bit of rehearsal, we could put it in the show.' But there was no time to discuss it, for they were surrounded by people shaking their hands and patting them on the shoulder.

Frances pointed to her watch again. 'We have to go. It's only an hour before the train leaves.' She grabbed Della's arm. 'D'you know where we can get the bus to the station?'

'Don't bother with the bus, love. I'll give you a lift.'

Frances turned to see Jerry Costigan standing behind her. Close up, she could see that he was rather good-looking, with startlingly pale blue eyes in a sculptured face. In this area of obvious poverty, he looked wealthy. His black suit was made of fine, smooth material, and he wore it over a crisp white shirt and plain blue tie. If Frances hadn't heard Della describing him as a crook, she would have imagined him a solicitor or a doctor. Respectable middle class at the least.

'No, thanks,' Della butted in. 'The bus will do.'

Jerry ignored her and remained looking at Frances. 'What time's your train, love?'

'Seven twenty-one.'

'You'll never do it.' He glanced at his expensive watch. 'It's gone six thirty now, and you'll have to get through all the traffic: the shift workers will be coming off, and the buses will be full. Look, my motor is in the street. It can take you three easy, and your bags.'

Frances looked at Della and then at Catherine. 'What shall we do?'

'We'll have to accept his offer,' Catherine said. 'I don't

want to miss the train. Lili and Maman are waiting for me.'

They turned to Della. She was scowling and shaking her head.

'Della,' pleaded Catherine, and Frances raised her eyebrows nervously.

'Oh, alright,' Della sighed. She glared at Jerry Costigan. 'No obligations, mind. D'you hear me?'

'Sure,' he grinned. 'Whatever you say.'

The girls went to say goodbye to Ma Flanagan and Maria. 'Bye, Ma,' said Della, giving her mother a hug. 'I'll try and get up again in a few months.' She kissed Maria and pressed some coins into her hand. 'Buy some sweeties, darling, and be a good girl.'

'I always am,' said the girl with a laugh, and turned to hug first Catherine and then Frances. 'Thank you so much. I'll never forget this afternoon.'

Ma Flanagan hugged Catherine. 'Try to remember that he's only missing,' she murmured in Catherine's ear, 'and there's every chance he'll come home to you. I'll light a candle for him in church on Sunday.'

'Thank you, Mrs Flanagan.' Catherine felt tears coming to her eyes again and turned away so that Frances could have her hugs and then picked up her suitcase.

'Ready?' Jerry Costigan walked across the courtyard towards the archway and the girls followed, waved away by the people who were drifting back towards their houses.

'That was fun,' said Frances, linking arms with Della, 'and I loved meeting your mother and your sister and brother.' She paused for a moment and then said, 'What's the matter with Maria?'

'Oh,' Della sighed, 'she was born like that. There's something wrong with her spine. Ma has tried everything, and she's seen loads of doctors, but they say there's nothing they can do. It's such a shame because she's so clever and pretty.'

'It is,' Frances agreed. 'But she's a good help to your ma with the moonshine business.'

'What?' Della blustered, and then laughed. 'Oh God, I thought you might have guessed. What about you, Catherine?'

But Catherine wasn't paying attention. As they turned the corner into the main street, where Jerry Costigan's shiny Humber limousine waited for them, she was looking across the road to where Eric Baxter loitered, pretending to look in a shop window.

Chapter 5

Over the next few months the troupe played in many different places. They did army and air-force bases, and even once on board a battleship. Military hospitals were a frequent and favourite venue, not only because the damaged soldiers and airmen were hugely appreciative of the entertainment – it was the hope that they seemed to exude that made the performers feel that they were doing something worthwhile.

Sometimes they performed in dark, busy factories, where weary-looking women loaded explosives into shells and bullet casings, and everyone pretended that they were working in car factories. The next day, the venue might be an open field, on a rickety, hastily erected stage, before hundreds of soldiers roaring out their approval.

In the middle of July, Beau gathered the troupe together after they'd finished a lunchtime performance on a London dock. The show had gone well, particularly when the girls sang as a trio. The dockers cheered and drummed their feet on the wooden floor of the huge warehouse, causing clouds of dust to rise up and fill the air with choking particles from the ancient cargoes.

'That was great,' said Beau, when they'd finished and stood beside the truck, grinning at each other and still breathless from excitement.

'You've changed your tune,' Della laughed. 'I thought you weren't keen on us doing it.'

'No, I wasn't,' he confessed. 'I didn't think it would work. Especially with Frances singing. I mean, come on – she was hired as my assistant, not an artiste.'

'But she's got a good voice,' said Catherine. 'You heard her.'

'And I can still do the organising,' Frances protested. 'I haven't let you down, have I?'

'No, you haven't, and I wouldn't dare argue with you. You three girls have become something of a formidable force.' Beau sat down suddenly on a packing case. Catherine thought he looked tired; his leg was obviously causing him trouble. She watched as he rubbed his hand on his thigh and massaged his knee. He'd been on his feet all through the show, introducing the numbers and encouraging the audience to join in with the singing. She'd also noticed that when they'd first arrived at the dockside, Eric had taken hold of his arm and spoken directly into his ear. Whatever he'd said had caused Beau's face to fall, and he'd shaken off Eric's hand quite sharply.

Now he looked exhausted. 'I think you need a rest,' she said. 'And I'd like to get home too.'

'Yes,' he said, 'but hang on a minute, before you get in the truck. I've a couple of announcements to make.' He stood up and nodded to Frances.

'Gather round,' she called. 'Beau's got something to tell us.' Her voice was drowned out by the sound of a crane moving overhead, and she waved at the Players to move back towards the warehouse, where it was quieter. The dockers had gone back to work as soon as the show had finished, but some were still working inside, at the far end of the building, moving crates around and shouting instructions to each other.

Catherine leant against a wall of boxes and took out her handkerchief to wipe a faint sheen of sweat from her forehead. A hot smell of oil combined with the other odours of machinery and packing bales filled the air and she could feel her stomach turning over. She was wearing a light coat to cover her stage dress and, after the heady excitement of the show, was feeling the summer heat of July. The weather had improved in the weeks that had passed since D-Day, and it added to the joyful mood that filled the nation; everyone seemed to have a grin on their face. She didn't feel like grinning, though. Christopher was still missing, and even though she'd written to the War Office for more news, she hadn't received a reply.

But she'd had another visit from Robert Lennox.

He'd called one morning, a week ago. She was in the scullery, doing the washing and singing along to Al Bowlly on the wireless, when she heard the gentle rap on the front door. Drying her hands on a towel, she'd opened the door thinking it was the postman, perhaps with a letter from Christopher, but her heart sank when she saw who it was.

'Good morning, Mrs Fletcher,' Robert said, tipping his hat. 'May I come in?'

Honorine had taken Lili for a walk to the shops and Catherine was alone in the house. She was tired. They'd done a show at an army camp the night before, somewhere north of London, and it had been a long drive back, down unlit country roads, before they'd reached the city. And tonight, she'd promised to sing with the Melody Men at a club in the West End. The last thing she needed was a visit from Mr Lennox, and for a second she considered saying, 'No, you may not come in,' and shutting the door rudely in his face. But she didn't and instead stood aside and indicated the front room.

He wasted no time. 'We wondered if you'd changed your mind,' he said. 'Because now that we've invaded France, I expect you'll be crossing the Channel to entertain the troops.'

'Will I? How d'you know?' she asked.

He shrugged. 'It's my job. We all have jobs to do. All of us.' This last was said casually, but Catherine knew what he was inferring and frowned. He had his back to her and was picking up the photographs on the mantelpiece and examining them. He stared at the wedding photo and then, turning round, saw that she was looking at him and put it back in its place.

'He looked like a nice chap,' he said slowly.

'He is,' Catherine replied, her eyes steely with determination. 'He is, not was, a nice chap, and he's going to come home.'

'A junior lecturer before the war, yes?'

'Yes,' Catherine nodded. 'He taught modern languages.' She thought back to when they'd been courting and she'd made fun of his French accent. 'You sound like a Parisian street trader,' she'd laughed.

'Do I?' Christopher had been surprised. 'I suppose I picked that up from my tutor, although God knows where he got it. You must tell me how to improve. I can't pass that on to my students.' He'd pushed a hand through his untidy straw-coloured hair and looked so worried

61

that she'd laughed again, and after a moment he'd relaxed and laughed with her. Oh, how she had loved him, how happy they'd been.

She was brought back to the present by Robert Lennox's voice breaking through her thoughts. 'Mrs Fletcher, Catherine. Did you take your husband to your grandparents' farm?'

'To Amiens?' she said, bewildered. 'How could I? We were already at war when I met him. The Germans were in Amiens. They still are.'

'Yes,' Robert said, 'of course. You didn't know him before.'

She shook her head. 'No.'

'And his parents, did you meet them?'

Anger was beginning to flood through her. 'They're dead,' she said sharply. 'You must know that. You know everything else.'

Robert nodded slowly but said nothing, and she felt forced to add, 'They lived in Hereford. Christopher's father was a teacher. Languages like Chris.'

'And they died before you were married?'

'Yes. Together, in an accident. They were abroad on holiday and were killed in a car crash.' Catherine remembered Christopher telling her about them with tears in his eyes. He'd loved them very much.

'So after that, Lieutenant Fletcher joined the army?'

'No.' She shook her head. 'Christopher's parents died before the war, about a year before, I think. He didn't join up until after it started.'

'And then what?'

Catherine frowned. 'I don't know what you mean. He did what everyone else did. Training and joining a regiment. When he came home on his last leave, he said nothing about doing anything else.' She bit her lip. 'It was just after Lili was born. We could only speak about the baby. He said that he knew that I would be a wonderful mother.' She tried to keep the wobble out of her voice, but judging from the look of concern on Robert's face, she hadn't succeeded.

He took out a packet of cigarettes and offered her one, and then, when she shook her head, put the packet back in his pocket. 'The thing is,' he said, not really looking her in the eye but turning to stare out of the window onto the street, 'I...er, I know a little about what your husband was doing. It was something similar to what I'm suggesting for you.'

'What?' Catherine asked, astonished. 'No, no, you've got it wrong. He was with his regiment. I don't know where, but somehow I thought it was in Italy. I've been following the war news and that seemed the most logical place. He's a soldier, not a...'

'Spy?' Robert raised his eyebrows. 'Is that what you were going to say? Well, my information seems to suggest that he was one of our operatives, gathering information for us. He was in France, close to Caen when we last heard from him. Then he simply disappeared. We think he was captured by the Gestapo.'

Catherine felt as though the room was whirling round her and sat down suddenly on the armchair. 'I don't believe you,' she whispered.

'I'm sorry,' Robert said, and reached out to put a hand on her shoulder. 'But it is true. The fact is that Lieutenant Fletcher was a man of the highest calibre, utterly brave and who believed in freedom, but' – Robert's hand was firm on Catherine's shoulder – 'now we have every reason to believe that he has been lost.'

Every word of that conversation had imprinted itself on Catherine's brain and even now, a week later, she couldn't stop going over it. Christopher in France? Surely that was wrong? But at the same time, a niggle of doubt began to worm its way into her mind.

I know you'll look after our baby girl, always. I love you. And whatever happens, my darling girl, try and remember that I loved you both. That's what Christopher had said before he kissed her goodbye. And she'd been so wrapped up with the baby that she only heard his words as the usual loving farewells that he always gave. Now, standing in the hot warehouse, she could only dwell on how stupid she'd been, how careless in not recognising that there was something different about him. He'd looked stronger, fitter, but now that she thought about it, there had been a sadness in his eyes. He was saying goodbye forever, she now realised, and as that thought hit her, her hand went to her mouth, and tears welled up in her soft brown eyes.

'Are you alright?' Della whispered, touching her arm and looking at her.

Catherine took a deep breath. 'Yes,' she said, 'I am,' and giving her friend a smile, turned her attention to Beau.

'First,' he was announcing, 'you'll be pleased to hear we've obtained a bus.'

'Thank God,' said Della. 'That bloody truck was killing me. I'm covered in bruises.' The rest of them nodded in agreement.

'Well, yes,' Beau grinned. 'It should be much more

comfortable, and Frances has assured me that she can drive it.'

'It can't be harder than the truck,' Frances said, and grinned. She glanced at Beau, waiting for him to tell the next piece of news. He'd told her earlier, before the show started, that he'd been to the War Office, but hadn't said what it had been about.

'Now for the really exciting news,' Beau said. 'In three weeks' time, we'll be in France.'

'Wow!' said Della, and Tommy Rudd raised a joyful fist in the air. Catherine took in a quick breath. Robert Lennox must have known. Maybe he even organised it.

Colin Brown punched Godfrey on the arm. 'There's no way the wee wifey can follow you there, eh, man?' He nodded to the dockside, where Godfrey's old Sunbeam was parked. Mrs James, banned from the show, was sitting in the driving seat, waiting for him. When they were performing in London, she always drove him to the venue and waited angrily for the show to be over.

Godfrey took a quick glance at her and then nodded happily. 'Oh dear,' he said, trying to keep the joyful bellow out of his voice. 'She will be cross.'

Only Eric Baxter made no comment. He stood slightly apart from the rest of the company, watching and listening, but refusing to join in with the conversation. The Bennett Players had become friends, enjoying each others' company and keen to help with lost greasepaint or outfits, if necessary. Della even performed as Colin's 'lovely assistant' when he was doing his act, posing beside his magician's table and pretending to be just as amazed at his tricks as the audience. Catherine had sung with Godfrey when he did pieces from popular musicals, and Tommy had brought along a drum and did drum rolls when Beau introduced the acts. The group had melded together, all except Eric.

'Beau should get rid of him,' Tommy had whispered. 'There's something funny about him.'

'He won't,' Frances replied. 'Eric's never missed a show, and he's popular with the audiences.'

But the rest of the company found him difficult. Della loathed him and made no secret of it.

'Hush,' said Beau, holding up his hand. 'I haven't finished. Now, because we're going into what is a war zone, we've been issued with uniforms. It'll be army officer's, not that we've been commissioned or anything, but apparently we can take advantage of the officers' mess wherever there is one. Look...' He paused. 'When we're in France, we must wear uniform, for our own safety, so I think we should wear it at home too. It'll show people that we're doing our bit. On stage, we can change into our performance clothes, but otherwise it's uniforms. Alright?'

The group nodded and Beau looked relieved. Catherine wondered if he'd imagined that anyone would object. She glanced quickly at Eric Baxter, but he had his face turned away and had picked up the case containing Captain Fortescue, ready to leave.

'Good. Then we'll meet again tomorrow morning at Victoria Station, nine o'clock sharp. Our venue is close to Windsor and another lunchtime performance. Frances will have the bus by then, so it should be an easier journey.' Beau started to walk out of the warehouse and then stopped. 'We've got three performances this week, all in the London area, and then you have ten days off.

Get some rest, because I think the next few weeks will be hectic. And Frances will tell you where you can pick up your uniforms. I'll give her the chitty.'

Two days later, the girls were in Beau's flat in Knightsbridge, where Frances had a room, trying on their new uniforms.

'What d'you think?' asked Della, looking at herself in the dressing-table mirror, then turning this way and that, and giving a little twirl.

'Very nice,' grinned Frances, 'but all the buttons have to be done up, and the skirt pulled down to regulation length. If you want to see yourself properly, go into Beau's room. He's got a long glass.'

'Oh good,' she said, dashing out of the door.

'We're not soldiers,' said Catherine, who was trying on the cap. 'So does it really matter?' She turned round to look at Frances. 'I don't know why we have to wear uniform, anyway. It won't make me sing any better.'

'But you heard what Beau said,' Frances protested. 'It's a precaution. Besides, I think it's rather smart.'

'You would,' Della laughed. She had come back into the bedroom. 'Anyone would take you for the real McCoy.'

It was true. The khaki jacket and skirt looked completely right on Frances. She'd tucked up her red hair under the cap, which she wore straight on her head, and with her ever-present clipboard could have been a real officer.

Catherine wore her cap at an angle, and Della, catching sight of herself again in the mirror, realised that she'd put hers on the back of her head and that her blonde hair was hanging to her shoulders beneath it. She looked as though she was in fancy dress and she laughed. There was no reason she couldn't adapt it to wear on stage.

'It's really for when we go abroad, just in case,' Frances said, taking off the cap and putting it down on the bed. 'If we wander away from the front line and are captured, we could be shot as spies.'

Della giggled. 'Some spies,' she smirked. 'I'd like to see the spy who looks remotely like any of us.'

Catherine said nothing as she took off the uniform and pulled on her summer frock. Robert Lennox had suggested that she could be a spy. He must think that she looked exactly like one.

'You're quiet today,' Della broke into her thoughts.

'Am I?' Catherine smiled. 'Well, you do enough talking for all of us, doesn't she?' She raised her eyebrows at Frances, who laughed and went to the door.

'I'm going to make some tea,' she said. 'Let's go into the living room. Beau's not here and we can have it to ourselves.'

She went out and Catherine waited for Della to get into her slacks and blouse, and to comb her hair. Frances's bedroom was small, with a single bed and a few other bits of furniture. On the bedside table, there was a studio photo of a small, red-haired boy, and a black-and-white snap of two youngsters, a girl and an older boy, with a pony.

'I expect that's Frances and her brother,' said Catherine. 'They're very close.'

'Mm,' Della replied, busy with her lipstick. She turned her head and whispered, 'You don't suppose they're sleeping together?'

'Who?' Catherine was astonished. 'Frances and her

68

brother?'

'No, you idiot. Her and Beau.'

Catherine shrugged. 'I don't know. Why don't you ask her?'

Della stood up. 'I might at that,' she laughed. 'I saw...' She stopped mid-sentence and then said, 'It doesn't matter, but now that I come to think about it, I'm pretty sure his fancies lie elsewhere. Haven't you noticed?'

'Noticed what?'

'Beau and Eric Baxter.'

'Oh no,' Catherine gasped, her cheeks going pink. 'He couldn't – Eric is vile.'

Della laughed and was still smiling when they went to join Frances in the living room. 'Wow!' she exclaimed, looking at the photographs that were scattered around the rather good furniture. They were of Beau with his famous show business friends. 'My God,' she exclaimed, picking up one glossy picture in a silver frame. 'This is Noël Coward with his arm around Beau's shoulder, and this' – she pointed to another – 'isn't it Laurence Olivier?'

'Come and have your tea,' Frances said, but Della was still intrigued by the photos.

'Look at this. Isn't he a member of the royal family? And this? Good God, it's George Formby with Beau,' she laughed excitedly. 'I know him, been on the same bill, but I didn't think Beau would. My God, he knows everyone.'

'Well, yes,' Frances smiled. 'He was on the stage for a few years before the war, and even did a couple of pictures. If it hadn't been for his injury, he might have been a Hollywood leading man. I mean, he's got the looks and is pals with everyone.'

Della gave Catherine a meaningful wink, but didn't say anything. Catherine had the uncomfortable feeling that Frances had caught the wink, and so quickly started a conversation about their tour into France.

'Where are we going?' she asked.

'I don't know,' said Frances. 'That's something they won't tell us, but we will have a liaison officer. I do know that we'll be going by sea so that we can take the bus with us.' She handed a cup to Catherine. 'Are you going to work for the government when we're there?'

'What?' asked Catherine, a feeling of panic rushing over her. How on earth did Frances know what Robert had suggested?

'You know. Translating.'

'Oh.' Her heart slowed to a normal beat and she gave a little smile. 'I suppose so,' she said. 'If I'm needed.'

'I bet you will be,' said Della. 'Who else speaks French? You're a godsend.'

'I know a bit,' Frances said. 'Only what we did at school and what my—' She stopped that sentence quickly before admitting that she and Hugo had been brought up by a Belgian governess. She swiftly changed the subject, and smiling at Della, she asked, 'Are you going home for a few days while we're on leave?'

Della shrugged. 'I don't know. I could, but I'll only fight with Ma over Paddy and his job with Jerry Costigan.'

'Is he really a gangster?' asked Frances.

'I should say so.' Della's mouth turned down. 'You don't know the half.'

Frances turned to Catherine. 'What about you?'

'Oh, I'll spend time with Lili.' She stood up. 'I've got

to go. I've an appointment.'

Della was curious. 'Who with?'

'It's nothing important,' she said. 'I have to take Lili to the clinic for a check-up. Maman gets confused at the doctor's.'

'Can't your father go with her?' asked Della.

There was a pause and then she answered, 'No, it is not possible. It is not possible because my dear papa died nearly three years ago. He was an ARP warden working in the East End and had just got everybody into an air-raid shelter when it was bombed.' Her voice broke slightly and Della got up and put her arms around her friend.

'I'm so sorry, darling,' she said angrily. 'Those bloody Jerries.'

Catherine picked up the paper parcel that contained her new uniform. 'I'll see you tomorrow evening,' she said. 'At the Savoy Theatre? Our show goes on before the play?'

Frances nodded.

'Alright, then.' She smiled at her friends. 'Bye.'

She was on the pavement outside Beau's flat walking towards the bus stop when Della and Frances caught up with her. 'Shall we come with you?' Della suggested. 'We'd love to meet your little girl, and your mother, of course. Besides, you seem to be a little down today.'

Catherine was surprised, but at the same time quite moved. It was good to have friends. 'Yes,' she said. 'Why don't you, and then you can come home and have a cup of tea. Maman would love to see you.'

*

71

They met Catherine's mother and her baby outside the church hall, where the children's clinic was held. Catherine immediately picked the baby up out of her pram and gave her a cuddle.

'Oh, give her to me,' said Della. 'I love babies.' She held the little girl up and cooed into her face. 'Hello, darling,' she warbled. 'What a lovely girl you are.'

Lili gave a delighted squeal and reached out to grab a strand of Della's hair.

'*Dépêche-toi*,' urged Catherine's mother. 'Hurry up!' and urged them towards the door.

Inside, about forty women with their babies sat on hard chairs waiting to see the nurses and one tiny, bird-like lady doctor, who looked as though she should have retired years ago.

'She's a bit terrifying,' whispered Catherine. 'She shouts if the babies cry. They seem to know too – haven't you noticed how quiet it is in here?'

'The old witch,' Della snorted, nodding towards the doctor, who was poking her bony finger into the little mouth of a bewildered baby. Della didn't bother to keep her voice down and one or two of the mothers sitting beside them grinned. Catherine's mother, however, clucked her tongue in dismay and whispered, 'Silence, mademoiselle.'

Frances laughed outright, and even Catherine giggled.

'Shall we give them a song?' Della asked. 'They must be bored hanging about for Madam Crippen to get round to them. What d'you think?'

But it was Lili's turn next and Catherine picked up her daughter and took her to the table at the front of the church hall, where the doctor was waiting. Della and

Frances got up too and followed. These days, they were used to doing things together.

'This child looks pale,' the old doctor growled. 'Does she get enough fresh air?'

'But of course,' Catherine said. 'My mother or I take her out every day. She is not pale. That is her natural colouring.'

'She's beautiful,' Frances said, touching Lili's soft cheek. 'There can't be anything wrong with her.'

'Be quiet,' snapped Dr Crippen. She pulled up Lili's vest to look at her chest and then, grabbing one of her little arms, pulled her onto her face to have a look at her back.

A howl of protest erupted from the baby and Catherine, horrified, pushed the doctor's hands away. 'What are you doing?' she cried.

'I'm looking for a rash, of course. There's a lot of measles about. Stop interfering at once, you silly girl. Really, you young mothers are hopeless. None of you knows how to look after a baby.'

'She hasn't got a rash,' said Della, a hint of menace in her voice. 'And there's no need for you to be so rough.'

'What?'

'You heard me. There might be a war on and you should be at home doing your knitting or drowning kittens, or whatever it is you do in your spare time, but in here, you're a bloody doctor, and these women and babies deserve to be treated right.'

'Here, here,' said Frances, and Catherine pulled down Lili's vest and picked her up. The women in the hall had given a collective gasp of shock and were leaning forward, eager to hear more.

The doctor stared at the three girls, her hands flat on the table and her grey head bobbing up and down like a toy bird's. She picked up Lili's medical card. 'I believe you're in show business, Mrs Fletcher,' she hissed. 'And I suppose these are friends of yours.'

'They are,' said Catherine. 'My best friends.'

'Well, we all know what goes on among that fraternity, so I'm not surprised that your bottle-blonde friend has a foul mouth.' She tossed Lili's card in the bin beside the table. 'I suggest you go to a different clinic.'

'I will.' Catherine grinned, suddenly emboldened. She looked at Della and Frances. 'How about a song?'

'Yes,' laughed Frances. '"Boogie Woogie Bugle Boy"? Time us in, Della.'

So in that bleak church hall, surrounded by mothers and babies, and an angry doctor and startled nurses, Della called, 'One, two, three, four,' and they started, 'He was a famous trumpet man from out Chicago way...' standing together with Lili in Catherine's arms.

Chapter 6

Frances alighted from the train at the station closest to Parnell Hall. She'd telephoned the evening before to say that she was coming home on leave, and her father, sounding a little absent-minded, had agreed to meet her. But there was no sign of him, or anyone else, on the platform.

'Damn,' she muttered, and picking up her suitcase, walked through the gate and onto the lane outside the little country halt. She would have to walk the three miles home.

It was a hot afternoon; bees and flies were buzzing around taking nectar from the wild flowers that grew in abundance at the edge of the dusty road. In the old days, before the war, the hedges and ditches had been managed properly, but now there weren't the men to do it and the hedges were overgrown and the ditches blocked with rotting vegetation.

As she walked along, Frances found herself singing the latest number that she, Catherine and Della had been rehearsing. 'It had to be you, wonderful you,' she sang, mentally counting the beats in the way Catherine and Della had taught her, pleased with her effort. It had been a revelation to her that she could sing well enough to perform on stage, and although at first she'd been nervous of letting the others down, they'd assured her that she was good. 'You've got a super mezzo voice,' Catherine had said, and Della nodded enthusiastically. 'And now that we've got matching frocks, we look the business.'

Surprisingly, for she never wore clothes like these new frocks, Frances loved dressing up for the show. The dresses were in a lavender blue, with tight halter-neck bodices and long, swirling skirts. Della had gone to a dressmaker she knew in Soho and had them made up. 'Ginger Rogers wore something very similar to this in *The Gay Divorcee*, or one of those films. I can't remember. Anyway' – she held up one of the dresses – 'what d'you think?'

'I like it,' Catherine said, fingering the fabric, and Frances had nodded, 'Me too.'

Now Frances was belting out the song and practising the few steps that Della had incorporated and was so lost in her performance that she didn't hear the ancient tractor that was coming up behind her until it was almost on her heels. Her song came to a sudden halt as she squeezed herself into the hedge, scratching her bare arms and legs on the hawthorn branches.

'Lady Frances.' The old man who leant out of the tractor cab looked at her in amazement. 'What the bloody hell are you doing here, prancing about like that?'

'I'm walking home, Jethro,' Fran said, ignoring the reference to 'prancing about'. 'My father was supposed to pick me up from the station, but he hasn't come.'

'His mind's taken up with his new troubles, I dare say.'

'What troubles?' Frances asked. Her father was always short of money, so that couldn't be something new. 'What are you talking about?'

But Jethro was not forthcoming. He scratched his beard and spat a glob of phlegm onto the dusty road. 'Get up on the trailer,' he grunted. 'I'll drop you by the back gates.'

'Thanks.' Frances heaved herself up and leant against the sweet-smelling hay. Oh God, she thought to herself, what's Pa done now?

There was no sign of her father's Rolls as she walked past the outbuildings and garages at the back of the hall. The battered old shooting brake, which had a temperamental clutch and wouldn't start at all if there had been even a hint of frost, was standing by the door to the boiler house. That meant that Pa had gone out, and Frances wondered if he was now outside the station, waiting for her arrival.

She walked in past the back offices and into the kitchen, and found Maggie at the scarred wooden table, skinning a rabbit, and Johnny sitting on the floor beneath the table, building a tower out of cake tins and copper jelly moulds.

'Lady Frances,' Maggie beamed. 'Oh my word, you're a sight for sore eyes.' She put down the rabbit and wiped her hands on a cloth before coming round the table to give Frances a hug. She looked at the little boy. 'And this young man will be really pleased to see you.'

Frances knelt down and held out her arms. 'Darling, come and give me a cuddle.'

He crawled out from under the table and then, standing up, ran over to where Frances was kneeling. 'Hello, Mummy,' he said. 'You've been away for ages.'

'Yes, my little love,' Frances said, holding him close and planting a kiss on his smooth pink cheek. 'Have you been a good boy?'

He nodded and Maggie grinned agreement before picking up the skinned rabbit again and starting to chop it into pieces ready for the casserole. 'He has, Lady Frances. He's a lovely boy and no trouble at all.'

Frances smiled and got up. 'I've got something for you, sweetheart,' she said to Johnny. 'Come and look.'

Opening her handbag, Frances pulled out a red-painted wooden car and put it in the little boy's hand.

'Oh!' he cried. 'A car!' He sat down again on the floor and pushed the little car along the quarry tiles, laughing in delight as the wheels went round and he discovered that the driver could be taken in and out of his seat.

'He likes that,' Maggie said.

'He does,' smiled Frances. Then watching the child, she asked, 'Where's my father gone? He was supposed to meet me at the station, but he didn't turn up.'

'Gone?' said Maggie. 'He hasn't gone anywhere. He was in the library when I took up the tea tray about half an hour ago.'

'But the car isn't there.'

'Ah.' Maggie shook her head. 'The Rolls. It's in the garage, up on bricks. Not to be used.'

'What?'

'Didn't you know?' Maggie frowned. 'I thought his lordship would have told you.' She slapped the rabbit pieces into seasoned flour before putting them into a black cast-iron casserole dish. 'Constable Hallowes caught him buying black-market petrol. He would have come up in court, which would have been a scandal, him being the magistrate and all.'

'Oh my God,' cried Frances. 'I told him months ago not to do it. Those spivs were in and out of the village all the time. But it was just too risky. I warned him.' She shook her head, exasperated. 'So what happened?'

'Well, he was let off, wasn't he. Bert Hallowes said that as your father has allowed the folks on the estate and in the village to help themselves to the fallen wood in the copses while the war is on, he'd turn a blind eye. But he made his lordship promise to put the Rolls up on bricks.'

Maggie started chopping carrots and onions, and throwing them in the casserole dish along with the rabbit. 'The countess is not best pleased, I can tell you. She's been stamping around the house for days now, saying she won't go out in the shooting brake. Anyway, his lordship couldn't get it to start this morning.'

'Oh hell.' Frances could imagine her mother's fury. She was a woman who stood permanently on her dignity. Even with war raging and the family going broke, she expected to live in the style she'd enjoyed all those years ago at her father's New York mansion. Then, she'd been a dollar princess, a good catch for anyone, and both her father and Lord Parnell's had been thrilled with the match. But it hadn't taken long for the Parnell estate to eat up her fortune, and the title she'd acquired when she married now seemed worthless.

'Look,' Frances said, 'I'd better go and see them. Will you keep an eye on Johnny?'

'Of course I will, lovey. Off you go.'

As Frances walked towards the stairs that led up to the main hall, she had a thought. 'Where's that girl – Janet, was it? The one my mother took on.'

Maggie snorted. 'Her? Pregnant. Her dad came to take her home.'

'Good Lord,' Frances said. 'She can't have been more than fourteen or fifteen.'

'She isn't. The father is one of those soldiers that were in the village before D-Day, but she doesn't remember his name.'

'Poor thing,' Frances said, as she went towards the stairs; she and Maggie didn't look each other in the eye. There was no need.

She found both of her parents in the library when she opened the door and went in. 'Hello,' she said, and her father, with a big grin, sprang to his feet.

'My dear girl, what a pleasure.' He gave her a hug and then turned to his wife. 'Look, Opaline, Frances is home. She'll sort things out.'

'I can see her,' Lady Parnell said coldly. 'I'm not blind.'

Frances bent and gave her mother a kiss on her thin, rouged cheek. 'How are you, Mummy?' she asked.

'Don't ask,' her mother replied, and bent to pick up the copy of *Vogue* that was on the threadbare rug at her feet.

'What's the matter?'

Opaline Parnell flicked noisily through the magazine pages, refusing to look at her husband or her daughter. Frances thought she wasn't going to answer, but suddenly her mother spat out, 'Your father, that's what's the matter. Your goddam father. As usual.'

'For Christ's sake, give it a rest,' Lord Parnell said angrily, and with less than his usual care crashed his teacup down on the tray and strode out through the French windows. Frances heard him whistling for Hero and Spartan, and soon the mad Irish setters came galloping up to him, ready, as always, for any activity.

As she watched them walking off across the parkland, Frances sat down beside her mother on the sofa. 'I heard about the petrol,' she said.

'Uh!' Her mother dropped the magazine back onto the rug. 'Who told you? Not your father – he wouldn't. It was Maggie, I suppose. And did she tell you that we have no transport now and that we're trapped in this mausoleum for eternity?'

'Come on,' Frances grinned. 'There's the shooting brake. It's not smart, I grant you, but it goes. At least, most of the time.'

'I absolutely refuse to go in that…that, vehicle. Hell, I'm supposed to be the goddam lady of the manor. What will people think if I'm seen in that piece of junk?'

'Nothing,' said Frances. 'They won't think anything of it. We're in the country; there's a war on. Most people don't have cars. Be reasonable.'

Lady Parnell snorted. 'I've been reasonable for twenty-five miserable years. And I've had enough. I'm going home as soon as I can.'

Frances stared at her mother. She'd often made these threats before, but somehow this seemed real. 'This is your home,' she said cautiously.

Opaline gave a cold little smile. 'No, it isn't. It never has been. It's the place I was sent to in exchange for my fortune. An arrangement made by my father and John's. And I've hated it.'

'But what about Pa and Hugo and me?'

'Face it, honey. Hugo is probably dead. You let the family down years ago and went your own way. You won't miss me, and I know your father won't either. He was forced into this marriage as much as I was.'

Her words were shocking and Frances could feel her heart beating rapidly as she stared at this brittle, hard-faced woman who was her mother. Had she always felt this way? she wondered. Had she never been happy? Frances could think of nothing to say, but just as she was getting up to leave the room, there was a knock at the door and Maggie came in, holding Johnny by his little hand. 'Can I take the tea tray, milady?' she asked.

Opaline nodded and, getting up, went to the door. 'I'm going to my boudoir,' she said. 'I'll have my supper on a tray there.'

'Oh Lord,' Frances said, picking up her son for a hug and then taking him to look out of the window onto the parkland. 'Things are worse than I thought.'

'I know,' Maggie sighed. 'I think the petrol business was the last straw.'

In the five days that followed, Frances saw her mother only a few times. Lady Parnell stayed in her room, reading and smoking, and whenever Frances passed her room, she could hear her talking on the telephone. Once, when it rang and Frances picked it up in the hall, a man's voice, said, 'Opaline, honey, Mabel said you were coming up to town next week. Great. We'll do the shows.'

'Er…it's not Opaline,' Frances said, and would have gone on to explain that she was the daughter, but her mother came on the line.

'Put the phone down, Frances. This is my call.'

The coldness in her mother's voice was chilling. She sounded like a stranger. Frances tackled her father about it when they were together leaning over the pigsty wall, looking at the big Tamworth sow that had recently farrowed. Ten piglets were attached to her teats, grunting and squealing over the abundant milk, and the old sow had a dreamy expression of contentment on her brown, whiskery face.

'By God, those are healthy-looking pigs,' Lord Parnell said with a grin. 'They'll bring in a few bob.'

'Mm,' Frances nodded. 'That's good.' Then she looked up at him and took a deep breath. 'Mummy is talking about leaving,' she said. 'I think she means it.'

'She won't go,' he said. 'She's just restless, that's all.'

'Not this time,' said Frances. 'It's different. She's different.'

It was if he didn't care. 'Well,' he said, turning away from the pigsty, 'it's up to her, isn't it? I can't stop her.'

The phone call Frances got that evening from Beau was a welcome relief from the strained atmosphere at the hall. 'Fran, darling, you have to come back to London,' he said excitedly. 'Our plans have been altered. We're going to France earlier than we thought and I need you here to organise the gang.'

When she went back into the library, her father was on his hands and knees playing with Johnny and his cars. He had accepted the little boy absolutely, even if her mother hadn't. Only this morning he'd been talking about buying him his first pony.

'I have to go back to London tomorrow morning, Pa. Beau needs me,' Frances said, coming to sit on the arm of the sofa.

He sat back on his heels. 'Must you, dear girl? You're such a help on the farm. The land girl isn't bad, but she needs telling what to do all the time. Not like you.'

'I must,' she said. 'We need the money. It's not much, I know, but it's something. Besides, what I'm doing is helping the war effort. You've no idea how much the servicemen and the factory people appreciate us.'

He sighed. 'I'll miss you, and so will Johnny.'

Frances sat on the rug beside them and gathered the child into her arms. 'I'll miss him too, but I know that you and Maggie will take care of him.'

'We will,' he said, and gave her a kiss on her cheek.

She went up to see her mother. Opaline was sitting at her dressing table painting scarlet varnish onto her fingernails.

'What d'you want?' her mother asked. 'If you've come to try and persuade me to make up with your father, you're wasting your time.'

'I hadn't, actually,' said Frances, 'but that would be good. I wish you would.'

'I won't.' Opaline looked at Frances through the mirror. Her elegant face was as hard as stone when she said, 'The bastard's cooked his goose this time.'

Frances felt sick. This was horrible, and not for the first time, she wished that Hugo was here. He'd always got on better with Opaline than she had. But he wasn't and she would have to deal with it on her own. Growing up, she'd always known that her parents had a rocky relationship, but something had tipped her mother over the edge. Surely it couldn't only be the black-market petrol; it had to be more. For a moment, she considered asking her, but what would be the point? Instead, she said, 'I'm going back to London in the morning, so I've come to say goodbye.'

Opaline looked up from her nails. 'Are you still staying with Beau Bennett?'

Frances nodded. 'I've got a room in his flat.'

'I wouldn't hold out any hopes there, honey.' Opaline

gave a short, sour laugh. 'He sure ain't a lady's man, you know. Not like his father.'

Frances thought about that last remark as she sat on the train back to London. She had guessed that Beau preferred men, but that was beside the point. Had her mother had an affair with Rolly Bennett, Beau's father? That brought further thoughts about the reason her mother appeared to be leaving Parnell Hall. Could it be that she had a boyfriend in London, a lover?

'God, I'm glad to see you,' said Beau, when she walked into the flat.

'That's nice,' she grinned, taking off her coat.

'Here' – he went to the sideboard – 'have a drink.' He poured a large measure of gin into a glass and a minuscule amount of Angostura bitters. 'How were the folks?'

For a moment, Frances was tempted to tell him, but only for a moment. 'Alright,' she said lightly. 'The same as ever.'

'Good. Now, let's get down to business.'

The Bennett Players' travel plans had been finalised. 'We get a troop transport ferry from Gosport,' Beau said. 'That'll take us to Arromanches, and then you'll drive the bus to our first venue. It's a field hospital and transit camp near Bayeux. They'll be glad to see us; at least, I hope they will.'

'Have you told everybody?' Frances asked. 'They all think they've got another four or five days off.'

'Not all of them. I sent a telegram to Colin Brown in Glasgow and he's coming to London tomorrow. I phoned Godfrey and had to speak to that dreadful wife for five agonising minutes before she let him on the line.'

Frances laughed. 'What about the girls?' she asked.

'I'm leaving that up to you. I've got their addresses. I did phone Catherine's house, but her mother answered and we didn't understand each other at all. She seemed to think that Catherine was away performing with the Players. So perhaps you can go round there first thing in the morning. As for Della, she hasn't answered my phone calls either.'

'She did say once that the phone was in the hallway of her digs and that she didn't always hear it. I'll go round.' Frances took a gulp of her drink. 'And Tommy?'

'Got him. I went to the Criterion the other night and he was playing with the band, so he knows.'

'And that leaves the hateful Eric Baxter,' sighed Frances. 'Can't we just forget to tell him and go to France without him? Everyone would thank you.'

'No, we can't.' Beau's face lost its normal pleasant expression. 'Don't worry about him. I'll do it.' He cleared his throat and then said, 'By the way, we're having a liaison officer. He'll be meeting us in France. It's someone you know.'

'Who?' asked Frances.

'Robert Lennox.'

86

Chapter 7

She could hear the rain beating against the window as she lay in bed with her eyes closed. It was time to get up, she supposed, but a few more minutes wouldn't matter, and she needed time to think about the last three days. About the new people she'd met and the things she'd been told.

It had started when Robert Lennox had met her at the station at Sevenoaks and had driven her the few miles out of that little town and into the lush Kent countryside. He had an open-top roadster and Catherine, surprised, because she'd imagined he would have something more sober, found herself enjoying the sensation of the wind blowing through her hair. It made her feel young and carefree, although considering the circumstances, carefree was the last thing she should have felt.

'Are you sure you don't mind this?' Robert asked again. He'd offered to put the top up when he'd led her out of the station to where the car was parked. 'It'll take us about twenty minutes to get to our destination, and it's a lovely day. I thought you'd quite like it.'

'Yes,' she'd said, staring at the well-polished red car with its big headlamps and shiny bumper. 'Leave the top down.' And now, with her hair streaming out behind her, he'd flicked a look at her and asked again.

'It's alright,' she assured him. 'It's fun.'

'Good,' said Robert, and grinned.

Catherine immediately felt uncomfortable. Should she be having fun when Christopher was missing or – she forced herself to think it – dead? And this outing to the Kent countryside was certainly not for fun. It was deadly serious. She swallowed the nervous lump that kept forcing its way into her throat and looked up to the blue summer sky. She could see vapour trails criss-crossing the heavens and wondered if they were enemy fighters.

Robert caught her looking. 'They're ours,' he said, glancing up briefly. 'The German bomber force is just about finished, but it's the doodlebugs we have to worry about now.' He frowned. 'We're struggling to counter them and the people in south London are paying a terrible price.'

'I know,' said Catherine. 'My mother has friends in Croydon who escaped from France in a fishing boat at the beginning of the war. They attend the Church of Nôtre-Dame in Leicester Square, where Maman goes. Last week, the priest told her that her friends were injured in a rocket attack two weeks ago.' She shrugged. 'Their neighbours were killed, so I suppose they were lucky. But I think life is very cruel: they thought they would be safe in England.'

'Yes,' agreed Robert. 'Life is cruel. But we're coming close to the end of the war and we'll be able to go home and get on with our lives.' He was quiet for a moment, concentrating on the narrow, winding roads, shaded with heavily leafed overhanging trees. Then he added, 'If there's a life worth getting on with.'

Catherine glanced round at him. He was looking

straight ahead at the road, his face expressionless. Did he mean something by that? Something personal?

He cleared his throat. 'This place we're going to is a training school for our agents. You won't be doing the full course, as it takes months, but you will be given an idea of what you might be able to do for us.'

Catherine bit her lip. She phoned him a week ago and told him that she would consider doing something in France. He'd sounded surprised but pleased at the same time. The next day, he'd phoned her back and asked her if she could get away for two days.

'Alright,' she'd said. 'I can tell Maman that I'm working.'

'Good.' He sounded relieved and then gave her the time of the train she was to catch and where she was to get off. 'I'll be there to meet you.'

At Victoria Station, she'd been tempted to walk off the platform and go home to Maman and Lili, but, almost without noticing it, she'd found herself on the train. Now her doubts returned and she looked about wildly. If she decided to leave, would there be a bus or a taxi that could take her back to Sevenoaks?

Almost as if he knew what she was thinking, Robert smiled. 'They're a nice crowd,' he said. 'The evenings are quite jolly.'

'Will you be staying?' she asked.

Robert shook his head. 'No, I have to get back to London. But I'll hang on to introduce you. Don't worry. You'll be fine.'

She was fine. The woman who met them at the studded oak door gave Robert a broad smile. 'Major Lennox,' she said. 'How very nice to see you again.'

Catherine looked up quickly. Major Lennox, she thought. So he isn't a civilian after all. There was no time to reflect on this for the woman was holding out her hand. 'Mrs Fletcher,' she beamed. 'I'm Veronica Bishop. How very nice to meet you. Come in, do, and I'll find you a cup of coffee. Only Camp, I'm afraid, but we do have biscuits.'

The coffee was served in a large sitting room, where she and Robert sat side by side on a deep, squashy sofa. The cover was worn out and torn in places, and it looked as if somebody had been picking at the threads and making it worse. Maman would be scandalised, Catherine thought, looking around at the other furniture. It was all in much the same state, old and rather tattered. The legs on the oak coffee table in front of her were chewed, the wood scarred and splintered. Miss Bishop, a heavy-breasted woman in her forties, caught sight of the dismay on Catherine's face. 'The brigadier's dog, I'm afraid,' she sighed, handing round the coffee cups. 'So very badly trained.'

Robert grinned. 'It makes it more homely, don't you think?' he said. 'Less military.'

'If you say so,' Miss Bishop replied rather glumly, obviously not agreeing with him.

She turned to Catherine. 'We have our lessons during the day, but we do relax in the evening.' She nodded towards a grand piano, which filled a corner of the room. 'Sometimes we have a sing-song, which should suit you.'

The brigadier and his young Labrador, Belter, came in then and more introductions were made. The dog immediately galloped over to the coffee table, but Miss Bishop slapped her hand loudly on it and Belter retreated to the seat in the huge bow window and, leaping on the cushions, proceeded to gnaw at one of the tassels that held back the curtain.

'He's a young devil,' the brigadier smiled fondly. 'He does love to chew, but' – he looked nervously at Miss Bishop – 'he will grow out of it.' He turned to Catherine, who had stood up to shake hands. 'Now, my dear, we've only got two days with you, so we'd better get to it.'

Catherine's heart started pounding again and her face must have shown it because Robert touched her arm. His hand was cool and comforting. 'Don't worry,' he said. 'It'll be nothing much. Just a recognition course, German Army insignia and suchlike, so you'll know who's who, if you ever come across them.' He smiled at her and then shook her hand. 'I've got to go,' he said. 'Good luck.'

She was taken through the house and out of the back door to the yard, where beside the brick coal houses and carriage house were a couple of Nissen huts. 'In here, Mrs Fletcher,' said the brigadier, holding open the door to the closest hut. 'Captain Jaeger is waiting for you.'

He was a short, older man with a ring of white close-cropped hair round a bald pate. Like the brigadier and Robert, he didn't wear uniform, but was dressed in a neat grey suit and well-polished brown shoes. In fact, in the two days Catherine was at the house, she only saw people in mufti, although they were always introduced by their military titles.

'How d'you do?' said Catherine, when the brigadier introduced her, and had a quick look around the hut. It was laid out like a classroom, with a blackboard at one end and wooden desks arranged in a row in front of it.

Maps were pinned to the walls, rustling slightly in the breeze that crept under the door and through the half-open window. Captain Jaeger wasted no time. After briefly shaking her hand and showing her to a wooden desk, he went to the blackboard.

'You are here to learn German insignia, Mrs Fletcher, which, I think, is not a difficult task, but there are many variations, so we start...now.' He turned the blackboard over and Catherine saw that there was a coloured chart on the back. She leant forward to examine the pictures of cap badges and shoulder boards, and the names beside them.

'You have the German language?' Captain Jaeger asked. Catherine realised that he had an accent; could it be German?

'No. I don't.' It was hard to keep the hostility out of her voice. The captain's countrymen were holding Christopher in a hell that she didn't even want to imagine.

If he noticed it, Jaeger gave no indication, but took a pointer from the ledge beneath the blackboard and pointed at the first badge. It was an embroidered white eagle with outstretched wings on a grey background. 'All German soldiers wear this emblem on their uniform blouses,' Jaeger said, 'but different ranks and different divisions have, as you will expect, slight variations.' He moved the pointer to another badge. 'I show you this as an example.' It was the same eagle but now in silver on a black background. 'It is the emblem of the Panzer Division.'

Catherine gazed at the blackboard. There must have been about fifty different badges and emblems pictured on the chart. Surely she wouldn't be required to learn all of them. It was impossible. Nobody could stop me if I got up and left, she thought, and put her hand down to her handbag, which she'd tucked in beside her feet.

Suddenly Captain Jaeger gave a short, barking laugh. 'Do not despair, dear Mrs Fletcher. You will understand very quickly. The German Army does everything in order. One step will follow on from the next.'

By the time Miss Bishop came to collect her, just before six o'clock, Catherine's mind was bursting with the information that Captain Jaeger had imparted. The sound of his pointer rapping on the board as he drilled the significance of the different insignia into her was still ringing in her head when she was led through the house and up the wide oak staircase.

'This is your room,' Miss Bishop said, showing her into a small, somewhat bleak, servant's room on the second floor. 'It isn't awfully nice, I'm afraid; we are rather strapped for accommodation at the moment. But,' she added brightly, and nodded towards a green-painted door, 'that's the bathroom next door to you, so it's very convenient. When you're ready, come downstairs. We gather in the drawing room for drinks before dinner.'

Standing uncertainly in the hall half an hour later, wondering which of the closed doors opened into the drawing room, Catherine was startled by a greeting called from the half-landing.

'Hello.' A woman of about Catherine's age skipped lightly down the stairs until she was in the hall. 'Are you Mrs Fletcher?' she asked, and her red-painted lips parted in a wide smile.

Her dark hair was rolled and curled and piled on top

of her head with a green ribbon threaded through the curls, which matched her glamorous green-beaded dress. It seemed remarkably over the top and Catherine wondered if her grey day dress and short-sleeved cardigan was too plain for a dinner at this house. The woman took Catherine's arm and led her across the floor.

'I'm Chantal. How d'you do? We heard we were having a temporary guest.' She opened a door. 'Come on in and meet the gang.'

The gang consisted of eight men and five women, who all turned their heads to look at her when Catherine followed Chantal into the room. 'I'll do the introductions,' Chantal laughed, 'but you'll probably forget all the names.'

Catherine did forget the names, shyly shaking hand after hand, until one man in a brown corduroy jacket with a livid scar on his face that stretched from the corner of his eye to his mouth stood in front of her and stared. 'I know you,' he said after a moment, and gave her a lopsided grin. 'I saw you sing at the Criterion. You have a terrific voice.'

'Thank you,' Catherine smiled.

'*Mon Dieu*, you're a famous person,' Chantal said loudly, so that everyone turned round to stare. 'How exciting.'

'Not that famous,' said Catherine, blushing.

'Let me get you a drink,' said the man who recognised her. 'Gin?'

'Thanks,' Catherine nodded, and after he'd moved towards the drinks tray on the sideboard, she turned to Chantal. 'What was his name again?' she asked.

'Larry Best. Major Larry Best. Nice man.' Chantal

grinned and adjusted the neckline of her dress, which was in danger of exposing her breasts. 'Sorry,' she said in a stage whisper. 'I've lost weight in the last few weeks and this frock doesn't really fit me any more.'

'I didn't bring any formal dresses with me,' Catherine said. 'I didn't think it would be necessary.'

'It isn't.' Chantal jerked her head towards the others. 'Look at them. It's only me. I like to dress up. Nobody else bothers.'

Catherine sat next to Larry at the table when they went into the dining room for supper. They were served at a long table by silent ATS girls, who handed round dishes of unidentifiable stew and boiled potatoes. The food was demolished eagerly, without anyone examining what was on their plate; it seemed as though everyone was hungry. Catherine only picked at her meal, and even when the next course, a sponge pudding, arrived, she still couldn't eat much.

'Not hungry?' Larry leant towards her, and in a lowered voice said, 'If you don't want the rest of that pudding, can I have it?'

'Of course.' Catherine smiled and pushed the bowl to his place. He only took minutes to finish and then leant back and took out his packet of cigarettes.

'Smoke?' he asked, offering the packet of Woodbines.

'No, thank you,' Catherine said. 'I don't smoke. My voice is my living, so I look after it.'

'Are you still at the Criterion?'

'Well, I did a couple of nights there some weeks ago, but I've joined a group now and we entertain the troops and factory workers. I'm loving it.'

'Are you all singers?'

'Oh no. Not all of us. We have a conjurer, a pianist, a ventriloquist, a tenor, and my friend Della Stafford does songs from the shows and dances brilliantly. Even Frances, who's our administrator, sings. We're a good troupe and the audiences seem to like us.'

'I'm sure they do,' Larry grinned. 'Perhaps you'll sing for us one evening, while you're here.'

'Maybe,' Catherine said, as they got up. The ATS girls were collecting the dishes and Miss Bishop was directing people out of the dining room and back into the drawing room.

'Coffee is being served as usual,' she called out, as Catherine followed the others.

The evening sun was going down and shone through the great bow window, lighting up the large room in a rosy glow. It picked out the dusty Edwardian carvings on the mahogany panelling above the fireplace and gleamed through the stained-glass half-windows around the bow, sending shafts of colour onto the faded carpet.

'How lovely,' Catherine breathed.

'It is,' said Major Best, handing her a coffee. 'This place must have been magnificent once.'

She was going to reply, but suddenly the room was filled with music, as one of the younger men had sat down at the piano and was thumping out a Noël Coward number. Some of the others were singing along with gusto. Catherine smiled. The pianist was dreadful and the singing pretty poor, but they were enjoying themselves. The man who was playing had a black eye and a cut on his cheek, and looked as if he'd been in a fight. One of the women had her arm in a sling and looked tired, but she was singing along happily, her good arm linked in Chantal's.

'Not up to your standard,' Larry grinned.

'It doesn't matter,' Catherine said. 'They're having a good time.' She looked at the group again. 'A lot of them seem to have been injured. Why's that?'

'Oh, the training is quite hard,' Larry grunted. 'They're always getting bumps and scrapes.'

For the first time, Catherine thought about what these people were doing. Robert and his boss hadn't actually said what this house was for, but you didn't have to be a genius to guess. The men and women who were gathered round the over-strung piano were training to be agents. Some of them would be smuggled into France and Holland to send back information to the War Office. Others would be required to fight, blow up buildings, railway lines and bridges. Dangerous assignments. It was a sickening thought and she nervously sat forward on the shabby armchair ready to jump up and leave the room.

'I see you're married,' Larry Best broke into her anxious thoughts.

'What?'

He nodded towards her wedding ring, which she had been winding fretfully round her finger. 'Is he in the forces?'

'Yes, Christopher is a para. At least...' She was going to say more but remembered that she'd signed the Official Secrets Act. Robert had said that Chris was an agent. God, he might even have been here, but she couldn't tell anyone that. Even here. Even to Larry Best.

'At least what?'

Catherine swallowed the lump in her throat and then

97

said in a rush, 'He's been posted missing. I don't know whether he's still alive. I don't even know where he is.'

'I'm sorry,' Larry said. 'War is God-awful hell.' He narrowed his eyes and stared again at her hand, where she was once again twisting her wedding ring round her slim finger. 'Christopher, you said? In the Parachute Regiment?'

'Yes,' Catherine nodded. 'Before the war, he was a lecturer, and we were convinced the army would post him to some sort of office job. But they didn't.'

Larry narrowed his eyes. 'When did you last hear from him?' he asked.

'I haven't heard from him,' she answered, trying to think back. 'Not since he left that last time. I assume he is abroad.'

'But you've been told he's missing.'

'Yes.' Catherine nodded her head slowly.

'And nothing more?'

She frowned and glanced up at him. He was asking questions about something that she knew she mustn't divulge, and from the change in his face and the quick crooked smile he gave it was obvious he recognised that.

'How about another drink?' he said, moving to get up.

'Thanks, but no.' Catherine stood up. 'I'm rather tired, so if you won't think me too rude, I'll go to my room.'

Larry Best stood up too and shook her hand. 'I'll see you tomorrow,' he said.

The next morning after breakfast, she was directed again to the Nissen hut classroom. To her surprise, it was Larry standing behind the teacher's desk.

'Hello,' he said. 'I'm going to give you a quick

rundown of military hardware.'

Catherine could feel her face falling. This is mad, she thought, but Larry must have noticed how miserable she looked because he grinned.

'Don't worry,' he laughed. 'We're just going to look at some pictures of tanks and armoured cars. If you can sort them out in your head and remember them, it will be useful.'

He reached up and pulled down a chart that had pictures of tanks on it. Catherine sat at her desk and stared at them. They looked all the same to her. Tanks? She could distinguish a tank from a lorry or a car, but from each other?

'Oh God,' she muttered, but if Larry heard her, he ignored it.

'This is the Panzer VI,' he said, rapping his pointer on one of the pictures. 'I'm showing you this first because this is the vehicle that is the most used now, but there are others in service.'

The lesson dragged on through the morning, and after a quick lunch of soup and cheese on toast, she was straight back into the Nissen hut to learn about the different identifying markings that might be found on the military hardware.

'Are you taking any of this in?' asked Larry after an hour in the afternoon.

Catherine, who was sitting with her eyes turned towards the small window, shook her head. She'd been watching the activity outside on the large back garden. Several members of the group were having what looked to her like wrestling practice; others were practising fighting with knives.

'Not much,' she said, dragging her face away from the window. 'I think, for me, this is a total waste of my time and yours. I will never be in a situation where it will be useful.' She looked back to the window. 'And I'm certainly not going to do any of that.'

'Mm,' Larry murmured. 'I agree. But the powers that be sometimes have odd ideas. And we have to go along with them.' He followed her eyes to the activities in the garden. 'Don't worry, Mrs Fletcher. Nobody is going to ask you to fight or even learn self-defence.' He sighed. 'I think we've done enough today. If only a little of what I've said sticks, it could be useful.' He paused for a moment. 'Why don't you tell me a little about yourself? I believe your mother is French. Where does she come from?'

In no time Catherine found herself talking about her grandfather's farm south of Amiens and how much she had loved her holidays there. 'We haven't heard from them since Dunkirk, really. Maman and I are so worried.'

'Did you go there for your honeymoon?'

'Oh no,' she laughed. 'Chris and I married after the war had started. It was impossible to get there. No, we went to Brighton for a couple of days. Then his leave ended.'

'And he went back to war.'

'Yes.'

Larry lit another cigarette and drew in a deep lungful of smoke. 'It's surprising that he wasn't posted to the Education Corps. After all, he was proficient in French and German.'

Catherine nodded. It had been surprising. He should have been in the Education Corps.

They walked together back to the house, skirting the garden, where Catherine's companions from yesterday evening trampled the neglected and overgrown flower-beds. The sun was shining brightly, and beyond the house and garden, a bucolic scene of farms and cottages covered the low rolling hills. 'On a day like this,' Catherine said quietly, 'you'd never guess that...'

'No, you wouldn't. It seems too peaceful out there, and almost wrong, when you think of what's happening across the Channel.' Larry's voice was halting, and when Catherine looked up, she saw that his damaged face was set in a bitter expression. What must he have gone through? she wondered.

He noticed that she was looking at him and he gave her his lopsided grin. 'Ignore me, Mrs Fletcher. I'm turning into a curmudgeon. But take it from me – things aren't always what they seem. Now, will you sing for us tonight? We'd love it.'

'Alright. I'd like to.'

She had one last conversation with the brigadier before supper. He and Belter were in the corridor when she walked inside and he beckoned her into the empty dining room.

'I realise that you think that these two days have been a waste of time, Mrs Fletcher, and you could be right. There might not be any opportunity for you to help us when you go to France' – he put a fond hand on Belter's head and scratched the young dog behind the ears – 'but in case there is, I hope you've understood just a few of the things you've learnt.'

'I have, Brigadier, and if the occasion arises, I will try

to discover something that might be useful.' Even as she said these words, Catherine knew that the occasion would never arise and her promises were meaningless. So she smiled at him, and when Belter came snuffling around her knee, she bent and stroked his golden head, which caused the lively dog to jump around in excitement.

'Down, sir,' shouted the brigadier, and then with an indulgent smile confided, 'He will learn, but he's really not much more than a pup.'

That evening, after supper, when they were all in the drawing room, Larry stood up and clapped his hands. 'We have a treat in store now. Catherine Fletcher, who is well known in the West End, is going to sing for us. George is going to play the piano for her, but has promised not to drown her out with too much hard pedal.'

Catherine handed George the score and he softly played the introduction. She sang 'The Very Thought of You', which was one of her favourites, and judging by the rapt attention of the group, who were lolling about on the battered sofas and chairs, they were enjoying it too. Veronica Bishop was sitting on a hard chair by the door and Catherine caught a glimpse of her surreptitiously dabbing her eyes with a lace-edged hanky. The brigadier, who was in an armchair, with Belter at his feet, led the applause when she'd finished.

'Wonderful,' he shouted. 'More, please.'

She followed up with a medley from *Show Boat* and then a couple of Ivor Novello songs. Miss Bishop got up and went out at one point and Catherine worried that she'd upset her; maybe she was not quite the martinet that she affected and had someone special that she was thinking about. But as Catherine was starting her last number, the door opened and Miss Bishop reappeared, followed by Robert.

'I'm going to finish with a song that means a lot to me,' Catherine announced, her eyes on Robert, and then, nodding to George, started 'I Will Wait'.

'*Mon Dieu*,' one of the men breathed, and when she sang it in French, several of them were looking lost, as though this was taking them home to a comforting place where there was no war.

Cheers erupted when she'd finished and Larry Best gave her a swift hug. 'You're just terrific,' he said.

Robert came to stand beside her. 'Hello, Catherine,' he said.

'What are you doing here?' She was strangely pleased to see him.

'I thought I'd drive you home. What d'you think?'

'I'd like that,' she said, looking into his eyes. Then she was surrounded by the group, and Veronica Bishop brought her another cup of the execrable coffee.

When everyone had calmed down, she sat on a sofa with Robert.

'Shall we go now?' he said. 'We'll be in London before midnight. You'll be able to see your little girl.'

'Yes, oh yes,' she answered, with an excited smile, and jumped to her feet. 'You arrange it with the brigadier while I get my things.'

It took less than ten minutes to pack her few belongings and put on her coat. Larry was at the bottom of the stairs when she came down with her small suitcase.

'You're leaving us tonight?' he asked.

'Yes,' she nodded. 'Major Lennox is driving me home. I'm longing to see my baby daughter.'

'A child? I didn't know that. So, all I can do is to wish you good luck.' He stretched out his hand, and over his shoulder, Catherine could see Robert standing impatiently by the front door.

'Thank you, Larry.'

He moved aside to let her pass him and then quickly caught her arm and bent his head to her ear. 'Remember what I said. Things aren't always what they seem.'

'What was that about?' asked Robert, as they drove through the dark country lanes. 'You and Larry Best.'

'Nothing,' Catherine dismissed the question. 'He was wishing me luck, I suppose.'

'Mm,' Robert grunted. 'You just seemed very close.'

What a strange thing to say, Catherine thought. It's almost as if he's jealous. 'He's a nice man,' she said. 'We chatted a lot.'

'What about?'

'Oh, Christopher and about my grandparents' farm. He said he was surprised that Chris wasn't posted to the Education Corps, what with his French and German.' As she spoke, a new realisation dawned on her. How on earth did Larry know that Chris was fluent in German as well as French, and for that matter, what else did he know? She thought back to the two conversations she'd had with him and was positive that she hadn't mentioned that Chris lectured in modern languages. She turned her head and stared at Robert.

'Larry Best knew all about me,' she said. 'I think they all did.'

'Not all of them,' Robert grinned.

She wanted to be angry, to be furious about being tricked into going to the spy school, but glancing again at Robert, found that he was smiling unconcernedly and she knew anything she said would be useless. So she settled down for the two-hour drive through unlit roads and was almost asleep when Robert drew up in front of her house.

'Thank you,' she said, turning to him and giving him a sweet smile.

'It's alright,' he nodded, looking straight ahead. 'I was glad to give you a lift.' Then suddenly he turned and, grabbing her shoulders, pulled her towards him. His mouth found hers and for the longest moment she relaxed into the embrace, loving to be held and only remembering the pleasure of intimacy. Then, opening her eyes, she pulled away sharply.

'Sorry,' Robert groaned. 'I don't know what came over me,' and he opened the car door and went round to her side. She had already alighted and pulled her suitcase from the back seat and was standing in front of her door.

'Let me,' said Robert, as she struggled to put her key into the lock, but the key turned and the door swung open. 'Forgive me,' he said again, as she stepped inside, and she looked down into his eyes when she turned back to him.

'I have a husband,' Catherine said fiercely. 'Don't ever forget that.'

Chapter 8

'*Chérie!*' Maman's voice broke into Catherine's confused thoughts and she sat up.

'Yes?' She got out of bed and looked out of the little front window. Across the road, two of her neighbours were chatting. One was pointing to her shopping basket and shaking her head. Catherine guessed that they were talking about the rationing.

She grabbed her dressing gown from the hook behind the door and went out of the bedroom onto the landing. 'What is it, Maman?' she called, leaning over the banister.

'You have a visitor. Get dressed.'

'It's only me,' Frances called up the stairs. 'Beau wants to get in touch with everyone. We're going to France sooner than we thought and we have to find Della.'

'Oh!' Robert knew, she thought. That's why he came to get me. 'Give me ten minutes,' she called. 'Maman will give you a cup of coffee.'

When she came downstairs dressed and made-up, she found Frances sitting in the front room with Lili on her knee. Maman had brought in a tray of coffee and some pastries.

'These little cakes are delicious,' beamed Frances. 'What are they called?'

'Nun's puffs. And before you ask, I don't know where she gets the sugar,' Catherine laughed, and reached over to take Lili.

'Oh, let me have her a bit longer – she's so gorgeous,' Frances begged, 'and the absolute image of you.' She stroked Lili's dark curls and popped a tiny piece of pastry into the little girl's mouth.

Catherine gave her a calculating glance. Frances seemed very at home with a small child on her knee. 'You've done this before,' she said quietly.

Frances said nothing for a moment and then looked up to the mantelpiece, where Catherine's wedding photograph stood. 'Christopher is very handsome,' she said. 'And he looks as if he's great fun.'

Catherine was grateful that Frances spoke of Chris in the present tense. In truth, she was beginning to lose hope, but she remembered what Larry had said last night: *Things aren't always as they seem.* Did he know something about Christopher? 'Yes,' she said. 'He is.'

The baby had reached up to Frances's pearl necklace and was trying to pull it into her mouth. Frances gently moved her little hand away. 'They always go for necklaces,' she laughed.

Maman put her head on one side and said in French to Catherine, 'Your friend, she has a family?'

Catherine started to shake her head, but to her astonishment, Frances smiled at her mother and replied in French, 'I have a little boy, madame. Johnny's nearly four.'

Catherine didn't know what surprised her more, Frances's admission that she had a child or the fact that she spoke and understood French. She remembered the photograph of the red-headed boy that had been beside Frances's bed at Beau's flat. That must be him. She stared at Frances. 'You didn't say anything.'

'No.' Frances shook her head. 'I've got used to not talking about him.' She looked down at Lili and muttered, 'You can guess why.'

Catherine leant over and touched Frances's arm and her friend looked up with eyes that were brimming. 'His father's dead,' she said bleakly. 'He was killed at Dunkirk.'

Catherine felt her own tears coming. 'I'm so sorry.'

'I should be used to it,' sighed Frances. 'It's more than four years ago. But I loved him so much.'

Catherine remembered the conversation on the train to Liverpool. Beau had mentioned Johnny Petersham, describing him as d'Artagnan to their 'Three Musketeers', and Frances had looked a little lost. Della noticed it and had given Catherine a meaningful look.

Maman, looking from one girl to the other, whispered in French to Catherine, 'Your friend is sad. Has something happened?'

'We were talking about Frances's little boy. His father was a soldier, but he was killed.'

'Oh là, là. Pauvre petite.' She kissed both of Frances's cheeks. 'War is terrible, yes?'

Frances smiled and thanked her, and then, standing up, put Lili into Honorine's arms. 'We should go,' she said. 'We have to find Della.'

They took a bus to Della's flat. On the way, Catherine asked, 'Does anyone else know about your boy?'

Frances shook her head. 'My parents, of course, and our housekeeper, but as far as anyone else is concerned, he's an orphan whom I adopted. My mother told everybody in the village that he's the son of a distant cousin who was killed at the beginning of the war and that his mother died soon after.' She sighed and looked out of the bus window as they journeyed through the centre of London. It was a busy morning; people were out and about, housewives queuing at the shops and men, some in uniform, others civilians, walking to and from their offices, but all, she thought, moving rather slowly. People were tired, tired of the war, tired of being frightened and, most of all, tired of hearing bad news. The exhilaration that had swept the nation after the invasion had filtered away. She was glad that she had a job that cheered people up, if only for an hour or so.

'Who looks after him when you're in London?'

'Oh, Maggie, our housekeeper, and my father too.'

'Not your mother?'

'No. She can hardly bear to look at him; besides, she's left. Left my father. She's here in London somewhere.'

Catherine said nothing for a few moments. She couldn't understand Frances's family at all. It sounded so different from hers, but Frances was her friend and she put an arm around her. 'I think you're very brave,' she said. 'And I'd love to see him.'

They grinned at each other, and Frances said, 'I'll tell Della, but not the others. It would involve too much explanation. And anyway, they might be shocked. I think Beau wouldn't be, but he'd tell his parents and then everyone in Wiltshire would know.'

Della's flat was above an empty shop in Soho, and as the girls alighted from the bus and walked into the narrow street, they looked around in surprise. It was so different from the West End, where Catherine normally worked, and Frances had no knowledge of this rather seedy part of town. They came across Gerrard Street, which seemed to be entirely populated by Chinese and where wonderfully exotic smells emanated from several restaurants, but turning into Della's street, the atmosphere changed again to one where pubs abounded and not a few women stood purposefully on the street corners.

'Goodness,' said Frances. 'It all goes on here.'

Catherine laughed. 'I shouldn't think Della worries about it much. She can hold her own in any situation.'

'Yes,' Frances agreed. 'I hope she's in. I tried to phone, but I got no reply.' She looked at Catherine. 'I meant to ask. Where have you been? When Beau phoned your house two days ago, your mother said you were away with us.'

Catherine blushed. 'I told her a lie,' she said. 'And please don't ask me where I was because I can't tell you.'

'Alright,' Frances said slowly. 'But you aren't in trouble, are you?'

'No. No trouble. I just can't talk about it.' Catherine swallowed the nervous lump that had come into her throat. 'Now,' she said brightly, 'where's Della's place?'

Frances looked at the piece of paper on which she'd written the address. 'It's here somewhere...er...number 24.' She stopped and grabbed hold of Catherine's arm. 'Good God. Look who's over there.'

'Where?' Catherine asked, but almost as soon as the words were out of her mouth, she saw who it was that Frances was looking at.

Jerry Costigan was standing in front of an open door, beside an empty shop, having what sounded like an argument with whoever was inside.

'Shall we stop?' whispered Catherine, but it was too late. A shoe came flying out of the door, followed by

Della, who was still in her dressing gown and wagging an angry finger at Jerry.

'You're a bastard and a bastard's son,' she was yelling. 'Get out of here and take the next train back to the 'Pool.'

Jerry was laughing and bent to pick up the shoe. 'Give over, Delia,' he said. 'It was a perfectly reasonable suggestion.'

'No,' she shouted. 'You leave my family alone.' It was then that she looked over and saw Catherine and Frances, who were standing across the street watching in astonishment. One or two passers-by had also stopped to take in the entertainment. Jerry Costigan turned to see what Della was looking at and, spotting the girls, gave them a big grin.

'Hello,' he called, and tossing the shoe back to Della, took off his hat. 'Well, this is a nice surprise.'

Della scowled. 'Bugger off,' she said, and turning to her friends, beckoned, 'Come on inside.'

Jerry was still grinning when they walked past him to Della's door. Frances looked back over her shoulder as she got to the step. He gave her a wink and she found herself smiling back. He might be a crook, as Della had said, but there was something awfully attractive about him. She kept smiling as she followed Della and Catherine up the stairs.

Della's flat was really only a large room with a bed pushed into the corner, an old-fashioned mirrored wardrobe against the wall and a table and a couple of chairs beside the window. In the opposite corner was a sink and a wooden cupboard, which held a two-ring Baby Belling cooker. Della filled a small kettle from the tap and set it on the cooker. 'Tea?'

111

The girls nodded. There was a plate of toasted teacakes and a small covered butter dish on the table, a bottle of milk and two dirty cups. Frances picked up the cups and went to the sink to wash them.

'What was that about?' asked Catherine. 'In the street. And why are you in your nightclothes?'

'Did he stay over?' Frances grinned, running hot water from the wall-mounted boiler into the sink.

'No, he bloody didn't,' snapped Della. 'He's just got off the train and came straight here. I suppose Paddy gave him my address, the silly idiot.'

'What did he want?'

Della frowned. 'He said he'd come to London to do a bit of business but wanted to look me up first. He had a bag of teacakes that he'd bought at the station, so I gave him a cup.'

The cold teapot stood on the sink and Frances picked it up to wash it. 'Where shall I put the tea leaves?'

'Give it here,' said Della, and went out of the room. After a moment, they heard a lavatory flushing and Della reappeared. She opened the cupboard underneath the cooker and, pulling out a tea caddy, put two generous spoonfuls into the pot before elbowing Frances aside to pour boiling water into it. 'Here,' she said, putting the teapot on the wooden table. 'Help yourselves. I'm going to the bathroom.' She took her underwear from the end of the bed and a dress from the wardrobe. 'I won't be a moment.'

Catherine and Frances looked at the teacakes and then, laughing, dived in. 'Good old Jerry Costigan,' said Frances. 'There's nothing like railway teacakes.'

'You've already had cakes at my house,' Catherine said. 'Didn't you have any breakfast?'

Frances shook her head. 'No, I don't generally bother. D'you know,' she said, licking her fingers, 'this is real butter.'

'It'll be him. Black market, I bet.'

'Mm,' Frances nodded, and then pouring tea in both cups, said, 'He's rather good-looking. Don't you think?'

'Listen to you,' laughed Catherine. 'I thought Della was the one for the boys.'

'I'm allowed to look,' Frances protested indignantly, and then burst out laughing too. They were still smiling five minutes later when Della returned, dressed and made-up.

'I heard you talking about Jerry Costigan.' Della sat down with the other two at the table. 'Yes, he is good-looking, but he's a right bastard and a criminal. You don't know the half.' She held up a brown paper bag. 'Guess what he brought me?'

'We know,' Frances said, pointing to the plate, where only one teacake remained.

'No,' Della groaned, 'besides those bloody cakes. These.' She upended the bag and two pairs of fishnet tights fell out.

'Stockings?' Frances looked puzzled.

'They're fishnet tights,' breathed Catherine. 'Gold dust. Wherever did he get them?'

'I told you. He's a criminal. Black market, fell off the back of a lorry or just plain stolen. Whatever, it makes me an accomplice.' She looked so angry that Catherine and Frances glanced at each other with raised eyebrows.

'Are you going to give them back,' said Frances eventually, 'or report him to the police?'

'Well, of course not,' Della scowled. 'But he's still a

113

bastard.' She picked up the teacake and took an angry bite out of it. The others watched her, and then Frances cleared her throat.

'I suppose it would be nosy of me to ask what his "perfectly reasonable suggestion" was?' she asked. 'And why did it involve your family?'

'Yes, it is nosy,' Della snorted, 'but if you must know, he wants Ma to make her tonic on a larger scale. He would sell it and divide the proceeds.'

'But I think that it must be against the law, if your mother's tonic is, well, really alcohol.' Catherine looked puzzled.

'It is,' Della said angrily, 'but as long as she keeps it local, nobody minds. If Costigan gets involved, the bobbies will be sniffing around.'

'Calm down,' Frances urged. 'You told him it wasn't going to happen, so it'll be alright.'

'Oh God, I hope so. But Paddy can persuade Ma to do anything, and he's under Jerry Costigan's spell. I'm going to write to Ma today and tell her to have nothing to do with the stupid idea.' She stood up and paced the room, still trying to simmer down. She stopped in front of the mirror on the wardrobe and glared at her reflection. 'I do need to get my roots done,' she grumbled.

'You'd better be quick,' said Frances. 'We're crossing the Channel on Friday. That's what we've come to tell you.'

'What!' Della turned to face her friends. 'Oh wow! Now I really must go to the stylist.' She grinned. 'Why don't you come with me? She's only down the street. We can all get our hair done.'

Frances and Catherine looked at each other.

'Do you want to?' asked Catherine.

'Yes,' Frances said. 'It's fun doing things together, and my hair does need a trim. Then we can grab a bite to eat at a Lyons Corner House.'

That afternoon, they ate macaroni cheese at a Lyons cafe. Della kept looking at herself in the wall mirrors, and even Frances touched her hair, pleased with the trim, which had smartened up her heavy neck-length bob. Catherine had only had hers washed and dried, but the stylist had massaged a little dab of special cream through it that made it shine.

'I might go to that place again,' said Catherine. 'They do a nice job.'

'Yes, they do.' Della flicked at her hair again. 'Now, let's talk about France.'

'Well' – Frances opened her large handbag – 'I've got forms for you to fill in and insurance policies that you must have, apparently. The forms are temporary passports, in case you don't have one.' She waved another piece of paper. 'These are will forms. We have to do them just like the soldiers do.'

Christopher had made a will and told her about it before he went away that last time. 'The house is yours,' he'd said. 'And what I've got in the bank. Not much, I'm afraid, but you'll get a pension.'

I didn't listen properly, Catherine thought, angry with herself. I was so besotted with the baby that I'd almost forgotten how much I loved him. And now, I have to write a will too.

'I've got nothing to leave.' Della's voice broke into Catherine's thoughts. 'Apart from clothes and a few sticks of furniture. Why should I bother?'

115

'You must,' said Frances. 'Anyway, who knows? You might meet a millionaire general in France.'

'Good thought,' grinned Della. 'I'll be on the lookout.'

'Then I've a list of bits and pieces we must take with us.' Frances lowered her voice. 'Women's things, you know.'

'What about our performance clothes?' asked Della.

'They'll go in the big baskets that Beau's organised. If you bring your stage outfits and make-up round to his flat tomorrow morning, then we'll pack them up. I've got in touch with all the boys and they'll do the same. Then we set off at six o'clock on Friday morning. We're sailing from Gosport and we'll be based near Bayeux.'

'Does everyone know?' Della leant back and lit a cigarette.

'Yes. We've got in touch with all the gang. And Beau said we'll be having a liaison officer, although we might be meeting him in France.'

Della giggled. 'I do love the thought of a real officer joining us. I wonder what he'll look like.'

'You've already seen him,' Frances said, clearing a space on the table for them to fill out the forms. 'At least, you have, Catherine.'

Catherine said nothing and waited.

'Not that bloke who wanted her to do translating, the one with the glasses?' Della's mouth turned down. 'Well, he's not what I'd call a dish.'

'But he's very nice. I remember him from years back when he, Johnny and Beau used to stay at our place during the holidays. Hugo and Beau always grumbled about me hanging around with them. But Robert was kind and included me in all their games. You liked Robert

Lennox, didn't you?' Frances had turned to Catherine.

'Yes,' she nodded, remembering that kiss. 'He seems pleasant. Anyway, let's fill in these forms. I want to get back to Lili and have a bit longer with her. And you' – she gave Frances a look – 'had better tell Della what you told me earlier, in case I blurt it out.'

'What? What?' squeaked Della, and later, after being told about Johnny, she lit another cigarette and gazed at Frances. 'I would never have guessed,' she grinned. 'Not in a thousand years.' She shook her head. 'So the toffs are at it too.'

'Of course,' Frances said with a serious face. 'We just breed and breed. How else are we supposed to keep you peasants down?'

Della's mouth dropped open and Catherine held her breath, waiting for the angry outburst that was sure to follow, but then a snort burst from her friend's red-painted lips, followed by a barely suppressed giggle, and the three girls burst into laughter, causing the other diners to turn their heads and stare at them.

Chapter 9

August 1944

'Oh God,' Della moaned. 'How much longer?'

'Not much,' Catherine said. 'We've already been on this boat for six hours. We must be near the French coast.'

'I'm never going on the sea again,' Della cried. She was sitting on the deck of the landing craft, one hand clasped to her mouth and the other braced against the metal side of the vessel.

It had been a rough passage, with heavy seas and driving rain. It had rained all the way from London and Frances had struggled to drive through roads packed with military traffic and the occasional farm vehicle. Very few civilian cars were on the road, because nobody could get any petrol. Frances's heart sank when she thought about her father and his black-market purchases. He'd been lucky not to get a prison sentence; only a few months ago, Ivor Novello had been given eight weeks at Wormwood Scrubs for doing the very same thing, and he was famous.

She sighed as she waited at a T-junction for a line of army trucks to pass in front of the bus. It was only a week since she'd been at home, but she did miss Pa and, most of all, little Johnny. They'd be happier without her mother, she was sure of that, but would they be able to manage? Maggie would have to take over. Then she wondered what Hugo would say about Opaline's decision to leave. He had been closer to their mother than she had, but nevertheless, he wouldn't approve of her going off with some man...if that's what she'd done.

'There's a barrier ahead.' Beau's voice suddenly penetrated her thoughts of home.

'Yes, I can see it,' she said, slowing down. They'd arrived at the port, and when she stopped the bus, Frances got out and showed their papers to the tin-helmeted sailors who were manning the barrier. One of them examined the documents and then looked at the bus. Beau had arranged for it to be painted red and had had a logo designed along the side that read, in a green script, *The Bennett Players*, and underneath that, in smaller, yellow letters, *Entertainment for Military and Civilian Workers.*

'You sure of what you're doing, miss?' the sailor asked. 'They're still fighting over there.'

'We'll be alright,' smiled Frances. 'They wouldn't let us go if they thought it was dangerous.'

'Well,' he grinned, 'they'll be very glad to see you, I'm sure. 'Specially if they're all corkers like you.'

'Watch it, cheeky,' Frances laughed, and looked back to the bus to where the other members of the troupe were waiting and watching the byplay through the windows. Della gave the young sailor a wink and he blushed furiously as he handed the papers back to Frances.

'Follow the road round, miss,' he said, pointing towards the harbour, where Frances could see ships bobbing restlessly on the water, 'and then there'll be someone to show you to the embarkation point.'

119

When they had arrived at the allotted place, the troupe had been astonished when they saw what vessel was going to take them across the Channel.

'Crikey! It's a landing craft,' said Tommy with a huge grin. 'Just like the ones that took over the invasion force. Good. I'll feel like a proper soldier.'

The others had not been so enthusiastic, but put on brave faces, all except for Baxter.

'Pretty poor show, old sport,' he brayed, in Captain Fortescue's voice. 'We're entertainers, artistes, not bloody soldiers.'

'Oh, shut up,' Della growled. She had noticed, as they all had, the looks that had passed between the sailors who were loading them on board. 'If it's good enough for the forces, then it's good enough for me.'

'Here, here,' said Tommy loudly, and the others nodded.

Eric shrugged and, lingering in the rear as they were helped aboard, crooked an imperious finger to Beau, who frowned and limped over to him.

One of the sailors had driven the bus on board. The Players had trailed after it up the broad gangplank and sheltered beside the small bridge until it had been secured with metal ropes. Then they'd got back inside, out of the wind and spits of rain, while they waited to sail. But it had been an hour before they set off, and they'd waited in the bus, enduring the swell of the harbour.

Della's face had drained of colour. 'I get sick on the Mersey ferry,' she whispered to Catherine before they left, and once the landing craft had manoeuvred out of harbour and passed the bar into the open channel, she was desperate. 'I can't stay in here,' she gasped. 'I'll take my chance in the rain.' And for the next five hours she'd lain against the bulwarks being sick into a tin bucket, which one of the crewmen brought for her.

They'd all been issued with waterproof gas capes, and those offered some protection from the weather, but Catherine, who had come to sit beside Della, could feel the damp creeping into her uniform.

'Go back in the bus,' Della sighed. 'I'll be alright.'

'No. I'd rather be out here too,' Catherine said. 'It's not much fun inside.'

Eventually other members of the Bennett Players left the bus, driven out by the stuffiness and thick atmosphere of cigarette smoke. Frances had come to sit with her friends, while Colin, Tommy and Godfrey had rigged up a small shelter out of capes and were playing poker.

They had a storm lantern, the light illuminating the play, but the cards slithered off the upturned ammunition box that they were using as a table whenever there was a particularly deep lurch over a wave.

'Bloody hell,' grumbled Colin. 'It's almost nae worth it.'

'You can't stop now,' Tommy grunted. 'You already owe me two quid, and I mean to make it five before the night's out.'

Godfrey held up his hand. 'Come now, gentlemen,' he said in his deep, rich voice. 'Don't let us argue. Tommy, deal the cards.'

He had become a different person since they'd left London and travelled to the south coast. At Victoria, where they'd all met up, his dreadful wife had hung on to his arm, issuing copious instructions about wearing his scarf and taking his cough medicine and not to forget his daily dose of laxatives. She had waved her passport at Frances and indicated the small suitcase she had brought with her.

'Not even remotely possible,' said Frances shortly, and returned to her seat in front of the wheel. The rest of the group had already taken their places on the bus and impatiently watched Godfrey and his wife out of the window. Beau kept sighing and tapping at his watch.

Eventually Frances got up and walked down the bus to the door. 'Godfrey,' she called, 'come on. We'll be late.'

He had looked over his shoulder with a desperate face. 'I'm coming,' he called, and turning back to his wife, said, 'Goodbye, my dear.'

'Not yet.' Mrs James grabbed the sleeve of his uniform. 'I haven't finished what I wanted to say.'

'Oh Christ!' Frances jumped down the steps of the bus and, taking Godfrey's other arm, marched him towards the door. 'Get in, now,' she ordered.

'But...' Mrs James flustered.

'But nothing,' said Frances firmly. 'We have to go. Please stand out of the way or I might be forced to run you down.'

'What a cheek!' Mrs James clutched her muskrat coat around her and shouted, 'I never heard the like. I'll report you.'

But Frances was already in her seat and letting out the clutch. As the bus slowly drove away, Godfrey waved a hand to his outraged wife, and then, when she was safely out of sight, he laughed out loud. 'I thought I'd never get away,' he said, and gratefully accepted a swig from Tommy's flask. Now, hunkered down on the damp, riveted floor of the landing craft, he was cheerfully playing poker, safe in the knowledge that Gertrude James was already hundreds of miles away.

Beau staggered over to them. He'd spent the entire journey in the bus, as had Eric, but now, both of them had emerged, Beau joining the girls and Eric sitting beside the card players.

'Frances,' Beau called, his voice hard to hear above the sound of the engine and the wind, 'the commander wants to talk to us. Bring your torch.'

Catherine watched as they went to join the commander and soon they were peering at a map, unsteadily illuminated by Frances's small torch. Catherine knew that they were discussing where they would land and she was getting excited. It would be somewhere in Normandy, possibly on one of the invasion beaches.

She looked down at Della, who had her head over the small tin bucket. 'We're nearly there,' she said sympathetically. 'You'll soon be on dry land.'

'I might die before then,' groaned her friend, and started dry-heaving again.

'Butterscotch, old fruit. A sovereign cure.'

Catherine turned to see Eric offering a small paper bag that contained a few wrapped sweets. She was astonished. Eric being nice? Impossible. She looked over to where Beau was standing with the commander and Frances. He was looking back at them, as though he was watching Eric's actions. He's spoken to him, Catherine thought. Our pleas have got through.

'Thank you.' Catherine gave Eric a brief smile and squatted down beside Della. 'Try this,' she said, holding out a butterscotch. 'It might help.'

'It won't,' Della wailed. 'I'll only chuck it up.' She

looked up from the bucket and saw Eric standing beside Catherine, an amused smirk on his face. 'Bugger off,' she growled.

Catherine stood up and put the sweet back in the paper bag. 'Sorry,' she said. 'Della's not herself at the moment.'

'Herself?' Captain Fortescue's voice cackled. 'There's a conundrum. Who is Della Stafford? A Liverpool moonshine merchant, or a tart from Soho?'

Catherine, furious that she'd read him wrong, shot up her hand and fetched a hard slap on Eric's thin face. He gasped and put his own hand on the reddening mark.

'You'll regret that,' he whispered, in his own voice.

'No, I won't,' Catherine smiled. 'You've been asking for it.'

The card players watched, open-mouthed, and as Eric walked back to the stern of the boat to sit beside the big suitcase that contained the doll, they grinned at Catherine.

'Good girl,' said Tommy, and Colin and Godfrey nodded in agreement.

Della's hand found hers and gave it a squeeze. 'You're a star,' she murmured.

Frances came to join them. 'What was all that about?' she asked. 'I saw you slap him.'

'It doesn't matter,' said Catherine. 'It was just something that had to be done.'

'I don't doubt it,' Frances grinned. 'Anyway, listen up, everyone. We'll be landing at Arromanches in about twenty minutes.'

'Hurrah.' Della gave a weak cheer.

'Then we'll drive to Bayeux, where we're billeted at a hotel. It'll be basic – the Germans were there only a few weeks ago – but at least we'll get a bed…of sorts.'

Robert was waiting for them on the beach at Arromanches, and introduced himself as their liaison officer. He shook hands with each member of the troupe before leading them up to the road to wait while their bus was driven off the landing craft and across the beach on the specially erected track. He was in the uniform of a Guards Regiment and drew salutes from the sailors and the many soldiers who were busy on and above the beach.

Catherine heard Tommy whisper to Colin, 'Look at his ribbons. That white-and-purple one. It's an MC.'

A Military Cross, Catherine thought. I wonder what he did to earn that? And as she shook hands with him, she remembered that kiss and felt strangely shy, as though he mattered to her, more than he should have.

'Your billet is in the town.' He stood up at the front as they settled onto the bus, and turning to face them all, said, 'The first concert is tomorrow afternoon, in the theatre. I'll discuss the arrangements with La— er, Miss Parnell, but you've time to have a bit of a rest and a recce. Look, there's something else. The Germans are not that far away and have by no means given up. There'll be some shelling probably and you'll be told where to go for shelter.' He smiled. 'But you're used to that, I'm sure. And you've been issued with tin helmets, so remember to take them with you at all times.'

Catherine and Della looked at each other. 'I thought it would be safe,' whispered Catherine.

'He's probably only saying that to make him seem more important,' Della whispered back. 'Anyway, with all these soldiers about, the Krauts won't come anywhere near us.' Since being on dry land, Della's sickness had abated. She still looked washed out, but her confidence had returned, as had her enthusiasm for the venture. She looked through the bus window as they drove along the cobbled street beside the Gothic cathedral. 'Look!' she squealed, grabbing hold of Catherine's arm.

'What?'

'Yanks!'

Catherine followed Della's pointing finger and saw what she was looking at. A group of GIs were standing beside the cathedral door. Nearby was a Jeep and Catherine guessed that they'd come to have a look at the sights during their few hours off duty. They turned round when Frances braked to let a military truck pull out in front of the bus and, spotting them, started to whistle; a couple of them ran over and banged on the windows.

'Hi, honey!' A young sergeant jumped up to Della's window.

She giggled, then daringly blew him a kiss.

The rest of the Players grinned at him and at his companions, who had got into their Jeep and driven it alongside the bus. The young sergeant hauled himself aboard and shouted, 'What's your name, good-lookin'?'

'Della!'

'What?'

She opened her handbag and, finding a pencil and a piece of paper, wrote, *Della Stafford…theatre tomorrow p.m.*, and held the paper up to the window as Frances drove on to their hotel.

'It takes me to drum up an audience,' said Della triumphantly.

The Hôtel Côte de Nacre was on a narrow street behind the cathedral. It was small with grey-painted shutters on the first- and second-floor windows, and a cafe at street level. A striped awning hung over the tables and chairs, which crowded the pavement on either side of the door, and even at now, at mid-afternoon, several people were sitting on the metal chairs, casually drinking glasses of wine and reading the newspaper. This, added to the relatively undamaged town that they'd driven through, was astonishing.

'You'd hardly think that there's a war on,' said Godfrey.

'It was the first town we liberated,' Robert agreed. 'The Jerries put up virtually no resistance. You'll see later that some of the others have been almost obliterated.'

Catherine felt a shiver run down her spine. She thought about her grandparents, further north at Amiens. What had happened to them?

'Stop here,' said Robert, pointing to the hotel. Then, turning to Frances, he continued, 'Beau and I will find somewhere to park the bus. You go inside with the others and find your rooms.'

The boys got out first and unloaded the suitcases. They left the baskets with the stage clothes and props where they'd been stored at the back of the bus.

'We'll unload them at the theatre,' Beau said. 'We'll be there for the next week, before moving on. Just like the old days.'

They laughed. Most of the company had done the

circuits, Glasgow one week, Birmingham the next, always on the move.

Della grinned. 'Audiences of fit young men, night after night. What could be better?'

'Della, you're mad,' smiled Catherine, as they picked up their bags.

'Why?'

'Flirting with an American soldier before we've hardly got here. A couple of hours ago, you were dying.'

Della grinned and walked towards the hotel door. 'I like Yanks,' she said. 'Harry was a Yank.'

'Harry?' Frances had joined them.

'Harry Stafford, my husband.'

Catherine and Frances looked at each other.

'Husband?' Frances stared at Della. 'Did you say "husband"?'

'Yep.' Della gave a little grin and leant on the shiny wooden reception desk that doubled as the hotel bar. A stern-looking older woman, dressed in black with her thin grey hair scraped into a high knot, stood in front of the rows of bottles. Della gave her a grin and then turned to her friends. 'Catherine,' she said. 'Come and do your stuff. Ask Madame Défarge here about our rooms and, more importantly, where the conveniences are. I'm absolutely bursting.'

The woman scowled. She patently understood a little English. '*Madame*' – she sniffed – '*les toilettes sont là*.' She pointed to a door beside the bar.

'Thanks.' Della nodded politely and then, turning to her amused friends, said, 'I'll join you in a minute…Find out where our rooms are.'

When she finally did join them in the room that the

three girls had to share, she was bubbling with indignation.

'The lav,' she grumbled, 'it was outside.'

'For goodness' sake.' Catherine shook her head. 'You must be used to that. I bet there aren't any inside toilets in the Courts.'

'No, there aren't, but it's years since I've lived at home. And worse than that, these French ones don't have a seat! You have to, well, you have to squat.'

Frances and Catherine burst out laughing, and after a moment, Della joined in. 'Oh God,' she gasped, wiping her eyes, 'what have we let ourselves in for?' She unbuttoned her uniform jacket and pushed off her shoes. 'Which is my bed?'

Frances looked around the room. It was furnished with three narrow iron beds and not much else. In one corner was a curtain and, behind it, a decorated porcelain washbasin and a bidet. 'Whichever one you want,' she answered. 'They all look uncomfortable.'

'This will do.' Della sat on one of the beds and lit a cigarette. 'Home sweet home, I don't think. Where are the boys?'

'They've got rooms on this floor. Tommy and Colin are sharing. Godfrey's on his own, and so is Eric. Beau is in the house next door. It's been commandeered by the army and they've found a place for him with the officers.'

'Who's a lucky boy, then,' Della smiled. 'I don't suppose he'd consider a swap?'

'Before we go into sleeping arrangements,' said Catherine, sitting on the bed next to Della, 'tell us about Harry Stafford. We thought' – she looked at Frances, who nodded eagerly – 'that Stafford was only a stage name. You never said that you'd married.'

'Didn't I?' Della drew on her cigarette. 'Well, it was a while ago now. He was an illusionist who I met when I was doing a summer season in Brighton.' She stood up and walked over to the window, which looked out onto the street. 'What can I say? I fell in love. So did he, I think. He was an American, you know, from Brooklyn, New York. He kept telling me how much I'd love it there. We were going, emigrating – well, I was. But I kept putting it off: there was Ma and Maria and Paddy. My money was helping. Then war was declared.'

She turned back to face them. 'And d'you know what that silly bugger did? He joined the army, the British Army, for Christ's sake. Said he believed in doing something against Hitler. He went to France right at the beginning and that's the last I heard. Reported missing, just like your bloke, Catherine. One of his friends told me he'd been blown up.' There was a choke in her voice as she said that last and Catherine walked over to put an arm around her, followed swiftly by Frances. They stood, arms wrapped about each other for several moments, gaining comfort from their friendship until Della broke away.

'Enough,' she said. 'The boys will be talking about us. Well, at least Eric will.'

'Oh Lord,' grinned Frances. 'We'd better get moving. Beau's arranged that we can rehearse in the theatre this evening at six o'clock, which we might need, and also he said something about a soldier joining us. He was a comedian before the war – worked all over, apparently.'

'What's his name?' asked Della.

'Um...' Frances tapped her lip. 'I've forgotten. Davey something, I think. Anyway, he was wounded in Italy, and when he came out of hospital, he was transferred to the Entertainments Division. He's been offered to us.'

Della frowned. 'There was a Davey Jones. I remember him at the Palace in Manchester, but he was the straight man for Lenny Locker. I don't think it can be him.'

'Anyway' – Frances went to the door – 'I'm going to ask the boys to gather on the pavement at half five. I'll find Beau and he can tell me where the bus is.'

'Any chance of a cup of tea downstairs?' asked Della.

'I shouldn't think so,' said Frances. 'We can use the NAAFI and the officers' mess. Major Lennox will give us the info.'

At half past five, the Players gathered on the pavement outside the hotel. Catherine and Della sat at a table sipping brandy, which was the only drink that Della recognised. Catherine warned her against the absinthe, which the workmen at the next table were drinking. 'That's the green fairy. It's a dangerous drink,' she said. 'It makes people mad.' But even as she said that, she looked over to the table where Eric sat with Captain Fortescue on his knee and saw him pour water from a dusty carafe into a glass of the *feé verte*.

The theatre was an old building that had seen many changes over the centuries, but it had a fine stage and Catherine enjoyed stepping out onto it to rehearse her first number. In discussion with Beau, she'd added a couple of different songs to her list and now, nodding to Tommy, who sat at a battered upright piano, she launched into the first one.

Some local workmen were in the theatre. They'd carried the wicker hampers from the bus and, under Frances's instructions, put them in the rather dingy dressing rooms backstage. As the rehearsals started, they had been noisy, shouting instructions to each other while they manoeuvred the hampers through the narrow corridors. But when Catherine started to sing, they gradually began to come to the wings, silenced now, and listening entranced as her voice floated across the theatre.

'*Bravo, mademoiselle!*' one of them called, and the others clapped their hands furiously.

'Praise indeed,' said Beau, grinning. 'From people who've seen and heard it all.'

'Thank you,' Catherine smiled, and turning to the workmen, said, '*Merci beaucoup, messieurs.*'

'Can we get on with it?' Eric snapped, dragging a wooden chair to the centre of the stage and sitting down. He put Captain Fortescue on his knee and looked up to where a technician was adjusting the spotlights. 'Have you got me?' he called in the captain's voice. 'After all, old fruit, this is a review, don't you know? Not a one-woman show, no matter how much she likes to hog the limelight.'

The rest of the company, who had been waiting for their turn to rehearse and listening with pleasure while Catherine sang, looked shocked.

'Bad show, sir,' said Godfrey, and Tommy and Colin muttered their disgust.

Frances looked at Beau to see if he would say something, but he merely walked away to talk to the stage manager. What is the matter with him? thought Frances, and taking Catherine's hand, she whispered in her friend's ear, 'Ignore him. He's just vile.'

'He's a bastard,' said Della, not bothering to lower her voice, 'but don't you worry. Let's look forward to the show, and somehow I'll find a way to do for him.'

'Della!' A voice came from the back of the theatre, and turning to face the soldier who was walking up the aisle, her angry face dissolved into a welcoming smile.

'Davey Jones, as I live and breathe.'

Chapter 10

'Well, well. Della Stafford. As glamorous as ever, and in uniform.' Davey Jones bent to give her a friendly peck on the cheek. He was tall, very tall, with sandy hair and pale skin. A livid scar ran down the side of his face and extended beneath his collar. It was puckered in places, which dragged his eye down slightly and gave him a look of constant sadness. But he wasn't sad, and when he was introduced to the rest of the Players, he had a cheery word for each of them.

'Mr James, how are you?' he grinned. 'D'you remember me?'

'I do, indeed, young man,' said Godfrey, and confided to Frances, 'Davey was a boy when I first met him. At Blackpool, wasn't it, Davey?'

'Yes, Mr James, we were on the same bill.'

Godfrey chuckled. 'You've grown a span since then.'

Colin hadn't met him before, nor Tommy or Catherine. 'You've got a lovely voice, Mrs Fletcher,' he said, when they were introduced. 'I could hear it as I came into the theatre.'

'Thank you,' she said, 'and please, call me Catherine.'

'So, this is the company,' he grinned, glancing around, and then his face fell when he saw Eric, who was arguing with the French workman who was adjusting the spotlight.

'D'you know him?' asked Frances.

'Oh God, yes,' Davey said. 'I know him. What's he calling himself these days?'

'Eric Baxter,' said Tommy, joining in. 'And the doll is Captain Fortescue.'

'Baxter, eh. He was Eric Lawford when I knew him, and I was told that he'd been Farley before that.'

'Why does he keep changing his name?' asked Frances.

Davey frowned. 'We all change our names. I was David Hardcastle before I teamed up with Lenny Locker.' He stared at Eric and then said in a lowered voice, 'He was a blackshirt, you know, before the war. One of Mosley's mob, and there was a rumour about him having been in prison.'

As the others turned their heads to gaze at Eric, Davey added in an urgent hiss, 'Look, I don't know that for sure, and I beg you, for God's sake, don't quote me.'

'He's not a bad ventriloquist,' said Godfrey, generous as ever. 'I've seen plenty worse.'

'That's as maybe,' Davey conceded. 'But years ago, before he had the doll act, he was an actor in rep and got terrible notices. Then the next thing, he was in variety. Singing, tap-dancing, all sorts. I was on the same bill once when he bombed and they actually dragged him off stage with the hook.'

Della laughed. 'Oh, I do hope you remind him of that.'

He grinned. 'You haven't changed.'

The rehearsal went well; Beau rearranged the running order so that Davey came on after Della's first song and then again later before Catherine closed the show. He was quite good; he told a few jokes and did a couple of funny monologues. His act was nothing spectacular, but it did fit in nicely with the rest of the show. Afterwards, they all went to the NAAFI for a meal. It was next to army headquarters.

'What's happened to Lenny?' asked Della, as she wiped the remains of her plate of pie and chips with some bread. 'Did he join up?'

'No.' Davey shook his head. 'He didn't fight at all. Cleared off to the States as soon as war was declared, tried to get into pictures, but I don't know how he did. I never heard from him again.' He lit a cigarette. 'What about you? Where's old Harry these days?'

'Killed,' said Della shortly.

Catherine and Frances, who were sitting on either side of her, edged closer, comfortingly.

'God, I'm sorry,' Davey said, looking embarrassed. 'I didn't know.'

'It doesn't matter.'

'D'you know' – Frances hurried to change the subject – 'they've got loose tea and tinned milk for sale here? I saw that there was a stove at the back in the theatre. We could have a cuppa before we go on. What d'you think?'

'Good idea,' Della agreed, grateful for her friend's tact. 'Let's all get some.'

That night, Catherine slept deeply. The iron bed was uncomfortable, but she was tired after the long journey on the landing craft and the excitement of the rehearsal. She tried, as she often did, to imagine that Christopher was lying beside her. That his arm was around her and that she could feel his body pressed into hers. Am I near to him? she wondered, as she closed her eyes. Is he close by? Somewhere in the French countryside, being hidden by kind friends, waiting to be rescued? Oh, please God. Then, as she was drifting off, she found herself thinking about Robert and how impressive he'd looked in his uniform. Stop it, she told herself. Don't let him, of all people, invade your mind; you're being stupid.

In the morning, she was the last to wake up. 'Come on, sleepyhead,' Della said, pushing her on her shoulder. 'I've brought you a cup of tea.'

'However did you get that?' asked Catherine sleepily, sitting up and pushing her hair out of her eyes. She picked up the cup and saucer that Della had plonked on the rickety table between the beds.

'It's the tea Frances bought last night,' Della said, sitting on the next bed. 'I took it down to Madame Défarge and persuaded her to put a couple of spoonfuls into a coffee pot. I think she was scandalised, but as we couldn't understand each other, it doesn't matter. She didn't have any milk, so I opened the tinned stuff.' She took a sip from her cup. 'I've had worse,' she said, pulling a face. 'But not often.'

'It's fine for me,' said Catherine. 'My French grandparents make tea with tinned or sterilised milk, so I'm used to it.' She looked at Frances's bed. 'Where is she?'

'Out already. Beau came knocking for her before eight. They're fixing up for us to do some matinees in the field. She's gone to talk to the military.'

Catherine got out of bed and, stretching her arms above her head, pulled a face. 'I feel sticky,' she said, 'and I'm sure I smell. I'd love a bath.'

'Ah,' smiled Della. 'I've found out that we can get a shower at the NAAFI. How about us going there? We can have some breakfast too. It's not far – we can walk.'

The streets were busy, full of civilians who seemed to be heading towards a covered market, and soldiers who strolled along the narrow thoroughfares and gave the girls the eye as they passed. There was a rumbling in the air and Della looked at Catherine. 'Thunder,' she groaned. 'It'll rain in a minute.'

Catherine looked around. 'I'm not sure,' she frowned. People had stopped walking and were standing staring towards where the sound was coming from, and then a siren started wailing in the air. She clutched Della's arm and started to say something when suddenly there was a louder boom, followed by a sickening crump, which made the buildings beside them shake. 'It's shelling,' she shouted. 'We must get under cover.'

'Should we go back to the hotel?' Della asked, wildly looking backwards and forwards as the people, who had a minute ago been strolling down the street, started to run.

'No.' Catherine hurried her along. 'The NAAFI. It's just round the corner. They must have a shelter.'

A group of soldiers who had just passed them turned and started to run back. 'Come on, girls,' said one of them. 'You need to get away from here. Bloody Jerries are at it again.'

Della and Catherine ran down the cobbled street, surrounded by the phalanx of young men from the Pioneer Corps, while in the near distance a constant barrage of explosions rattled the old buildings and caused panic to the few people who were still about.

'Whoosh!' A boom, followed by another crash and another and another, and finally they reached the building that housed the NAAFI and ran inside and down into the packed cellar.

'Wow!' said Della, her face white. 'I thought this town was supposed to be safe.'

'It is, mostly,' said the sergeant who had run with them. 'And there's probably nothing damaged in the town. The Jerries are too far away. But better safe…'

'…than sorry,' Della finished the sentence, and grinned at the young man. 'I'm Della Stafford,' she said, holding out her hand. 'Part of the Bennett Players. We're giving a performance in the theatre after lunch. You should come and see us.'

'Oh yes,' he said. 'We heard about you, didn't we, lads?'

They nodded and grinned, and one of them said, looking at Catherine, 'Is she in it too?'

Della laughed. 'You bet,' she nodded. 'Just wait till you hear her sing.'

The shelling stopped almost as soon as they'd reached the shelter and they went upstairs into the canteen, where the NAAFI workers were already pouring tea from steaming urns and scrambling dried eggs.

'Look,' Catherine said, pointing towards the back of the room. 'The gang's already here.'

They joined their friends at a table and ate fried tomatoes on toast and drank dark tea out of thick china cups.

'Did you get caught in the raid?' asked Godfrey.

'Yes,' Della nodded. 'We were in the street and ran here for the shelter.' She frowned. 'We didn't see you down there. Where were you?'

'Here,' laughed Davey. 'The NAAFI girls didn't bother to move, so neither did we. Some bugger might have eaten our breakfast if we'd left it.'

'Aye,' Colin agreed. 'I've paid for this.'

'There's Beau and Frances.' Catherine stood up and waved. Spotting the company, the pair came over. Beau was limping badly, as though he'd further damaged his leg.

Catherine put a gentle hand on his arm. 'What's happened to you?' she asked, her voice full of concern. She could see that as well as the more pronounced limp, his face was pale and he didn't look well.

'It's nothing.' He shrugged off the enquiry, but Frances wasn't having it.

'He fell,' she said, 'or so he says. I think he should go to the military hospital and see what the doc says, but he won't.'

'For Christ's sake, stop fussing,' Beau growled. He was leaning heavily on his stick. 'Now...' He took the rolled-up paper that Frances had been carrying and showed it to them. It was a brightly coloured advert for the show, with a list of their names and the times of the performances. 'Robert Lennox got this done,' he said. 'I'll put one up in here and a couple at HQ. As well as this, I have to tell you that we're going to a field hospital tomorrow afternoon, to give a show, and then at the end of the week, we're moving on.'

'Not back home?' Godfrey asked, his face falling.

'No.' Beau smiled at him. 'I'm afraid that the redoubtable Mrs James will have to do without you for some time yet. We're going to the front. Well, as close to the front as is safe.' He waited for questions, but they were all slightly stunned and he said, 'Look, I'm going to get these posters put up and I'll see you at the theatre. One o'clock, alright?' He limped away to talk to the woman who was in charge at the NAAFI.

It was exciting news and the Players looked at each other with a mixture of apprehension and delight.

'This is what we volunteered for,' said Tommy. 'I'm glad we're going.'

'There speaks a man who hasn't been at the sharp end,' Davey muttered.

'No, I haven't.' Tommy's face reddened. 'But it's not for want of trying.'

There was an awkward silence; then Davey grinned. 'Sorry, mate,' he said. 'I didn't mean anything.'

Tommy nodded, but Catherine could see that he was still simmering. She turned to Frances. 'What happened to Beau?' She looked over to where he was talking to the NAAFI woman behind the counter and showing her the poster.

'He says he fell,' Frances murmured, 'but, you know, I don't believe him. He has bruises on his arms as though...' She shrugged. 'Well, I don't know, but one of the officers in the billet told me that he was brought back last night by a bloke from our troupe. Apparently Beau was in a bit of a state.'

'It wasn't me,' said Tommy, 'or any of us boys here. We were playing cards until late.'

'Oh God,' Della snorted. 'We all know who it was. That bloody Eric Baxter, or whatever his name is.'

'I'll speak to Beau again,' Frances sighed. 'He has to get rid of that bullying bastard.'

The rest of the company was silent for a second, as they'd never heard Frances speak like that before, but there was a succession of nods from about the table.

Davey stood up. 'I'd be careful,' he warned. 'Things might not be as they seem. You might make enemies.'

There was that expression again, Catherine thought. *Things are not always what they seem.* It was almost sinister and she shuddered, causing Della to look at her in surprise.

'I've known Beau since...well, since forever,' Frances said firmly. 'He'd never be my enemy, and as for Baxter, well, I couldn't care less. The sooner he goes, the better.'

Della nodded enthusiastically. 'Hear, hear,' she said, and the others murmured their agreement.

'Anyway,' Frances said, consulting her clipboard, 'enough of that. We have to get ready.'

When the curtains swung back to reveal the audience on that first show, the troupe were both astonished and thrilled to see how full the theatre was. Soldiers jostled with each other for seats, and some were standing up at the back of the house. They were ready for a bit of entertainment after the hard and terrifying slog of the invasion.

'Ready?' asked Beau as the company gathered in the wings. Everyone was breathing hard, nervous and excited at the same time.

'Ready, willing and able,' Della said. 'Bring up the curtain,' and as cheers rang out, she stepped onto the stage, while Tommy banged out her opening tune.

She'd gone on stage in her uniform jacket and a pair of the fishnet tights. After she'd belted out her first number, she threw off the jacket, revealing a figure-hugging red costume with a minuscule pair of shorts, which drew whistles of excitement as she launched into her acrobatic dance.

'Bravo!' the crowd yelled, hugely enthusiastic, applauding wildly after every spin and cartwheel. And when she jumped into the air and came down doing the splits to end her piece, the place erupted.

The American GIs who had flirted with her on the bus were in the front row and led the cheers, stamping their feet and yelling, 'Go, girl!'

'Great house,' Della said breathlessly, coming off and pushing Colin into the spotlight. 'I loved it!'

Colin bamboozled them with his tricks, and Della went on again to pose with his props and pretend to be astonished when paper flowers poured out of the front of her bodice. When they came off, Godfrey went on. He was cheered too, especially when he got the audience to sing along with 'Keep the Home Fires Burning' and 'On the Road to Mandalay'.

Davey, who was dressed in his own uniform of the Royal Artillery, with his corporal's stripes and campaign ribbons in place, was well received. His jokes and monologues fitted in nicely with the rest of the review, particularly when he told the tale of Young Albert, who went to Buckingham Palace to get his medal.

'Well done,' said Beau, when he came off, shaking his hand, but then Eric and Captain Fortescue did their turn.

Catherine could hear the gasps of indrawn breath from the audience as the doll, using the crudest of language, made vulgar innuendoes that seemed to make even the most cynical soldier look at his companion before nervously joining in with the laughter. As he went on, though, the audience became inured to the rudeness and were screaming with mirth.

'He's going too far,' said Catherine to Frances, who was standing beside her in the wings. 'I haven't heard him do this stuff before.'

'I know,' she said. 'It's horrible.'

When Beau limped over with the running order in his hand, she grabbed his arm. 'Listen to Eric,' she whispered. 'Don't you think he's a bit close to the knuckle?'

'Maybe,' he whispered back, 'but these are men. That's what they like.'

Robert Lennox was backstage too and he looked worried. 'You'll have to talk to him,' he said to Beau. 'The authorities will clamp down on you if they get to hear any of his act.'

Beau looked nervous. 'I'll see what I can do,' he said.

'I mean it,' said Robert, and when Eric finished and joined the company in the wings, Robert gave Beau a nod, to enforce what he'd said.

The mood changed when Catherine walked onto the stage. She was wearing her long lavender-blue dress and elbow-length black gloves. She had let her dark, wavy hair hang loose onto her shoulders, and as the spotlight picked out her lovely face, there were a few wolf whistles. She nodded to Tommy and he started the introduction to her song. When she sang the first line, there was an appreciative groan as the audience recognised 'P.S. I Love You', and Della, peeping through a gap in the curtains, saw that several of the soldiers had tears in their eyes.

'They're like putty in her hands,' Della whispered to Frances. 'She could sing them the telephone directory and they'd cheer.'

Cheer they did, and she followed up with 'The Very Thought of You' and could hardly get to the end before the audience stood up and hollered.

'You were just wonderful,' Robert murmured as Catherine walked off the stage. 'Just wonderful.'

'Thank you,' she replied, and caught up in the moment, allowed herself to look into his eyes. They were glistening. 'Thank you,' she said again, and touched his hand.

The second half went just as well, although Eric refused to go on after Beau had told him what Robert had said about the authorities. 'Who the hell does he think he is?' he said, in his own voice, and then reverting to the captain's, said, 'Tell him to fuck off, old sport.' With that, he picked up the suitcase containing the doll and walked out of the theatre.

'Good riddance,' said Della. 'Please God he doesn't come back.'

The girls closed the show, singing in harmony one of their upbeat numbers. Cheers and whistles rattled the rafters of the old theatre, and afterwards, the Players gathered in the bar of the best hotel in Bayeux and relived every moment, grinning at each other and buying quantities of drink.

Beau held up his hand. 'Listen,' he said. 'Before you all get too hammered, remember we have a show tomorrow afternoon, at the hospital. It'll be shorter than usual, bearing in mind that some of the patients can't sit for long. I've redone the running order – Frances will show you.' He looked at Robert, who was sitting at a table with Tommy and Catherine. 'Major Lennox has organised our transport for this trip.'

Robert stood up. 'Yes. We'll be travelling in army trucks. It's a field hospital near to the front line, and we'll have guards riding with us.'

Della was standing by the bar with her American sergeant, who'd followed them in, and said, 'Bloody hell, Robert. We didn't sign up for danger.'

He grinned. 'You did, Miss Stafford. Don't you remember? Make sure you bring your tin helmet.' He looked at the rest of the company. 'That applies to all of you. Ten thirty sharp outside the Hôtel Côte de Nacre. The army doesn't like to be kept waiting.'

'I wonder if Eric will be with us,' Catherine said to Frances, when she joined them at their table.

'Who knows?' Frances said. 'Beau hasn't mentioned him.'

'They've got some sort of thing going,' Tommy butted in. 'Everyone knows that.'

'Do they?' Catherine was surprised. 'I didn't know.'

'You saw them, in Liverpool. Beau was giving him money. I'll bet it wasn't a loan.' Tommy laughed. 'Look,' he said, 'I couldn't care less about Beau being a queer – God knows there's plenty of them in show business – but with Eric?'

'Did you know?' Catherine asked Frances.

She nodded slowly. 'I think I knew. Johnny Petersham hinted at it, years ago, but I don't believe he would go with Eric. It has to be something else.'

Robert had said nothing during the exchange and Catherine wondered why. He been one of 'the Three Musketeers' and he must have an opinion, but when she turned to him, he suddenly stood up and asked to be excused. 'I have to meet someone,' he said. 'I'll see you later, or tomorrow, if you've gone home by then.' He picked up his peaked cap and turned to go and then paused. 'Why don't you go to the officers' mess for a meal? You'd be very welcome, and I've told the stewards to look out for you. It's in the HQ building.'

'Good idea,' said Tommy. 'Let's round up the gang.'

'Not me,' called Della, when Tommy went to get her. 'Chuck and I are going to stay here and have a few more drinks.' She turned to her young GI. 'Isn't that right?'

'Sure thing, honey,' he grinned, and clicked his fingers to the barman.

The food at the officers' mess was much the same as they would have got at the NAAFI, but it was served on china plates on a table with a cloth. Not many officers were in, but those who were welcomed them and asked about the show.

'I'm coming to see you tomorrow night,' said one of them, an older man with a neatly clipped moustache. 'My chaps have told me that it's a damned fine show. Damn fine.'

He sounded a bit like Captain Fortescue and Catherine struggled to keep smiling at him. 'I do hope we'll live up to expectations,' she said, and was startled when he slapped his hand on the table and roared, 'I know you will, little lady.'

Frances laughed about him as they walked back to their billet. 'I wonder if Hugo spoke like that when he was with his friends in the mess.'

Catherine linked arms. 'Have you heard anything lately?'

'No.' Frances shook her head. 'Not a word. I feel we're in limbo.'

'Like me,' said Catherine, wondering if Christopher's face was beginning to fade from her memory. 'In limbo.'

Chapter 11

It was an uncomfortable ride to the field hospital on a very wet day. They had been loaded into the back of a three-ton army lorry with a driver at the front who refused to slow down at corners and managed to drive over every pothole along the way. Two squaddies sat with the company under the canvas on the hard benches that ran along the inside of the truck. The soldiers were close to the open flap at the back, which allowed the mud from the road to rise up and splatter them so that they kept up a continuous barrage of grumbling and cursing. They seemed more concerned about keeping their rifles dry than getting their uniform dirty.

The pouring rain made the ride even worse, and Frances, leaning forward and looking at the wet and misty road behind them, wondered if the whole trip would be worth it. Beau had said that they would be performing in the open air, as the hospital was under canvas and there was barely any room between the beds. If the weather didn't clear up, she couldn't imagine how the show could go on.

'Where are we?' asked Tommy. He was sitting opposite her.

Frances shrugged. 'Somewhere in Normandy. I wasn't told exactly where we were going, but it must be behind our lines. They wouldn't put a hospital in a place that could be overrun.'

'It's quite exciting,' Catherine said. 'What d'you think, Della?'

'Mm,' her friend grunted. She had her head in her hands and hadn't opened her mouth since the journey began.

'Della?' Frances looked at her closely. 'What's the matter?'

'I'd say it was a hangover,' said Colin, with a grin. 'She took a few good drams last evening.'

'Oh, shut up,' Della groaned, and then looked up and gazed desperately around the company. 'Has anyone got any water?'

'Here.' Davey passed over a small green canteen.

'God love you.' Della grabbed the bottle and took a long swig. 'You're a saviour.'

Davey chuckled. 'First time I've been called that.'

'I don't believe you, darling,' she said, perking up. 'Not with all those medals on your chest.'

The two soldiers who were sitting with them looked at each other with raised eyebrows. It was obvious that they thought these people who were wearing army uniform and whom they had to treat as officers were a pretty rum bunch. Tommy noticed the look and blushed. Of all the company, he seemed to be the one who felt the most uncomfortable among the real military.

He pulled over the wooden Bennett Players advertising board that was propped up against the wall between the cab and the back, and arranged it on top of his and Colin's knees. 'Cards, anyone?' he said, pulling out the battered pack that went with him everywhere.

'Good idea,' said Godfrey, and Davey moved up and said, 'I'm in.'

'Girls, what about you?'

'No' – Frances shook her head – 'you take too much money from me.'

Catherine shook her head too, and Della didn't even look up.

Tommy cocked his head to the two soldiers. 'Poker?' he asked.

'Better not, sir,' said one of them who had a lance corporal stripe. The other looked quite keen but didn't dare argue with his superior.

When the boys were busy with their game, Catherine looked at Della. 'Feeling a bit better?' she asked.

'Mm.'

She lowered her voice. 'What time did you come back?'

Della sighed. 'After midnight, I think. Chuck took me on a round of all the bars that were still open.' She groaned. 'There were millions of them.'

'Did you...?' Catherine whispered.

'No. At least, I don't think so.'

Frances laughed. 'He's awfully good-looking.'

Della managed a little grin. 'He is.' She looked to see if the boys were listening before saying, 'But there was nowhere to go.'

That set them off giggling, and Frances whispered, 'You're quite shameless.'

'Yes, I know.' Della took another swig of water from the canteen. 'But it's fun.'

They arrived at the field hospital after a journey of about an hour and a half. It was in a large field, with rows of big green tents and some hastily erected Nissen huts. The paths between the tents were deep with mud, and Frances, looking out of the window, noticed that the uniformed nurses walking from one tent to another all wore army boots. Duckboards had been laid, so that trolleys could be wheeled to and from the operating theatre, or to the wards.

The lorry came to a halt in front of one of the Nissen huts and the two squaddies jumped out and unfastened the back.

'Come on, miss,' said the lance corporal. 'Take my hand.'

Frances shuffled over and, swinging her legs out, jumped out of the truck. 'Thanks,' she said to the corporal, and straightening up, had a look around. Beau had arrived before them, riding in a staff car with Robert and, to Frances's surprise, Eric.

'Look who's there,' hissed Della, nodding towards the ventriloquist, who was standing beside Beau. 'I hoped we'd seen the back of that bugger.'

'I thought Beau was getting rid of him,' said Catherine, joining them. 'Robert said he must.'

'No,' Frances corrected her. 'He said Beau had to talk to him. Perhaps he has.'

The boys had jumped out of the truck and stood with them, eyeing Eric with annoyance. 'Why does he get to ride comfortably in the car?' Godfrey bellowed, not caring that he could be overheard. 'It smacks of favouritism.' The others mumbled their agreement.

'Would you rather he was with us?' Frances asked.

Nobody had an answer to that, and they waited in the drizzle while Beau limped over to them. 'Come on,' he said. 'Into the hut.'

It was stuffy inside, the small windows misted up, and the metal tables and chairs, for this was the canteen, had a sheen of dampness over them, which Della looked at in disgust. 'I'm not sitting down,' she whispered. 'I'll get a wet arse.'

A small upright piano with an attached seat and wheels stood against one wall, and Tommy walked over to it and lifted the lid. 'Jesus,' he whistled in dismay. 'Is this it?'

'Shut up,' Beau growled. 'We're not at the Kit Kat Club now.' He would have said more, but an army doctor and a youngish-looking matron, dressed in her triangular cap and short red cape, came into the hut.

'Welcome!' said the doctor. He was young too, with wild red hair that needed cutting and weary lines under his eyes as though he had too many days without sleep. 'We're very much looking forward to the show, although' – he frowned and looked out of the window, to where the rain was getting heavier again – 'I'm not sure when we'll be able to get on with it. The rain makes it impossible for us to get the patients outside right now. Maybe in an hour or so.'

'In the meantime,' Matron spoke up, 'how about a cup of tea, or coffee?' She smiled. 'We've been very lucky with coffee at this camp. The locals seem to have an endless supply.'

'What about us performing in here?' said Beau. 'We've done our show in canteens lots of times.'

'That would be fine for the ambulatory patients,' the doctor answered. He had a soft Irish accent, pleasant to the ear, and a manner that made Catherine think that he'd never be able to impart bad news. 'But it's our boys confined to their beds. We couldn't get them in here – the door's too narrow – and they'd miss out.' He smiled again. 'Sure and it's a fine soft day; the rain will go over soon. Now, if you'll excuse me, I have a leg to take off.' He nodded to Matron and, with a goodbye wave of his hand, went out of the door.

'Oh my God,' muttered Della. 'I think I'm going to be sick.'

'No, you're not,' said Frances very firmly. 'This is a hospital. These things go on.'

They waited in the canteen, drinking coffee and eventually, after a good deal of wiping with handkerchiefs, sitting on the chairs. Catherine leant back and looked at the tin walls of the hut and thought about the one at the country house where Captain Jaeger and Larry Best had tried to get her to remember military insignia and vehicles. They must have been mad, she decided. There was no way that she could do what they suggested, even if she wanted to. And she didn't want to.

She looked up. Robert was standing by the door, watching her. It was as if he knew what she was thinking and her cheeks coloured up and she looked away.

'What's up?' asked Della. 'Your face has gone pink.'

'Nothing's up,' Catherine replied crossly. 'It's just stuffy in here. I could do with some fresh air.' She got up and walked to a window that was slightly open and leant her face against the glass.

Rain was beating down hard, and under the low cloud, the tented hospital seemed sad and dismal. A few nurses ran from tent to tent, hands over their caps to stop the starch melting out, and now and then a patient could be seen, helped along on crutches or in a wheelchair, being taken along the metal tracks between departments. How terrible for them, Catherine thought. Only a few days ago, these had been healthy young men, and then, in a heartbeat, they'd been wounded and their lives altered, perhaps, forever.

She could see a soldier at the entrance to one of the big tents. He was in a wheelchair, with a red blanket covering his legs, and was looking up at the rain. His nurse was holding an umbrella over his head, and when she bent down to push off the brake, Catherine saw him attempt to pinch her bottom. The gales of laughter that ensued from the pair of them were carried on the wind so that Catherine could hear them clearly and she smiled too. How brave they both were, she thought, and then suddenly she felt ashamed of herself.

Why can't I be more like that? I'm not brave. I've been moping about for months now, drifting like a piece of flotsam on the tide of misery. If Christopher is gone, and, she steeled herself, that is the most likely thing, then I have to accept it and get on with my life. Lili needs a cheerful mother, not one who's always looking backwards. She looked over her shoulder into the room to see Della painting her nails and Frances with a book propped up on her coffee cup. They've got on with their lives, she thought, and now, so must I.

Pleased with herself for having to come to a decision, she looked back at the soldier and nurse, but they had gone – hurried across the walkway into another tent, she supposed. But something, or someone else attracted her attention.

In the room behind her, Della yawned. 'This is so

bloody boring,' she moaned. 'How about us doing a bit of rehearsal?'

'I'm up for it,' said Frances, putting down her book. 'We could do that new number you suggested.' She looked over to the boys. 'Tommy! Come and play for us. We want to rehearse.'

'Give us a moment,' he called back. 'I'm on a roll here.'

The boys were playing poker, a game that had been going on for weeks for three of them, and now Davey had become a keen participant. He was quite good but, surprisingly, not as good as Godfrey. The tenor gave off an air of being a bumbling old fool, but he was a clever player and often got the better of Tommy. Colin wasn't. Often he would forget the rules and complained when the others corrected him.

'I was brought up a Wee Free,' he cried. 'Card playing, along with drinking and music are works of the devil. You know fine well that you've tempted me. Led me astray.'

'Rubbish,' cried Tommy. 'Christ knows you do enough card tricks. You should be better than the rest of us.' He dropped a shilling onto the table. 'Come on, show us what you've got.'

Della sighed. 'It's hopeless. We're never going to get to rehearse.'

'I know,' said Frances, and then, looking around, asked, 'Where's Eric? He's disappeared again.'

'Who cares?' Della snorted.

'He's outside,' Catherine called from the window. 'I can see him.' She'd been watching him for a while, curious to know why he was talking to a soldier who wore an orderly's white coat. As she watched, Eric delved into his army greatcoat and withdrew a carton of cigarettes. The soldier, after quickly looking around, put them in his own pockets and, after another few seconds of conversation, walked away. 'He's doing a deal,' she whispered to Frances, who had joined her at the window.

'What sort of a deal?'

'I don't know, but it looks like it, don't you think?'

'What were you whispering about?' asked Della when they rejoined her. Catherine quickly told her and Della raised her eyebrows. 'Black market?' she asked.

The girls shrugged. It was war; everyone was doing deals of one sort or another. 'Perhaps he's getting a supply of coffee to sell when we get home,' said Catherine. 'I wouldn't mind some, and I know Maman would be delighted.'

'Listen up.' Beau and Robert had been talking with the medical officer, who had returned to the Nissen hut. His cheerful face was downcast and remained so when Beau announced, 'I don't think we can do a performance here today. The rain hasn't stopped and doesn't look as if it's going to. It's a pity, but there it is. Captain O'Brien here' – he nodded to the doctor – 'can't let his patients lie outside and get wet.'

The company groaned. They'd endured a long ride in an uncomfortable lorry and now they were going to have to endure another one back without having done what they came for.

Tommy stood up. 'Excuse me, Beau and Doctor. If the patients can't come to us, why can't we go to the patients? That piano' – he jerked his head towards it – 'is on wheels, and I suppose it was going to be taken outside for the show. Why can't we wheel it into the wards? It'll be a smaller show than usual, and Della won't be able to do her somersaults, but the girls and Godfrey can sing, and Colin and Davey can do their turns. Even Eric, if he bothers to turn up. What d'you think?'

'Grand,' said the doctor before Beau and Robert had a chance to speak. 'We'd love it. That is, if you don't mind. Some of our boys are quite badly injured, so... well, there'll be some sights in the ward that the young ladies will find difficult.'

'We don't mind,' Della said quickly. 'Not at all. Anything to cheer up the troops.'

The doctor beamed at her, while Catherine and Frances raised their eyebrows at each other. Della was notoriously squeamish.

It was decided, and twenty minutes later, they were in the centre of the big tent, where recovering soldiers were lying on narrow cot beds.

The light was very poor inside, and when the company took their places beside the piano, they took up even more room in the packed tent. There was hardly any space between the beds, with the nurses squeezing this way and that to tend to their patients.

'How can they bear the smell?' Della muttered, putting a hand to her face.

'Shush,' said Catherine. She had noticed how young most of them looked, and how pale. Several had plaster casts, and one or two had extensive bandages over their heads. One man had both eyes covered, and a dressing over his jaw.

'We'll be moving Lieutenant Strange back home tomorrow,' whispered Matron, noticing where Catherine was looking. 'He's been blinded.'

Della opened the show as usual with an upbeat number, sitting on top of the piano, with her uniform skirt hitched up to her thighs. 'You are my sunshine,' she crooned, and in the second chorus jumped down from the piano and walked around the beds, encouraging the soldiers to join in. They did, and cheered when she finished and begged for more.

'Later,' she promised, and blew a kiss to a young man with a bandage round his chest who was lying flat on his cot.

The boys went on next, Colin doing a shortened version of his act, mostly card tricks, which intrigued the men, and then Godfrey sang 'There'll Always Be an England', followed by 'I'll Take You Home Again, Kathleen'. Captain O'Brien joined in with that, singing in a high tenor voice, which harmonised brilliantly with Godfrey's rich voice.

'Well done, sir,' boomed Godfrey to the doctor, and the soldier patients clapped and called out a mixture of congratulations and insults.

'You'd never be out of work in showbiz,' laughed Della, punching Captain O'Brien on his arm. 'If you decided to give up the doctoring, that is.'

He grinned. 'Now wouldn't that be a great offer, Miss... Sorry, I didn't catch your name.'

'Stafford, Della. Call me Della.'

'I will indeed, and let me tell you, I thought you were grand.'

'Flatterer,' she smiled, and punched his arm again.

Davey did his monologues and sang 'Kiss Me Goodnight, Sergeant Major', which drew howls of approval from the men.

The nurses quietly moved from bed to bed while the company was performing, and at one point, during Davey's act, the matron requested a pause while they moved one patient, who was obviously in pain, out of the ward.

'Poor man,' whispered Catherine, and Frances nodded her head and then she dug Catherine in the ribs.

'Look,' she said, jerking her head to the doorway, where the patient had been wheeled out. Eric had come in, his hair black and slick with rain, and he was carrying the suitcase that contained Captain Fortescue.

'He's going to do his turn,' said Catherine, and Della leant over and growled, 'I hope Beau's spoken to him.'

Eric waited for Davey to finish and then, after a nod from Beau, walked forward. As he bent to open the case, Robert appeared by his side. 'Remember what I said,' he whispered.

Eric ignored him, fiddling with one of the latches, which seemed to be stuck, when suddenly Robert jammed his foot on top of the case.

'I mean it.' His voice was harsh and Catherine looked at him with new eyes. 'I'm quite prepared to send you home, and' – he leant forward – 'I can make sure you never work again.'

The girls, shocked, looked at each other and waited.

'Alright,' Eric muttered, still refusing to look up.

'Good,' said Robert, and lifted his well-polished shoe off the case, which immediately snapped open, revealing Captain Fortescue lying on his purple cushion.

The doll was picked up and settled on Eric's arm. Its head turned slowly to stare at Robert. 'This won't be forgotten,' it said in the captain's fruity voice. 'No, by God. Never forgotten.'

Eric did his act, keeping his remarks and jokes well within the bounds of decency, and the other members of the company breathed more easily. If Eric was sent home in disgrace, who knew what might happen to the rest of them?

'Now,' called Beau, standing up in front of the row of beds when Eric had finished to a laughing round of applause, 'we have a further treat for you. Catherine Fletcher, who some of you might have heard on the radio or even seen at various London clubs, is going to sing for us.' He turned to her and held out his hand to draw her forward.

She nodded to Tommy, who started the opening bars of 'As Time Goes By' and a hush descended throughout the tent. When she opened her mouth and started to sing, the bedridden audience lay back on their pillows and listened. Somehow, in this small space, her voice seemed even more intimate, as if she was singing to each soldier individually, and they were spellbound.

'Wow,' breathed Captain O'Brien, when she'd finished and the patients were clapping wildly.

'She's good, isn't she?' Della said.

'Not as good as you, Miss Stafford.' He pushed a hand through his untidy hair and grinned down at her.

'Oh,' she said, pleased and surprised. 'You really are a flatterer.'

There was no time for the conversation to continue, because Catherine was singing again. She decided to sing her French song, and when she started, one or two locals who had been delivering bread to the camp came in to listen to her.

It went down as well as the first, particularly when she walked between the beds and even along to the far end of the tent, where three beds were partially curtained off. She looked at the nurse standing by the curtain, and when she was given nodded permission, she walked behind the curtain to sing to the three patients who were there. One of the boys was sitting up. He was very young, perhaps fourteen or fifteen years old, and he looked as if he'd been crying. Catherine noticed the dried tears on his cheeks first, and then with a stab in her heart saw the blue-grey jacket that he wore over his hospital gown. It was a German uniform.

If there was a pause in the lyrics, it was unnoticeable. She had nearly stopped singing, such was the shock of seeing a German soldier, but her professionalism kicked in and she carried on. Turning, she walked back to the centre of the ward, singing now in English and smiling at the patients and nurses until she was beside the piano.

The tent rang with cheers and Catherine, acknowledging them with a bow and a wave, was concerned that it would make the patients worse.

Dr O'Brien had much the same worries and stood forward and gestured for them to calm down. 'Enough, gentlemen,' he said. 'The old blood pressure will be rising.'

'More,' shouted a soldier lying close to the piano. 'Let's hear the girls again.'

'Yes,' more of them yelled, and the doctor looked hopelessly at Beau. 'Perhaps one more song,' he said.

Beau beckoned Frances over. 'The three of you, but go easy.'

'Alright,' she said, and looking at Della and Catherine, said, 'What'll it be? Got to be something quiet.'

'What about "Lili Marlene"?' whispered Della. 'You always like that, Catherine, because of baby Lili.'

'The men behind the curtain are Germans.' Catherine's face was set in a frown.

Della shrugged. 'All the more reason,' she grinned, and nodded to Tommy.

While they sang, Catherine couldn't keep her eyes off the Germans at the end of the ward. It was clear that they were enjoying it, but the youngster started to cry again, and some part of her felt sorry for him. The British patients joined in and Della grabbed the doctor and even made him sing with them.

The whole company was exhausted at the end of the show and Matron led them to the canteen, where sandwiches and beer awaited. 'Lovely show,' she said. 'You've really bucked up the blokes. One or two of them would like autographs, if you don't mind, and we thought a photograph would be good.'

Frances looked at the others and said, 'We don't mind that, do we?'

They posed all together for the photograph in front of a row of beds, the girls sitting on chairs hastily arranged by the nurses and the boys at the back. Eric had disappeared again, much to Beau's annoyance, and he held up the photographer while they waited for him.

'We'll get on with it without him,' said Robert, and in a lowered voice muttered, 'It's your own fault. You've allowed him too much leeway.'

Afterwards, they mingled with the patients and staff, Della chatting to Dr O'Brien most of the time.

'I'm on leave in Bayeux at the end of the week,' he said. 'I'll come and see your show, and,' he added shyly, 'we could go out for a meal afterwards, if you'd like to.'

'I'd love to,' she said, and smiled.

Frances went over to the blind patient, Lieutenant Strange. She touched his arm and he moved his head towards her. 'Did you enjoy the show?' she asked.

'It was brilliant,' he answered, shuffling off his bed and standing up. 'I loved it. Which one are you?'

'I'm Frances Parnell,' she said. 'I sang with the other two girls at the end of the show. I'm the administrator, really.'

He put out his hand for her to shake. 'How d'you do?' he said. 'Felix Strange.' Then, 'Parnell?'

'Yes.'

'You're not related to Hugo Parnell, by any chance?' He chuckled. 'No, ignore me. I'm so desperate to hear about people back home, you see. And that would be too much of a coincidence.'

'Hugo's my brother. However d'you know him?' Frances found that she was still clutching Lieutenant Strange's hand.

'If it's the same Hugo Parnell, he was a couple of years ahead of me at school. He was my head of house.'

'Oh!' Frances gasped. 'How amazing. But then you must know Beau. Beau Bennett, our leader.'

'I got that he was a Bennett,' he said. He was quite animated now. 'Dr O'Brien introduced him as Major Bennett.'

'Well, it's Beau,' laughed Frances, 'and what's more,

Robert Lennox is here too. He's acting as our liaison officer.'

There was a pause, and then to her dismay, Felix Strange's shoulders began to shake and he sat down heavily on his bed and put a hand up to his bandaged eyes. 'Oh God. I don't want them to see me like this,' he muttered.

Frances sat beside him. 'Listen to me,' she said in her no-nonsense manner. 'Beau has a badly damaged leg and he's barely able to walk. Hugo is a prisoner of war in the Far East and I haven't heard from him for a year. Robert is uninjured, but he's sad...I don't know what's happened to him. Johnny Petersham, d'you remember him? Well' – she swallowed the lump in her throat – 'he was killed at Dunkirk.'

He was silent, sitting on his bed, and she took his hand. 'Felix,' she said, 'remember that you're absolutely not alone. The war has taken its toll on everyone, us girls too. We're all affected.' She got up. 'Now, I'm going to bring Beau and Robert over. They'll want to meet you.'

She left him then and looked around for Beau and Robert. She spotted them, walking towards the door, both their faces closed and angry. They've been rowing again, she thought, as she hurried after them, and I know what about.

'You have to come and meet Lieutenant Strange,' she said, running to stand in front of them. 'He was at school with you – Felix Strange, in your house.'

'I remember him,' said Robert. 'He played the piano, rather well.'

'Well, he's in there' – she jerked her head back to the tent – 'and blind. He needs some reassurance.'

'We haven't time,' Beau said, scowling. He was clearly still furious. 'We've got to get back to Bayeux.'

'Two minutes,' Frances pleaded. 'It would cheer him up.'

'I'll go,' said Robert, and turned back to the tent. After a minute, Beau limped after him, and Frances, joining Catherine by the piano, where she was signing autographs, was relieved to see Felix Strange's face break into a smile when Robert took his hand and introduced himself.

'Robert is such a good man,' she said to Catherine when they were in the lorry on the way back to Bayeux.

'I know,' her friend murmured. 'I do know.'

Chapter 12

The week in Bayeux was hugely successful, and despite the war waging only about twenty miles away, they played to full houses. For Catherine, it was a revelation. Previously, she'd performed at nightclubs and grand hotels, with the occasional foray into radio, but she'd never been a theatre star. Now she embraced it wholeheartedly and enjoyed the excitement and noisy audiences as much as Della did.

'Wow,' said Della, as she came off stage after their last performance. 'It's been absolutely fantastic.'

'It has,' laughed Catherine, joining in the general backstage exhilaration. 'Who'd have thought it?'

When the lights finally dimmed and they had all quietened down, Beau called for a meeting. They sat, still in their performance costumes, on the dusty boards of the stage.

'Listen,' he said. 'We've been asked to go further inland. This side of the front, of course, but we'll be closer to the action.'

The company looked at each other. It sounded dangerous.

'I can understand completely that this isn't what most of you signed up for. I mean, factories and dockyards back home are one thing, but being at the front is different. So if anyone wants to leave, it'll be no reflection on them. We are, after all, performers, not soldiers.'

Tommy broke the silence. 'I'm up for it,' he said. 'I'll even hold a gun, if necessary.'

Beau grinned. It was a rare sight these days, him being happy. Since they'd been in France, he'd seemed to be more troubled than before, not only with his leg but angry about something else. Frances knew it was Eric Baxter who was the cause of much of Beau's aggravation and she quickly looked around to see what his reaction to the news might be. As she'd half expected, he wasn't there.

'I don't think they'll let you touch a gun, Tommy,' Beau said. 'Your hands are much more valuable on the keyboard. But you'd better bring your guitar. I don't know where they'll have a piano.' He paused and glanced about rather nervously. 'What about the rest of you?'

'Of course we'll come,' Godfrey boomed. 'Wouldn't miss it for a fortune. Girls too?'

The three girls nodded. 'You bet,' said Della, looking at her friends. 'Playing to hordes of frustrated men! What could be better?'

'Good.' Beau looked relieved. 'Now, you've got the day off tomorrow and then the escort will come for us eight o'clock sharp, Monday morning, outside the hotel.' He glanced at Frances. 'Sorry, Fran, although we can use the bus, the army has decided that they want a couple of soldier drivers as well as the escort. But it will be more comfortable than a lorry. So pack up your bags because we probably won't be coming back here, and make sure you've got your tin hats.' He looked around, waiting, Catherine thought, for any objections, but there were none forthcoming. 'Good,' he said. 'Now, I've got some things to do, so I'll see you all Monday morning.'

After he'd gone, the company sat for a moment looking at each other and grinning at the prospect of performing on the front line. Despite it being dangerous, it was tremendously exciting, and absolutely what they'd come for.

Tommy held up his hand. 'Before we go…to get a drink, which is what we've been looking forward to' – everyone laughed – 'there's something we have to talk about.'

'Baxter,' snorted Della. 'That's who we have to talk about.'

'Aye,' Colin nodded. 'How long do we have to put up with yon bastard?'

'He has to go,' boomed Godfrey. 'The man's a charlatan.'

'Look,' Davey said, 'he's trouble. He always has been. I could tell you stories about him that would make your hair curl.'

The others were intrigued. Della begged him to say what the stories were, but he wouldn't.

'Trust me. He's a bastard. He'll drag you down,' was all he said.

'Are we agreed, then?' Tommy sought nodding assent from the company, and then, getting it, he turned to Frances. 'You're closest to Beau. You must tell him what we've decided.'

'Oh.' Frances looked so appalled that Catherine reached for her hand and gave it a squeeze. 'God,' Frances groaned. 'Surely it would be better if one of you men told him, or even Robert Lennox.' She looked around for him, but he'd already gone. ' Alright,' she sighed. 'I'll do what I can.'

With that, they got up and went to change before

going out to the big hotel, which was their usual after-show haunt. It was packed. British, Canadian and American officers filled the bar area, and those of them who had seen the show whooped and cheered when the members of the Bennett Players came in.

'Jolly good show, little lady,' beamed the elderly major whom they'd met in the officers' mess.

'Thank you,' said Catherine, smiling, but she was still put off by the similarity between his voice and that of Captain Fortescue.

A glass of red wine was put into her hand and she turned her head to see Robert standing beside her. 'I thought you'd like this as a change from gin,' he said. 'It's not bad.'

He looked more relaxed this evening. The intense frown that was usually in place had gone, as though something that had been worrying him had melted away. 'How about dinner? We could go to the officers' mess, or there is a cafe in one of the streets at the back of the cathedral that does pretty good food, considering...'

'Yes.' Catherine smiled quickly. 'I'd prefer that.' The thought of spending time alone with him was exciting, and although part of her brain told her that it was disloyal to Christopher, she remembered that she'd decided to move on. She turned to tell Della that she was going, but was stopped by Della giving a yell of 'Hello' to Dr O'Brien, who was working his way towards them through the noisy crowd at the bar.

'I saw the show,' he grinned. 'You were all wonderful, 'specially you, Miss Stafford.' This last came out a little breathlessly and he blushed. 'I mean...yes, you were all wonderful.'

'Idiot,' laughed Della. 'Have a drink and, for God's sake, tell me your name. I can't keep calling you "Doctor", and you can drop the "Miss Stafford" nonsense and call me "Della".'

'Timothy O'Brien...Tim, that's what my friends call me.'

'Well, Tim,' said Della, grabbing him by the arm, 'let's go to the bar, find another drink and you can tell me all about yourself.'

'Wait, Della.' Catherine smiled at Tim O'Brien. 'I was just going to tell you that Robert and I are going to get some dinner.' She glanced quickly at Robert before adding, 'Come with us, if you like.' He didn't look particularly pleased but nodded politely.

'Oh,' said Della. 'I don't know. What d'you think, Tim?'

'Now wouldn't that be grand,' he beamed, 'but I have Lieutenant Strange with me. You know, the man who's been blinded. I'm escorting him to hospital in England. Normally they travel in the ambulances, but as I'm going back for a couple of days to sit my fellowship exam, I thought...' He looked slightly embarrassed. 'Well, I thought it would make him feel more normal.'

'You're an old softie,' grinned Della. She looked around. 'Where is he?'

'Oh, he's in the officers' mess. He's not well enough to have fought through the crowds at the theatre, but' – he looked at Robert and Catherine – 'if you wouldn't mind, I'm sure he'd enjoy a meal out.'

Frances, drink in hand, emerged from the braying throng at the bar. She'd been with Beau, Catherine thought, and she looked angry. It wasn't difficult to guess that Beau had rejected their request.

'Did you tell him?' Catherine asked anxiously. 'Did you tell him what we said?'

'I did,' said Frances. She shook her head slowly. 'He wouldn't have it. He said we were exaggerating and that Eric was a good act. I told him that the company loathed him and he was poisoning the atmosphere, but' – she shrugged – 'it made no difference. Beau is adamant. Baxter stays. In fact, he said that if anyone refused to work with him, then they could go home.'

'But you told him what Davey said?' Della demanded.

Frances nodded. 'Yes.'

Tim O'Brien glanced from one of the girls to the other, patently confused about what was going on, and looked to Robert for an explanation. But he said nothing and had a still, rather menacing expression on his face.

Della and Catherine looked at each other, and then Della said, 'What's the matter with Beau, anyway?' She shook her head. 'It's as if he's scared.'

'Remember when we saw him giving Eric money?' whispered Frances. 'D'you think it could be blackm—'

'You'd better stop right there,' Robert butted in, causing Catherine and Frances to stare at him with astonishment.

Della snorted with fury. 'But—' she spat.

He turned his head to look at her. 'No "but"s.' His voice sounded as though it was sliding over ice. 'You're treading on dangerous ground, Miss Stafford.'

She opened her mouth to say more, but before the words came out, Robert said, 'End of discussion, I think.' Then, as suddenly as the edge of steel had appeared, it melted away. He smiled and took Catherine's arm. 'I'm hungry. Let's get some food.'

As they were walking through the hotel lobby, Frances felt a hand on her arm. She turned and, to her surprise, saw that it was Davey.

'Can I have a quick word?' he asked.

'Er...yes, of course,' she answered, and called to the others, who were looking back, 'Carry on. I'll catch you up.' Then, turning to Davey, she said, 'What can I do for you? Is it about your act?'

'No.' He looked around, checking the people in the lobby. She looked too, wondering whom he was concerned about.

'What is it? Tell me.'

'Have you spoken to Beau yet, about Baxter?'

'Yes. I have.' She sighed. 'Nothing doing, I'm afraid.'

'D'you think I could have a go?'

'Of course,' said Frances. 'Why not? But I warn you, he's not in the mood to listen.'

For a moment, he looked as though he was going to say something else; then he smiled and said, 'I suppose it can wait. Baxter's bound to make another mistake. Then he'll be finished.'

'Are you sure?'

'Positive. Go on. Have a nice evening.' He started to walk away towards the bar and then turned back and said, in a lowered voice, 'Don't say anything to the others just yet. I don't want to rock the boat, being the new boy and all that. If they ask, tell them I was wondering about putting a different monologue into my act.'

'Alright.' She watched him go towards the bar and frowned. She hated the fact that a member of the company was so disliked by everyone else.

Della was still grumbling when she caught them up,

but Tim was surprisingly good at calming her down, and by the time they'd been to the officers' mess and picked up Lieutenant Strange, she was in a happy mood again and skipping along the street.

At first, Felix Strange was reluctant to join them. He was sitting by himself in the officers' mess waiting for someone to bring him supper. Frances noticed that his fingers, placed on the table in front of him, were running over imaginary keys. He's playing the piano, she thought, and a wave of sympathy washed over her.

'Hello,' she said, going up to him before the others. 'It's Frances, Frances Parnell.'

'Frances?' He moved his head towards her and smiled. The dressing that had been on his jaw when Frances had seen him at the field hospital had been removed and she could see the evidence of the shrapnel damage he'd suffered. Flesh had been torn out of his chin and the wound hastily stitched together, and she could tell that it still hurt, for he gave a little gasp of pain when he smiled at her.

'What are you doing here?' he asked.

'We've come to collect you.' Frances sat down beside him. 'We're going to a cafe Robert knows, to have some dinner. Dr O'Brien has said you're fit enough, so come on.'

'Who's "we"?' he asked.

'Oh, me and Catherine and Della, plus Robert and Dr O'Brien.'

He took his hands off the table and nervously put them on his lap. 'No, I'll hold you back,' he said. 'Go and enjoy yourselves.'

'Sure and I'm not having that, son.' Tim O'Brien had joined Frances. 'You're fit enough to go to a cafe, and in

173

my opinion it'll do you good. Therapy, of the best sort. On your feet, Lieutenant.'

He was going to argue, Frances could see that. 'I'd love it if you came,' she said quickly, and took his hand. 'I'd like to hear about Hugo at school. I miss him so much, and we haven't had a letter or any information for over a year.'

Reluctantly, Felix stood up. 'If you're sure,' he said, 'and you don't mind leading me.'

'I don't mind at all,' said Frances, and tucked her hand under his arm.

It was quite late when they all walked in, late for England but not for France, it seemed, for the place was busy with locals, men in blue workmen's clothes and women with sleepy children on their laps, using spoons to drink up the heavy garlicky sauce in their bowls of mussels.

'Oh Lord,' groaned Robert from where they were standing by the open door. 'I don't think there's room for us.'

'Wait,' said Catherine, and went over to the thin black-clad woman behind the counter. 'Madame,' she asked in her perfect French, 'perhaps you have room for us, for supper? We are six, and very hungry.'

'Wait, if you please.' The proprietress used a bony finger to beckon a waiter who was placing tiny cups of very black coffee on a tin tray. She spoke rapidly to him and Catherine waited while they looked around the cafe. Eventually the waiter jerked his head towards a table where a mother and three children were beginning to get up and move away. Beside it was a smaller, empty table.

'Mademoiselle, we will push the tables together, there.'
She pointed. 'Yes?'

'Yes, thank you, madame,' Catherine smiled.

There was no choice of menu, but everything they ate was delicious. Onion soup, complemented with shavings of cheese, croutons and garlic mayonnaise, followed by bowls of steaming mussels.

'I love this,' mumbled Della, in between mouthfuls. She had been suspicious at first, never having seen, let alone eaten, a mussel before, but persuaded by Tim O'Brien, she had dug in and squealed with laughter when spurts of liquid shot across the table. 'I'm sorry,' she gasped. 'I'm being so bloody clumsy.'

'It doesn't matter,' laughed O'Brien. 'Eat up.'

'Let me help you,' Frances muttered to Felix. She had watched him feeling for his spoon when the soup was brought and then putting his other hand on the edge of the bowl.

'I'm alright,' he said. 'It's just that I don't know if I'm making a mess.'

'You aren't,' she assured him, but when the mussels arrived, he struggled again. 'I can open them,' he said, 'but where do I put the shells?'

'There's a big bowl in the middle of the table.' Frances guided his hand towards it.

After a minute, he got it right and laughed out loud.

'Good,' she said. 'Now, tell me how this' – she put her hand gently on his face – 'happened.'

Robert and Catherine hardly spoke during the meal but sat in companionable silence. He said, 'I suppose this is the first time you've been to France for years.'

'Mm,' she answered. 'I was here in '39, just before war

175

was declared. It was difficult. My grandparents knew that it was coming and were so worried. Their farm, you know, is just outside Amiens, about a hundred hectares, mostly dairy.' She leant back and looked away, remembering. 'It's a lovely place and I was always so happy there.' A deep sigh escaped her lips. 'We haven't heard a word since the middle of 1940.' She paused. 'No, that's not quite right. A young man who escaped to England in 1941 came to the house and gave us a message from them. Apparently they were well, but the Germans were in the village and taking all the milk from the farm. After that, nothing.'

'Our armies are pushing forward,' Robert said. 'Perhaps you'll hear from them soon.'

'It is my hope, but I would love to see them for myself.'

Robert smiled. 'Maybe we can arrange for the company to move north. The whole area is gradually being liberated.'

Della leant over. 'What did you say? Are we going north?'

Robert shook his head. 'Not yet. We're following the army. We'll go where they go.'

'They're going east,' said Tim. 'When I come back from leave, I'm being posted to a field station further on. On the front line.'

The girls looked at each other nervously. If the field hospital was on the front line, that was certainly where they'd be going.

'Oh well.' Della took a swig from her wine glass. 'I always said I'd probably peg out on stage.'

'But not in your twenties,' Frances objected.

'No, I hadn't planned that. Perhaps we shouldn't…'

'You signed up for danger,' said Robert. 'No backing out now.' He looked serious. 'I mean, haven't you all signed the Official Secrets Act? Walk away now and you'll be sent to the Tower.'

'What?' squeaked Della, a dripping mussel halfway to her mouth. 'The Tower?'

Frances and Catherine stared at Robert and then Frances noticed the slight grin that was playing around his mouth. She giggled. 'Robbie Lennox, you're an absolute rotter.'

He laughed. 'Got you going, though, didn't it?' He wiped a thin, yellowy piece of bread round his bowl and with a contented sigh put it in his mouth.

Della watched him, still not entirely sure. 'It'll be quite safe, won't it?'

Robert wiped his mouth. 'I told you. Behind the lines at all times. Besides, Mr Churchill would be furious if we got you killed. Lord Haw-Haw would have a propaganda field day, and Winnie would hate that.'

Even Della laughed at that, and another carafe of wine was ordered. Frances was surprised at the availability of alcohol. She'd discovered that bread and meat were rationed here like they were at home, but there seemed to be no problem with drink.

'Have some more wine,' she said to Felix. 'It's not bad.'

'Alright.' He groped on the table in front of him until he found the stem of his glass. 'Is this mine?' he asked.

'Yes,' she smiled. 'Well done.'

He took a sip and then, turning to her, said, 'They've told me that in a few weeks I'll be going to the training school for blind servicemen.' His voice sounded sad and

Frances wished she could say something that would make him feel less despairing.

She glanced quickly at her friends. Della and Tim O'Brien were sitting very close, talking and laughing, taking no notice of the others. Catherine was telling Robert about her grandparents, describing their farm, and he was listening intently. She put her hand over Felix's long fingers. 'Are the doctors certain that your sight has gone? In both eyes?'

'Yes,' he nodded. 'Or at least, in my right eye. That's certainly gone. The left too, probably, but apparently the eyeball is still there.' He gave a little shudder and she squeezed his fingers. 'Sorry,' he whispered. 'I'm being stupid.'

'Nonsense!' she whispered back. 'You have every right to be shocked by what's happened. Who wouldn't be?'

He turned his hand over and grasped hers. 'Thank you,' he said, and grinned.

When they were all walking back to the hotel, Felix suddenly said, 'Frances, what d'you look like?'

She smiled. 'Do you remember Hugo? I look a bit like him.'

'Red hair and all?'

'Oh yes.'

'Good,' he said. 'Now, when I'm back home and I think about this evening, I can picture you.'

'Where is home?'

'Well, my mother is in Salisbury. I suppose I'll go there after I've been in hospital.'

Frances, who had her arm tucked in his in order to lead him down the street, held it a bit closer. 'That's good. We don't live too far apart. I'll come and see you when we get home.'

'I'd like that,' he said.

When they reached the hotel, Della said, 'How about us all going out tomorrow, a picnic or something? Tim and Felix are leaving on a night transport, so will have to hang around until the evening, and we've got a day off.'

'I'm up for it,' said Frances. 'What about you, Felix?'

'I'd love it,' he said, and then, his face turning this way and that, asked, 'Dr Tim, wherever you are, will that be alright?'

Tim stepped across and patted him on the shoulder. 'Sure 'twill do you the world of good. And won't I be there too, so with me and Frances to look after you, you'll be in safe hands.'

That left Catherine and Robert. 'I'd like to,' she murmured, giving Robert a quick glance, 'but...'

'I've got a meeting at nine,' he said, 'but after that' – he looked down at her – 'I'm all yours.'

Chapter 13

When Catherine awoke, the sun was filtering through the slats in the shutters, lighting up the dusty shadows in the room. She could hear a church bell outside and then another and remembered that it was Sunday. At home, Maman would be pushing Lili in her big pram to church and then sitting with her on her knee while the priest intoned the prayers for redemption and peace. I haven't been to Mass since I heard about Christopher, Catherine thought. I couldn't. It seemed pointless. Devoid of hope. But now, lying here on the narrow bed, she wondered if she'd been wrong. Perhaps, if I'd prayed, things would have been different; Chris would be alive. Certainly Maman and Father Clement tried to persuade me. 'Come to confession,' he'd said kindly. 'It will cleanse your soul and you'll feel better.' And Maman had nodded anxiously, standing beside him in the little front room of their house. Catherine had shaken her head. 'I don't want to feel better,' she'd said. 'Leave me alone.'

But now, in this room, with her friends sleeping in adjacent beds, she felt at ease. I could go to church, she thought. I could pray for Christopher's soul and then get on with my life.

She rolled over and looked at the photographs of Christopher and Lili that she had placed on the rickety cupboard beside her bed. The one of Christopher had been taken in the park. She smiled, remembering that day when they'd planned their future. Chris was on leave, but he'd refused to talk about the war. 'Forget it,' he'd said. 'Let's talk about after.'

'I've been to the doctor,' she said, as they strolled, hand in hand, beside the lake.

He'd stopped and turned to stare at her. 'Oh God. Are you ill?'

'No,' she'd laughed. 'We are going to have a baby.'

'You clever girl,' he'd said, and there in front of all the other Londoners who were enjoying the park, he'd picked her up and twirled her round.

'Stop it,' she'd protested. 'Everyone's looking.'

'I don't care,' he'd said, and bent his head down to kiss her. 'I want all the world to know how much I love you.'

Later, sitting on a bench, she'd told him that she wanted to give up show business. 'You and the baby are the most important things now. I will be a proper housewife.'

'In that case,' Christopher had said eagerly, 'shall we leave London and go and live in the country? I'd like that, and I think country life would suit you. You're always saying how much you love your grandparents' farm, and anyway, it'll be a good place to bring up the children.'

'Children?' she'd smiled. 'Let me have this one first.' She'd leant her head on his shoulder. 'I love you so much, Christopher. I want us to be together, always.'

'I did mean it,' she whispered to the photograph, and Chris smiled back at her, his fair hair brushed away from his face and his spectacles dangling from his hand. I'd forgotten about the glasses, she suddenly thought, and swinging her legs out of bed, sat up. He wore glasses for reading. Why haven't I remembered that? Oh God. What else is drifting away?

Now, above the sound of bells, she heard a different noise. From the distance came the boom of big guns. That will be at the front, she thought, and if I can hear it, it can't be that far away.

Since that first day, they hadn't been troubled by the sirens warning them to go to the shelter, but they had heard the sound of cannons. 'It's miles away,' Robert had said. 'The noise is carried on the wind.' But tomorrow they would be travelling towards those explosions, and although Beau had been positive that they'd never be put in danger, a tiny frisson of fear curdled her stomach.

She picked up Lili's photo and kissed it. My little girl, she thought. Christopher gave me a lovely child. I must stay safe for her.

'She'll be OK.' Della's voice broke the silence of the room.

'I know,' said Catherine, looking over her shoulder. 'But I do miss her.'

If Della noticed the trace of tears on her friend's face, she said nothing, but swung herself out of bed and walked over to the window. 'Shall I open the shutters?' she asked. 'Will it wake Frances?'

'I'm awake,' Frances spoke from her bed. 'I've been awake for a while, listening to the bells and the guns and thinking.'

'What about?' asked Della, swinging back the shutters and letting the bright morning light flood the room.

'I don't know. Everything.'

'Lieutenant Strange, perhaps,' said Della with a wicked grin. 'You two seemed very cosy last night.'

Frances laughed. 'Don't be silly,' she said. 'Anyway, what about you and Tim O'Brien? Talk about cosy.'

Della turned away from the window. 'He's so lovely,' she said with a surprised look on her face. 'I've never met anyone like him before.'

'You mean, someone respectable?' Frances grinned.

Della shrugged. She seemed genuinely baffled by her feelings and Frances gave Catherine a conspiratorial wink before picking up her wash bag and going towards the door. With her hand on the doorknob, she paused and looked back. 'And what about you and Robert Lennox?' she said to Catherine as she went out. 'Anyone can see that he's mad about you.'

They walked to the NAAFI canteen to get breakfast. Tommy was there with Godfrey and Colin, eating powdered-egg omelettes, each topped with a sausage.

'They've got sausages in today,' called Tommy, spotting them. 'Good breakfast!'

'It doesn't look good,' muttered Catherine, turning down her mouth, 'but I'm hungry,' and she followed Frances and Della to the counter.

When they were all together at a table and had nearly finished eating, Tommy asked, 'Where did you girls get to last night?'

'We went to a cafe.' Della popped the last of her sausage in her mouth and leant back. 'We ate mussels!'

'Jesus!' Colin shook his head in disgust. 'I wouldnae look at those.'

'They were delicious,' said Della. 'You should try them.'

'Never.'

'Where's Davey today?' asked Frances, looking around the canteen. 'Still in bed?'

'No,' boomed Godfrey. 'He didn't come back to the hotel last night and still wasn't there this morning.'

'He's picked up a bit of skirt,' Tommy asserted, grinning widely. 'These local ladies are not half bad.'

The girls rolled their eyes at each other. 'Charming,' said Della, and would have said more but there was a commotion at the entrance to the canteen. People were standing up to get a better look, and even as the company scraped their chairs back too, a group came into the room. Clapping erupted and a few shouted cheers came from the diners before Frances suddenly saw who had come into the canteen.

'Bloody hell!' squealed Della. 'It's George Formby!'

The performer had arrived with a small entourage, including a woman in uniform who appeared to be directing the whole operation of meeting and greeting.

'Give us a song, George,' called one of the soldiers, who'd been eating breakfast with a group of mates.

'Too early, lad,' George grinned. 'Me bloody chest's not working yet. I just popped in to say hello.'

The Bennett Players got up and walked over to where he was standing to join in the general applause. He spotted their uniforms and recognised that they were army entertainers like he was and came over to shake their hands. When he got to Della, he stopped and gaped at her, then grasped her hands more tightly.

'By 'eck, it's Della Stafford.' He turned to the woman beside him, who was giving Della and the other girls a glowering look. 'Beryl, love. Look who's here. You must remember Della Stafford. She was on the same bill as us – in Blackpool, was it? Aye, Blackpool.'

Beryl gave Della a brief nod and tried to direct George on to the rest of the excited crowd, but he was having none of it. Still holding Della's hand, he turned to his entourage. 'Take a look at her, lads. Gorgeous Della Stafford. This girl's got the best legs in the business.'

He grinned widely, and Della laughed and said, 'Hello, George. Meet my pals.'

The Bennett Players were introduced and he had a kind word for each of them. 'Still doing the magic act, Signor?' he said to Colin, and then patted Godfrey on the shoulder. 'How's the wife?' he asked, and with his back turned to Beryl, he gave Godfrey an enormous wink.

'Now, who are these two pretty lasses?' he said, looking appreciatively at Frances and Catherine.

Before Della could introduce them properly, Beryl stepped in front of him. 'We have to go, George. We're due to meet the general.' She grabbed his arm and pushed him towards the door.

He went, reluctantly, shaking hands on the way with the soldiers and the canteen staff who had thronged to see him. 'Goodbye, everybody,' he called from the door. 'Keep the old flag flying.'

'That was fun,' said Frances, when they were sitting back at their table. 'But who was the gorgon?'

'Beryl?' Della shook her head and laughed. 'She's his wife. And his manager and an absolute cow. She thinks he's doing it with every girl he meets and causes no end of trouble for him.'

'He probably is,' grinned Tommy. 'Wouldn't you,' he said to the boys, 'with that waiting at home for you?'

'He was right about your legs, though, Della,' roared Godfrey. 'I've never seen a finer pair.'

'Why, you old smoothie,' Della blushed. 'This French air is certainly suiting you. Mrs James won't know you when you get back.'

'If only,' he sighed, and they laughed.

Tommy went to get more teas as Beau limped into the canteen, followed by Robert. Catherine looked up and smiled, but Robert didn't smile back. His face, like Beau's, was still and serious. 'Hello,' she said. 'Finished your meeting?'

'Gather up,' said Beau, and waited while Robert pulled over a chair for him and one for himself.

Tommy came back with the teas and immediately offered to get more for them.

'No. Sit down,' said Beau. 'We've got something to tell you. It's about Davey Jones. There's...no easy way to say this, but he's been found dead.'

'Dead!' There was a gasp round the table. Catherine and Della reached for each other's hands, and the boys stared, open-mouthed.

'He can't be,' said Tommy. 'He wasn't ill.'

Frances remembered the conversation she'd had with him last evening and wondered if it was somehow connected. 'How did he die?' she asked.

'His neck was broken,' said Beau.

Catherine went white and put her hand to her mouth. 'How horrible,' she whispered.

'My God,' Tommy breathed. 'Where was he found? Did he have a fall?'

'He was in an alley behind the hotel,' said Beau. 'Just lying on the cobbles. The police don't think he fell, but...'

He didn't finish the sentence and turned to Robert for help.

'We don't know anything for sure,' Robert said. 'The local police are liaising with the redcaps because Davey was still a soldier. Despite his injury, which made him unfit for active service, he wanted to do his bit. As an entertainer.'

The company were still shocked and silent; it was almost too much to take in.

'Look,' said Robert calmly, 'it'll have been nothing to do with the company. It could have been a drunken brawl or a robbery gone wrong. Crime does go on, even during wartime.'

Frances shot a glance at him. Somehow, he didn't seem as confused as the rest of them. Beau was clearly stunned, but Robert, well, he was behaving almost as though he'd been expecting it. She turned to Beau. 'Did he speak to you?' she asked, fixing him with a stare. 'He had something to tell you.'

'What?' muttered Beau.

'He was asking about Baxter. Whether you were getting rid of him.'

The colour drained out of Beau's face. 'For Christ's sake,' he shouted. 'Will you all stop going on about Baxter? I'm sick of hearing his name.'

'Well, you know what to do, then,' said Della, and got a poisonous look in return.

'But,' Frances persisted, 'perhaps you saw him this morning?'

Robert came to Beau's rescue. 'Mr Jones was killed in the night. The police have established that,' he said. 'Nobody saw him after the show. Except Frances.'

Catherine turned to her with a frown. 'When I asked you what he wanted, you said it was about changing his act,' she said.

'I know.' Frances bit her lip. 'He didn't want me to say anything. I think he was scared of rocking the boat.'

Beau suddenly had a bout of coughing, and dragging a hanky from his sleeve, he covered his mouth. Frances noticed that his hand was shaking. He looked as if he was about to pass out.

She reached out her hand and covered his shaking one. 'Can I get you a glass of water, Beau? You don't seem very well.'

He shook his head. 'No. No, thank you, Frances.' He pulled his hand away from hers and dug into his pocket. From it he produced a small, round box. 'My leg is giving me hell this morning,' he said, opening the box. It was half full of small white pills. 'If you'd let me have a sip of your tea to get a couple of these down, I'd be grateful.'

Frances watched as he swallowed the pills. Somehow the whole coughing incident looked fake, as though it had been done to stop further questioning. She turned her head to look at Robert and found that he was staring back at her, almost daring her to go on.

I will, she thought, but before she could speak, Della said, 'I'll bet it was to do with Baxter. Davey knew something about him. Something bad.' She looked round. 'And where the hell is he? Where does he go between performances?'

Robert stood up. 'Never mind that now. I've come to take you to the officers' mess. The redcaps and the local police want to question you and are waiting there. We' – he looked down at Beau – 'thought it would be better if we told you the news first. He was a colleague, even if only for a brief time, and I understand that you're all upset.' His face softened as he looked down to Catherine. 'I am very sorry, but we have to go. They're waiting.'

They trooped out, nobody talking. Davey had only been with the group for a short while, but he'd quickly melded in, and they'd liked him.

'I wonder if this will stop us going to the front,' muttered Tommy.

Nobody answered. Each had their own thoughts.

The three girls walked together down the street towards the old hotel that housed the officers' mess. Della was, as always, the first to speak. 'It's a rum do,' she said.

'Yes,' Frances replied. She looked over her shoulder to where Robert was walking slowly alongside Beau. They were deep in conversation. 'There's something going on. I'm convinced of it. And they're in on it.' She jerked her head and the other two girls looked over their shoulders too.

'What did Davey want to know?' asked Catherine.

'About Baxter, of course. Whether Beau had sacked him.'

'We've seen things,' Catherine muttered. 'Remember at the field hospital he was exchanging cigarettes for something? I don't know what.'

'It'll be drugs,' Della growled. 'What else do you pinch from a hospital?'

'And he's selling them to Beau,' Frances whispered. 'We saw Beau giving him money ages ago in that factory in Liverpool.'

Catherine thought about her two days at the spy

school. Was this connected? But no. It couldn't be, not really. That was all about tanks and uniforms, not about murder.

'We'd better say something to the police,' said Della. She looked at Frances. 'You have to tell them that Davey spoke to you last night.'

'I suppose so.' Frances nodded, but she felt uncomfortable. Robert and Beau wanted her to keep her mouth shut and it seemed to matter an awful lot.

When they walked into the officers' mess, Robert caught up with them. The boys had gone ahead and were out of sight now, and Beau was still limping up the street behind them. Robert took Frances's arm and stopped her. 'Before we go into the dining room, where the police are waiting,' he said, 'can I have a quick word? With all of you.' He looked up and down the corridor and, seeing that it was empty, opened a door on one side. 'In here, I think.'

They were pushed, not too gently, into a white-tiled room that echoed to the tap of their high-heeled shoes. It smelt rank.

'Bloody hell,' said Della, pinching her nose and looking at the three cubicles and the row of urinals. 'It's the gents'. What the hell are we doing in here?'

Robert quickly pushed open the cubicle doors, and satisfying himself that no one else was in the room, he turned to the three startled girls. 'I'm going to be quick, so listen carefully. None of you will say anything to the police or to the redcaps. Whatever they ask, you know nothing.'

'That's ridiculous,' said Frances.

'Nevertheless, I insist.'

Catherine remembered her first interview with him at the airfield. He'd looked then as he did now, serious and rather intimidating, and she was scared. Della and Frances were not.

'We're not stupid,' said Frances. 'We know something is going on.'

'And we know that it has to do with Eric Baxter,' Della added, wagging her finger at him. 'You and Beau can't get away with it.'

Robert took off his glasses and slowly polished them on his khaki tie. Frances guessed that he was thinking of something to say. Would it be conciliatory or threatening? Whatever it would be, she felt prepared.

He looked at Catherine. She wouldn't meet his eye and stared beyond him to the rather grubby tiles on the wall, but when he transferred his gaze to Della and Frances, they, not intimidated, glared back at him.

'Alright,' he said finally, 'I agree that you're not stupid, and yes, there is something going on. But I can't tell you what it is. We are at war, and in war there are secrets, secrets that affect our military security. So I am asking you to trust me. Please.' He looked at each of them in turn, trying to convey the seriousness of the situation. 'Don't voice any of your suspicions to the police or the redcaps. Play it as neutral as you can, because I promise you, it matters. It matters a lot.'

'Is the tour going on?' asked Della.

'Yes. I can't see that there is any need to postpone it. That is' – he glanced at Catherine – 'unless you're too upset to carry on.'

'No,' Frances said. 'It isn't that. But what about Baxter?'

'He'll be with you. I'll speak to him about his behaviour – don't you worry. He won't upset you again, but he is going on with the tour.'

The girls looked at each other, and then Della nodded. 'Alright, we won't say anything, but, Robert' – she narrowed her eyes – 'stop trying to bully us, and don't take us for fools. Never again.'

The door suddenly swung open and a young officer came in. He gaped at the sight of the three young women and started to back out. 'It's OK – we're leaving,' said Robert, smiling. 'Our meeting is finished.' And as the startled officer held open the door, the three girls glided out, followed by Robert. Catherine was the last to leave, and when they were out in the corridor, Robert caught her hand. 'Did you understand?' he asked, his voice quietly anxious. 'It is for the best reasons.'

'Yes, I think so,' she said. 'And…I do trust you, Robert.'

He looked down into her dark eyes and smiled. 'I don't know what you've done to me,' he said. 'You're making me soft.'

'Is that bad?'

He took a deep breath and then gave a short laugh. 'In my line of work, yes. Now, we must hurry.'

The questioning didn't take up much time. The boys had gone first and said they didn't know if Davey had enemies, and although Tommy said that Davey hadn't got on with Eric Baxter, as did Godfrey and Colin, nobody took much notice. The two redcaps looked at each other with raised eyebrows and a hint of a grin. It was obvious that they imagined that these theatre people were prone to having little tiffs.

'Where is this Eric Baxter?' asked the redcap sergeant.

'We don't know,' said Tommy, shrugging.

'He's gone on ahead to prepare our next venue,' Beau suddenly announced. 'I asked him to go straight away after last night's show. He got a lift with some BBC reporters who were heading the same way.'

The members of the company looked at each other. This was the first they'd heard of it, and Della opened her mouth to say something, but then thought better of it and, sitting back in her chair, lit another cigarette.

The redcap frowned. 'You wanted to speak, Miss Stafford?'

She drew heavily on her cigarette and, after blowing out a lungful of blue smoke, grinned at the soldier. 'Me, darling? No. Nothing to say.'

The French police were more persistent and Catherine, who had been called to interpret, was careful in her translation.

'Mademoiselle,' the police inspector said, 'ask Monsieur James when he last saw Monsieur Jones. Indeed, mademoiselle, ask everybody, if you please.'

Frances seemed to have been the last person who saw Davey, and with one eye on Robert, she told the inspector that Davey had wanted to add something into his act.

'And that was all, mademoiselle?'

'Yes. A new monologue, he said.' Frances let Catherine interpret. Her ability to speak and understand French was something she'd mostly kept to herself.

There were no more questions, and when Robert asked if they could go on with their tour, both the redcaps and the French police inspector nodded. 'We'll know where you are,' said the redcap sergeant.

The inspector turned to Catherine. 'You must give us your schedule, mademoiselle.'

'Yes, monsieur,' she said. 'Monsieur Bennett knows where we're going. I'll ask him.'

Before he turned away, the inspector spoke to her again. 'Are you sure you've told us everything, mademoiselle? Interpreted correctly?' There was a suspicious edge to his voice and Catherine felt suddenly nervous. She knew Robert was watching her.

'I have, monsieur,' she said, keeping the tremor out of her voice. 'Absolutely. And, monsieur' – she lifted up her left hand to point to her wedding ring – 'I am Madame Fletcher, not Mademoiselle.'

He blushed and bowed his head. 'My apologies, madame.'

'Well done,' said Robert when the police and the redcaps left. 'You got him on the back foot.'

'Not deliberately,' she smiled. 'I was being correct.'

Tim O'Brien came into the dining room arm in arm with Felix, and Della jumped up and went over to greet them.

'What's going on?' asked Tim, and Frances went to join them and explanations were made.

'Jesus,' said Tim. 'Sure and that's dreadful.'

'It's bloody awful,' Della cried. 'I knew him from before. He was a nice bloke.'

Felix reached out his hand. 'Frances,' he said, 'are you alright?'

She went over to him and took his hand. 'I'm fine,' she said. 'But how about us getting away from here? I need some fresh air. Remember? We had planned a day out.'

194

'Let's buy some cheese and perhaps bread, if we can find some, and a bottle of wine,' Tim suggested. 'I'm told there's a fine park, here in the city. We could go there. It'll be a grand picnic.'

'Yes,' enthused Della, 'I love the idea.' She looked around for Catherine, who was standing beside Robert. He was gathering up the papers scattered on the canteen table. 'What about you two?' she called.

Robert looked up. 'I need Catherine to look through these documents that the police left. They're copies of our statements and they're all in French. Perhaps we'll join you later.'

Della gave a little smirk before they left. 'He wants her all to himself,' she whispered to Frances.

Alone with Robert, Catherine felt strangely vulnerable. She knew that he spoke and understood French perfectly, so his excuse for keeping her behind was exactly that, an excuse. But what for?

Robert stuffed the papers in his briefcase and then turned to look at her. 'I have a Jeep outside. How would you like to go to the coast for the day? It's only a few miles away, quite safe, and I know a place that's relatively unspoilt by the war.' He grinned. 'Maybe you could dip your toes in the water.'

Catherine nodded. She didn't want to walk with Robert in the park – that's what she did with Christopher – and the thought of a few hours at the seaside was entrancing.

'Yes,' she smiled. 'I'd like that.'

Chapter 14

The road to the coast was crammed with lorries bringing supplies to the advancing army, and with soldiers, each heavily laden with the equipment of war, marching in single file along the edges of the road. One or two waved to her as she and Robert drove past them in the open Jeep and she waved back and smiled. They looked young, eager and excited. The thought of what might lie ahead didn't seem to be bothering them at all. Some locals had gathered at the road junctions to cheer on the invasion force and throw flowers. Catherine saw one old man press a bottle of wine into a young soldier's hands and a girl run forward to kiss the cheek of the man behind him.

It was an exciting sight and Catherine laughed out loud. 'Isn't it wonderful?' she said. 'These people are so happy to see the army.'

Robert braked slowly and, turning the steering wheel, drove off the main road and onto a narrow country lane. It was empty of trucks and people, and led away through meadows and high hedges towards the coast. 'Yes,' he said, eventually responding to her remark. 'They'll be glad to be free. The sooner the war's over, the better. For everyone.'

This last seemed heartfelt and she gave him a quick glance. It occurred to her that she knew nothing about him except for the fact that he'd been at the same school as Frances's brother. He knew all about her, everything; but even last night, at the cafe, when she'd spoken about her grandparents, Robert had given nothing in return. Did he have a family? Was he married? The thought made her uncomfortable, but not as uncomfortable as it should have done. She was simply happy to be with him.

Ahead, the light was changing. The pale summer sky was taking on a translucent gleam as it reflected the sea beneath it. Catherine couldn't see it yet but knew it was close, for she could smell the salt in the air and feel it sharp on her face.

'Where are we going?' she asked.

'Ah,' he said, concentrating on missing the bumps in the road. 'I'm keeping that as a surprise, but I'm reliably informed that it's the one area around here that hasn't been damaged by the invasion and that we'll be able to get some lunch.'

Soon they crested a little hill and the whole coastline lay ahead of them. 'Oh,' Catherine said, entranced by the view, 'it's so beautiful.'

'From here, yes,' Robert agreed with a sigh, 'but when we get closer, signs of the war will become evident.'

He was right. As they drove along, Catherine could see the beaches more clearly and was shocked at the sight of yards of barbed wire, damaged vehicles and all sorts of military debris. She wondered if there would be dead bodies lying in the sand, washed constantly by the incoming and outgoing tide, and then assured herself that was silly. What had happened here was weeks ago now, and those poor soldiers who had died would have been buried.

At one point, the broad sweep of the coastline horse-shoed into a narrow cove before straightening out again to continue on. Above the cove, a small group of houses clustered on a flat meadow, which after a hundred yards dropped gently down to the sea. Robert turned towards the largest house. It was square with a low-pitched grey-tiled roof and a white veranda running round the front of the building. The windows were open, with curtains blowing out against the pale blue shutters, and a thin plume of smoke spiralled up from the chimney.

'Are we going here?' asked Catherine, intrigued. 'What is it? A small hotel?'

'No.' Robert chuckled as he drew up on the sandy gravel in front of the veranda. 'Not a hotel, a house. My house.'

She was still taking in that remarkable announcement when a middle-aged woman with wild black hair came out of the house and ran down the steps. 'Oh, Monsieur Robert,' she cried. 'How wonderful.' She enveloped him in her arms and kissed him several times on the cheeks. 'I thought I'd never see you again.' Tears came then, which were dabbed away with the corner of her red velvet shawl.

'I'm here now, Agathe,' Robert smiled, disentangling himself, 'as you see, and as I told you on the telephone, I'm alive, quite safe and undamaged. Now' – he turned to Catherine – 'I'd like you to meet my friend. Madame Fletcher.'

Agathe gave her a searching look when she shook hands. 'Ah,' she beamed. 'Such a pretty girl.'

'And half French,' Robert warned. 'So mind what you say – she'll understand it.'

'Silly boy,' Agathe growled, and then took Catherine's arm. 'Come inside, madame. Lunch is ready.'

Sitting on the veranda after a delicious meal of soup and mushroom omelettes, and with a glass of white wine on the basketwork table in front of her, Catherine asked Robert about the house.

'It was my uncle's,' he said. 'He came here after the Great War to live and to paint. Surviving the trenches left him in a bad way and he couldn't face going home, so my grandfather bought this house for him and gave him an allowance to live on. I visited here often as a child, particularly after my mother died. Uncle Matthew was a kind man, and closer to me than my own father.' He leant back, holding his glass up to the light before taking a deep drink. 'He left me the house when he died, on the understanding that Agathe could live here for her lifetime. I was happy with that.'

How strange, Catherine thought, leaving the house to his nephew but insisting that his cook should live in it too. She leant back and looked out over the green meadow to the sea. It sparkled in the afternoon light, serenely peaceful and inviting. I must go down there, she thought, before we leave, but now that Robert's finally giving something of his life away, I want to hear it.

'Was he a good artist?' she asked.

'No.' Robert shook his head. 'Not really. His seascapes weren't bad, and he sold a few of those, but what he really wanted to do was to paint nudes.' He lowered his voice. 'Agathe was his model and his lover.'

'What?' Catherine was astonished and looked back into the house to see if she was there. She was clearing away the lunch dishes and, seeing Catherine looking at her, gave her a pleasant smile and waggled her fingers.

'Oh yes. It was quite the scandal in the village below here. But she didn't care. I think she loved him.' He paused. 'No. Not think. I know she loved him, and he adored her.'

'But why didn't they marry?'

'Because she already had a wife at home. Aunt Dorothea. A first-class bitch. I hated her.'

He was scowling again, that grim face that Catherine had seen before, and she stood up and leant on the veranda railing. She wanted to ask more about him, but not now – it seemed that he'd hit a raw spot.

'How far away is the sea?' she asked, not looking at him. 'My toes are dying for a dip.'

He looked up. 'What?'

Catherine turned to him. His face was set as though unhappy memories had pushed themselves into the foreground. 'Can we go on the beach?'

He gazed at her and then his face cleared and he stood up too. 'Come on, I'll take you down.'

A winding, narrow track led down through the meadow as it fell towards the sea. Soon they were clambering through sand dunes and Catherine stopped to take off her shoes.

'Give them to me,' said Robert, and stuffed each high-heeled shoe into the pockets of his battledress. The deserted little beach curved out before them, surprisingly untouched by military hardware, although in the distance to the left and right of them Catherine could see that the coastline was covered in barbed wire and wrecked bits of machinery.

'The sand shelves away very quickly in this little bay,' said Robert, pointing out to sea. 'The Germans knew that the marines couldn't jump out of a landing craft here. Half of them would drown, and you'd never get the vehicles off. So our beach was left alone and undefended.'

'Well, I'm going for a paddle,' said Catherine, taking off her jacket and dropping it onto the sand. She held out her hand. 'Come with me, Robert.'

'Yes,' he said, and took off his jacket too and, bending down, rolled up his trouser legs. They held hands as they ventured into the sparkling water. It was cold and Catherine gasped at first and then went further in. She ignored the wind, which blew gently off the sea and sent her hair into a shining dark cloud around her face, and she laughed as she pushed it back with her free hand.

The little waves splashed against her legs, and as she went deeper, she had to hitch up her khaki skirt to stop it getting wet. 'This is wonderful,' she said. 'I can't remember when I last paddled.'

'Nor me,' said Robert; then he grasped her hand tighter. 'No further, Catherine. It is dangerous.'

She allowed him to lead her back up the beach until they reached the place where they'd dropped their jackets. The sand was warm on her bare feet and she sat down and pushed her legs out in front of her to let the sun dry them. 'We should have brought bathing suits,' she said.

Robert sat down beside her, loosening his tie and opening the top buttons on his shirt. 'Have you got a bathing suit in your luggage?' he asked.

'No,' she laughed. 'Have you?'

'There was one at the house, I think. If it's still there. Agathe said that the Germans went through all the rooms when they came to the village, but surprisingly, as far as she can see, they didn't pinch anything. I'd imagined that the house would have been commandeered by some of the officers, but it wasn't. They took over the hotels further along the coast. We were lucky.'

'Mm.' Catherine closed her eyes and put her face up to the sun. 'It's a lovely house,' she said dreamily. 'Will you live there after the war?'

Robert lay back on the sand and folded his arms under his head. 'I don't know,' he answered. 'It depends.'

Catherine opened her eyes and looked down at him. He seemed relaxed. The most relaxed she'd ever seen him, his glasses lying on the sand beside him and his hair, ruffled by the wind, dragged out of its usual neat side parting.

'On what?' she asked. Half of her didn't want to hear his answer. It could be about whether he could earn a living, which would be reasonable, but what if it depended on what his wife wanted to do? There had to be a wife. Robert was – what? About the same age as Hugo and Beau, and pretty well off, she suspected. He would have a wife.

He propped himself up on one elbow. 'On many things,' he said. 'But' – he put a hand out and touched her face – 'I don't want to talk about me. I want to kiss you.'

For the briefest of moments, she thought of getting up and walking through the dunes back to the Jeep, but she didn't. Instead, she put her face down to his and felt his lips cover hers. And when he put his arm around her waist and pulled her onto the sand beside him, she didn't struggle. It felt right. It was what she wanted.

She could hear the tide rolling in and gulls wailing overhead as Robert held her very close and explored her face and neck with his mouth. His hands ran over her back, pulling her to him, and she could feel that he was as aroused as she was. Let him. Let him take you, one half of her brain was screaming. It's been so very long. And she melted further into his arms.

But then, as Robert pressed his mouth on hers and started unbuttoning her shirt, an indistinct image of Christopher came into her head and, shocked, she drew back. 'No,' she gasped. 'No, Robert. I'm sorry. I can't.'

He stopped immediately, sitting up, breathing hard and running a shaking hand across his face. 'Alright, Catherine,' he murmured. 'Perhaps it's for the best.'

Without speaking further, they both got up and started to walk across the beach and through the dunes to the meadow. When they were nearly back at the house, Catherine grasped Robert's arm and drew him to a halt. 'I wanted you to kiss me,' she said with a slight choke in her voice. 'I wanted more than that. But the fact is, Robert, I'm not free.'

He gazed down at her troubled eyes. A curling strand of her brown hair trailed across her mouth, and lifting his hand, he gently hooked it behind her ear. 'You are the loveliest girl I've ever seen,' he said. 'And I think I'm truly in love for the first time in my life. But I understand what you say. You're not free, any more than I am.'

That evening in the hotel room, while she and the other two girls packed up their cases, ready for the morning's departure, Catherine thought about what Robert had said. He'd spoken of love. But what was it he'd said afterwards? *You're not free, any more than I am.* That's what he'd said. It could only mean that he has a wife, possibly children, and his feelings for me are no more than a wartime romance. They go on all the time, everybody knows that they do. Perhaps that's what he meant and I should simply treat it as that.

Putting Christopher and Lili's photos in her case, she sighed. Is that all it was?

'That was a big sigh,' said Della. 'Are you sorry to leave Bayeux?'

'Not really,' Catherine answered. 'Davey's death has cast a bit of a pall over this place.' She looked at the other girls. 'Has anyone heard anything new?'

They both shook their heads. 'I asked Beau,' said Frances, 'but he said he was as much in the dark as we were.'

Della looked up from spitting into her rock-hard mascara. 'Dr Tim said that Davey's body would probably be flown home. So that there could be an inquest and a murder inquiry, even though it happened here.'

Catherine turned down her mouth. 'It's horrible,' she said, as she finished her packing and closed her suitcase.

'But it won't put us off doing our best at the front,' Frances tried to cheer her up.

'No.' Catherine sat on her bed. 'I'm excited about going, really looking forward to singing to the troops.'

'Me too,' said Della. 'It'll be fun.'

'Where did you go today?' asked Frances, glancing at Catherine, who was deep in thought. 'We thought you were going to join us in the park, where, incidentally, we had a fabulous time.'

'We did,' agreed Della. 'We talked until I was hoarse, and we found out so much about each other.' She plonked herself down on Catherine's bed and, with one wicked eye on Frances, said, 'Did you know that Frances is a lady?'

'Of course I did,' Catherine smiled. 'She has beautiful manners, she's very well behaved, and she doesn't swear all the time like you do.'

'No,' Della laughed. 'I don't mean that. She's a real lady. She's called Lady Frances. Her father is a duke or something.'

'What?' Catherine stared at Frances. 'Really?'

'No,' growled Frances. 'Della's got it wrong, as usual. My father is an earl. And Felix should have kept his mouth shut.'

'Goodness,' said Catherine. 'Are you terribly rich?'

'Oh, I wish,' Frances sighed. 'We've barely two pennies to rub together now. That's why I was working on the farm. We can't afford to pay men's wages.' She grinned at Della. 'I bet your mother is much better off than my pa. 'Specially with the moonshine.'

Della frowned. 'I just hope to God she hasn't gone in with that bastard Costigan.' She threw a pair of white high-heeled shoes into her case almost as though she was throwing them at Jerry Costigan. Then she looked at Catherine again. 'Anyway, Catherine Fletcher,' she demanded, 'what did you get up to today?'

'Well, we went to the seaside. I paddled.'

'And how was Robert? Did he manage to crack a smile?'

'He was fine,' said Catherine. 'He took me to his uncle's house, where the housekeeper made us omelettes. Then we went for a walk to the beach. All around, the coast was littered with wrecks and rubbish, but his little cove was lovely and clear.'

'Was the uncle there?' asked Frances.

'No, he's dead. It was just the housekeeper, Agathe. She was very nice and it was a lovely day.' A day I'll hold close all my life, thought Catherine, and the memory of Robert's mouth on hers and his hands running over her body made her heart beat a little faster.

'I'd say you've taken the sun,' said Della, getting up and going for her wash bag. 'Your cheeks are quite pink.'

The weather had changed again the next day, and rain spattered the windows of the bus as they were driven further inland. The Bennett Players were quiet: none of the usual shouting back and forth between them had happened this morning, and although the poker game was going on as usual at the back of the bus, the card players kept their voices down to an agreeable banter. Frances sat with Beau at the front, going over the schedule of performances and venues. She was rather alarmed to find that there had been nothing arranged for their accommodation.

'They'll probably give us a tent wherever we perform,' said Beau, 'or we'll have to sleep on the bus.' He looked back over his shoulder. 'We could take out some of the seats, you know. We don't need them.'

The soldier driver who was manoeuvring the vehicle through the rutted and potholed roads turned his head. 'Me and Walter can help with that, sir, if you want us to.'

His mate Walter, who was sitting on the opposite front seat, nodded. 'Piece of cake, sir.'

'Thank you, Corporal,' said Beau. 'We'll certainly consider that.' He seemed more cheerful today, his hands weren't shaking, and Frances hadn't seen him reach for his pain medicine once during the journey.

'What about the playlist?' she asked. 'Shall we rejig it? Now that Davey's...' Her words trailed away. She didn't know how to put it.

'Yes,' said Beau. 'I think Eric should open the second half, followed by Della. What d'you think?'

'I suppose that's alright,' said Frances, pencilling in names on her clipboard. 'And who closes? Catherine?'

'Oh, I think so. She's really the star, but for an encore, you three girls can do another number. Are you up for that?'

Catherine, sitting in the aisle seat beside Della, looked at the back of Frances's head as she and Beau discussed the running order. She'd caught some of the conversation and said to Della, 'Beau wants us to do a third number. Can we think of something?'

'I expect so,' her friend replied. She was quiet too this morning, quite unlike her normal gregarious self.

'Did you have a lot to drink yesterday?' Catherine asked sympathetically.

'No, not much.'

'Then what's the matter? You seem a bit upset today.'

Della scowled. 'There's nothing the matter with me,' she snapped. 'Don't know what you're going on about. Minding everybody's business.'

Catherine was astonished; this was so unlike Della. She turned to face her friend. 'Della, *chérie*, what's up?'

Her friend took out her packet of cigarettes and, lighting one, drew a couple of deep lungfuls before putting her hand on Catherine's. 'Sorry, darling,' she said. 'Didn't mean to snap. It's just that...'

'That you're missing Tim?'

Della nodded. 'Stupid, isn't it? Missing someone you've known for only a week. And someone like him too. I mean, he's so bloody...innocent.'

Catherine laughed. 'What does it matter if he's different from all the other rogues you pick up? He's a nice man, and he seems to like you. In fact, from what I saw, he's crazy about you.'

'D'you really think so?' Della pressed Catherine's hand. 'D'you think he is?'

'Yes,' said Catherine. 'He's mad for you.'

Della relaxed then, and her usual grin lit her face. 'D'you know, he was going to be a priest? That's what his mammy wanted, but after a year in the sem...' She paused. 'I can't remember the name of the place where men go to be priests, but anyway, he left. His mammy was furious, he said, still is. Silly old cow. I'd like to give her a piece of my mind.'

By the time they'd reached the first roadblock, Della was back to her old self and had gone to sit beside Walter. 'Where are you from?' she asked him.

'Birkenhead, miss.'

'Well, I never,' Della giggled. 'We're neighbours. I'm from the 'Pool. D'you come across the water ever?'

'Hold on, folks,' called the driver. 'We're stopping.' They were on the edge of a wood, and a barrier had been placed across the road. It was manned by four guards, who were armed with rifles, and another two were at the edge of the trees with a machine gun, which was aimed at the bus. The Bennett Players stared out of the window at it as the driver climbed down and showed the guards their pass.

'Crikey,' said Tommy, jumping up to get a better look. He suddenly sounded more scared than excited. 'That looks the business. I think we really are going to the front.'

'Of course we are, old chap,' Godfrey bellowed, and Colin tapped a finger on his cards. 'Come away, Tommy. It's your turn.'

Catherine stood up and went to the front of the bus. She could see Robert in his Jeep on the other side of the barrier. He was with two more soldiers, and when she turned to look out of the back window, she could see an armoured car behind them with yet more. 'We must be important,' she said to Frances, who was standing beside her. 'Look at all the soldiers escorting us.'

'I suppose we are,' Frances nodded. 'Troop morale and all that.'

The soldier driver climbed back into the bus and the barrier was lifted. Soon they were on their way again, as the rain got heavier and the road muddier. They went through a small village where many of the buildings were badly damaged. Through the rain, Catherine could see large bullet holes in the walls of some of the town houses, and others were almost totally demolished. A few people wandered about, still dazed, she thought, by the extent of the damage, but a couple of food shops were open, with women queuing outside to get whatever provisions they could. An army lorry was pulled up in front of the little town hall, and soldiers were unloading supplies of flour and cooking oil, and further on, an army ambulance was parked in front of a lightly damaged house. Another queue of people, some with bandages round their heads and others with crutches, waited outside.

'Look at that,' whispered Della. 'It must have been awful.'

'No worse than the bombing at home,' said Catherine.

'I suppose so,' Della agreed. 'The 'Pool was pasted, but those bullet holes in the walls are something else.'

A shape loomed up at the side of the road. It was a wrecked tank with German markings on its side. The turret was completely blown off, and the tracks at the front wrecked. That's a Panzer VI, thought Catherine, recollecting her lessons at the spy school. However did I remember that? she smiled to herself. I thought everything had gone in one ear and out the other.

'Nearly there,' called the driver after another half-hour, and soon the bus was driving into a square clearing where there was one very big tent to one side and many smaller ones on the other sides of the quadrangle. It seemed like hundreds of soldiers were waiting to greet them, lined up in front of the tents and cheering as the bus came to a halt.

'Wow!' said Della, quickly powdering her nose and fluffing up her hair before arranging her army cap on the back of her head.

'Ready, everyone,' called Beau, struggling to his feet. 'Look your best and don't forget your tin helmets.'

The soldier drivers jumped down first and helped Beau and then Frances to alight. The rest of the company came after, to welcoming cheers and whistles from the military.

'Hello, boys,' called Della, and did a sexy pose before blowing kisses to the men, while the rest of the troupe waved and smiled.

'Goodness,' whispered Frances, 'are they glad to see us!'

'We must give them a good show,' said Catherine, and smiled as a senior officer came up to welcome them and show them into the large tent.

'Oh Christ,' groaned Della, as they walked into the tent. 'Look who's here.'

It was Eric Baxter, standing beside a small platform with Captain Fortescue on his arm.

'What ho!' brayed the captain. 'The extras have arrived.'

Chapter 15

That first concert at the front went better than they'd expected. Playing to an audience of exhausted men should have been difficult, because many of the soldiers had experienced things that they could never talk about and which would trouble them in their dreams for years to come. Could they be bothered to watch a troupe of performers when only days ago they had faced death? Frances, coming out of the latrine, overheard one of the senior officers, on the other side of the canvas, complaining that 'The variety troupe performance will be all silly nonsense and a waste of time.' She heard murmurs of agreement from the men he was talking to.

'Some of them don't want us here,' she said to Beau, as they, and the rest of the Players, set up the lights and the microphone.

'And others do,' he replied. 'So we'll put on a super show.'

From somewhere, probably one of the destroyed houses in the village they'd driven through, the colonel had found an upright piano. It was a little battered, and it had a splintered chip out of its lid, but when Tommy tried a few bars, he declared it 'not bad' and left his guitar on the bus. He'd brought the guitar to play in places where there would be no piano, and over the last few months he'd given Colin some drum lessons. The magician turned out to be remarkably good. 'All we need is for Godfrey to find himself a double bass and we could be a pretty good combo,' said Tommy.

The girls changed into their lavender-blue dresses in the colonel's office. Della had adapted hers with a split up the front so that her legs could be seen. Underneath, she wore her acrobatic costume shorts and her beloved fishnet tights.

'I don't think there's room for somersaults,' said Frances. 'That platform is quite small.'

'I know, darling. I've checked it out, but I'll shorten the dance and do the splits. The boys love that.'

Catherine arranged a lavender silk flower in her hair. She had gone over her music with Tommy but hadn't yet decided what she would sing. Beau left it up to her now, trusting her judgement entirely, and she had never let him down. It always depended on the mood of the audience, but tonight it also depended on her own mood.

She'd spoken briefly to Robert when they'd all been given a tin mug of tea and some bread and jam in the canteen before going to set up the show.

'Hello,' he'd said, looking intently into her eyes.

Her mouth felt dry. She yearned to touch his hand, wanted him to bend his head and kiss her. I'm mad, she thought. Whatever has come over me? 'Hello,' she'd said, hastily taking a swallow of the tannin-laden tea.

He glanced around. The officers who'd joined the Players in the canteen were looking appreciatively at her, and a couple were moving towards them. He cleared his throat. 'I...' but he could see that they were no longer alone, so instead he asked, 'What are you singing tonight?'

'I don't know yet.' She smiled at the young lieutenants who joined them and said, 'I'll see how it goes.'

'Excuse me, Miss Fletcher,' one of the young men said. 'I saw you once at the Savoy. You were wonderful.'

'Thank you.' Catherine smiled and shook hands with him and his colleagues. They looked tired and dirty, their hair curling over their collars, and their uniforms, worn every day for weeks, were scruffy and torn in places. The man who'd first spoken to her had a drying scab along his cheek, and another had his arm in a sling. Catherine thought about the shows they'd done in army camps at home, where the troops had neat battledresses and short back and sides. Even at the theatre in Bayeux, the men were clean and looked as though they'd eaten well. This was such a contrast.

'You've been hurt,' she said to the young lieutenant.

'Oh,' he shrugged. 'It's nothing. An argument with a Jerry sniper.'

'You got him, though, Danny, didn't you?' another boy laughed, and punched Danny on the shoulder.

Catherine kept smiling, but inside she felt a little sick. Was this how Christopher had been with his friends? Pretending that nothing mattered. Pretending to be brave.

She had turned her head to see what Robert thought of these young men. He'd fought, she knew that. You didn't get medals for nothing. But he'd gone, moved away into the crowd and was deep in conversation with Beau.

Now, getting ready to go on stage, Catherine knew what she would sing first, and having a last quick look in the long mirror that travelled with them, she went outside to find Tommy.

Della opened the show with her usual upbeat number, belting out the song so loudly that Tommy had to keep his foot jammed hard on the pedal. She high-kicked across the platform and ended her act with a jump and the splits, which drew cheers from the audience.

She was followed by Eric. The rest of the troupe, none of whom had spoken more than two words to him, watched from the sidelines. As he stepped onto the platform, he passed Robert, who grabbed his arm and spoke quickly into his ear. Whatever Robert said seemed to have worked, because Captain Fortescue's performance was clean and funny and well received.

Godfrey followed, his rousing song filling the tent, and during the second chorus, he encouraged the audience to sing along to the familiar words. They loved it. Then Colin fascinated the men with his card tricks and knotted strings that magically fell into straight pieces of cord. At one point, he got so excited with the applause that he reached up with his hand to calm them down and accidentally knocked his wig askew. This drew roars of laughter, the men thinking it was all part of the act, and Beau whispered to Frances, 'We should keep that in and expand on it. We need a comedian.'

Finally Catherine closed the first half. She sang 'You'll Never Know', her voice rising into the air and reaching into the hearts of all who were listening to her. She left the platform and walked into the audience, still singing while shaking hands with the soldiers. They were awestruck by her voice and her beauty, and by the words of her song. It meant so much to these men who were away from home and who had so recently been in danger and knew that they would be again.

Frances saw the officer who had spoken disparagingly of the troupe. He was standing, open-mouthed, against the door of the tent, and when Catherine finished, he cheered and whistled along with everyone else. Idiot, thought Frances. You couldn't have been more wrong.

They went into the colonel's office for a breather between the first and second halves of the show and grinned at each other. 'It was great,' said Della, jigging up and down with excitement.

'You all did very well.' Beau limped in, his face wreathed in a big grin. 'And, Colin, I was especially impressed with that bit of slapstick. Let's get together and see how we can combine it in the act.'

Colin frowned. 'I didnae do any slapstick, boss. I had a wee accident with the wig, that's all.'

'Precisely,' Beau nodded. 'It was brilliant.'

'A loose definition of "brilliant", old sport,' sneered Captain Fortescue, who was sitting on Baxter's arm, the doll's head moving this way and that, and its eyebrows jerking up and down.

Della shot round, ready to say something, but Beau stepped in front of her. 'Anyway,' he said, trying to regain his grin, 'let's get back out there and wow them again.'

They did.

Catherine sang 'Long Ago and Far Away' and saw Robert leaning by the entrance, his eyes fixed on her. She turned her head and sang a few lines directly at him, before looking back to the rest of the audience.

'Wonderful!' the soldiers yelled, and, 'More, more!' and when Catherine beckoned Della and Frances onto the stage, they went wild. It was hard to get them to calm down, and although both Beau and Tommy tried to hush the audience, it was Della who yelled, 'Shut the hell up!' and who finally got them to be quiet.

They sang 'Don't Fence Me In', wearing the cowboy hats that Della had managed to buy from a theatrical costumier in London. The audience loved it, and after a nod from Beau, Della had a quick word with Tommy and he struck up with 'Boogie Woogie Bugle Boy'.

'Just wonderful,' said the colonel, when the show was over and they were in his office having a drink. He'd produced two bottles of whisky, which they were drinking out of tin cups. 'I can't tell you how grateful we are. These lads have had a hard time, and we'll be going forward again next week.'

'How far away is the front?' asked Tommy. 'I mean, are the enemy close?'

'No, not that close,' the colonel smiled. 'No need to worry. They're at least ten miles down the road. The next village is liberated, and the one after. They're in the one after that. We'll be clearing them out soon.'

Frances thought of the bullet holes in the walls of the village they'd come through. That's what's going to be happening there, she realised, and how many of the young men who'd whooped and cheered tonight would be injured or even killed? It was a very sobering thought and she sat down, suddenly very tired.

'There's food for you in the canteen,' announced the colonel, 'and then we can put the ladies up in the first-aid tent. There is a regular tent with the men for the gents.' He looked at them anxiously. 'It won't be what you're used to, being show business people, but it's the best we can do.'

'We don't mind at all,' rumbled Godfrey, knocking

back his whisky and holding out his glass for another. 'We're just glad to do our bit.'

Later, the girls settled into their cots in the first-aid tent. It had stopped raining, but the ground was very muddy all around and their shoes sank into it.

'We'll have to get gumboots, you know,' said Frances. 'It's going to be like this everywhere we go.'

'You're right,' Della yawned. 'You organise it.'

Catherine lay thinking about Robert, to whom she'd had no opportunity to speak. He hadn't joined them in the colonel's office after the show, and neither had Eric Baxter. That was odd too. And as she was thinking about it, Frances said, 'Where d'you think Baxter went? I didn't see him. Did either of you?'

'No,' said Catherine. 'You wouldn't think there'd be anywhere for him to disappear to around here.'

'He'll be doing some buying and selling,' snorted Della. 'Mark my words.' She yawned again. 'Christ, I'm tired.'

'Well, get some sleep,' Frances said. 'We've got a ten o'clock start tomorrow, so there'll be time for whatever breakfast they can give us and a bit of a wash.'

When they got into the bus the next morning, they found that Beau had organised overnight alterations. With the help of the soldier drivers and a couple of volunteers, he had removed the four back rows of seats and begged three camp beds from the quartermaster. They were complete with sleeping bags and a sheet that could be hung from screwed-in pegs to provide some privacy for the girls. The hampers had been squeezed into the luggage compartment at the side of the bus, and he'd even found a little collapsible table for the card school.

'We should have thought all this out before,' Beau

grumbled, when Frances had exclaimed in delight over the arrangements. 'We really are bloody amateurs when it comes to touring.'

'Never mind,' she said. 'It'll do fine. If you men don't mind mucking in with the military.'

'Of course we won't,' he grinned. 'They're all geared up for men. It's the women who are a bloody nuisance.'

'That was simply tremendous,' said Della, climbing into the bus and then hanging out of the door, laughing and waving to the soldiers who'd come to see them off. 'What could be better?'

'Well, this could,' smiled Catherine, looking with delight at the new interior of the bus. 'Beau,' she called, 'you've worked miracles.'

'Thought you'd approve,' he said awkwardly. Catherine wondered if Robert had spoken to him and pointed out that he was in danger of losing the trust of his company. Whatever had happened, he seemed to be back with them these last two days.

'Anyway, we have to get going,' he said. 'Where are the drivers?'

They were climbing on board, arms full of more equipment. 'Thought you'd like these, sir,' said Corporal Trevor, the one in charge. He had a small paraffin stove, a kettle and a couple of storm lanterns. 'It's best to be prepared.'

Walter was carrying a box containing biscuits, tea and sugar, and eight tin cups. 'We noticed, sir, that you hadn't brought any provisions with you, so we took the liberty.'

Beau was very grateful. 'That's incredibly generous of the commanding officer,' he said. 'I'll make sure to thank him when I next see him.'

'I wouldn't do that, sir,' Trevor grinned. 'He doesn't exactly know.'

'Aha,' bellowed Godfrey from his seat next to the table, where the cards were already being dealt, 'nothing like a bit of pilfering from the stores. It's what we all did in the first show. And, Beau, dear boy, very well done.'

'A matter of opinion, old fruit,' Captain Fortescue's voice came from where Baxter was sitting on his own in the seat behind Walter. He had a new kit bag clutched in his arms, which he wouldn't let out of his sight. 'Not much fun being all squeezed up, I'd say.'

'No danger of you being squeezed up, Baxter,' said Della, her voice dripping with poison.

'Stop it, Della,' said Beau, and tapped Trevor on the shoulder. 'Time for the off.'

For the next three weeks, it was shows every day. Many were at much smaller camps than the first one, and often there wasn't time to put on the full performance, or space to change out of their uniforms, but they clambered up onto makeshift stages and performed to the best of their ability. In most places, there wasn't a piano, but Tommy accompanied the singers on the guitar, with Colin giving rhythm on the drums.

The girls slept happily in the bus and got used to diving behind bushes for the necessary comfort breaks. They made themselves tea and washed their underwear in a bowl that they'd begged from a quartermaster sergeant, along with a collection of gumboots. It was, as Della put it, 'almost fun', and the days slipped away as they criss-crossed backwards and forwards along the front line.

After nearly a month of touring, they turned up at a small camp in the middle of a forest, where they had to perform on the back of a lorry. Della could only sing, but was a knockout, perched on the lorry with her skirt hitched up her thighs and her cap at a saucy angle on the back of her head. When Catherine sang, a soldier spontaneously accompanied her with his clarinet, which had been with him throughout the invasion.

'I know you,' said Tommy, shaking hands with the young man afterwards. 'Weren't you with Geraldo, or one of the bands at the Criterion?'

'I played everywhere, mate,' the soldier grinned, 'until I was called up. I even played for Miss Fletcher here, with Bobby Crewe's Melody Men, although I bet she doesn't recognise me.'

'Let's ask her,' said Tommy, and called, 'Catherine, Catherine, come over here.'

She looked over from where she was signing autographs, and smiling goodbye to the soldiers, she went over to where Tommy was leaning against the side of a tank chatting to the clarinettist. 'Hello,' she said to the soldier. 'I must thank you for accompanying us. You played so well.'

'D'you remember him?' asked Tommy excitedly.

She shook her head, puzzled. 'I don't think so. Have I met you before?'

'Gino Olivero.' He put out his hand for her to shake. 'I played with Bobby Crewe in 1938 for a week. You were singing.'

She frowned, trying to think back. 'Did you replace Pete Lincoln when he had bronchitis?' She clapped her hands. 'Yes, you did. I remember you now. Bobby was really pleased with you. Didn't he ask you to come back?'

'He did,' grinned Gino, 'but I'd already signed a contract to go to the States with a big band. I came home when war was declared and was immediately called up. That was nearly five years ago: no wonder you didn't recognise me.'

'You're a sergeant now,' said Tommy, looking a touch enviously at the white chevrons on the man's sleeve. 'You must have seen it all.'

'I have, mate,' Gino grinned, 'but I'd rather have your job, any day.'

Suddenly, in the distance, there was the rattle of gunfire and Gino looked round. 'Shit,' he muttered, and then dragged Catherine towards a sandbag-covered trench. 'Get in there, quick.'

Soon she was joined by the rest of the troupe, Della giving little squeaks of fright as she was manhandled in by a couple of squaddies. 'Keep your heads down,' one of them grunted, and Beau, who had struggled in, shouted, 'For God's sake, put on your tin helmets.'

'We can't,' Frances shouted back. 'They're in the bus.'

'I'll get them,' said Tommy, and started to climb out of the trench.

'Come back,' Beau yelled. 'It's too bloody late now.'

A big gun started up with a boom, boom, boom. It was very close and Catherine put her hands over her ears as the whole trench reverberated to the sound.

'Oh my God,' wailed Della, and Frances put her arm around her and held her close, and Catherine moved towards them so that the three girls sat on the muddy floor of the trench in a tight huddle.

'Just as well we didn't put our frocks on,' said Frances, trying to calm Della. 'It would have been hell trying to get the mud out of them.'

'Ha, ha,' Della muttered. Then, as another huge boom shook the trench, she burst into tears. 'I hate this,' she cried. 'I bloody hate it.'

The boys were sitting in silence, all of them smoking furiously, and Tommy lit another cigarette and, with a shaking hand, passed it to Della. 'Here you go, girl,' he said. 'Have a drag on this.'

The gunfire rattled above them for another five minutes and then there was silence. Frances held her breath, waiting for the next explosion, but nothing happened. To her astonishment, she thought she could hear birds twittering in the trees above them, and from all around them came the noise of men talking and laughing.

An officer jumped into the trench. 'Excitement over, folks. Come on out.'

It was almost the same scene as it had been when the firing began. Frances could see no damage, but spent cartridge cases littered the ground, and the smell of cordite hung in the air. 'What was that?' she asked the officer. 'Who was firing?'

'Oh, it was some Jerry platoon,' he said cheerfully. 'Got lost probably and barged into one of our outposts. We'll know in a minute when the men come back.'

As he spoke, a group of men walked out of the trees, one of them carrying a body dressed in German uniform over his back.

'*Mon Dieu*,' whispered Catherine, but she watched as the soldier gently put the body on the ground and called, 'Medic!'

'Captured a live one, then?' asked the officer.

'Yes, sir. The others are dead. He's got a bullet in his thigh.'

The German opened his eyes and gazed up towards the soldier who was bending over him. '*Kaput*,' he said urgently. '*Kaput*.' He looked very young, almost like a schoolboy, and there, lying on the ground, he raised his trembling hands above his head.

'It's alright, boy,' said the soldier who'd captured him. 'The doc's coming to look at you.'

The medic arrived and did a cursory examination. 'Broken femur,' he said. 'Will need surgery. I'll organise an ambulance.'

'Good,' the officer grinned. 'Bind the bugger up in the meantime and then I'll have a few words with him. Be nice to know where Jerry is heading.' He turned to Beau. 'Your officer, Major Lennox, is it?' He nodded to where Robert was standing, examining a map with their drivers. 'He thinks you should get your skates on. Back the way you came, I imagine. We don't know what the buggers are up to.' He grasped Beau's hand and pumped it up and down. 'Very good of you to come and all that – the men really enjoyed it – but now I think you should get the hell out of here.'

With a last look at the injured soldier, who widened his eyes in amazement when he saw the women, the company left.

'Tin hats on,' said Beau firmly, when they were back on the bus. 'And keep them on.'

Robert was in the bus with them, this time, leaning over the driver and pointing out the route. For the first time, Catherine noticed that he had a revolver in its holster on his belt and that the drivers had stacked their rifles on the floor beside them. Strangely, she felt quite safe. Robert wouldn't let anything happen to them.

Frances sat with Della, still holding her hand. 'Have I made an awful fool of myself?' Della sniffed.

'Not at all,' whispered Frances. 'We were all scared. I nearly wet my pants, and I'm pretty sure Godfrey did. Didn't you see that damp patch by his flies?'

Della took a deep, shuddering breath and gave a half-smile. 'Thanks for saying that, darling,' she murmured. 'You know, you're not half bad, for a toff.'

When they were on a larger road that had plenty of army traffic, Robert came to sit down beside Catherine.

'Are you alright?' he asked, and moved his hand so that it was touching hers.

'Yes, I am,' she said, then looking out of the window, asked, 'Where are we going?'

'Back towards the coast. We'll find a place somewhere near Caen where the Players can have a couple of days off. We've had to cancel the next few shows because the Germans have broken out of the pocket we had them in and it's not safe.'

'That sounds good, about going to a hotel or some-where.' She grinned. 'I hope it has a shower.'

After about an hour, Beau struggled to his feet. 'Colleagues,' he said, 'I have to say that in the last few weeks, you've been extraordinary. You've performed in the most difficult of circumstances, and today, you've witnessed what our troops go through every day. Now, we're going to Caen. It's been very badly damaged, but I think we'll find somewhere to stay and you can have a couple of days off.' He paused. 'I was wondering, though, after what you've all been through, if you might want to go home.'

'No,' roared Godfrey. 'For Christ's sake, no, sir,' and the laugh that followed that strident plea broke the tension that had been lingering since they'd left the camp.

'We'll carry on,' said Tommy. He stood up and looked at his companions. 'Won't we?'

'Yes,' they all called, even Della, who in her mercurial fashion had got over her upset and was now as cheerful as ever.

'Good,' said Beau. 'Well, I have a few announcements to make. As you know, Paris has been liberated, and for those of us who know and love the city, it was achieved without any major damage. The Allies are moving forward on various fronts. Brussels, Antwerp and Dieppe have fallen to our armies, and Catherine' – he looked at her – 'I believe you have family in Amiens?'

She nodded.

'Well, that's been liberated too.'

'Oh, thank God,' she whispered, and wondered about her grandparents. Then the thought came to her that Christopher had last been known about in that area. She looked at Robert. 'He might be alive,' she whispered.

He shrugged, understanding whom she was talking about. 'I don't know. I'll try and find out.'

They stopped at a roadblock just outside the city of Caen. Robert jumped down from the bus and went to speak to the officer in charge of a group of soldiers. Out of the windows, the Players could see the city. It was a terrible sight, damaged buildings standing starkly raw amid streets full of rubble.

'My God,' breathed Frances, gazing with horror at the

ruin. 'It must have been dreadful for the civilians as well as the military.'

'There won't be anywhere for us to stay in there,' said Della. 'It doesn't look as though there's a building left standing. What a mess.'

'I think we're being directed back along the road.' Tommy had his face glued to the window.

After getting and returning salutes with the officer and his men, Robert got back on board. 'Right,' he said to Corporal Trevor, flourishing the map and pointing. 'We go down this road. It's not very far.'

'Oh Lord,' groaned Della, as they drove along a narrow lane where fat blond cows in the fields on either side of the road gazed at them over green hedges. 'Where the hell is he taking us? It'll be some little hovel or another bloody campsite.'

She couldn't have been more wrong. Under Robert's instruction, Trevor turned in through stone entrance pillars. 'Nearly there,' said Robert, as Trevor followed a long, winding drive. They turned the final corner, and magically, their accommodation came into view.

'Wow!' shouted Della, and Frances and Catherine laughed.

A pretty eighteenth-century chateau lay before them, shimmering in the late-afternoon sun.

'Will this hovel do?' asked Robert.

Chapter 16

Della sat in front of the mirror on the rosewood dressing table in the huge bedroom she shared with Frances and Catherine, and stared at her reflection. Her face, with its high cheekbones and startlingly blue eyes under straight, dark brows, stared back at her. She examined her hair, darker at the roots now, showing up her natural chestnut colouring, and tried to remember how long it had been since she'd decided to become a blonde. 'Donkey's years,' she muttered.

'What?' asked Frances. 'What did you say?'

Della swivelled round. 'I said, "Donkey's years." I was wondering how long I'd been a blonde.'

'Oh,' said Frances. She was sitting on her bed with paper and envelopes on her knee. Mail had been delivered today, sent on from the PO forces box that the Players were told to use. Frances had two letters. One was from her father, with news about the farm and the village, and thanks for the money that she was having forwarded to him.

An owl got stuck in the library chimney and made a hell of a mess before we could get it out, he wrote. *Mr Rogers, senior, the old vet, came with his gloves and yanked on its leg. It pecked the hell out of him before it was forced down; then it flew around the room, making more mess, before it saw the window was open. I had to give old Rogers a couple of bob.*

228

Rainwater is dripping into the attics in the north wing, and part of the bell tower on the stables collapsed during the gales.

We're alright. Johnny is a boy to be proud of. I've got him up on a young Welsh cob I bought at the horse fair. He loves it. They can grow up together.

How much did that damn pony cost? Frances wondered, turning over the page. Had her father no sense?

In the few more lines on the back, he had written that there was no news from Hugo, but sent fondest love from him and Johnny. There was a little drawing that Johnny had done of a pony; at least, Frances thought that it was a pony and she got up to show it to Della.

'My little boy did that,' she said proudly.

Della gave it a brief glance. 'What is it? A train or something?'

Frances laughed. 'I think it's supposed to be a pony. My father has gone and bought him one, though where he got the money from, I have no idea.'

'He sounds as bad as my ma,' Della grumbled, and picked up the flimsy sheet of airmail paper that lay on top of her make-up bag. 'She's taking Maria to London to see a new specialist, but unlike you, I'm pretty sure that I do know where the money is coming from. Jerry bloody Costigan.'

'He does take a very close interest in your family,' said Frances. 'Is he related to you in some way?'

'No,' said Della. 'He isn't.' She changed the subject abruptly. 'Who's your other letter from?'

Frances's face lightened. 'It's from Felix. Remember, Felix Strange? He's in a convalescent hospital on the south coast. And guess what?' She picked up her other letter. 'He writes that he can now see light and dark with one eye and sometimes shapes. The doctors are pleased and think that he'll get some sight back.'

'Good for him,' Della grinned. 'You really got fond of him, didn't you?'

'I suppose I did,' said Frances slowly. 'He's another link to my brother.'

'And that's all?' Della raised her eyebrows. 'Looked like more than that to me...In fact, I'd say you were definitely sweet on him, you baby-snatcher!'

'Shut up,' Frances growled. 'He's only a year younger than me.'

'He looks more like four.' Della grinned. 'Anyway, let's go down. Catherine will be back any minute.'

Arm in arm, they walked down the long corridor to the grand staircase that led down into the magnificent rooms below. The chateau had been commandeered by the army as extra accommodation, but apart from the Bennett Players, it was practically empty. An elderly caretaker and his wife lived in a few of the back rooms, she popping out now and then with a broom and mop, and he doing mysterious things with the old hot-water boiler, but otherwise keeping themselves to themselves. Catherine had introduced herself to them and had persuaded the wife to come and cook some meals for them.

'We will, of course, pay,' she said.

Madame Farcy had eagerly agreed. 'But' – she'd shrugged, lifting her hands, palms up, in a gesture of resignation – 'we have very little food. Some vegetables, yes, but meat is hard to get.'

'We could supply the food,' Catherine said. 'We can buy provisions from the army.'

Madame Farcy smiled. 'I would be very glad for that. For tonight, Monsieur can take trout from the river, if that would suit.'

'It would suit very well,' Catherine said, and on that first night, grilled trout and small sautéed potatoes had been served to the company in the echoing dining room.

'This is delicious,' Frances had said. 'Best meal we've had for weeks.'

Today, Madame Farcy had agreed to cook again, but only if Catherine would get hold of some rations. 'Perhaps meat?' Madame had pleaded. 'Could you buy some, from...the army, perhaps?'

'I'll see what I can do,' Catherine said.

That morning, Robert had arrived at the chateau. He'd been staying in Caen so that he could use the communications centre. 'This place is yours for the foreseeable future,' he told Beau. The rest of the company, who'd gathered to listen, stared at each other. 'It is to be your base and you will tour from here.' He'd looked around the grand salon, with its magnificent plastered ceilings and huge fireplace. It also had a grand piano, which Tommy had been trying to tune. 'Not bad, I suppose.'

'Who does it belong to?' asked Frances. 'It looks in pretty good condition, and surely now that the invasion has happened, the owners will want to return.'

'I suppose they will,' said Robert, 'but so far they haven't turned up, and in the meantime it's been taken over. Apparently, a German general lived here up until a few months ago. In some style, I believe. He's in a POW camp now.' He buckled the straps on his briefcase.

'The caretaker should know more about the family, if you're really interested.'

'So,' said Beau. 'Where do we go next?'

'You'll do the camps around Caen and the field hospitals. And we are liaising with our American colleagues, so some of your performances will be for them.'

'Great,' said Tommy, giving Colin a punch on the arm. 'They're good audiences, the Yanks.'

'What about further afield?' asked Beau. 'We're very willing to entertain at the front, you know.'

'Yes,' Robert grinned, 'I know you are, and we'll be pencilling that in for later. But things are a bit haywire at the moment. The "front" isn't always where it should be, if you understand what I mean.'

'The Jerries broke through, didn't they?' said Della. 'One of the boys at the last camp told me.'

'I'm afraid so,' Robert agreed, 'but we're pushing them back all the time. Now' – he opened his briefcase and withdrew a bundle of envelopes – 'I've picked up your mail, and if you've any letters you want to send home, I'll get them this evening.'

He put the bundle on the table, letting Beau undo the string that was tying them and distribute them. Everyone had some mail, even Beau himself. Frances wondered who had sent him a letter and then decided it must be from his mother. It occurred to her that she knew nothing about his private life in London. His family in the country were near neighbours, and she'd played with Beau and his two sisters when they were all children. But in town? She knew nothing about his friends, and nobody had visited his flat when she'd been there. But of course, she reasoned, he'd been in the theatre and then the army. He'd have tons of pals.

'Robert,' Catherine said, holding her letter from Maman tightly. She was anxious to read it, but had questions first. 'What about food? The caretaker's wife here will cook for us, but she hasn't any provisions.'

'I was coming to that. The NAAFI can supply what we need, and if any of you want something in particular, make me a list.' He looked at Catherine. 'Perhaps you'll come back with me into Caen. We can get food and cigarettes and anything else from the NAAFI there.'

Frances and Della winked at each other. 'He really is stuck on her,' Frances whispered.

'What about her?' Della grunted. 'She keeps giving him cow eyes.'

Catherine knew they were whispering about her, but she didn't care. A trip out with Robert was all that mattered.

Fifteen minutes later, armed with ration books and a lengthy list, they set off. In her handbag was the letter from Maman, which she had read twice and would read many more times.

Lili can walk two steps, Maman had written. *She says 'Mama' and 'Papa' when I show her the pictures on the mantelpiece. Please come home; we miss you. Father Clement took this to remind you.* Enclosed in the envelope was a small black-and-white snap. It was of Lili in Maman's arms, outside the church, and Catherine's heart melted.

I should go home, she thought. They need me. I could easily earn enough money in London to keep us and then I would be able to watch Lili growing up. What is the point of me being here in France?

'You're very quiet this morning,' said Robert. They

were on the outskirts of Caen and she could see the devastated city in front of her. 'I hope there wasn't bad news in your letter.'

'No,' Catherine sighed. 'Nothing bad, but…'

'…but you feel guilty about leaving them.'

'Yes. I do. Lili has walked two steps and I haven't been there. Her four front teeth are through and she's beginning to talk. All the things that matter in her little life and I'm missing them.'

'All the things that matter in a little life,' Robert repeated. His voice was bleak and Catherine glanced at him. Was he making fun of her, or had he experienced something similar?

They were entering the ruined city. One side of the street they were driving along had been bombed or shelled to complete destruction. Only rubble remained. But a few buildings on the other side had survived. They were horribly damaged, but Catherine could see that people were living in them: washing hung out of the windows, and children were playing on the pavement, chasing each other and laughing, seemingly without care. The locals as well as the military were on the streets, walking along with purpose, all of them used now to the destruction and ready to carry on. She imagined that a couple of months ago, when the town had been fought over, these same people had been in a similar stunned and confused state as those she'd seen in the villages at the front. It is remarkable, she thought, how quickly the status quo becomes reality.

'Are you married, Robert?' There. She'd said it.

At first, she didn't think he was going to answer, for he was silent, his face closed and unreadable. Then he drove to the side of the road and drew to a halt. It was a warm, late-summer day, with puffs of white cloud drifting across an azure sky, and as Catherine waited, she watched a young woman who was wheeling a battered pram along the street in front of them. Two infants sat up in the pram, and another toddled along beside her. The woman stopped frequently to let the toddler catch up and to switch the bag she was carrying from one hand to the other. It looked heavy, and Catherine kept thinking, Put it on the pram. It will be easier.

'I am married,' said Robert, breaking his silence. 'I have a wife and a son.'

It wasn't a shock. She'd guessed it all along. When he'd kissed her, it had been done with almost desperation, as though he'd known it was wrong.

'I thought you might be,' Catherine said. She looked down at her fingers, twisting the leather handle of her bag, and at her wedding ring. 'But my husband is missing, probably dead, as you keep insisting, while your wife lives in happy ignorance somewhere at home, bringing up your son. Perhaps I'm not as guilty as you.'

He sighed. 'I don't think that either of us is guilty,' he said.

'But your wife...' Catherine kept her eyes fixed on the pram. 'Does she know?'

'No.' Robert took off his cap and ran a hand through his thick brown hair. 'How could she? I don't know where she is. I haven't seen or heard from her for five years, or my son. She took James to see his grandparents in Berlin in May 1939 and never returned.'

Catherine gazed at him. 'Your wife is German?'

Robert nodded.

'*Mon Dieu!*' And then another, terrible thought came to her and she took his hand. 'Your wife, she is Jewish?'

He slowly shook his head. 'No. She isn't Jewish. In fact, I rather think that like the rest of her family, she was in love with the Nazi Party. We had so many arguments about it, and in those last months we were drifting apart. Then she left.'

Catherine looked back at her fingers again and at her wedding ring. In a way, she and Robert were in the same boat. Christopher was missing and so was his wife. 'I'm very sorry,' she said. 'I shouldn't have asked.'

'It doesn't matter.' The finality of those words signalled an end to the conversation, and Robert started up the Jeep and drove on.

At the NAAFI, they bought food and cigarettes. The list Catherine had been given included toiletries and newspapers, and she was able to get most of those too.

'What did you get?' asked Robert, as they were driving back.

'Tinned stuff mostly,' sighed Catherine. 'Spam and some sort of canned stew, as well as beans and powdered eggs. But I'd love to get some fresh meat and vegetables. I can't imagine where from, though.'

'I can,' said Robert, and drove down a side road until they reached a small warehouse. 'Stay here,' he instructed, and jumping down, walked over to a door and went inside.

Ten minutes later, when Catherine was beginning to feel nervous, he reappeared, followed by a couple of Canadian soldiers carrying large boxes.

'Ma'am,' said one of them to her, tipping his helmet, and then went to the back of the Jeep and loaded the box. The other one did the same, while Robert got out his wallet and handed over what looked like quite a lot of cash.

'Say nothing,' Robert grinned, glancing at Catherine's astonished face as they drove away. 'It's all in a good cause.'

A fresh side of beef came out of the first box, much to everyone's, including Madame Farcy's, delight, and in the second they found eggs, flour, butter and chocolate.

'You have done well, madame,' cooed the old lady, examining Catherine's purchases. 'I will start the cooking.'

In the days that followed, the company settled into the chateau. Tommy and Colin went out fishing with the caretaker, coming home with a catch more often than not. One afternoon, Tommy arrived back with a couple of live chickens, which he'd bought from a farmer. 'You don't speak French,' said Frances. 'How did you do it?'

'I speak barter,' laughed Tommy. 'I swapped my watch for them.'

'Oh.' Frances was impressed. 'But don't you need your watch?'

'Nah.' Tommy shook his head. 'It was junk. I bought it off a stall in Lambeth. It only goes now and then.'

In the mornings, they rehearsed, slotting in new numbers, and Beau and Colin worked up a comedy act. At first, Colin wasn't keen, but Beau insisted, and after a few tries at making his tricks go wrong and knocking his wig askew, it started to come together.

'I thought the appalling Baxter was supposed to be the comedy act,' said Godfrey, watching Colin hide a glass of water under a series of tall black cups and then not be able to find it. It was quite funny and the Players clapped enthusiastically.

'Baxter isn't a comedian,' snorted Della. 'He's just a creep.'

'And he's disappeared again,' said Catherine.

The ventriloquist had begged a lift into town with Robert and Beau a couple of days ago and hadn't come back. 'He's requested permission to stay in the officers' quarters in town,' Beau said. 'I couldn't stop him, really. I couldn't stop any of you.'

'Good riddance,' laughed Della. 'Hope he never comes back.'

They wondered about Davey Jones and if his killer had been found. 'It seems wrong that we're here enjoying ourselves when he's six feet under,' said Della. 'I liked him.'

'Beau hasn't been able to find anything out,' Frances said. 'At least, that's what he told me when I asked him.'

That was not quite what he said. He'd been quite irritated when she mentioned him. 'For God's sake, let it go,' he'd said with a frown. 'These things happen in war.'

'Alright,' Frances said, surprised, and remembered Robert warning her not to mention that Davey had spoken to her on the evening that he'd been murdered.

They had ten days' rest and recreation, and then it was back to performing again. They played at camps and field hospitals, and once back at the theatre in Bayeux. Eric Baxter turned up ready with Captain Fortescue at the first venue and subsequently rejoined the company as they toured in the bus. Frances was driving again with Beau giving her directions from the map. As they weren't at the front, they didn't need their military escort, and even Robert had stayed behind in Caen. After each of the shows, they made their weary way back to the chateau, to be greeted by Madame with a handshake for the men and a kiss on both cheeks for the girls. No matter how late they arrived, she was there with coffee and some little titbit.

They had all become used to buying what they could at every place they performed. Once, they went to an American camp, where their version of the NAAFI was like a wonderland.

'God,' said Frances, wandering into the PX along with the others before the show. 'Bacon, bananas. I haven't seen a banana for years.'

The audience was good too. Della went down a storm, cartwheeling and somersaulting all over the large stage. She had worked on a new dance routine, tap as well as show dancing, which the audience cheered.

'Those guys are fantastic,' she panted, coming off after blowing kisses to the crowd.

'Guys?' queried Frances, one eyebrow raised.

'You have to get into the swing of things. Use the lingo,' laughed Della. 'Don't be so stuffy.'

Only Baxter and Captain Fortescue bombed. None of his remarks or jokes had any resonance with the American audience, and they started talking and getting up and walking about. Beau hovered anxiously in the wings, beckoning him to come off. 'I'm leaving you out of the second half,' he said, as Baxter left the stage to desultory clapping.

'Thank God,' Baxter brayed in the captain's voice. 'I'm not used to playing to lower-class colonials.'

The American corporal who was working the curtain scowled and bunched his fists, but Della put a hand on his sleeve. 'Ignore the bastard,' she said loudly. 'That's what we all do.'

The audience was a little restless after that, but when Catherine stepped on stage and started to sing 'As Time Goes By', they quietened down and listened attentively.

'She's got them back,' breathed Beau with a sigh of relief, as cheers rang out and there were cries of 'More, more!'

'This next song is for my husband, who is missing in action,' Catherine said, when the audience had resumed their seats, and she sang the opening bars of '*J'attendrai*' in English before going on to the French words. Even though most of the men didn't understand the language, they understood the sentiment and loved it. The place rocked with cheers and continued on when the three girls sang a medley of Andrews Sisters numbers.

'Gee,' said the American colonel, when they were treated to drinks afterwards. 'Who'd have thought a bunch of Limeys could put on such a good show?'

'Not you, obviously,' said Frances.

Beau frowned and hurried to stand in front of her, but Catherine giggled and took her hand. Della broke off from flirting with the young officers and laughed out loud.

'Aw, shit.' The colonel blushed and ducked his head. 'I guess that didn't come out right. I truly thought you were all pretty damn good. Honest Injun.'

'It's alright,' said Frances, smiling at him. 'I was only kidding.'

On the way back to the chateau, Beau said, 'You

nearly caused a diplomatic incident there, Frances.'

'Hardly,' she answered, her eyes on the dark road. They'd reached the turn-off that led up to the chateau. 'That colonel knew he'd made a mistake. He was fine afterwards. We even got presents.'

'Scent,' grinned Della, holding up the square Chanel No.5 bottle. 'Such big bottles, and where the hell did they get them from? Must have been pinched.'

'One of the officers told me that they'd been confiscated from a German HQ,' Catherine added from her seat beside Della. 'Apparently, one of the generals had been getting the perfume from manufacturers in the south and was selling it in Paris. A good little business.'

'I'd say,' Frances started, but then gasped and swerved the bus to one side.

'Watch out,' grunted Beau, looking out of the window. 'What was it? A rabbit?'

'No.' Frances looked swiftly in the driving mirror. 'It was a man, walking up the drive towards the chateau.'

She looked again, wondering if she'd imagined it, but the road behind was very dark. How strange, she thought, and then decided that if she really did see someone, he would be a friend of the Farcys and going to visit them. But at nearly midnight?

Madame was waiting for them as usual, with a tray of coffee and an apple pastry cut into little squares.

Tommy struggled in carrying an orange box full of food from the American PX. 'For you, madame,' he said. 'I'll take it through to the kitchen.'

'*Oh là, là,*' she squealed with joy, hurrying after him, while the others flopped onto the couches in the salon with cups of coffee and plates of pastry.

'It was a good house,' Godfrey said, pouring a dram of whisky from his hip flask into his coffee.

'Aye,' agreed Colin, and held out his hand for the flask, which was readily passed. 'I like those Yanks. Very appreciative.' He turned to grin at Della. 'You were a fine assistant, lassie. You really looked surprised when ma tricks went awa. You know, boss' – his eyes turned to Beau, who was lying back on a couch looking exhausted – 'I've thought of something else we can put in. I'll tell you in the morning, though.'

'I think that would be better,' Beau yawned. 'I've had it for today.' He started to get up, but stopped when Madame Farcy bustled into the room, looking back over her shoulder.

She went over to Catherine, her face full of joy and excitement. 'Madame,' she said excitedly, 'he has come home.'

'Who?' asked Catherine, smiling at her. 'Who has come home? Your son, perhaps?'

'No, madame, not my son, but someone I love like a son.'

Catherine looked past her into the grand reception hall. A man was standing there. A man dressed in a blue workman's jacket and crumpled black trousers. His dark, untidy hair flopped over an unsmiling face, and while Catherine stared, he started to enter the room.

Madame Farcy turned and, rushing back to him, took his elbow and ushered him in. 'I present to you the owner of the chateau,' she said, and as everyone started to get to their feet, she continued, 'I introduce Monsieur Guy. Monsieur le Compte de Montjoy. You are his guests.'

Chapter 17

There was a stunned silence as the company stared at the man, who shifted his feet impatiently and stared back. Beau was the first to move. 'Monsieur de Montjoy,' he said, thrusting out his hand. 'I'm Beau Bennett, the leader of this company. How do you do?'

Guy de Montjoy took Beau's hand and answered in French that he was well and what the hell were they doing in his house? Frances understood his words and knew that Beau did too, but he turned his head to Catherine and beckoned her forward to explain.

'Monsieur le Compte,' she said, shaking hands with him. 'I am Catherine Fletcher, and I'm so sorry to have to tell you that the army have commandeered the chateau for extra accommodation for the military. Although, we' – she gestured towards the Players, who were all standing up now, looking concerned and confused – 'aren't exactly soldiers. We are entertainers in uniform.'

Guy was silent, slowly taking it in. He twitched, and scratched his chest, then raising a grubby hand, raked his nails through his dusty, untidy hair. Catherine took an involuntary step back. He's got fleas, she thought.

'Bloody hell,' muttered Della from where she stood with Frances beside the fireplace. 'He's alive.'

Guy de Montjoy briefly flicked his eyes to Della before returning them to Catherine.

'We were told,' she said quickly, 'that the owners of the chateau couldn't be found. And Madame Farcy could tell us nothing of the family's whereabouts.'

'That is true, monsieur,' Madame Farcy cried. 'I knew that your father had died and that your dear mama was in Switzerland, but you? I had no knowledge. Not for two years. And I would not say because...' She looked at the group of Players, who were watching, and then lowered her voice. 'Well, you know why.'

Catherine turned her head to Beau to see what his reaction would be and was alarmed to see that he looked nervous and rather upset. Oh hell, she thought, we're going to be turned out of here, and she looked back at the dusty stranger and tried to think of something else to say.

But for the first time since his rather dramatic entrance, Guy de Montjoy had allowed his face to relax. 'It is alright now, Manon,' he said to Madame Farcy. 'We are no longer so secret.' And turning back to Catherine, he explained, 'Madame Farcy would not tell you about me because I have been working with the Resistance. She, of course, did not know where I was, nor did she know that for the last four months I have been in prison.'

'Oh! *Mon Dieu!*' The old lady gasped and clamped a hand over her mouth. 'The Germans? They caught you?'

Guy sighed. 'They caught me,' he confirmed. 'But I was lucky. The Americans overran the prison before the Gestapo shot me. Now I have come home.'

Catherine's mind whirled with a thousand questions. Guy had been imprisoned by the Gestapo. Was it possible that he had known Christopher? Was this her opportunity?

'Monsieur—' she started.

'For Christ's sake, Catherine,' Della called. 'Give us a bit of translation. Who the hell is he?'

'He's…the owner of this place. He's called Guy de Montjoy, and he's a count.'

'A count?' Della asked impatiently. 'What's that when it's at home?'

'A sort of lord, like my father,' Frances hissed.

'Bloody hell. Not another toff,' Della groaned.

'What else did he say?' begged Tommy, and Colin and Godfrey nodded.

'He said he'd been working for the Resistance and that for the last four months he's been in prison,' Catherine translated.

'No wonder he's crawling,' Della laughed. 'I'd tell Madame F. to get the water boiling and dump him in the bath before he infests the rest of us.'

Guy, who had seen and heard Della's mocking laughter, scowled. 'What did she say?' he asked Catherine.

Beau rolled his eyes and looked daggers at Della, and was about to tell her off when Catherine said quickly, 'She said she thought you should have a bath. She thinks you might have fleas.'

The grin that widened Guy's lips and showed up dirty yellow teeth broke the moment. 'Yes, the lady is right. I do have fleas, and many sore places on my body, which are, I think, infected. Perhaps I smell? In the prison, everyone was the same – you stop noticing.' He smiled at Madame Farcy. 'Lead me away, Manon. I need food and hot water.'

He looked at Beau. 'In the morning, monsieur, we will discuss this further,' and nodding to the rest of the company, he turned and followed Madame Farcy out of the room.

'Crikey,' said Tommy. 'That's a turn up.'

'Yes,' said Beau, looking worried. 'Now I'm going to bed. We'll see what he says in the morning.'

As the girls climbed into their beds in the large room that overlooked the parkland at the front of the chateau, Frances said, 'I bet this was the main bedroom. I bet his parents slept in here and now he'll want to do the same.'

'He's welcome to join us,' giggled Della sleepily. 'He's quite a looker under all that filthy hair.'

Robert drove in the next morning with more mail. Catherine, who was strolling in the neglected grounds, spotted him and waved. He hurried over to where she was standing beside a big oak tree and, dropping his briefcase, took her in his arms.

'I've wanted to do this for days now,' he said, and passionately kissed her mouth and face, making her gasp with pleasure. She wound her arms about his neck, as anxious as him for this intimacy, and it was only when she began to feel her knees buckle and knew that at any moment they would be rolling on the grass that she stopped him.

'It's too public,' she whispered.

'We'll find somewhere quiet,' Robert said. 'Come on.'

'No.' Catherine gazed up at him, longing to be kissed again. 'I have to tell you. The owner of the chateau has turned up. I don't know what his plans are, but he wasn't too happy last night when he found us here.'

'Good Lord.' Robert looked quite surprised. 'We were told he was dead.'

'The father's dead. This is the son, Guy de Montjoy. It seems that he was in the Resistance and that he was captured. The Americans opened the prison some days ago.'

'Interesting,' said Robert, all passion now forgotten. 'I can't wait to meet him.' He started to walk back to the house, but Catherine grabbed his arm.

'I'm going to ask him about Christopher,' she said. 'He was captured by the Gestapo, and so was Chris. He might have met him.'

For a moment she hoped he would agree. Say, 'What a good idea,' and that he would question Guy de Montjoy with her, but the words were hardly out of her mouth before he said with a voice hard as steel, 'No, Catherine. Absolutely not.'

'Why not?' She could hear the whine in her voice but didn't care.

'Because your husband was on a secret mission. It must not be mentioned. Remember you signed the Official Secrets Act. There is a penalty to pay for breaking your promise.'

'But—'

'No "but"s,' he said, and took her arm to urge her along. 'Come on, let's meet the new arrival.' He was smiling again now, as though nothing had happened, and she, confused, walked with him.

Strangely, and even after that cold and swift rebuttal of her suggestion, Christopher and his whereabouts were not uppermost in her mind. It was of Robert she pondered. How could he turn off his desire so abruptly?

Guy was in the dining room with Della and Frances. The boys had eaten and were in the large salon rehearsing new numbers. The rousing chorus of the drinking song from *The Student Prince* suddenly resounded through the rooms and Guy looked up in astonishment.

'They are rehearsing,' smiled Frances. 'We have to keep adding new things to our acts to keep them vibrant, alive.'

'You can speak French,' said Della accusingly, spreading some of the American PX butter on one of Madame Farcy's bread rolls. 'You didn't say so before.'

'Nobody asked me,' said Frances.

'What act do you do?' Guy asked her. He was wearing a clean shirt, one of Monsieur Farcy's, and a pair of blue trousers, courtesy of Tommy, who had offered them when the count had first appeared downstairs with a blanket wrapped round his waist. He looked clean, but was terribly thin and covered with small sores and scabs. Frances guessed that he was in his late twenties or early thirties.

'I'm the administrator, really, and I drive the bus, which you will see at the back of the chateau,' said Frances, 'although I do sing with the other girls at the end of the show.'

'And Mademoiselle Della?'

'She dances and sings. She's wonderful. The audiences love her.'

He grinned at Della. His teeth were cleaner now, as was his hair, and although his skin looked pale and there were lines of exhaustion around his eyes, it was possible to see the handsome man he'd been. 'I'm sure they do,' he said. 'And Mademoiselle Catherine?'

'Oh, she sings too. She's awfully good.'

Della poured herself more coffee. 'What's he saying?'

248

she asked. 'I heard my name and Catherine's.'

'He wanted to know what you did. I said you sing and dance.'

'Oh.' Della grinned at him and Guy smiled back. 'Tell him he looks better this morning and that I've got some ointment for those sores on his arms. I'll put it on for him, and for any other patches he's got on his body.'

When Frances gave her the raised-eyebrow treatment, Della laughed. 'It's all part of our job,' she said. 'Bringing comfort to the troops.'

Frances was translating this when Robert came in, slowly followed by Catherine and Beau. 'Monsieur le Compte,' he said, saluting and then putting out his hand, 'I'm Major Lennox, liaison officer for this group.' His French was perfect. 'Perhaps, if you've finished your breakfast, we could go into the small salon for a little chat.' He turned to Catherine and reverting to English, added, 'We won't need you this time for translation, Mrs Fletcher. Major Bennett and I can manage quite well.' He handed her a bundle of letters. 'Perhaps you'd like to distribute the mail?'

It was all said very formally, and although Robert smiled politely, Catherine gave him a bleak stare. She had been dismissed and didn't much like it.

'That was a bit cheeky,' said Della, when the men had left the room. 'Leaving you out like that.'

'I suppose they're going to discuss something top secret,' said Catherine, undoing the string on the bundle, 'that they don't want me to hear.'

'With Beau?' said Frances. 'I do hope not. If he's anything like the rest of his family, it won't be a secret for long. All the Bennetts are dreadful gossips.' She looked at the letter Catherine had put in her hand. 'Oh goody,' she beamed. 'Another one from Felix.'

'Anything for me?' Della eagerly looked at the letters as Catherine riffled through them.

'Mm, yes.' Catherine held up a flimsy airmail envelope. 'This is for you.'

Della grabbed it and tore it open. 'It's from Tim,' she said excitedly.

Catherine wandered through to where the boys were practising. 'Post,' she called, and put the letters down on the table. She was keen to open her mail. There was one from Maman – she recognised the writing, but the other one she didn't recognise.

Sitting on the second step of the grand staircase, she opened the envelope. A single sheet of paper was inside with one line of writing: *Find Father Gautier somewhere south of Amiens. He'll tell you about your husband.*

She flipped the sheet over and back again. There was nothing on the back, and no signature. I'll show it to Robert, she thought. He'll be able to explain. But then, would he? Looking at it again, she began to have doubts. This brief note was for her only. Not to be shared.

The door to the small salon suddenly opened and the men came out, smiling and shaking hands. Catherine hastily folded the sheet of paper and put it in her pocket, and then opened the one from Maman.

Robert was watching her, and taking a deep breath, she smiled at him. 'Lili is well and growing,' she said, holding up Maman's letter.

'And your other one?'

Had he been checking up on the post? On all the mail that came to the Bennett Players, or just on hers?

She swallowed. 'It's from Bobby Crewe,' she lied. 'The band leader. He wants to know if I'm interested in a show going on at Christmas. If we'll be home then.'

'Oh.' Robert stared at her for a moment, his eyes narrowing, and then gave her a brief nod. Somehow, she thought, he knows I'm lying, and she put a hand in her pocket where the flimsy envelope, with the note inside, lay crumpled. Her fingers were slightly damp and stuck to the paper, and she felt a little sick. I ought to tell him now. Admit I've been telling a fib. But she looked at Guy, who'd been a Resistance fighter and suffered for it, and a wave of anger came over her. How dare Robert look at her letters, as well as everything else? she thought. I won't let him stop me searching for Christopher, no matter how hard he tries. She stood up, and refusing to look at him, she walked down the single stair and went into the large salon, where her friends had gathered.

Della was breathlessly reading out bits of Tim O'Brien's long letter. 'He can't say where he is, but I'm sure he's at the front,' she said. 'Listen to this: *We are hectic, here. Wounded arriving constantly, many of them in a bad way.* And what about this bit?' She turned the page and ran her red-painted fingernail down the close-written script until she found the place she wanted. '*I have a house in the west of Ireland, and after the war we could live there. They need a doctor in that town.*' She put the letter down and looked at Frances and Catherine. 'Did you hear that?' she whispered, her eyes round. 'He said "we".'

'He can't mean it,' said Frances. 'After all, you barely know him, and more than that, he barely knows you.'

'I know that,' Della said crossly. 'Still...' She didn't

finish the sentence, but half turned away and started to read the letter again.

Godfrey had three letters, all from his wife. After he read each one, he crumpled it up and threw it in the fireplace.

'What's she say?' asked Tommy.

'Oh, just rubbish, dear boy. Complaining that I've been away too long.' He gave a loud, barking laugh. 'Not long enough for me.'

'Do you have children, Godfrey?' Catherine asked.

He shook his head. 'Sadly no. But' – he smiled gently – 'it's maybe for the best. A child could have taken after me and she would have nagged it senseless, or, God forbid, it would have been like her and I'd have two harpies after me.'

Robert, Beau and Guy came into the room, and Beau rapped his hand on the table. 'Listen up, everybody. The count has very generously allowed us to stay here.' He nodded his thanks to the young man, and the company murmured, 'Hear, hear.'

'So, we still have a busy tour in this area, but in a couple of weeks we'll be going further afield. As you know, several towns north-east of here have fallen to the Allies, and we'll be touring up there. Robert has been liaising with the army and has picked out some venues. Field hospitals again and camps similar to the ones we've already been in. So you'll know the drill. Tin hats at all times!' Everyone laughed and grinned excitedly at each other, before Beau held up his hand again for silence.

'We're taking our bus,' he said. 'It's more convenient, as we know, and, Frances, you will drive – they seem to trust us not to get in any trouble. But here comes the best news. We're going home in the middle of December. So you can have Christmas with your families.'

'Wow!' said Della, and Catherine and Frances gave each other a hug. Colin and Tommy shook hands. Only Godfrey looked miserable.

'Don't tell her, laddie,' said Colin. 'Come away with me up to Glasgow. Ma wife and bairns will welcome you and we'll have a grand time.'

Later, when everyone was chatting excitedly and planning to write home, Robert asked Catherine to walk in the overgrown garden with him.

'You'll be happy with that news,' he said. 'Going home to see your mother and your little girl.'

'Oh yes,' Catherine nodded. 'It is so wonderful.'

'And you might be able to join your old band leader for his show. Bobby Crewe, is it? Wasn't that what he asked you in his letter?'

She stopped walking and turned to stare at him. 'Stop questioning me, Robert. I don't like it. Nor do I like you telling me what to do.'

His face flushed. 'Sorry,' he said. 'It's become a habit. I exist in a strange world where I'm never sure of ... But,' he said quickly, 'I didn't mean to hurt you when I excluded you from the discussion with de Montjoy. The thing is, it might have been something that we needed to keep secure.'

Catherine shrugged. 'I wasn't hurt,' she said coolly. 'It meant nothing to me. Although, including Beau in your discussion might have been a mistake. Frances says he's a terrible gossip.'

'Just as well, then, that there was nothing secret in what the count had to say.' Robert gazed at the sky. Grey clouds were rolling in from the west, threatening that rain would soon ruin what had been a perfectly sunny morning. 'I'm paranoid, I think. Too long in my job.'

He reached to take her hand, but before he could touch it, she pushed it into her pocket and started walking back to the chateau. 'Sorry,' she said. 'Tommy's waiting for me. We have to rehearse a new number.'

Catherine could feel his eyes on her back as she hurried to the house. I don't believe him, she thought, her stomach churning, that him questioning me was just a habit. He meant it, and despite all the kissing and pretence of love, he doesn't trust me.

I know that there's something very wrong about Christopher's disappearance, and he's determined I won't find out about it. But then, another part of her brain questioned, why was he so keen for me to come to France? He arranged the tour; I know he did. And why was I taken to that country house for a few stupid lessons? After all, nothing more has been mentioned about them, or of me doing anything undercover. Then another thought struck her and she paused at the studded oak door and looked back to Robert, who had reached his Jeep and was climbing into the driver's seat. Was that letter she'd received this morning a fake? Some sort of test of her loyalty?

That's it, she determined, as she watched him drive away. Any suggestion of a romance, wartime or no, is over. And I will carry on looking for Christopher. Robert just won't know about it.

Tommy was waiting for her in the hall. 'Where've you been?' he asked, waving pages of sheet music at her. 'I haven't got all day, you know. Colin and I are going fishing after lunch. Old man Farcy is taking us to a new place. Come on.'

'Sorry,' she smiled. 'On my way,' and the normality of rehearsal calmed her fears. This is who I am, she thought, and allowed her voice to rise in the air and fill the grand but dilapidated rooms with glorious melody.

Madame Farcy, listening with Guy in the reception hall, smiled. 'That girl is wonderful,' she whispered. 'And half French.'

For the next several weeks, the Bennett Players toured Normandy, performing in many different venues, large and small. They played to British, American and all sorts of colonial troops, as well as men of other nationalities.

'Who are these blokes?' asked Della, at one camp, as they looked at the audience who were eagerly awaiting the show. 'They're wearing funny uniforms.'

'They're Polish, I think,' said Frances. 'They might not understand English. That's why Baxter hasn't come with us today.'

'Good,' said Della. 'I already love them. Here goes,' and Della stepped onto the makeshift stage and started to sing.

The reception she – and indeed, all of them – got was tremendous and they came away clutching bottles of Polish spirit that had been thrust at them as they left.

'Find us some more Poles, Beau, dear boy,' boomed Godfrey, working on the screw top of a bottle. 'This is what I call gratitude.'

On some occasions, Guy came with them. He was keen to know the people who were living in his house, and even when he didn't understand the jokes that Baxter and Colin made, he clapped enthusiastically.

'You didn't get a word of that,' laughed Frances, shaking her head at him when Colin came off stage to ringing cheers.

'It doesn't matter,' Guy said. 'You are my friends; it is good that you are successful.' He had put on weight, and the sores that had covered his body had healed, leaving only the reddened marks from where they'd been. In time, those would fade too. But the lines around his eyes remained.

'I have seen too much,' he told Frances, one day, when she remarked about how tired he looked. 'These lines are not from lack of sleep, not now. They are from memory.'

'Of the prison?' she asked, her voice full of sympathy.

'Yes,' he said. 'That and other things. Acts of war, acts of cruelty. Mine as well as others'.'

'I'm sorry,' she said. 'I shouldn't have asked.'

'You should,' he sighed, massaging his fingers. Some of them were bent and were obviously painful. His interrogators had broken them. 'There will come a time when I tell it all. But not yet. The war isn't over.'

He and Frances talked often. She told him about her home in Wiltshire. 'My father's title means nothing now. We have a huge house, bigger than your lovely chateau, but no money, and it's falling to pieces. My brother had plans, but he's a POW in the Far East and we haven't heard from him for over a year. So I don't know what's going to happen.'

'You have farms?' Guy asked.

'Yes,' Frances nodded. 'But since the war, no one to

work them, until I got in a land girl. Besides which, my father has made some bad decisions.'

'I have farms,' said Guy, 'but I'm planning to concentrate on orchards. Normandy is famous, is it not, for apples? And Calvados. That is where money can be found. Cider and Calvados.'

'Mm.' Frances thought about it. Could that work at Parnell Hall? She thought not: her father needed money now, not in the ten years that it would take to establish such a business.

Guy changed the subject. 'Tell me about Catherine. She is married, yes?'

'She is,' Frances said. 'But her husband has been declared missing in action. He was, she says, a para.'

'He was lost during the invasion?'

'Well, no, and that's the strange thing. He has been missing since the spring, and apparently somewhere in France. Perhaps near here. She talks about him but doesn't give any details. I don't think she knows. She has a little girl too, at home with her mother...' Frances stopped, noticing the frown on Guy's face. He'd been listening attentively, but now he was staring at her. 'What?' she said. 'What is it?'

Guy's face cleared. 'Nothing. I was just interested, that's all.'

As the weeks went on, the weather became cooler. Autumn storms whipped across the country, stripping the trees of their remaining leaves. It rained heavily, so that driving in and out of the camps became difficult, and often it required a troop of men and, once, a tank to push the bus out of the mud.

'I'm freezing,' Della grumbled. 'I need different clothes.'

Robert arranged for them to be supplied with army greatcoats, but the girls hated them.

'They're horrible,' Della said. 'Surely you can find something better.'

'No, I can't,' snapped Robert. 'Take them or leave them.' He was angry all the time these days. Catherine would barely speak to him, and every time he tried to get her on her own, she found an excuse. She was convinced that he was keeping something from her and that she was, in some way, being used.

'What's the matter with you two?' Della asked, one night after a show when Catherine had ignored his offer of a drink. 'I thought you fancied him.'

'Well, you were wrong. I'm a married woman.' Catherine glowered at her friend and marched off to where Beau was leaning against the bar of the hotel where they'd stopped.

'When are we going to Amiens?' she demanded, not bothering with any niceties. 'It's been liberated for months now and I want to see if my grandparents are alright.'

'Calm down,' he said, swallowing his drink with one gulp. 'We're going the day after tomorrow. Robert has arranged it.'

'What?' she said, shocked.

'He knew you were anxious and he's been working on the schedule. I was going to tell you all when we got back to the chateau.'

'Oh.' Now she felt a little foolish. 'Good.' She glanced around and noticed Robert was looking at her, but she turned away from him. 'I'll tell the girls, if you don't mind,' she said.

'I don't mind.' Beau clicked his fingers at the barman for another drink. 'Anything to stop you shouting at me. Tell them all.'

Chapter 18

Guy came to sit beside Catherine on the journey to Amiens. Frances was driving, and Della was sitting behind her, with another letter from Tim O'Brien, which she was going over and over. 'Listen to this,' she was saying, and reading out bits and pieces of the letter. Catherine had moved to another seat on the pretence that she wanted to read her book, but in reality she needed to think. Della's overwhelming excitement over Dr Tim was getting in the way.

Catherine had had a letter too, from Maman. In it, she'd written that there was no news of the grandparents in Amiens. *Father Clement tried to get information for me about Papa and Maman but to no avail*, she wrote. *They seem to have disappeared from the face of the earth. I feel so sad.*

I took Lili to the clinic for her check-up. The nurse was kind and helped me. They gave us orange juice, which you know she likes, and now cod liver oil. I didn't understand what it was for, but I give her a teaspoon every day.

'You have bad news from home?' asked Guy, watching Catherine sigh as she put her letter back in its envelope.

'Yes, I suppose,' she said, dropping into French, which was easier for Guy. 'My mother says that there has been no news about my grandparents in Amiens. They have a farm to the south of the city, but they aren't there. Maman writes that they have disappeared from the face of the earth.'

'People have been displaced,' Guy said. 'And, of course, the postal service can be difficult. I expect they're still at home, wondering why they haven't heard from you.' He smiled. 'Will you try to see them when we reach Amiens?'

'Of course,' Catherine nodded. 'It was my main reason for coming on this tour, that and ...' She stopped speaking, remembering what Robert had said about Christopher's mission.

'And to look for your husband?'

She looked around the bus quickly to see if anyone was listening, but the others were all occupied. The boys were well into their card game, and Della was still talking to Frances. Beau had a notepad on his knee and was writing some sort of invoice. It was for the War Office, Catherine thought, to make sure that the Players got their money.

Only Baxter, who sat alone on the seat behind Beau, was doing nothing. He had Captain Fortescue on his knee and was making the doll look out of the window, raising its neck if they passed something of interest, like a burnt-out tank or other discarded military hardware. But every now and then the doll would turn its head right round and look straight at Catherine. It made her feel uncomfortable. Captain Fortescue seemed as if he was constantly checking up on her.

She lowered her voice. 'How did you know about Christopher?' she asked.

'Oh, Frances told me. She said he was missing in this

261

area, but' – he lowered his voice too – 'I am confused. It was before the invasion, was it not?'

'Yes.'

'And?'

Catherine bit her lip and looked out of the rain-spattered window. It was a bleak day, cold as well as wet, and on the flat landscape, bare-branched trees stood like sentinels, warning of danger ahead. Through the rain she could see that they were passing a neat cemetery, with a tall white cross at its gates. She realised that it was a memorial from the Great War and wondered how many more cemeteries would be built in the next few years.

'And?' Guy prompted her again.

'I'm sorry,' she murmured. 'I'm not allowed to talk about it.'

He was silent for a moment and then said, 'Major Lennox? He's stopped you?'

She nodded and then, turning to him, said, 'Will you come with me when I go to the farm? Just in case they aren't there and I have to discover someone who might have information. I think you will be better than me at finding out.'

'I will, Catherine. I will be happy to help you.'

As she smiled her thanks to him, she saw that the other members of the company were pointing out that they were coming into the city.

'We're here,' called Frances, and Beau, looking up from his invoices, grunted, 'Find the hotel. It's called the Normandie. It's in between the station and the cathedral, I think.'

It was only when Catherine moved to the front to look

out of the big window that she noticed that Captain Fortescue was still staring at her. 'What is it?' she snapped at Baxter.

He ignored her, but Captain Fortescue winked his painted wooden eye. 'Nothing,' he brayed. 'As long as you don't think Major Lennox will mind you cosying up to the Frog Prince.'

'Oh.' The colour drained from Catherine's face. 'I wasn't.'

'Just tell him to shut up,' said Della, turning away from the window, and glaring at Eric, she shouted, 'I'm going to take an axe to that bloody doll. Just see if I don't.'

'Then you'd be very sorry. Very sorry indeed.' This last was said in Baxter's normal voice, which was even more chilling.

As they walked into the hotel, Guy said, 'That man, Baxter, he insulted you, yes?'

Catherine, who was still simmering, nodded, but said, 'It doesn't matter. He does it to everyone.'

'But why does Beau keep him on the tour? I don't understand.'

Frances, who had caught up with them, said, 'None of us understand.' She gave a small, sour laugh. 'Unless it's because of—' She was stopped by a dig in the ribs. Catherine was warning that Beau was behind her and looking like thunder.

When they were all gathered in the lobby, Beau announced that they would be performing that evening at an army camp. 'Six o'clock, on stage. Running order as per usual. The bus will be waiting outside the hotel at five o'clock, but I suggest you change into performance

263

clothes here, as I doubt there'll be anywhere at the camp. See you later.'

As he was leaving, Catherine hurried over to him. 'Beau,' she said, 'what's happening tomorrow?'

He looked at his notebook. 'Another evening perform-ance. It'll be at the NAAFI, which is in town apparently – not sure where yet.'

'So you wouldn't mind if I went to see my grand-parents, who have a farm outside the city?'

He gave her a strange look. 'Um…' he hesitated. 'I suppose so,' he said, 'but I thought they'd disappeared from the face of the earth.'

Disappeared from the face of the earth? That was how Maman had written it and what she'd told Guy. The letter had only come this morning, and nobody else knew. She hadn't even had time to tell Frances and Della. How on earth had Beau got wind of it?

'How did you know that?' she said slowly, her voice cold.

Two spots of colour came into his pale aristocratic cheeks and he hunched his shoulders awkwardly. 'I don't know,' he said. 'I suppose I assumed it, or perhaps' – he was clutching at straws now so obviously that she wanted to slap him – 'someone said something. That's right – you mentioned it the other night.'

The temptation to call his bluff was almost over-whelming. She was certain now that there was something underhand going on, and far from being afraid, as she should have been, her anger made her all the more deter-mined to discover more. She gave him a brief smile. 'Well, perhaps I'll go to the civic authorities first, then,' she said. 'To the town hall. They might know something.'

The relief on Beau's face was patent. 'Yes,' he said. 'That would be a better idea. Now, if you'll excuse me, I have a few phone calls to make.'

I'll bet one of them is to Robert, she thought, as she walked back to join her friends, who were by the reception desk waiting for their keys.

'What was that about?' grinned Frances as she joined them. 'You looked at one point as if you wanted to smash Beau's face in.'

'Wait till we get to our room, then I'll tell you,' Catherine muttered. To hell with the Official Secrets Act, she thought to herself. The whereabouts of her grandparents couldn't possibly be a secret, and if it was, then it was one that she had no intention of keeping.

The hotel was full, not only with the Bennett Players but with senior military and visiting civil servants from the Allied powers. The manager apologised that he could only offer the girls one room. 'It is a nice room, on the first floor.' He was sweating slightly as he tried to deal with the throng of guests who were waiting impatiently at the desk. 'But,' he continued with a shrug, 'it is not how we usually treat our guests.'

'We don't mind,' said Frances. 'We're used to sharing. And there is a war on.'

'Yes,' he said, taking out a handkerchief and mopping his brow, before reaching behind him to take a key from the row of hooks. 'But we have no porter, I am sorry to say. You will have to find your own way.'

'Cheer up, cock,' grinned Della. 'We've stayed in worse dumps than this.'

The room had a double and single bed, and they tossed

a coin for the single. Della won, much to her delight, and crowed as she flung herself on it.

'I'm glad,' said Frances. 'If we were sharing, you'd be reading out bits of that damned letter again. At least Catherine doesn't read out hers.'

'That's the thing,' said Catherine. 'I want to tell you something that was in the one I had today.'

The three girls sat on the double bed while Catherine showed them the letter and translated to Della what Maman had written. 'You poor thing,' she said, and put her arm around Catherine's shoulders.

'No, but listen,' said Catherine. 'I asked Beau if I could go to the farm tomorrow and he said, "I thought they had disappeared from the face of the earth."'

Frances and Della looked blank. 'But don't you see?' said Catherine. 'He couldn't possibly have known that. I only had the letter today. I didn't even have time to tell you. So someone has been reading my letters.'

'Robert.' Della and Frances spoke in unison.

Catherine nodded miserably. 'I'm pretty sure that he's playing a dirty game and that he's using me.'

'The thing that puzzles me,' said Frances, frowning, 'is that Beau is in on it. I wouldn't have thought that he was the safest person to hold a secret.'

'Nor me,' Della joined in. 'After all, he's being black-mailed, isn't he? That bastard Baxter has got something on him – we all know that.'

'I am going to the farm tomorrow,' Catherine said slowly, and there was a determined tone in her voice that her friends hadn't heard before. 'I told Beau that I'd go to the town hall and ask there, but that was a lie. Somehow, I have to get out of town.'

'And we're coming with you,' Frances grinned. 'This isn't something you can do alone. We just need an excuse that works.'

'I'll tell you what,' said Della. 'Why don't we say we need to go shopping for warm clothes? We've been nagging about them for ages: nobody would be surprised.'

'Alright,' smiled Catherine, and gave each of her friends a kiss on the cheek. 'Oh,' she said, remembering, 'I told Guy about the letter when we were on the bus. He said he'd come with me too.'

'The more the merrier,' laughed Della, and got off the bed. 'Now, we must unpack and get ready for tonight.'

Catherine felt happier than she had all day. The oddness of her grandparents' disappearance somehow added to Christopher's and a new determination came over her. Isn't this war about freedom? she thought. An end to secrecy? Well, damn them. I won't let Robert or anyone else stop me.

But later, when they were walking down the stairs in their performance clothes, Frances said, 'I've been wondering. Why has Guy offered to come with us to Amiens? Don't you think it's strange?'

'Oh God,' muttered Catherine, and doubts began to worm themselves into her stomach. Had she made a terrible mistake? Had Robert made Guy come with them to keep an eye on her?

Despite or maybe because of all her worries, Catherine was the hit of the show. Somehow the tension that was whirling about in her mind made her sing with more depth and emotion, and the audience at the army camp shook the rafters with their cheers. 'You're hot tonight, kid,' said Tommy. 'What's got into you?'

'I don't know,' she muttered, smiling and acknowledging the applause. Her eyes flicked around the hall, looking for Robert, but she couldn't see him. He hadn't been at the hotel either, and afterwards, in the colonel's office, she asked Beau about him.

'No,' he said. 'He hasn't come on this trip. In fact, I think he may have gone back to London for a few days.' He frowned. 'Why d'you want to know? Is there something I can help you with?'

'No,' Catherine replied. 'There's nothing at all.' His look of consternation was telling. He's scared, she thought. He thinks I'm going to tell Robert what he said. She gave him a little smile, but her eyes remained cold. 'I'll wait and talk to him,' she said, and turned away.

The next morning, the girls got themselves ready for their trip. They had put on their warmest clothes, and after Catherine had said that the farm would be muddy, they'd gone to the back of the hotel, where the bus was parked, and collected their gumboots.

'We're going shopping,' Della told Beau after breakfast.

'Who's "we"?' he asked.

'Us girls. Catherine's got to do something at the town hall first and then we're all going to see if we can find some warm coats. These army coats are shit. They're too big and absolutely gruesome. We want something more fashionable.'

'For Christ's sake,' Beau growled. 'You're supposed to be in uniform, not on the catwalk.'

Della giggled. 'Oh, come on, Beau,' she said. 'You're dying to put on something glamorous yourself. One of those little cocktail numbers I saw in the wardrobe in your flat in Knightsbridge? When we went to get our uniforms.'

He was silent and for a split second she thought that she'd gone too far and that he was going to explode with rage and throw her off the tour. She held her breath; then suddenly he burst into laughter.

'You're such a saucy bitch, Della Stafford,' he said, getting out his handkerchief to wipe his eyes. 'I don't know why I don't fire you.'

'It's because you love me, darling,' she laughed, 'and because I'm great in the show. And, Beau, my duck' – she patted his cheek – 'everyone knows. And nobody gives a hoot.'

He gave a rather sad smile. 'Except the law,' he sighed. 'Except the law.'

Catherine had decided that they'd go without Guy – she wasn't sure that he was to be trusted – but to her surprise, he was waiting on the street for her when she came out of the hotel accompanied by Frances and Della.

'What,' he said, 'all three?'

'Yes,' Catherine nodded. 'My friends have offered to come with me, so I don't really need you.'

'I should like to come. I am interested to find out about your grandparents. Remember, I was in the Resistance. I still am, I suppose. I do know people.'

'Let him come,' said Frances, who had been following the conversation. 'He might have contacts.'

They walked off down the street towards the town hall. Frances looked behind them a couple of times to see if anyone was watching, but she could see no one and they carried on.

'So,' Guy said, pointing to a side street, 'we go this way.'

'You don't know where the farm is.' Catherine was suddenly suspicious again. 'It might not be this way.'

'No, you mistake me.' Guy gestured to a saloon car parked in front of a boarded-up shop. 'The car, there. We can go in that.'

'Is it yours?' Catherine was astonished.

'No,' he laughed. 'I borrowed it. For the trip.'

'Pinched is more like,' snorted Della, as they clambered into the black Citroën. 'We're going to get bloody arrested before the day is out.'

The road out of town was surprisingly quiet, with little traffic, neither military nor civilian.

'It's about four kilometres,' Catherine said. 'At the edge of a village. In the summer, it's beautiful.' She turned her head to her friends, who were sitting in the back. 'My father was here in the Great War. His regiment was fighting all around this area, and one day he and some of his pals came to my grandparents' farm to see if they had any fresh milk or eggs. He met my mother and they fell in love, just like that. Sometimes it happens.'

'Does it?' asked Della quietly.

'It did for them,' Catherine smiled. 'After the war, he came back. And they were married.' She turned her head to the front again. They were coming to the village now, a church and a few houses surrounded by bare fields and low hedges. In one of the fields, a man holding a plough was walking behind two huge horses. The churned-up ground seemed difficult to walk on, and the rain lashed at him, driving the waterproof gas cape he was wearing into a shroud-like covering around his body.

'God,' said Della, her mouth turned down in disgust. 'Who'd live in the country?'

'You will,' laughed Frances, 'if Tim has his way.'

Catherine was peering along the road. 'Look.' She pointed to a cluster of buildings. 'It's here.'

Guy parked the car beside the low stone entrance pillar and they all stared out of the steamed-up windows. Catherine craned her neck to look beyond the bare trees to the house and barns. She could see nothing moving, and glancing up, she noticed with despair that no smoke came out of the chimney. The place seemed deserted.

She opened the car door. 'I'm going to look,' she said, and getting out, walked along the muddy path that led into the farmyard and to the house. She heard the others climbing out after her, but she went straight round the house to the back door. Bending, she pushed aside a clay flowerpot and, finding the key, unlocked the wooden door.

Inside, it was dark and felt damp. Even with rubber boots, her steps echoed on the flagstone floor and bounced off the white plastered walls. 'Grandmère,' she called, her voice loud in the small room. 'Grandpère.'

As she'd half expected, there was no reply.

'I don't think there's anyone here,' said Frances from behind her, and she jumped in fright. 'Sorry,' Frances apologised. 'I didn't mean to scare you.'

The three girls looked all over the house. In the kitchen, the range was cold, and only dead ashes filled the space below the oven. Rainwater from a slightly open window had trickled over the sill and onto the floor beneath, gathering in a little puddle. Catherine, with an angry 'tch' forced the window shut and went into the small front room. Neat chairs dressed with lace antimacassars looked as though they'd never been sat in, but they had been roughly turned over, and the doors of the tall oak armoire were hanging open, exposing the lace cloths of which Grandmère had been so proud. In the two bedrooms above, one bed was made and the other tumbled and awry, but the cupboards were open, and drawers had been pulled out.

Catherine's heart sank. What on earth had gone on?

'Look,' said Della, holding up a frame holding a black-and-white photo. 'Isn't this you?'

'Yes.' Catherine took it, tears coming into her eyes at the sight of her fifteen-year-old self standing by the field gate hand in hand with her grandparents.

Suddenly there was a shout from downstairs. 'Catherine!' It was Guy and he was outside in the yard with a man in a gas cape, who stretched out his hands to her as she walked towards them.

'Catherine,' he said, grinning and taking off his cap to reveal tufts of white hair round a bald pate. 'Ah, Catherine, *ma petite*, how long, how long?'

'Jacques?' she said uncertainly. 'Is it you?'

'It is me.' He shook her hand enthusiastically and then, emboldened by the occasion, pulled her towards him and gave her a hug.

'This is my grandfather's cousin,' Catherine said to the girls, who had followed her out of the house. 'I've known him all my life.' She turned back to him. 'Where are they? Tell me, please.'

To her dismay, tears welled up in the old man's eyes and she knew that he was going to say something

272

dreadful. Frances and Della came to stand beside her, and each took a hand.

'My cousin Jean,' he sobbed, 'is dead. He was shot, by the Germans, in April. He hid Allied soldiers in the barn and in the cellar. No one knew, not even me. But he was given away and they took him and your grandmère.'

'*Mon Dieu*,' Catherine cried. 'They shot them both?'

'No. Béatrice was put in prison, but now she has been freed.'

'Where is she? I must go to her.' Catherine turned towards the car.

'Wait, wait, little one. She is with the sisters at the convent in Amiens. The prison did something to her mind. She knows no one. I think she will not know you.'

The words were devastating and Catherine could barely take them in. Her poor grandfather, how frightened he must have been when they took him away. And Grandmère? Did she see him being shot? She shuddered at the thought.

She could hear Frances translating to Della what had been said and heard Della's sad cry.

'The Jerries are pigs,' Della spat. 'Absolute pigs.'

Catherine struggled to gain control of herself. We must go back to Amiens, she thought. I have to go to the convent, and then something else struck her. She took Jacques's arm. 'My mother, Honorine, has written here several times to find out. Why are there no letters in the house?'

The old man shrugged. 'But she should have known by now. All the letters that came to the house were collected. I was told that your mother would be told, so

273

I waited for her to come if she could, or perhaps you. And' – he gave a sad smile – 'here you are.'

Catherine stared at him, trying to take in all the information that was bludgeoning her brain. She looked at Guy, who was looking back at her with a puzzled frown. There was a question to be asked. 'Who,' she asked finally, 'collected the letters?'

'Oh.' The old man put on his cap. 'It was Father Gautier.' She heard the sharp intake of breath from Guy as Jacques continued. 'He is our priest. A man of great honour.'

On the road back to Amiens, Catherine asked Guy to stop the car so that she could get out and stand for a moment in the cold air. Her head felt as though it was bursting. The news she'd received was so terrible that it was almost too much to take in. She wanted to cry for her grandfather, but found that she couldn't. Not yet. Jacques had said he was buried in the churchyard in a grave that was only marked by a small wooden cross and a number. She would come back to visit and arrange a headstone, but first she must find her grandmother.

'Are you alright, darling?' asked Della, getting out of the Citroën to stand beside her. 'It was awful news you had.' It had started to rain again and Della held her coat over her newly styled hair.

'Yes, I'm alright,' said Catherine. 'But there are so many questions.'

'Not least for this Father Gautier,' Frances joined in. 'What on earth was he playing at?'

'Let's get back in the car,' Catherine said. 'I want to show you something.'

When they were in their seats, with the rain driving against the steamed-up windows, Catherine opened her handbag. But before she took out the flimsy piece of paper, she turned to Guy. 'Why did you gasp when Father Gautier's name was mentioned?' she asked.

He shrugged. 'I don't think I gasped.'

'Yes, you did,' said Frances, and when she translated it to Della, she too nodded vigorously.

'I heard you, and I saw you. You looked quite sick.'

He was smoking a Gauloises Bleu and its strong aromatic smell filled the car, but after a moment he unwound the window and threw it out. 'Father Gautier's name is familiar to me,' he said at last. 'And I have met him. He was trusted by the Resistance fighters, and he was with me the night before I was arrested. What I do not understand is why he didn't let you know about your grandfather's death.'

Catherine took out the letter she'd had some weeks ago. 'Look at this,' she said. 'It came for me last month. And I don't know who sent it.'

It was handed round and Catherine translated the sentence into French for Guy. *Find Father Gautier somewhere south of Amiens. He'll tell you about your husband.*

'Who sent you this?' Guy asked.

Catherine shook her head. 'I don't know,' she said. 'But I'll tell you something. I'm certain Robert Lennox has read it.'

Chapter 19

The convent was in the quiet part of the old city, which had escaped the devastation of the invasion. Small houses, painted in pastel colours, lined the canal sides, lending a surprisingly bright note to the dreary day. Catherine, who had been mostly silent on the journey, gazed out at them and marvelled at the sight of a few market stalls, which had been set up. Winter vegetables were being sold, mostly cabbages, turnips and a few potatoes. Apples, taken from the store and slightly wrinkled, were fingered carefully by tired-looking housewives, and she even saw a few bottles of what she supposed was cider or even Calvados.

Half an hour before, they'd stopped at a cafe on the edge of the city for omelettes and a glass of wine. 'Eat up,' commanded Frances to Catherine, who was listlessly pushing her omelette around with her fork. 'You've had a terrible shock, but you're going to need your strength for the next bit.'

'I know,' she said. 'But it's so hard getting it all straight in my head. My grandfather being shot dead, and my poor grandmother losing her mind. I can hardly believe it.'

Frances and Della looked at each other. They didn't know what to say.

But Guy did. He put his arm around Catherine's

shoulders. 'Listen to me,' he said firmly. 'Your grand-father was a very brave man. Braver than many of us could be, because I have to tell you that I was frightened all the time, and it would have been the same for him and for your grandmother. You never knew who to trust or who to turn to for help.' He frowned. 'People you thought were on your side often weren't. I know now that there were many collaborators, not just the ones we saw, day in, day out, helping the Nazis, but those who were in the shadows, who pretended to be our friends.' He took her hand. 'Take comfort, Catherine. Jean Albert's name will never be forgotten. Not as long as I and the others who fought alongside me are alive.'

'Thank you, Guy,' she murmured, and wiped away the tears that were finally beginning to flow.

'What I don't understand,' Frances said, after finishing her wine and leaning back, 'is who this Father Gautier is. Why hasn't he got in touch with Catherine's mother? It's months now since the liberation – surely the post is working again.'

'Mm,' Guy frowned. 'That is strange.' He turned to Catherine. 'Was Father Gautier the parish priest of the village when you were last visiting?'

She shook her head. 'No. It was Father Bernard. I remember him so well. He would often come to the farmhouse for dinner. I don't know this Gautier at all. But remember, it was five years ago.'

Frances was translating the conversation to Della, who said to Guy, 'You know him. You said so. What's he like?'

Guy lit yet another cigarette. 'He's a priest – what is there to say? He's young, though, and not from around

277

here. From the east, I think, by his accent. He collects food and clothes for the refugees who have been bombed out, and he let us store our weapons in the vestry. He's a good man, I think.' Then added, 'Everybody likes him.'

Frances nodded. 'That's exactly what old Cousin Jacques said. Father Gautier is well respected; everybody likes him. He does sound like a good man. Anyway' – she got up from the metal cafe chair – 'let's get moving. Catherine wants to see her grandmother, and we've got a show tonight, in case you've forgotten. Beau will kill us if we're late.'

They left then and got into the car and drove quickly into Amiens.

'D'you know where we're going?' Frances asked Guy. He'd stopped for directions a few streets back, asking a woman with a shopping basket the way to the Convent of the Grey Sisters. He seemed confident that they were heading the right way, but after driving down a few streets, she'd pointed out that he'd missed the turning and he had to reverse and go back.

'It's down here, I think,' he said. 'A brick building with a stone chapel at the side – that's what the woman said.'

'Is it there?' called Della, pointing ahead. 'There's a couple of nuns going in. It must be it.'

It was the right place. A small painted sign beside the oak front door announced that it was the *Hôpital des Sœurs Grises*.

'Hospital?' said Della. 'Is this a hospital?'

'Perhaps,' Frances replied.

'Take your time,' said Guy, when he'd parked in front

of the convent. 'They won't appreciate a man who isn't a priest going inside. I'll walk up the road to the *tabac*. I need cigarettes.'

The girls climbed out of the Citroën and went up the broad stone steps to the door. When Catherine knocked, a square grille at eye level opened and a face looked out. 'Yes?'

'I believe Madame Béatrice Albert is staying with you. I'm her granddaughter and I would like to see her.'

The face gazed at Catherine for a moment and then the grille banged shut.

'Crikey,' said Della. 'What did you say?' But as she was speaking, the door was opening and the nun who had peered through the grille beckoned them inside.

'Wait, if you please.' Leaving them by the door, the little nun folded her hands into her grey sleeves and walked swiftly away from them down the corridor.

'It doesn't look much like a hospital,' said Frances, frosted breath coming out of her mouth when she spoke. She gazed around at the spotless, unadorned walls and down to the shiny tiled floor. 'I've never been in a convent before. Are they always so cold and so...stark? And that disinfectant smell...I swear it's the same stuff we use in the glasshouses at home.'

'Oh Christ, yes,' answered Della. 'It was just like this where I was. Jeyes Fluid and floor polish. The nuns believe that not scrubbing the pattern off the floors is a mortal sin. And as for lighting a fire? Not a cat in hell's chance.' She shuddered. 'I hated them.'

'Shush,' said Catherine as the little nun returned.

'You must speak to Mother Paul,' she whispered, and indicating that they were to follow her, walked before them towards a door at the far end of a bare and icy hall. Taking a deep breath, she rapped on the door.

After a moment, a deep voice begged them to enter and the nun opened the door and ushered them through.

Mother Paul was a tall, imposing woman with strong, almost mannish features, which her religious habit didn't soften. She was standing behind a large oak desk, which was bare of papers but had a telephone and a small brass bell. She gave each of the girls a long stare, her eyes taking in their uniforms, before saying, in English, 'Which one of you is Madame Albert's granddaughter?'

Catherine stepped forward. 'I am. My name is Catherine Fletcher.'

'And your companions?'

'They are my friends. Frances Parnell and Della Stafford.'

To Frances's surprise, Della bobbed a little curtsey when she was introduced, keeping her eyes lowered, and Mother Paul acknowledged it with a brief nod before drifting her hand to the chairs that were placed against the wall. The girls sat down.

'I see you are in the British Army. Are you nurses?'

'No,' said Catherine. 'We are entertainers.'

The atmosphere in the room got even more chilly, and Mother Paul folded her lips together as though to stop herself from yelling, 'What!' Instead, she said, 'How can I help you?'

'I want to see my grandmother,' said Catherine. 'I have only today been told that she is here with you. We, my mother and I, have been very worried about her and, of course, my grandfather. I have now learnt that he is dead.'

Mother Paul nodded slowly. 'He has been remembered

in our prayers. But, mademoiselle' – she looked at Catherine's hand and saw the wedding ring – 'er...madame, your presence is a surprise, perhaps a shock. We believed that dear Béatrice had no family left. That you and your parents were killed in the bombing.'

The girls looked at each other. 'As you see, Reverend Mother,' Frances said, not in the least awed, 'Catherine is very much alive. As are her mother and her daughter.'

'Yes.' Mother Paul's strong eyebrows drew together in a slight frown. 'Of course, I have no proof that Madame Fletcher is who she says she is. And you say she is.'

'But I am,' Catherine said angrily. 'However could you doubt me? I have my identity papers, and my father's cousin, Jacques Albert, could vouch for me if you don't believe those. He was the one who told me to come here.' She stood up. 'My grandmother, if you please, Reverend Mother. Take me to her.'

The nun didn't move from her chair, but brought one of her hands from her lap and opened the drawer in front of her. She withdrew a small black notebook. 'I will telephone to get permission.'

'Permission?' asked Frances. 'I think not.' Her voice was very much that of an earl's daughter. 'Catherine is Madame Albert's next of kin. She doesn't need permission. If you refuse to let her see her grandmother, we will return with the authorities.'

Della, finally overcoming her nervousness, stood up. 'Bloody hell,' she said, 'enough of this nonsense. Let's go and find her. This place isn't very big, so we'll look in every room.'

This last galvanised Mother Paul into action. 'No,' she said quickly. 'That won't be necessary.' She picked up the small brass bell that was on her desk and gave it a determined ring. The door was immediately opened and the little nun came back in. 'Take these ladies to Madame Albert.'

As they were going out of the door, Frances stopped and turned back to Mother Paul. 'Who were you going to call for permission?' she asked. The black notebook was still on the desk, and the reverend mother's hand was hovering over the receiver.

'Father Gautier, of course. He is Madame Albert's legal guardian.'

'Not any more,' said Frances. 'Her family have found her. Madame Fletcher will make the decisions now.'

As she left the room and followed the girls up a broad, uncarpeted staircase, she knew that in the room below Mother Paul would be dialling Father Gautier's number.

They found Grandmère Béatrice in a cold, bare day room. She was sitting on a hard chair by the window and was leaning forward, looking out at the buildings opposite and the road below.

Frances grabbed Della's arm. 'Let Catherine go alone to her,' she whispered, and the two girls stood by the door as Catherine went to kneel beside the old lady.

'Grandmère,' she said softly. 'It's me, Catherine.'

At first, Béatrice didn't move and Catherine took hold of her gnarled, veiny hand. 'Grandmère,' she repeated. 'It's me.'

Slowly, the old woman turned her head away from the window and gazed at Catherine. As her eyes scanned her face with seemingly no recognition, Catherine was certain that what Jacques had said was true. Poor Grandmère had lost her mind. She didn't know her.

Catherine looked over her shoulder to her friends, who were standing by the door. 'She doesn't know me,' she said, with a sob in her voice, and they nodded sympathetically and moved forward to comfort her.

But as they did, the old woman suddenly spoke. 'Catherine, *chérie*? Is it you?' Her voice was filled with wonder. 'Are you a dream?'

'Oh no, Grandmère.' Catherine put her arms about her and held her tight. 'I'm here. I've found you.'

In the minutes that followed, there was much kissing and many tears. 'How have you got here?' asked Béatrice. 'Is the war over?'

'It is in this area,' Catherine said, smoothing back Grandmère's tight grey chignon, which had become dislodged with all the hugging. 'I'm going to take you back to England. Maman has been so worried about you. And you have a great-granddaughter to meet.'

'Lili,' said the old lady, and Catherine looked at her in amazement. 'How—'

The door opened suddenly and a different nun came in, carrying a small steel tray that contained a medicine bottle and a little glass. She wore a stiff white apron over her habit, as though she was afraid that her clothes were about to be stained. 'Madame Albert,' she said briskly, 'it is time for your medicine.'

Béatrice clung to Catherine's hand. 'No,' she cried. 'I don't want it. I have told you, over and over.' She was shaking and Catherine held her and scowled at the nun.

'What medicine is it?'

The nun ignored her and measured a dose into the glass. 'No spitting it out, this time, if you please, madame.'

'Tell me,' said Catherine angrily. 'What is the medicine?'

'Oh, for Christ's sake.' Della stepped forward and grabbed the bottle off the tray. She held it up to the light and peered at the label. 'It says, "*L'hydrate de*...something,"' she muttered, and Frances had a look.

'"*L'hydrate de chloral*,"' she read. 'Chloral hydrate.'

'Bloody hell,' Della spluttered. 'I've heard of that. It's a Mickey Finn. It'll knock her out.'

The nun approached Béatrice with the glass of medicine and Catherine stood up. 'Take that horrible medicine away,' she said, giving the nun a steely glare. 'I refuse to let you anywhere near her.'

'But, madame,' the nun faltered, looking confused, 'it is my duty. Madame Albert must have this three times a day.'

'Three times?' cried Della. 'No wonder they say she's losing her mind. They're poisoning her.' She snatched the glass off the tray and upended the contents onto the polished floorboards. An unpleasantly musty smell rose up and Della shivered. 'Jesus and Mary,' she said, 'do I remember that stink.'

The nun gazed at the floor with horror.

'Yes,' said Della. 'A bit more cleaning to do.'

'We must get your grandmother out of here,' said Frances urgently. 'I'm sure Mother Paul was about to telephone Father Gautier. He'll be here any minute, and unless you want a stand-up row with him, we have to go.'

'I know,' said Catherine, and hooking an arm under her grandmother's, she said, 'Can you walk, Grandmère?'

'Yes, of course.'

'Then you're coming with me and my friends. Is your room close by, with your clothes?'

Béatrice nodded towards a door at the side of the room and Frances and Della ran to it. It was a small cell with a little cupboard that contained a few underclothes and her rosary beads. Behind the door was a hook carrying another dress and a coat. Della looked for a bag to carry them in and, finding none, emptied the feather pillow out of its case and used that. They helped the old lady into the coat, and then with Della on one side and Catherine on the other, they walked to the door.

'This is wrong,' shouted the nun, trying to bar the way. 'Madame Albert must stay here. Father Gautier says so.'

'And is he the one who told you to drug her?' asked Frances.

'But it is a kindness,' she wailed. 'So that she doesn't suffer mental torment at the end of her life.'

'Nonsense,' said Frances curtly. 'Now get out of the way.'

They were in the hall when Mother Paul, alerted by the cries of alarm from the medicine nun, came out of her office.

'You cannot remove Madame Albert from this house,' she said, moving to stand in front of them. 'I insist that she stays.'

'No, Mother Paul.' Catherine spoke with her newly found determination. 'You have no authority to insist, and I'm taking her to her family, where she'll be loved and properly looked after, so if you will step aside, we'll be on our way.'

'I've telephoned Father Gautier.'

'I'll bet you have,' said Frances, 'but it's none of his business. And if you try to stop Madame Albert leaving, I'll bring the police and the whole British Army into this convent. I don't think you'd like that.'

For the first time, Mother Paul looked alarmed, and as she stepped aside, the girls helped Béatrice to the door. Opening it, a blast a fresh air hit them and Béatrice breathed in deeply. 'Oh, how I've missed the outside,' she said, tears coming again to her old eyes. 'I've been in prison for so long.'

Della turned at the door and looked back. Mother Paul stood in the corridor, and in the background, several nuns, who had come to see what excitement had disturbed their endlessly peaceful days, hovered anxiously.

Della bobbed a curtsey and shouted, 'Goodbye, you old cow,' and with a final rude gesture with her fingers ran to the car, where Catherine and Guy were waiting for her.

'What have you been doing?' said Frances crossly, getting into the front.

'Something I've wanted to do for ten years,' laughed Della, getting into the back seat beside Catherine and Béatrice.

As he put the car in gear, Guy asked, 'Did you have trouble in there?'

'We did,' said Frances. 'At first, they weren't keen to let us see her, and getting her out was worse. Anyway, we'd better get moving. Mother Paul has phoned for backup.'

'Who'd she call?'

Frances looked ahead as they pulled away from the pavement and sped along the road. She pointed towards a tall, athletic priest who was walking swiftly towards the convent. 'I rather think she called him.'

'Father Gautier,' breathed Guy, and he pulled down the brim of his navy-blue cap.

The first person Catherine saw as they walked into the hotel was Robert. He was sitting at one of the little round tables in the lobby, deep in conversation with Beau. Papers were scattered on the table, and Robert's holdall was on the floor beside him. Catherine guessed that he'd just arrived back from England. I wonder what he's been doing, she thought, and what he'll say when he notices that Grandmère is on my arm?

'We're going to have to get another room,' said Frances, going to the reception desk. 'Grandmère Béatrice needs pampering.'

'God, yes,' said Della. 'Who wouldn't after spending time in that lunatic asylum?' She banged her fist on the bell. 'Let's get the manager.'

The clang of the bell made Robert and Beau look up. Robert glanced at Frances and Della; then, knowing that the girls would be together, he looked around for Catherine. When he spotted her, his eyes, behind the tortoiseshell glasses, softened. Catherine, looking back at him, found herself giving him a defensive smile because she knew that his expression would change within the next few seconds.

'Good God,' he said, standing up so suddenly that Beau, who was still studying the papers, looked up in alarm.

'What is it?' he asked, and then when he saw Catherine with Madame Albert, the colour drained out of his face.

Robert walked across to Catherine and, taking off his cap, bent and kissed her cheek. 'Hello,' he said. 'Who have we here?'

She was utterly disconcerted by that kiss, as she knew he had intended her to be. It was his way of getting back at her. Bastard, she thought, having picked up one of Della's favourite words, and turning to Grandmère, she explained, 'This is a friend, Major Robert Lennox.

'Robert,' she said slowly, 'let me introduce my grandmother, Madame Béatrice Albert.'

His surprise was so obvious that Catherine's frown turned into a small, triumphant smile, but he took no time to collect his wits and thrust out his hand. 'How d'you do, madame,' he said, giving Béatrice a slight bow, and she, casting a careful look at him, shook his hand and replied that she was well.

He turned to Catherine. 'Clever you,' he said. 'You found her. And...your grandfather?'

'He's dead. The Gestapo shot him.' Her voice was sharp, and at the mention of the Gestapo, several people in the lobby turned to look at her.

Robert said nothing for a moment, and then he turned back to Béatrice. 'My condolences, madame,' he murmured.

For all her previous anger with him, Catherine thought his sentiment sounded sincere. Perhaps he did already know about Grandpère, and by refusing to tell her was trying to save her the added heartbreak of losing both her husband and her grandparents. But he seemed genuinely surprised at seeing Béatrice. He'd thought she was dead. So that meant that his intelligence network had broken down somewhere.

'When you've settled her,' Robert muttered, 'I need a debrief. Where was she? Who was keeping her?'

Before Catherine could reply, Beau had joined them and was staring at the old lady. 'This is your grand-mother?' he asked.

His hand trembled as he was introduced and Béatrice asked if he was in pain. 'I see you have been injured, young man,' she said kindly. 'Sit, do. Standing can't be good for you.'

'Oh, he's alright, Grandmère,' said Catherine. 'He's just surprised to see you. After all, it was only this morning that he told me that you had disappeared. How wrong he was.'

Robert's face hardened and he slid a sideways glance at Beau. Catherine felt like laughing out loud. Both of them were now in trouble.

Frances called from the desk, where the sweating manager was shrugging and waving his arms about in exaggerated despair. 'He says that there aren't any vacant rooms. But Della and I have decided that we'll sleep in the bus and you and Madame Albert can have the room to yourselves.'

Della nodded her head vigorously. 'Just let us use it to change, but otherwise, OK, as the Yanks would say.'

'No,' Robert intervened, and looked at Catherine. 'You can have my room. I'll put up at the officers' mess. No need for the girls to sleep in the bus. It's far too cold.'

Beau cleared his throat. He'd got over whatever it was that had frightened him. 'If you don't mind me butting in,' he said. 'We do have a show tonight, so we need to get a shift on. It's at the NAAFI and not too far from here, but nevertheless...'

'Alright.' Frances had joined them. 'We'll be ready.' She smiled at Béatrice and then said to Catherine, 'What about Madame Albert? I'm sure she's tired. Will she stay here?'

But after Catherine had explained to her grandmother what was about to happen, the old lady was adamant that she wanted to see the show. 'It's been so many years since I heard you sing, *ma chérie*. Jean so loved the sound of your voice when you came to visit that it will bring back some happy memories.'

Chapter 20

The NAAFI was crowded that evening with soldiers and airmen, as well as some patients and nurses from the military hospital, who'd all come to see the show. There was no stage, but a large space at the far end of the room had been cleared and a piano brought in. Tommy and the other boys carried in the hampers and set up the microphones.

'I'll do the comedy stuff first, boss,' Colin said to Beau. He was looking in the hamper for his magic wand. 'And then finish with some of the better tricks.'

'Alright,' said Beau absently. 'Whatever you want.' He seemed distracted this evening and was constantly looking at the door. 'Has Eric arrived yet?'

'Haven't seen him, boss,' Colin said, arranging the curls on his luxuriant black wig and brushing down his velvet, star-studded cape.

'He'll hang on until the last minute,' sighed Tommy. 'Thinks it makes him more important.' He blew his nose hard and coughed. He had caught a cold in the last couple of days and now his chest rattled and two spots of colour brightened his cheeks.

Beau looked round at him. 'You alright, Tommy?' he asked.

'Mm,' he wheezed. 'I'll go to bed with a whisky after the show. That'll cure it.'

'Good man.'

'Don't be generous with your infection, dear boy,' said Godfrey. 'None of us want a cold. I think we should have a dram now as a precaution.'

'After the show,' warned Beau. 'Not now. I've told you before.'

Godfrey heaved a sigh and raised his eyebrows to Colin.

'Your wee man's at the door,' Colin called to Beau, and watched the boss limp away to the entrance before getting out his hip flask and handing it round.

The girls were in their room changing into their show clothes. Catherine had left her grandmother asleep in the bed that Robert had given up for them. The excitement had been too much for the old lady and Catherine had wondered if she would be fit enough to come with them to the NAAFI.

'I think I'll have to let her sleep,' she said to Della. 'And that could be a problem. Should I stay with her?'

'She seems like a tough old bird,' said Della, who was attacking her hair with a curling iron. 'Leave her a note telling her that you'll be back later. Damn!' The iron had got tangled up in Della's fringe and wisps of smoke and the smell of burning filled the air. 'Bloody hell, I'm doing a Joan of Arc here.'

'You can't miss the show,' Frances said. 'One of the officers downstairs said that they were all looking forward to it.'

'My grandmother's more important than that,' snapped Catherine. 'I'll go and see her now.'

'Oh Lord,' Frances groaned when Catherine had left. 'I don't know how we're going to manage this new situation.'

'It'll be OK,' said Della. 'She won't let us down.'

And fifteen minutes later, Della was proved right. Catherine and Madame Albert were waiting in the lobby when she and Frances came downstairs.

'I thought you might be too tired to join us tonight,' said Frances, taking the old lady's hand. 'You've had such an ordeal.'

'It has been very hard,' Béatrice conceded, 'but I must get back to work now. My Jean would want that. Tonight, I will hear my granddaughter sing,' she smiled at Frances and Della, 'and you two dear girls as well. Tomorrow, I return to the farm. There is much to be done.'

'But, Grandmère,' Catherine said, alarmed by the outlined plan, 'you can't. I want to take you to England, so you'll be safe and looked after by Maman.'

'Looked after?' Béatrice growled. 'You want to treat me like the nuns did? Wrapped in cotton wool, fed medicine to make me drowsy, while all the time waiting for me to die? No. No, *chérie*. I'm not ready for that.'

'But…'

Béatrice held up an imperious hand and Catherine knew she was defeated. She couldn't find an argument against her grandmother's decision, so she tucked her arm into the old lady's and they all walked outside.

'She's one feisty old girl,' grinned Della when Frances explained what Béatrice had said, and when they got to the NAAFI, Della gave her a big hug and a kiss on both cheeks, before showing her to a seat in the front row.

'Will you be alright, Grandmère?' Catherine asked, still doubtful. 'The show lasts about an hour and a half.'

'Of course. Off you go.'

As Catherine walked back to the performance area,

she remembered something else, which hit her like an express train. Grandmère had mentioned Lili. How could she have possibly known about her? Unless...

Tommy was playing the opening music, and Della was stretching her legs behind the curtain, which the NAAFI staff had rigged up for them. 'OK, kid?' she said when Catherine came to join her.

'Yes, I'm fine,' she smiled. 'But there's still something to think about. Do you remember when we were in that day room and Grandmère said—'

'Later,' Della grinned, and taking a deep breath, leapt through the curtain.

When Catherine came to sing, she opened with 'Blue Moon', and then 'The Very Thought of You', which entranced the audience and left some of them, both male and female, in tears. 'Bravo!' they shouted after, and cries of 'More!' rang around the room. She glanced down to Béatrice, who was sitting, her hands clutched together on her chest, with tears spilling down her cheeks.

Catherine went over to Tommy and whispered what he was to play, and then going back to the microphone, she held up her hand for silence.

'Oh hell,' muttered Beau. 'She's going to sing some-thing new.'

'She knows what she's doing,' said Robert, who was standing beside him against the back wall. 'Why can't you just trust her? I do.'

Catherine gazed at the audience, who were looking back at her and grinning in anticipation. 'I am half French,' she said. 'My mother's family had a farm just south of this city. Earlier this year, the Gestapo raided the farm, looking for the Allied airmen and the Resistance fighters that my grandparents hid. They found no one, but…' her voice faltered a little before she carried on, 'but their courage had been exposed by a traitor.' She paused again and swallowed the lump in her throat. 'My dear grandfather was shot dead, and my grandmother was put in prison, and we didn't know where she was, until today. We found her; she is sitting here, in the front row.' The audience craned their necks to see her, and encouraged by Frances, who had gone to sit beside her and was whispering a translation, Béatrice stood up and gave a little wave. Soldiers, airmen and civilians of all nationalities broke into respectful applause and Béatrice, overcome, sat down and fanned herself with one of little printed programme sheets that Beau had placed around the room.

'Now,' said Catherine, 'for her, for my own happy memories of days gone by, I will sing one of my grand-father's favourite songs, "*Parlez-Moi d'Amour*".'

As soon as Tommy played the opening bars, the audience recognised the familiar English version, 'Speak to Me of Love', and clapped in anticipation. Two hundred voices joined in the chorus, and Catherine walked along the aisle singing and shaking hands with men who stretched out to grab at hers. Still singing, she walked back and, reaching Béatrice, took her hand and led her onto the makeshift stage.

The cheers that rang around the room were probably heard out in the street, and as Catherine acknowledged them, Béatrice held on to her arm tightly, overwhelmed by the noise. Catherine held up her hand once more, and when the cheers had died down, she said, 'I present to you Madame Béatrice Albert. She is living proof that most of the French people do love their country and are prepared to fight and to die for it.'

Some Free French soldiers who were in the audience stood up and began to sing '*La Marseillaise*', the French national anthem, and Tommy struck up to accompany them. In the end, Catherine and Béatrice and all those who knew the words were joined by the company, who hummed and lah-lahed along to the tune. Catherine was close to tears again when the whole audience scrambled to their feet and drove their fists in the air in time to the music.

Nothing could have bettered that moment and Beau signalled to the company that it was the end of the show; the audience filtered out, exhausted by cheering and quite ready to carry on with the war.

Catherine, Frances and Della, with Béatrice stumbling along between them, walked back to the hotel. Robert, who had gone on ahead, was waiting for them.

'Your grandmother should rest until the morning,' he said to Catherine, 'but tomorrow, if she is able, we have to ask her some questions. I'm sorry – I know she's had a hellish time – but it must be done.'

'I do know,' said Catherine. 'And she will be ready. Besides, there is something I need to ask her myself.'

She waited until Béatrice was gently snoring in the double bed they shared before going down to the bar. Adrenaline was still surging through her and although she was tired, she found sleep impossible. It was after midnight and only a few of the guests were still wandering about. The bar was almost empty. There was no sign of her friends, and although she was tempted to go to their room, to see if they were awake, she resisted and ordered a brandy instead.

Robert was at a table, on his own, nursing a glass of Calvados; she went to sit beside him.

'How do you do it, night after night,' he asked, 'with the same intensity?'

'Because I love it,' she replied. 'Singing is my life.'

He swirled the liquid round in his glass, watching it gleam as it caught in the glow of the orange-shaded lamp behind him. 'We haven't been friends in the last month. If I've done something to hurt you, I'm truly sorry.'

She turned to face him. 'Don't pretend ignorance, Robert,' she said. 'Don't keep up this lie about being fond of me when I know that you've only been using me to root out a traitor.'

It was strange – she'd never actually put that realisation into words in her head, never really understood what was going on, but now, just saying it made everything clear. 'Those two days at the spy school were not for me to learn about how you go about your trade, but for you to learn about me,' she continued. 'About my husband and about my grandparents. They are linked. I know that now.'

'How d'you know?' He seemed surprised.

'Because Grandmère mentioned Lili this afternoon. She could only know about her if she'd met someone from home. That someone must have been Christopher.'

'Oh.' He narrowed his eyes and stared at her. 'Are you certain? What exactly did she say?'

'She just said her name and then we were interrupted. But I intend to find out more tomorrow.'

'Yes. But let me sit with you when you do. I have many questions for her, and she could be so helpful to us. I need to debrief her before she's...um...got at.'

'What?' Suddenly Catherine felt very afraid and started to get up. 'Is she in danger? I must go to her.'

'Don't worry.' Robert glanced to the bar, where the weary manager was flicking through a newspaper, desperate for the last few customers to go to bed. He put a hand on her arm and lowered his voice. 'I've got men stationed outside your room. She's quite safe.'

Catherine frowned at him. 'I didn't see anyone when I came down.'

He grinned. 'Well, that means they were doing their job properly. Believe me, they are on your corridor and closer than you think.'

She relaxed then and took a sip of her brandy. She watched Robert polishing his glasses on his tie and rubbing his hand over his face before replacing them. 'You've been reading my letters,' she muttered.

'I'm afraid I have,' he said almost cheerfully. 'It's part of the job.'

'But why did you have to share them with Beau?'

He looked genuinely astonished. 'I've never shared them with Beau. Whatever makes you think that?'

'Because when I told him this morning that I was going to the farm to look for my grandparents, he said, "But I thought they had disappeared from the face of the earth."' Those were exactly the same words as in my mother's letter. I hadn't shown it to anybody. But he knew.'

'Perhaps it was an assumption.' Robert spoke carefully, not giving anything away. 'Everyone knew that you had family in this area.'

Catherine gave a short laugh. 'You don't believe that any more than I do.'

He was quiet, thinking. 'Are you absolutely sure you told no one else?'

'Absolutely,' she said. 'I hadn't even had time to tell the girls.' Then a memory struck her and she clapped a hand to her mouth. '*Mon Dieu*,' she whispered. 'I told Guy de Montjoy, on the bus, when we were driving to Amiens, and I told him about Father Gautier. I showed him the other letter.'

'The one about you doing a Christmas show with Bobby Crewe?' he asked, one eyebrow raised, and laughed when she scowled at him. He got up and, taking her hand, helped her out of her chair. 'Come on,' he said. 'It's too late for all this now. We'll sort it out in the morning. You must get some sleep, and so must I.'

He walked with her to the staircase and then bent and kissed her. Almost involuntarily her arms went round his neck and she found herself kissing him back. This is all wrong, she thought, but it was what she wanted, and didn't care that she might part of his intelligence gathering. Being in his arms was wonderful.

'See you in the morning, my love,' he said, when they broke away, and she nodded and went up the stairs.

When she awoke the next morning, she found Béatrice already up and dressed. She was washing her underwear and stockings from yesterday in the washbasin and humming a little tune. Catherine recognised it as '*Parlez-Moi d'Amour*' from last night's show. She looked full of energy and almost back to how Catherine remembered her from before the war.

'Good morning, Grandmère. Did you sleep well?'

'Ah, *chérie*. You are awake at last. I am glad.' She squeezed out the water from her washing and, after looking around the room for somewhere to hang it, chose the wheezing old radiator. 'Now, there are things to do today. I must go to the market and get food to take to the farm, but first, I need to see if there is any money in the bank.' She came to sit on the bed beside Catherine. 'Do you think that the Boche will have emptied your grandfather's account? They might have, you know.'

'I don't know, Grandmère, but I have money if you need it. Let me get up and we can have some breakfast and then decide what to do. Major Lennox wants to talk to you. He has to know about the raid on the farm.'

Béatrice's face paled. 'It was dreadful, *ma chérie*. I cannot bear even to think about it.'

'But you must, Grandmère. So that the people who did those terrible things can be brought to justice.'

The old lady sat for a minute, and then nodded her head. 'You are right, Catherine. It would be cowardly of me to indulge in grief and not tell all that I know. So' – she stood up and went back to arrange her washing, which was dripping on the floor – 'you will get up and we can get on with the day.'

When Catherine came back from the bathroom, she found Frances and Della sitting on the bed chatting to Béatrice. They looked up when she came in.

'Get a move on,' said Della. 'We want to find some breakfast. And then Grandmère Béatrice is going to the market.'

'She can't,' Catherine said. 'Robert wants to ask her some questions. Besides...'

'Besides what?' asked Frances.

Catherine frowned. 'Besides,' she muttered, concerned that although she was speaking in English, which her grandmother wouldn't understand, some hint of what she was saying might get through, 'it isn't safe.'

'What?' The two girls looked amazed. 'Who isn't safe?' Della looked at Béatrice, who had got up to look out of the window. 'Not her, surely?'

Catherine quickly repeated what Robert had said last night and told them about him placing guards in the corridor.

'My God, I saw one of them,' said Frances. 'He was loitering on the corridor next to the staircase, pretending to read a French newspaper. He was so patently English.'

'Anyway' – Catherine put on her coat – 'we'll all go to get breakfast and then Robert will interview her here. He wants to find out about Father Gautier, among other things.'

She needed to know about the other things as well.

'Can we sit in on it?' asked Della. 'I'm dying to know what's going on.'

Catherine shrugged. 'I suppose that's up to him.'

They breakfasted on coffee and very inferior croissants at a cafe next door to the hotel. Béatrice got out of her seat to grumble furiously to the owner, who stood morosely behind his counter, a cigarette hanging out of his mouth.

'Call this a croissant,' she said, holding it up like some sort of specimen.

'There's a war on,' he shrugged. 'Can't get the flour.'

Frances smiled and looked to see what the other diners in the cafe thought, but as she looked around, her eyes were caught by someone standing outside, looking in through the window. She gasped and gave Catherine a dig in the ribs. Look,' she whispered. 'Isn't that Father Gautier?'

'What? Where?' squeaked Della, who had her back to the window.

'Don't look round,' Frances said urgently. 'I think he's watching Béatrice and waiting for her to come out.'

'What shall we do?' asked Catherine, trying not to stare at the tall, rather good-looking priest, who was casually watching while all the time smiling at people walking by and greeting him. 'D'you think there's a back way out of here?'

'Probably,' said Frances. 'Look, he knows that she was rescued by you and some friends, but he doesn't know what we look like. I don't think so, anyway. And I don't think he's been outside for long, and Grandmère Béatrice is over there giving the cafe owner grief, so as far as Gautier is concerned, we're not necessarily connected. If Della and I go outside and create a diversion, you can get Béatrice out of the back of here and into the rear entrance of the hotel. What d'you think?'

'Good idea,' Della grinned immediately. 'I can divert anyone.'

The two girls got up as Catherine took out her purse and went to the counter. 'In a moment, Grandmère,' she whispered, as she paid their bill, 'you and I are going through that door there.' She nodded to a half-open door through which could be glimpsed a courtyard and some bins. 'The other two are going out of the front. There isn't time to tell you why, but it is necessary.'

The old lady immediately understood and gave up her haranguing of the proprietor. Suddenly there was a noise outside and Catherine said, 'Ready?' and grabbing her grandmother's arm, hustled her through the door. She looked quickly back over her shoulder as they entered the courtyard and caught sight of Della helping the priest to his feet as Frances brushed down his black suit.

By the time she and Béatrice had wandered through the back offices of the hotel and were once again in the lobby, Frances and Della were already there, breathlessly squawking with laughter.

'What did you do?' asked Catherine.

'I barged into the bugger, accidentally on purpose,' giggled Della. 'It gave him a hell of a shock. I didn't realise I was so strong.'

'He couldn't possibly have seen you,' said Frances. 'But it does make you wonder what he's up to.'

'Who were we hiding from?' asked Béatrice, a tremor in her voice. 'Not the Nazis again?'

'No.' Catherine shook her head. 'They have gone from here. It was someone else.'

'Who?' the old lady demanded. 'Tell me now, Catherine. I am not a child.'

Catherine glanced at Frances, who nodded. 'It was Father Gautier,' Catherine said.

'What's this about Father Gautier?' None of them had seen Robert arrive, but all were glad to see him. 'Don't tell me you encountered him this morning.'

'We have,' Frances said, 'and—'

Robert interrupted her. 'Not here,' he said. 'Let's go somewhere more private.'

He led them into the manager's office. How he'd persuaded the manager to leave Catherine couldn't imagine, but he sat Béatrice down on the most comfortable chair, and dragging a wooden one from its place against the wall, he sat in front of her.

'You don't need to stay,' he said to Della and Frances. 'Catherine can help her grandmother.'

'They're staying,' said Catherine firmly. 'They are as much part of it now as I am. They helped me rescue Grandmère from the convent, and they helped me get her away from Father Gautier just now. So, Robert, take it or leave it.'

Della and Frances grinned as Robert looked a bit nonplussed. He opened his mouth to argue, but Catherine bent as though to take Béatrice's arm and lead her out, so he shut it again. 'Oh Christ,' he said eventually. 'Let them stay.'

He began his questions by asking Béatrice about what she and Jean had done at the farm for the Resistance.

'We let the boys stay with us,' she said. 'We fed them, and Jean drove them in his van when they needed to get somewhere. Sometimes they would bring weapons for us to hide. We put them in the barn, in the hay. Once, they brought us an English pilot who had been shot down. Him we hid for three weeks before he was handed on to someone who was going to get him on a fishing boat.' She paused, thinking back. 'I don't know what happened to him, but then another Englishman came; Father Gautier brought him.' She turned to Catherine and reached out her hand. 'He said he was your husband, *chérie*. Christopher. He told me all about you and baby Lili. He said he missed you very much.'

Catherine struggled to hold back the tears, but Robert said sharply, 'When was this? Can you remember the date?'

Béatrice shook her head slowly. 'I am not sure. It was in the spring, before they came for us. March, perhaps.

But,' she added with a smile, 'he was a good man and so handsome. He told me that Lili looked just like you.'

'What happened to him, Grandmère?' Catherine said, unable stay silent any more. 'Please tell me, because they are saying that he's dead.'

'Oh, *ma pauvre petite*.' Béatrice stood up and took Catherine in her arms. 'I don't know, child,' she said sadly. 'One day, he left with Father Gautier. We never saw him again.'

'Tell me about Father Gautier,' said Robert. 'When did he come to the village?'

'That was last year, in the summer. Poor Father Bernard had to go into hospital. He was taken ill one night and then we heard that he'd died. Father Gautier came to replace him, and a good thing too. He's very active in the parish. He does so many good things. Why, when the British Army came in and opened the prison, he came himself to get me and took me to the sisters. He said I needed to rest.' She shrugged. 'I didn't need that much of a rest, but how would he know? He's a man, even though he's a priest.'

She turned to the girls. 'I don't believe that he ordered that awful medicine for me, no matter what the reverend mother says. He wouldn't do that.'

'One more thing, for now,' said Robert. 'We'll talk again, but tell me this. Had you seen Guy de Montjoy before yesterday? The man who was driving the car when you left the convent.'

'Oh, the handsome one with the beautiful speaking voice. No.' She shook her head. 'I had never seen him before, but I tell you one thing: he was in the Resistance; he has that look about him.'

Chapter 21

Afterwards, to Catherine's relief, Béatrice pronounced that she was tired and she would have a little rest. 'I was up so early, *chérie*. It is habit, I suppose, but now what is to become of me? There is much to think about.'

It was as if reality was suddenly breaking through and she needed time to understand her changed circumstances. 'You rest, Grandmère,' said Catherine, giving her a kiss. 'We'll decide what to do later.'

Robert sat with the girls in the bar after Grandmère had gone upstairs. 'What exactly was Gautier doing this morning?' he asked.

'We were having breakfast and he was standing outside the cafe, watching Béatrice,' Frances said. 'Della and I managed to divert him so that Catherine could get her out the back.' She fixed Robert with a gimlet eye. 'What the hell is he up to? If you know, Robert, tell us, for God's sake.'

They had cups of coffee in front of them and Robert, after taking a sip, pushed his away. 'I'm not entirely sure,' he said. 'We knew about him, of course, and trusted him entirely. He was part of the line.'

'The line?' Frances was puzzled. 'What d'you mean?'

Robert didn't immediately answer. He was considering how much to say – that was obvious – and impatient, Frances said, 'Come on, Robert, we know about the Resistance: Guy and Madame Albert have vouched for that. France is mostly in Allied hands, so I don't think that Father Gautier's activities have to remain a secret.'

'You are extremely persistent, Frances Parnell,' Robert smiled. 'I know organisations who would love to have you on their books. So, I can tell you this much. Father Gautier was part of a network that helped Allied airmen and a few POW escapees get away from France. Each town had a link, and if such a pilot or whoever it was managed to contact them, they would be kept safe until they could be passed on to the next along the line. It worked well. Of course, the Resistance groups were key to all this. Now, in this area, Father Gautier was a contact. Guy de Montjoy was further south, near Caen. He was involved in the more vital activities, particularly leading up to the invasion.'

'And Christopher?' Catherine looked up. 'What was his role?'

'He was one of our agents. We dropped him into France to assist with the preparations for the invasion. But' – he shook his head slowly – 'he was betrayed and captured by the Gestapo. I told you that much before, Catherine. We lost contact with him in March, about the time your grandmother says he was at the farm.'

Catherine swallowed hard. 'Was he sent there deliberately? Did you know about my grandparents?'

Robert was silent again. It was as if he'd held secrets for so long that he couldn't bear to give them up. Finally he nodded. 'Yes,' he said. 'We knew that the line had been broken: too many of our agents had been captured. We suspected everyone in this area. Even your grandfather. Christopher's job was to root out the traitor, or traitors.'

As Catherine put her hand to her mouth, he added quickly, 'Your grandfather wasn't a traitor; we know that now. He paid a terrible price for his courage.'

'But what about Father Gautier?' asked Frances. 'Everybody loved him. Even Guy admired him, and Madame Albert won't hear a word against him.'

'I agree,' said Robert. 'We trusted him entirely, but' – his face clouded – 'there's no doubt about it, his behaviour recently has been tricky.'

'Guy said he was with him the night before he was arrested. D'you think...?' Frances left the question unsaid, and the three girls looked at each other, trying to digest this astonishing information. Robert seemed agitated; he was drumming his fingers on the table, as though counting off the possibilities of what might have happened.

They were still there at the table when Beau came in through the main door. 'Good,' he said. 'I was coming to look for you ladies and you, Robert. We'll have to call the show off for the rest of the week. Tommy's cold is worse, and I think Colin's coming down with it too. All we need is for you girls to catch it and Godfrey to get bronchitis or something and we're finished.' He turned to Robert. 'I'd be grateful if you could get in touch with the military authorities at the places where we were due to perform and explain what's happened. And as for the rest of us, well, I've spoken to Monsieur de Montjoy and he's quite happy for us to return to the chateau, so we'll pack up and set off after lunch.'

'Lovely,' said Frances, and Della gave a little whoop of joy.

'It's not that I don't like performing, you know,' she told Beau. 'But I just love being at that chateau. It makes me feel like a proper lady.' She caught his grin. 'And don't you say anything, Beau Bennett. I'm changing my ways. You won't know me soon.'

'I'll always know you, Della Stafford,' he smiled. 'Didn't George Formby say you had the best legs in the business?'

'What about my grandmother?' said Catherine. 'I can't leave her here on her own. I'll have to stay with her.'

Beau frowned. 'We won't be coming back this way, and next week we're going up to the front again. We can't take her there.'

Robert finally stopped drumming his fingers and stood up. 'Take her with you to the chateau, Catherine. I'm sure the housekeeper will look after her when you go on tour. And then a couple of weeks after that, we're going back to England, so she'll be safe at home with you and your mother.'

As Robert was leaving, Catherine ran after him and took his hand. 'Are you coming with us to the chateau?' she asked.

'Not immediately,' he said. 'Why?'

She found her cheeks growing pink. 'Oh, I just wondered,' she muttered.

He looked into her eyes. 'I'll be there in a couple of days,' he said. 'Unless something happens.'

'What sort of something?'

He smiled. 'Don't ask me, sweetheart, because I won't

tell you.' And with that he dropped a kiss on her cheek and walked away.

'It's all on again, is it?' asked Della, coming up behind Catherine.

'No. Yes. Oh, I don't know,' said Catherine impatiently. 'And there shouldn't be anything going on at all. It's so wrong.'

'I don't think falling in love is wrong.' Frances had joined them. 'I think it's wonderful and should be grabbed with both hands whenever it happens and with whoever it happens.'

'Who would have guessed that you were a romantic?' Della laughed.

'Not you, I suppose,' Frances sighed. 'Anyway, enough of this. We've got about three hours before we have to get on the bus. What shall we do? A bit of sightseeing?'

'Not me.' Catherine had spotted Guy de Montjoy entering the hotel. The smart black Citroën was parked outside, and he was dangling the keys from his hand. An idea occurred to her, and waving her hand, she walked towards him.

'Guy,' she said after they'd shaken hands, 'can I beg a favour from you?'

'Of course.'

'I see you still have the car. Will you take me to my grandmother's farm so I can pick up some clothes for her and a few other bits and pieces? She's coming back to England with us so that my mother can look after her. The company won't be returning to Amiens, so I have to get her things now.'

Guy nodded. He lifted his wrist and looked at his

watch. Catherine noticed that it looked expensive, as did, now she came to look at him properly, all of his clothes. What a difference from the tramp-like person he was when they'd first met.

'When d'you want to go?' he asked.

'Well, right now, if that's possible.'

'Give me ten minutes,' Guy said. 'I have a phone call to make and then I'll be glad to take you.'

Catherine ran upstairs to her room. Grandmère was still deeply asleep and Catherine quickly packed her bag and wrote a note for Béatrice, which she put on the bedside table on top of the old lady's rosary beads. She'd certainly find it there. Then she hurried along to the girls' room. 'I've begged a lift from Guy,' she said a little breathlessly. 'He's going to take me to the farm so I can pick up some of Grandmère's things. She's only got the stuff of hers that we took from the convent, and I'm sure she'd like some warmer clothes and possibly something of my grandfather. A photo, perhaps.'

'Can I come too?' Della pleaded. 'I'm all packed, and if I stay here, Frances will drag me around the cathedral or some other bloody place.'

Catherine laughed. 'Yes,' she said, 'of course.'

Frances grumbled, 'You miss all the culture of these places we visit. It's such a waste.'

'Never mind that.' Della put on her cap and set it at a jaunty angle. 'Are you coming with us, or are you going to wander around a freezing old church?'

'Oh hell.' Frances got her coat. 'I'm coming with, but I know I'll regret missing the opportunity.'

They were laughing when they walked into the lobby and were immediately stopped by a couple of officers who wanted their autographs. It was still a strange sensation for Frances, being asked to sign her name on odd pieces of paper, but Catherine and Della were used to it and could dash off several signatures in seconds.

'You girls put on a cracking show,' one of the officers grinned. 'Better than anything I've seen in the West End.'

'Thank you,' giggled Della, and pursing her lips, gave him a kiss on the cheek.

'Wow,' he said, and would have moved in for more but Frances saw Guy standing by his car and rattling the keys at them.

'Sorry, mate,' Della laughed. 'Different fish to fry.'

It was another cold day. Soggy grey mist hung in the air, obscuring the view so that the trees and buildings in the distance were wavering images, only becoming real when they drove close to them. They passed the village church, grey stone melting into the mist, looking almost insubstantial, as though if they came back tomorrow, it would have disappeared.

'This is a weird day,' Della shivered. 'The fog seems to be sucking the life out of everything.'

'Very poetic,' Frances grinned. 'Is that the sort of stuff you write to Tim?'

Della stuck out her tongue but made no other reply.

The farm buildings appeared out of the mist and they drove into the yard. There was another car parked in front of the barn, a small black Fiat, and the girls stared at it as they got out.

'Is that your grandfather's car?' asked Guy.

'I don't know,' said Catherine. 'He always had a van, as I remember, but maybe this was his too.'

'It wasn't here when we came last time,' Frances called.

312

She'd gone over to it to have a look through the windows. 'I wonder to whom it belongs?'

'Maybe that cousin, Jacques? Was that his name?' Della said.

Guy suddenly looked worried. He grabbed Catherine's arm and softly called to the other girls. 'Stay here,' he said. 'I'll go in first. You never know.'

'What's he talking about?' whispered Della, as they stood by the barn, watching Guy stop outside the back door. 'Jesus, look,' she squeaked, as they saw Guy take a pistol out from under his jacket. 'He's got a gun.'

'Everybody's got guns,' hissed Frances, trying to calm her down. 'There's a war on.'

'I haven't,' Della moaned, and then, 'Jesus, Mary and Joseph, he's going inside.'

They waited, staring at the back door for several minutes, and then Catherine said, 'There's nothing happening. Let's follow him.'

'Alright,' Frances agreed, and with Della clutching on to her hand, she walked towards the door.

Suddenly a shot rang out, followed almost immediately by another. The girls froze and instantly a figure stumbled out of the door and started to run across the yard.

'Stop him!' Guy was at the door, waving his pistol towards the running man, and without thinking, Frances dived at him and caught him round the ankles, just like Hugo used to do to her when he was practising rugby tackles. The man fell heavily to the ground, air expelling from his chest in a loud groan, and he uncontrollably rolled over and over, ending up with a sharp crack as his head made contact with a stone horse trough. A gun flew out of his hand and Frances yelled, 'Get it!' and watched as Della, stepping delicately through the mud in her high-heeled shoes, picked it up.

She pointed it at the man with a shaking hand and screamed, 'Shall I shoot him?'

'No, for Christ's sake, don't,' grunted Frances, scrambling to her feet. 'And give me that bloody gun.' Almost reluctantly, Della surrendered it, but stood over the man, staring down at him.

Catherine stepped forward to look at the person lying on the ground, his eyes closed and blood spurting from a wound in his chest. '*Mon Dieu*,' she cried. 'It's Father Gautier.'

Guy ran over. 'He shot at me,' he said. 'I shot back. Did I hit him?'

'I'd say.' Frances unwound her scarf from round her neck and stuffed it under Gautier's black jacket and pressed down hard on the wound. 'We'd better get him to hospital.'

'What about you?' asked Catherine. 'Are you hurt?'

'No.' Guy shook his head. His voice was shaky. 'He missed.'

'What the hell was he doing' – Della had found her voice and was now furious – 'in the house?'

'He was upstairs,' Guy said. 'I think he'd been in the roof. Look, he's covered in dust.' He gave himself a little shake. 'He shot at me as I came up the stairs.'

Frances looked up. 'We've got to get him to the hospital, now. Catherine, you go and get your stuff and Guy and I will get him into the back of the car.'

'We could leave him and call the police and an ambulance,' said Guy. 'I saw a phone box in the village.' It was as though Guy couldn't bear any more contact with the priest.

'But he could die while waiting for an ambulance,' Frances said, staring hard at Guy. 'If we take him, he might have a chance.'

The battle going on in Guy's mind was obvious on his face. He wanted nothing more to do with Father Gautier. He'd made up his mind that the man was a traitor.

But Frances stood firm. 'We have to,' she said.

'Alright,' said Guy, giving in, 'but get him into the back of his own car. I don't want him bleeding all over mine.' He thought for a moment. 'Frances, you drive his car, Della can hold the scarf in place, and Catherine can hold the gun on him. I'll drive mine and lead you to the hospital.'

'We didn't sign up for this,' Della wailed, as they manoeuvred the helpless body of Father Gautier into the back of his little car. She got in beside him and pressed her hand over his wound. 'What if he dies?'

'Then he'll be dead. Stop moaning,' Frances said, the fright of the shooting making her angry. She looked down at Gautier. 'Is he still unconscious?'

'Yes,' Della whispered, 'and I hope he stays that way. I couldn't bear to talk to him.'

Catherine hurried through the house, picking up clothes for Grandmère and some toiletries. She found Béatrice's favourite Coty talcum powder, in its ivory shaker, and wrapping it in a towel, added it to the collection of clothes. Finally she picked up the photo frame with the picture of her with Béatrice and Jean, and put everything in an old leather travelling case. With a last look round, she went outside, and carefully locking the door, put the key in her purse.

'Ready?' asked Guy. He still looked shocked.

'Are you alright?' she asked.

'Mm,' he nodded. 'It's just that we trusted him and now... I don't know.'

The drive back to Amiens was the worst twenty minutes Frances had ever known. Apart from finding the Fiat difficult to drive, she kept looking in the driving mirror, trying to see if Father Gautier was still alive. Catherine held the gun, but it was unnecessary. The man was motionless.

'Is he still breathing?' she asked, and Della nodded.

Then she gave a little scream. 'He's opened his eyes.'

Catherine leant over the front seat and looked at him. His eyes were flickering, opening and closing as though he was coming round and wasn't sure where he was. Blood was seeping onto his white dog collar and onto his chin, and he slowly lifted a hand to wipe it away. As he did so, he gave a little groan of pain and Della looked up at Catherine. 'What shall I do?' she whispered.

'Do nothing,' commanded Frances, from the driving seat. 'Except what you're doing.'

Gautier opened his eyes properly; they were brown, which sat oddly with his fair hair and pale skin. He looked puzzled, as though he couldn't remember what had happened, and when he raised his head to Della and then across to Catherine, they could see the recognition dawning.

'You are Catherine,' he whispered, looking directly at her. Strangely, he didn't try to move. He seemed to have given up entirely.

She nodded, hating him speaking to her.

'You have Béatrice?'

She nodded again and Frances, looking in the driving mirror, spat, 'No thanks to you.'

He coughed and a trickle of blood slipped from between his lips and onto Della's hand. 'Oh God,' she squealed, 'the bugger's spitting blood on me.'

'I am sorry, mademoiselle,' he murmured, still staring at Catherine. 'Forgive me.'

'I can never forgive you. You're a traitor,' she answered, her voice choking. 'And a murderer.'

'Not a murderer.' His eyes closed again, his voice fading away.

'He knew who I was,' Catherine whispered. She shivered and her hand shook so that the gun waved in the air.

'Put that bloody gun down,' shouted Della. 'You'll kill me, not him.'

'But how did he know?'

Frances, concentrating on following Guy through the now pouring rain, said, 'He saw your photograph in the farm. You haven't changed much since then.'

Catherine nodded and looked down at the unconscious man. He was barely breathing, and blood continued to dribble down the side of his mouth. He'll be dead soon, she thought, and wondered why she wasn't triumphant.

'I think we're nearly at the hospital,' shouted Frances. 'Guy is turning through some entrance gates. And, Catherine, make sure you've still got that gun on him.'

'I don't think it matters,' she answered. 'I think he's dead.'

'I'm going to be sick!' Della screamed, and tried to push Father Gautier off her lap.

'Hush!' commanded Frances, as she parked behind Guy's car, outside the hospital entrance. It took a couple of minutes for him to go inside and come out with a doctor and two nurses, who were wheeling a trolley.

Catherine put the gun in her handbag as the medics approached and Frances nodded. 'Good idea,' she whispered.

The back passenger door was opened and the doctor looked in. 'How long ago did this happen?' he asked, removing the scarf and looking at the bloody mess that was Father Gautier's jacket and shirt.

'As I said,' Guy replied, 'we found him like this beside his car about fifteen minutes ago. These ladies have bravely driven him back into town.'

'Right' – the doctor nodded to the nurses – 'get him onto the trolley. No time now for further explanations, but if you'll wait inside, monsieur, and also the ladies, I'm sure the police will have some questions.'

They watched for a moment as Father Gautier was wheeled into the hospital; then Guy said, 'Come on, into my car. Let's get away from here. We don't need to be involved.'

The girls looked at each other, then without further comment got into the black Citroën and were silent on the short drive back to the hotel.

'Will you tell Major Lennox?' asked Frances, as they got out.

'Of course,' said Guy. 'If I can find him.'

Grandmère was cross that they'd been to the farm without her, but pleased that Catherine had brought her clothes. She clutched the photograph to her heart and shed a few tears. 'I don't know where Jean is buried,' she sobbed. 'How can I mourn him?'

'We will find him, after the war,' promised Catherine. 'And he'll be buried in the churchyard with the other war heroes.'

They sat together on the bus and Catherine explained that they were going to a big house that was the company's base in France. 'You'll like it,' she said. 'The housekeeper, Madame Farcy, is very kind and cooks lovely food.'

'Lovely food, eh?' Some of Béatrice's old spirit had returned. 'We'll see about that.'

After a while, she closed her eyes and drifted off. Catherine got up and went to sit beside Della. She had changed out of her uniform skirt and was wearing a pair of green slacks.

'D'you think that blood will sponge off?' she said miserably. 'That bugger bled all over me.'

'I'm sure it will,' Catherine smiled, and thinking back to her conversation with Béatrice, she said, 'Just think, now you're a real war heroine. Bloodied in battle.'

'I suppose I am,' said Della, looking more cheerful. 'But what a thing to happen. I can't quite believe it. Me, holding a dead body.'

'We don't know for sure that he was dead. I wonder what Robert will say when Guy tells him.'

'If he tells him. He didn't seem too keen to me.'

No, he didn't, thought Catherine. He's another one playing a strange game.

'The tarts are subdued today!' Captain Fortescue's fruity voice broke into Catherine's head. 'What can have happened?'

She looked across the aisle and there, a couple of seats ahead, the doll's wooden eyes were staring at her. Baxter himself was looking to the front, but she could see his arm and shoulder move as he worked the levers on the doll.

'Oh Christ,' groaned Della, and made to get up, but before she could, the lumbering figure of Godfrey hove into view.

'Stop your bad manners, immediately, sir,' he roared, pointing his finger at Baxter. 'Your behaviour is unforgivable. Beau' – he walked unsteadily up the bus until he was beside the leader – 'sack him now or I'm finished. This cannot go on.'

How Frances kept the bus on the road Catherine didn't know, because she kept looking over her shoulder at Godfrey and Beau, and furiously nodding her agreement. Catherine looked back at Tommy and Colin, but they were asleep, having dosed themselves up with quantities of aspirin and whisky. Godfrey hadn't bothered with the aspirin but had made full use of the half-bottle of Teacher's that he had in his jacket pocket.

'Oh God, is there no end?' said Beau angrily. 'You're drunk, Godfrey. Sit down.'

'Drunk possibly,' he agreed, desperately grasping on to the back of the seat to keep his balance. 'But correct in all other aspects.' He sat down heavily in the seat opposite Beau and immediately went to sleep.

'What a toper,' cackled Captain Fortescue, then turned his head back to Catherine and Della. 'Off for a foursome with the handsome count, were we?'

Catherine stood up. That's enough, she thought. I won't put up with this for one more moment.

Beau walked down the aisle. 'Sit down, Catherine,' he said softly. 'Let me deal with this.' And he bent his head down to Baxter's and whispered in his ear. Whatever he said worked. The doll's head was lowered into its body and peace was restored. When Baxter and Beau were dropped off at the officers' club in Caen, everybody breathed a sigh of relief.

'I'm glad we're going home soon,' said Della to Catherine. 'I think I'll go up to Liverpool to stay with Ma and the kids. I need a bit of family. I want to tell them about Tim.'

'Are you really serious about him? If you married him, it would mean a totally different lifestyle for you. And, Della, think. You hardly know him.'

'I know all I need to know,' Della said. 'I think I've been searching for him all my life. If he wants me, and I'm pretty sure he does, he can have me. I'll be the best doctor's wife in Ireland.' She was quiet for a while and then said, 'There's just a few things I have to tell him first.'

'What things?'

'Just things.' Della wouldn't be drawn further.

Chapter 22

Béatrice woke up as they were driving along the tree-lined approach to the chateau. 'Where is this?' she asked, looking out of the window.

'It's where we are going to stay,' smiled Catherine. 'Look.' They turned the last bend and the chateau came into view.

'Oh,' Béatrice gasped. 'Not truly?'

'Yes, truly.'

Guy was already there, his car parked by the front door, and was standing with Madame Farcy waiting to greet them. He had obviously explained Béatrice's situation, so that when Catherine helped her grandmother off the bus and went to introduce her, Madame Farcy fell upon the old lady and went into an excited greeting with many remarks about the horrors of the occupation and effusive praise for all those who'd worked for the Resistance.

'Now, Madame Albert' – she'd taken Béatrice's arm – 'I can show you to a room on your own on the ground floor. I think it will be easier for you,' and she and Béatrice had gone off together, chatting happily.

The girls flopped onto their beds in the big room on the first floor. 'Isn't this heavenly?' said Frances, pushing off her shoes. 'It's like coming home.'

'It might be for you,' Della mumbled. She had stripped

off her uniform jacket and was pulling on a green ribbed jumper. 'You've seen my house. You could fit the whole of it into the kitchen here. Still, I do love this place.'

They were at the chateau for five days, enjoying being in the house and even the grounds, although the weather was freezing. Tommy and Colin got over their colds, but Tommy, although he said he was alright, seemed to have been left a little more breathless, and there was a pinched look about his cheeks.

'I'm fine,' he insisted when Catherine expressed her concern. 'Don't fuss.'

The card game had resumed, and in the evenings the girls found themselves joining in too.

'I'm hopeless at this,' said Catherine, and turning to the other girls, said, 'We shouldn't play. They're taking all our money.'

'Speak for yourself,' Della answered. 'I'm getting the hang of it now. I'll bankrupt the lot of you.'

'You'll have to give up poker if you marry Dr Tim,' Frances warned.

'No I won't,' Della shouted, slamming down her hand with a cry of joy. 'The Irish love playing cards.'

Guy came and went, but never wanted to talk about the shooting at the farm.

'Will the police catch up with us?' asked Frances one morning, when she encountered him on the corridor outside the big bedroom. He was sleeping in his old room, next door to theirs.

'No,' he said. 'They won't. They have no need.'

'But,' she protested, 'surely they have every need. A man was shot, and you were shot at.'

He twitched his shoulders. She could see that he didn't

want this conversation. 'They have understood the circumstances,' he muttered.

'You mean,' Frances said, 'that Robert or someone like him has leant on them.'

'Precisely.'

'Doesn't it mean anything to you?' As she said it, Frances noticed a tic at the side of his mouth where a muscle was involuntarily twitching, and knew that her question was foolish. This was a man who'd seen too many shootings, too much death.

'It means something,' he said slowly. 'Perhaps it means that I never want to do it again. That I just want to be a farmer, with an orchard and, perhaps, a wife and children.'

'Yes,' she said, 'I can see that.'

Robert turned up one morning, with a bundle of post. There was a letter for Béatrice from her daughter, which she read with much joy and many tears. Catherine had written to her mother on the day that they'd rescued her and already here was the reply. Honorine was so excited about seeing Grandmère after all these years. *I have told Lili that her great-grandmother is coming to live with us. Maybe she doesn't understand exactly, but it makes it more real for me.*

Catherine was sitting with Robert in the large salon when Béatrice came in with her letter. 'Today, I am happy,' she said. 'I thought that feeling had gone forever, that never again would there be something to look forward to. But now,' she smiled, 'perhaps my life will take a new turn.'

'I'm glad for you, Grandmère,' said Catherine, and the old lady leant down and stroked her cheek.

'It will happen for you too, *chérie*. Just wait. Now, you will excuse me. Madame Farcy and I have to make the lunch. Her soup is good, but' – she bustled to the door – 'I can improve it.'

Robert laughed. 'I'd love to be a fly on the wall when those two old biddies argue about recipes.'

'I wonder who wins,' said Catherine.

'Oh, your grandmother, I think. Every time.' He took her hand. 'Can you get away for a night?' he asked. 'I want to take you to my house again.'

Catherine lifted her face to stare at him. 'Why?' she said.

'You know why,' he answered. 'We need to be alone together. We have to know if it means something.' He waited for her to speak, and when she didn't, he groaned and grasped her hand tighter. 'Don't be naïve, Catherine,' he said. 'You know how I feel about you.'

She could feel her cheeks going pink and looked to the door in case one of her friends burst in. 'What excuse could I give?' she whispered. 'To Grandmère and to the girls.'

'I've thought of that,' he answered. 'I could say that the military authorities want to quiz you more about your husband and you'll need to stay the night in Bayeux. Madame Albert will accept that, don't you think?'

'I suppose so,' said Catherine slowly. 'The girls will guess it's a lie, though.'

'Do you mind that?'

She looked down at his hand clasped in hers and thought about what Grandmère had said about being learning to be happy again. 'No, Robert. I don't mind at all.'

They left before lunch, driving away from the chateau in Robert's Jeep. It was raining and he'd put the canvas roof up so that sitting beside him, cut off from the outside, Catherine felt that she and Robert could be the only two people in the world. She was excited and nervous at the same time, and glancing at him out of the corner of her eye, she knew that he felt the same. He was tapping his fingers on the steering wheel in a familiar movement, and when they were held up at a road barrier outside Caen, he barked at the corporal manning it for not carrying his rifle and being sloppily dressed.

It wasn't like him, and once back on the road again, she said, 'We could go back to the chateau if you're regretting this idea.'

He suddenly screeched the Jeep to a halt at the side of the road and she had to reach for the door handle to stop herself falling forward. Before she could draw breath, he shouted, 'I'm scared, you stupid girl. Don't you realise?'

She was bewildered and then she peered through the windscreen and her heart skipped a beat. 'Are we in danger here? Have the Germans broken through?'

'No,' he groaned.

'Then what? What are you scared of?'

'Of you, Catherine. Of you.' And he grabbed her by the shoulders and kissed her hard on the mouth.

'Of me?' she said, when they had broken away and stared at each other. 'How could you be?'

'Because you're beautiful and talented, and I'm neither,' he muttered. 'I see you on stage, lifting an audience to the heights of emotion, and I am so in awe of you that I can barely breathe.'

'But that's my job, Robert. It's only a job.'

'No, I can't believe that.'

She smiled. 'Well, maybe not, but it shouldn't make you scared.'

He shrugged, moving tense shoulders awkwardly. 'Then, perhaps,' he said, 'it's because of Christopher.'

Her smile disappeared and the suppressed anxiety of guilt started up again. 'What about him?' she asked.

'You loved him. Still do, I think. I suppose I'm jealous.' He had his face turned away, looking out of the windscreen at the raindrops trickling down the glass, and Catherine followed his eyes, watching the rain too.

'I did love him,' she said, 'and if he returned today, tomorrow, next month, next year, I would feel the same.' She took a deep breath. 'But you know, Robert, the truth is, I'm beginning to forget what he looks like, how he sounds when he laughs, and' – she swallowed the nervous lump in her throat – 'the feel of his hands on me.'

As she was saying it, the realisation of its meaning was washing over her. Was this admission, spoken out loud for the first time, the reason I've been feeling guilty? she wondered. Am I ready, like Grandmère, for life to take a new turn?

She turned to face him and found that he was looking at her with an expression that could only be called hope. 'I think that you've been telling me the truth all along, Robert,' she said. 'My husband is dead. I must move on.'

'Oh, my sweet girl,' he said, taking her in his arms again, and they remained locked together for many more minutes until their embrace was disturbed by a short convoy of heavy trucks passing by, tooting their horns and making the Jeep rock in their wake.

'Oh God,' laughed Robert. 'Let's get away from here. Besides,' he added, starting up the engine, 'I'm starving. We need something to keep our strength up for...well...' He grinned at her. 'Well, I'll leave that. You're already blushing.'

An Atlantic storm had blown in, but the house on the headland was standing strong, bravely looking out to sea, while the wind and rain blasted sand from the beach below onto the veranda and sifted it through the closed shutters.

'Will Agathe be there?' asked Catherine, as they approached along the stony lane. 'The shutters are closed.'

'But smoke is coming from the chimney,' Robert pointed out. 'She will be in the kitchen or in her studio at the back. Those are her favourite places.'

He was right. When they walked into the hall, she came out of a door at the far end with a shout of joy.

'Monsieur Robert,' she crooned. 'At last. You haven't been here for weeks. And' – she grabbed Catherine's hand – 'with the beautiful Madame Fletcher. What could be better?'

Catherine shook hands and smiled. Agathe looked as wild as ever, her long black hair uncombed but with a pencil holding some of it in an uncertain twist on top of her head. Her bright red smock was decorated with splashes of paint, and there was even a dab of it on her cheek, and another streaked along her wiry forearm. She was quite the most unusual person Catherine had ever met, but she found her impossible not to like.

Agathe clung on to Robert's arm. 'Since your phone

call,' she said, 'I have made up the beds, and there is a fire in the salon. There is fresh bread, wine and a rabbit stew in the oven, but if you don't mind, I must go to the village. My mother is ill' – she shrugged her thin shoulders – 'and because of this she has consented to my helping in her care. She forgets that she would never speak to me again. It is good.'

'Go, Agathe,' said Robert. 'Build a bridge while you can. We will be fine.'

'Thank you, dear boy.' She picked up a small canvas bag and swung a green waterproof cape from a hook by the door. 'I will come in the morning with bread and milk.'

'I'll give you a lift,' said Robert. 'The weather's too bad for your bike.' And turning to Catherine, he said, 'I'll be five minutes. Go and warm yourself by the fire.'

By the time he'd returned, she'd stripped off her uniform jacket and was sitting on the thick, brightly coloured rug, toasting her stockinged feet in front of the log fire. She felt strangely at peace with herself, as though something that had worried her for months had simply faded away. Whatever happens now, she thought, is fine. Christopher has gone and I'm ready to love again.

Robert knelt down beside her. 'Your cheeks are glowing,' he said.

'It must be the heat from the fire,' she murmured, putting a hand up to feel them.

'I'm not sure,' he whispered. 'Perhaps it's because you know what's going to happen next.'

And when his mouth lowered onto hers, she put her arms around his neck and pulled him to her. Whatever happened next, she was ready for it.

They made love there, on the rug in front of the fire. Outside, the wind howled and rain beat sharply against the shutters and rattled the shingles on the roof, but they didn't notice it. He paused once, as he was unbuttoning her blouse. 'Are you sure?' he asked, his voice breathless, and she opened her eyes and looked him fully in the face.

'Yes, Robert. I'm sure.'

Afterwards, they lay together, spent by lovemaking and each reliving the passion. She had been startled by his power, by the almost ruthless way he'd taken her, but she'd been equally excited and without shame explored his muscled, willing body.

'I love you,' he said, rolling over and looking at her. 'I think I have for months, even though...'

'Even though what?'

'Even though you didn't feel the same.'

Catherine reached over and pushed a lock of Robert's hair off his face. 'I didn't feel the same,' she said slowly. 'I was attracted to you, but it wasn't love.'

'And now?'

'Now? Now I think I do.' She sat up and stared at the flames and listened to the logs splitting – bursting apart with little showers of golden sparks. 'No,' she said, and alarmed, he sat up too. 'No,' she repeated. 'Not think. I know. I love you, Robert.'

He held her then, each revelling in the intimacy until the feelings became too much and they made love again.

Catherine cried afterwards and Robert, worried, tried to comfort her.

'What is it?' he asked, his voice full of concern. 'Did I hurt you? Are you sorry we did this?'

'No,' she laughed through her tears. 'I'm just so happy, that's all. I couldn't hold back the emotion.'

'Never hold back, my darling,' Robert said. 'I want to experience everything with you. Everything.'

They lay in each other's arms barely noticing that it was getting darker and that the light from the fire was beginning to fade, until with a groan, Robert sat up and looked at the flickering embers in the grate. 'It's going out,' he said, 'or it will be if I don't attend to it. D'you mind if I get up?'

'No, you idiot. And I should go and look at the casserole that Agathe left. For some reason,' she grinned, 'I feel suddenly hungry.'

They ate rabbit stew and drank red wine that evening, barely talking, but gazing at each other, in a sort of wonder. 'Did that really happen?' asked Robert, looking at the curve of Catherine's cheek and at the tiny ringlets that danced on her hairline above her ears.

'Well, I think I felt someone interfering with me,' Catherine teased. 'Was that you?'

'Let's go to bed.' He put down his glass and grabbed her hand.

Later, they slept, both exhausted by overwhelming emotion. She woke once in the night and for a moment she was back in her little house with Christopher lying beside her. But only for a moment. Robert turned and, muttering in his sleep, put his arms around her and she drifted back.

When she woke, it was morning and pale grey light was streaming through the shutters. Robert wasn't beside her and she looked at the dip in the mattress that his body had made and smiled to herself. What a night, she thought, and then got up to find the bathroom.

'Agathe's here,' he said, walking into the room with two cups of coffee. She was standing by the windows looking out on a restless sea. Gulls swooped and dived over the headland, their presence forecasting the approach of another storm.

Catherine bit her lip. 'What will she think?' she asked, suddenly embarrassed. 'Will she think I'm a terrible slut?'

'God, no,' Robert laughed. 'That's not Agathe. Besides, wasn't she a terrible slut herself? Here, get back into bed and drink your coffee. Make room for me.'

When they finally went downstairs, they found that Agathe had made a breakfast for them with fresh warm rolls and apricot jam. She'd put slices of ham and cheese on the table and hard-boiled eggs.

'I won't ask where you got the ham,' said Robert, 'because it's probably black market.'

Agathe wagged her finger at him. 'Still the cheeky boy,' she said.

'How is your mother?' asked Catherine.

'She is no better and no worse. Not as bad as she thinks she is, but prepared to let me in her house as long as I wash her linen and make a few meals. The neighbours were surprised to see me,' she laughed. 'The priest's mouth fell so wide open when he saw me that if it had been summer, he would have swallowed a quantity of flies!'

They left soon after, with hugs for Robert and a kiss on both cheeks for Catherine. 'Come back, very soon,' Agathe told them. 'I can see that it has done you good. Oh' – she looked beyond the veranda to the sea, smiling – 'I remember so many wonderful nights in this house. The days were good, but the nights, magnificent.'

Catherine laughed all the way to Bayeux. 'I do like Agathe,' she said.

'I'm glad,' Robert nodded. 'My wife hated her. She thought she was a trollop.'

It was the first time he'd talked about his wife since all those weeks ago, when she'd asked him whether he was married. Now the mention of her was like a little stone dropping into her stomach and her laugh faded away. He'd said that they'd been drifting apart before she'd gone to Berlin and she guessed that he would divorce her, if she was still alive. But there is a child, Catherine thought. And I have a child too. Darling Lili who needs a father.

'What was she called?' Catherine hoped the question sounded casual.

'Ulrike,' he said. 'She was the daughter of the professor who taught me languages in Berlin. We were happy at first, but she loathed England. Couldn't settle at all, and in the end she went home. She said it was for a holiday, but I think I knew she wasn't coming back.'

'Did you miss her?'

'Not really. No, not at all. We'd argued constantly in those last two years. But' – his face dropped into sadness – 'I miss my son. I wonder about him all the time. He would be about eight now, if he's still alive.'

Catherine put her hand on his shoulder. 'There's no reason why he shouldn't be,' she said softly.

'We've bombed the hell out of Berlin. Thousands have been killed.'

'And thousands haven't,' she argued. 'They've got shelters like we have.'

He drove on for a while and then took his hand off

the steering wheel and put it on hers. 'Thank you,' he said.

'Robert, can I ask you something else?'

'Of course. Anything.'

'Why won't you get rid of Eric Baxter?'

There was silence and Catherine thought that for some reason she'd overstepped a mark, that she'd strayed into territory that was somehow denied to her. But then how could it be? she thought angrily. The Bennett Players were all as important as each other, and if one of them was upsetting the others and hadn't been sacked, then she needed to know why.

She was just about to say all this when he said, 'I can't. Baxter has to stay. I can only tell you this, Catherine. He is useful to us.'

'Who's us?' she replied crossly. 'Certainly not anyone in the company. And, Robert, admit it. He's blackmailing Beau; we all know that. We've seen what he's doing, and God knows he'd probably blackmail the lot of us if he could.' She stopped speaking then, realising what she'd just said. He could have easily blackmailed Della over her mother's moonshine business, and what if he'd got wind of Frances's little boy? And then there were the others, Tommy and Colin and Godfrey. Why hadn't he had a go at them? Or had he?

'He won't touch you,' Robert said. 'I promise you that. He won't blackmail you or any of the rest of the company.'

'How d'you know?'

'I know. Leave it, Catherine.' His voice was hard and clipped. He was back in Major Lennox mode and she knew that it would be useless to argue. And that was a pity, because she wanted to know about Davey Jones and his mysterious death. The more she thought about it, the more strange it seemed. He turned up, out of the blue, did a couple of shows and then he was killed. She shot a sideways glance at Robert. Did she dare mention that?

'You're quiet,' he said suddenly.

'What d'you expect?' she sighed. 'I have a lot to think about.'

'Good thoughts, I hope?'

'About last night?' she smiled. 'Of course. It was wonderful. It'll show all over my face and everyone will know and I don't care.' She laughed. 'Such a slut.'

'You are,' he agreed cheerfully. 'But you're my slut.' Then his smile faded and he turned his head to look at her. 'You are mine, Catherine, aren't you?'

'Yes,' she said simply. 'I love you.'

When Robert dropped her back to the chateau with a swift kiss and a promise to see her soon, Della greeted her with joy. 'Thank God you're back,' she grinned. 'I'm bored to death.'

'Where is everybody?' asked Catherine, taking off her coat and going into the salon to warm herself by the fire.

'The boys are off with old man Farcy,' grumbled Della. 'They've gone to some bloody local horse race. I ask you, a horse race in the middle of the war. They've only gone for the betting.'

'Well, where's Frances?'

'Don't talk to me about her.' Della was really furious. 'She and Guy are messing about in the fields.'

'Messing about?' Catherine was astonished. 'Surely you can't mean…'

'No, I don't.' She shot an amused look at Catherine.

'I think you're the one who's been messing about, and don't deny it. It's written all over you.'

'Alright, I won't deny it. But where's Frances?'

'Yesterday, she and Guy were pulling out old fruit trees with chains and the tractor. Frances was driving that tractor like she'd been born at the wheel. And early this morning, they went to buy some cattle. They're in the field with them now.'

Catherine laughed. 'We knew she was a farmer. She told us.'

'That's at home,' Della growled. 'She's a performer here.'

'Well, I'm back now, and when I've said hello to Grandmère, we can have a good chat.' Catherine grinned as she left the room. 'And no. I won't tell you the details.'

They were a jolly group that evening. The boys had returned from the races flush with money and in high spirits.

'It was a local thing,' explained Tommy, 'but we enjoyed it, didn't we, lads?'

'We liked the free drinks,' Colin said, 'especially Godfrey.' It seemed that after the point-to-point finished, the participants had retired to a hotel, where Tommy played the piano in exchange for a few beers. Godfrey, who'd been dozing on his chair, woke up and said, 'Did I hear someone offering a beer?'

Frances was happy too. She'd been doing something she loved and her face had an outdoors glow that suited her. 'I wish my father had money like Guy,' she confided to Catherine and Della. 'I could really boost up the stock and make the place into a going concern. But he hasn't, so we can't.'

'Oh, something will turn up,' said Catherine. 'It always does.'

'Oh, isn't she the happy one,' Della whispered so that the boys wouldn't hear. 'There's nothing like a bit of "how's your father" to buck you up. Come on, Catherine, tell us. Was he any good?'

She didn't answer. Her smile told them all they wanted to know.

Two days later, she had a visitor. They were in the salon, rehearsing, when Madame Farcy came to tell her that there was a man waiting for her in the hall. 'I thought he had come for Monsieur le Compte,' she said. 'He looks like an official. But I told him that Monsieur is in Paris for a few days. He asked for you. Take him to the small salon. I'll bring some coffee.'

'Thank you,' said Catherine, and walked into the hall. Her heart was doing somersaults. Had someone come with news of Christopher? Standing there in the gloom of another November day was Larry Best.

'Good heavens,' Catherine said, trying to calm her breathing. 'You're the last person I expected to see. Whatever are you doing in France?'

'I've been here for a few days,' he said, and gave her a lopsided grin. 'I thought I'd come and see how you are.'

'Have you come to tell me about my husband?' Half of her wanted to know, but the memory of lying in Robert's arms clouded out Christopher's face and she could feel a flush rising up her neck and into her cheeks. Fortunately Madame Farcy arrived then with a tray of coffee and some little cakes, followed by Béatrice, who had come to see who her granddaughter's visitor turned out to be.

Catherine introduced him as a colleague of Robert's and left it at that, allowing the two old ladies to believe that he was some sort of entertainments officer.

When they'd gone, Catherine turned back to Larry. 'Those two days in the country,' she said. 'I wasn't really there for you to teach me, was I? You wanted to see what I knew about Chris. Have you found him?'

'No,' he said. 'Sadly, not a trace of him. I'm so very sorry. We did think that Father Gautier might be able to help us, but he died last night without regaining consciousness.'

She didn't know what to say or even to think. The one person who might have told her was dead and she was still in limbo.

'He told me he was sorry,' she said bleakly. 'In the car, when we were taking him to hospital. I called him a traitor and a murderer. He said, "Not a murderer."'

'I suppose it depends on how you define murder.' Larry Best took a gulp of the coffee and nodded his appreciation of it. 'He was certainly a traitor, but his motives for giving away our agents are blurred. We don't know what happened, and we lost track of him for a while. But you found him.' He grinned again. 'I thought you would.'

'It was you,' she said, realisation dawning. 'You sent that note.'

'Mm,' he nodded. 'Lennox wasn't keen, but I knew you'd go after him.'

'I might have been killed,' Catherine said.

'You might have, indeed. But we are at war and it's what agents do.'

'*Mon Dieu*,' Catherine said. 'You are very ruthless, and I am not an agent.'

338

'No, and that's a pity. I wish we had found you sooner, because I'm sure there's an element of ruthlessness about you too. You sing like an angel, but underneath you're as hard as I am.'

'I don't think so,' smiled Catherine, getting up. 'I have a heart.'

The next morning, Robert turned up, with Beau limping along beside him.

'Good news,' said Beau, when everyone was gathered in the salon. 'We're off tomorrow to some camps at the front.' He looked at a piece of paper. 'Yes, a forward camp first and then to a field hospital. So, a bit of rehearsing today, I suggest, and packing. And don't forget your tin hats.'

Della beamed. 'Maybe the field hospital is where Tim is. Oh, I do hope so.'

Frances was the only one who didn't look particularly pleased. 'Guy wanted to get in some ploughing,' she moaned. 'He's way behind this year. I hoped we would be staying here a bit longer.'

'For Christ's sake,' snorted Della. 'You're supposed to be an entertainer and an administrator, not a bloody farm labourer. He can get on with it by himself.' She stretched her legs and did a couple of squats. 'I do need exercise,' she groaned. 'Or I'll never be able to do the splits again. That's what the men like and I intend to give it to them.' And using the back of the sofa as a barre, she bent and pliéd, while Frances discussed the tour with Beau and attached his piece of paper to her clipboard.

Catherine followed Robert back into the hall, where

after a swift look round, he took her in his arms. 'I've missed you,' he said.

'It's only been a day,' Catherine whispered.

'And a night, my darling.'

They were still kissing when Frances and Della came to find them. 'Oops,' laughed Della, hands on hips and enjoying the scene. Frances pulled her back out of the hall, saying, 'Sorry, we didn't mean to disturb you. Er...carry on.'

When they'd gone, Catherine asked, 'Are you coming with us tomorrow? To the front.'

He nodded. 'I am, tomorrow and the day after, at the field hospital, but then I have to go back to England with Major Best. He didn't get anything out of Gautier, so although we know who blew all our agents in the area, we don't know why.'

'He was a collaborator. Isn't that enough?'

He twisted his uniform cap round in his hands, taking his time to answer. 'Possibly,' he said. 'But I can't tell you more. Now' – he put on his cap and straightened his jacket – 'I have to get back to Caen. I'll see you tomorrow, darling girl.' And with another kiss on her willing lips he walked out and into his Jeep.

Chapter 23

They drove into the camp in the early afternoon of a day where the weather had closed in and the rain had changed to sleet. The bus had been left at the chateau and they were in the lorry, driven by the same two soldiers as before, who had willingly volunteered for this assignment.

'Hey up, Walter,' called Della, when she saw him, and when Corporal Trevor went to climb into the cabin, she blew him a kiss and yelled, 'Hello, Trevor, darling.' He ducked his head in embarrassment and grinned before starting up the engine.

Robert, Beau and Eric Baxter were in Robert's Jeep and set off before them, with an armed soldier sitting beside Robert in the front passenger seat. The Players watched them drive on ahead, and Godfrey grumbled about Eric having a comfortable ride again while he and the rest of them had to be tossed around in a ten-ton truck.

'I'd rather he was with them, any day,' said Frances. 'He just poisons the atmosphere. So let's settle down and try and enjoy the ride.'

Nobody enjoyed the ride. The road was threaded with potholes so that the lorry jerked and swayed around, making Catherine feel a little seasick. Because of the driving rain and sleet, they had to keep the canvas back flap closed, so that the only light came from a couple of storm lanterns that the drivers had fixed up for them. It was enough for the boys and now Della to continue with the poker school.

'She's really got into it,' smiled Frances. 'So quickly.'

'Not that quickly,' Catherine whispered. 'She's been playing it for years – she just didn't let on.'

Frances laughed. She was examining a bruise on the back of her hand, which was gradually changing from purple to yellow.

'That looks nasty,' said Catherine. 'How on earth did you get that?'

'From the tractor,' Frances sighed. 'I had the bonnet up to look at the carburettor and the damn thing fell on me.' She laughed. 'Guy was most concerned.'

'Worried that you'd broken your hand?'

'God, no. He was worried that I'd damaged his beloved tractor. Mind you, he's not half as clever as he thinks when it comes to an engine. Ours at home is always breaking down and we can't afford to replace it, so I'm quite au fait with the innards of farm machinery.'

'But despite that, you enjoyed yourself with him on the farm,' said Catherine. 'And you were out with him last night too.'

'Yes, we were discussing the cattle. He wants to build up a beef herd, to keep the place going while the new orchards grow. I didn't really know about the breeds they have over here and it was fascinating to hear about them.' Frances leant back against the canvas cover. 'Yes, fascinating.'

'And what about him?' asked Catherine with a twinkle. 'Is Guy fascinating too?'

342

Frances lowered her voice and looked across to the card school. 'He is rather,' she grinned. 'But don't tell Della. She'll only rag me about it.'

'I heard that,' called Della, 'and yes, he is, and I will. You saucy minx.'

Trevor opened the partition window from the cab. 'We're going to be about another hour, folks. The road is shit – begging your pardon, ladies – so we'll have to take it slow. Sorry.'

'Leave that partition open, then, please,' called Frances. 'So at least we'll have something to look at.'

'Will do.'

It did take an hour, and by the time they reached the large clearing, which was carved out of dense pine woodland, the company felt exhausted. Walter drew the truck to a halt in front of a large, hastily erected hut that was the officers' quarters and they stumbled out of the back, stepping onto cartridge boxes, which the soldiers had hastily arranged to help them down, and then across duckboards to the open door of the hut. Soldiers, scruffy and tired-looking, gathered around to greet them, whistling their appreciation when Della posed and blew kisses to them.

'Welcome, welcome,' said the young colonel in charge. 'We are so looking forward to this show. The weather is beastly, so we've put up a canvas cover for you over the stage. You shouldn't get too wet.'

The company looked at each other, but nobody said anything. They'd done plenty of outdoor shows before. They were used to roughing it.

Beau and Robert joined them and Catherine had to work hard not to run over to Robert's side. He looked at her with eyes softened by love, but said nothing while

Beau discussed with the colonel how much of their show they could do, considering the weather and what the camp could provide as a stage.

'We've commandeered a piano,' said the colonel triumphantly. 'It was in the village school, just down the road, and the school mistress said we could borrow it. Not a Steinway, of course, ha, ha, but I'm sure it will do.'

'It will, and thank you,' said Beau.

'I can offer tea,' said the colonel, 'or perhaps something stronger? We captured a Jerry position a week ago and found a few cases of schnapps. It's not bad ... a little hard on the gullet, going down, but' – he looked at his fellow officers – 'we think it does the trick.'

Godfrey nodded eagerly, but Beau said, 'Perhaps we'll leave the schnapps till the end of the show. Don't want to wreck our voices, do we, Godfrey?' He gave the tenor a hard look. 'Now, Colonel, our pianist and I will look at the stage, if you don't mind, and then we'll see about setting up the mikes.'

In the distance, they could hear the boom, boom of cannon fire, a sound that they'd almost forgotten about, and Robert asked how far away it was.

'Oh, ten, fifteen miles, I should think,' said a fresh-faced young lieutenant, keen to be part of the conversation. 'We've cleared them out of here, and they are retreating. But they are determined buggers. You have to admire their guts.'

'I don't,' said Robert coldly. 'If you'd seen what I've seen, you wouldn't admire anything about them.'

The officer blushed to the roots of his gingery hair, and the colonel frowned. It was obvious that he didn't like his men being told off by this visiting officer. He turned to the girls. 'There's nothing to worry about, ladies: if we don't get them, the RAF will. As soon as the weather clears, the spotter planes will be up, and then they'll send in a light bomber.'

'We're not worried, Colonel,' said Della, giving him a flirty look. 'We've been bombed before. None of us turned a hair.'

Catherine and Frances, remembering how frightened Della had been when they were last bombed, looked at each other but said nothing.

'Let Hitler do his worst. We can take it,' Godfrey's voice boomed out, almost as loud as the cannons.

'That's the spirit,' the colonel laughed, before taking Beau and Tommy outside to inspect the stage area.

The young lieutenant organised tea and biscuits. He was still embarrassed, but Robert said, 'Sorry, Lieutenant. That was clumsy of me. No hard feelings,' and he thrust out his hand.

'Thank you, sir,' the lieutenant said, and Della gave him a wink, which made him blush even more. But the atmosphere improved markedly and the other officers chatted animatedly with the Players, while one of them offered Godfrey a nip out of his hip flask.

'You're a gentleman, sir,' roared Godfrey, and begged a drop more to put in his tea.

Robert caught Della's arm. 'I thought you'd like to know. Your Dr Tim is at the field hospital where we're going after the show. They're providing the overnight accommodation, so you'll have time to be with him.'

'Oh!' She looked at him with glistening eyes. 'Thank you, Robert.' And she turned to the others and said, 'Did you hear that? I'm so thrilled.'

She sounded thrilled too when she opened the show with 'Happy Days Are Here Again' and tap-danced across the improvised stage of boards over oil drums. The audience loved her, especially as, despite the cold, she had stepped out of her uniform skirt to reveal her tiny red shorts and fishnet tights. They whistled and cheered, and were still cheering when Colin came on stage complete with wig and spangled cape over his uniform to do his act.

Godfrey sang 'I'll Walk Beside You', his few belts of schnapps making him very emotional, and tears rolled down his cheeks as he got to the last line, 'I'll walk beside you to the land of dreams.' He wasn't the only one in tears. Hardened soldiers wept, and even the young lieutenant blew his nose.

Only Beau stared critically at him. 'He's been on the drink again,' he grumbled to Catherine.

'It doesn't matter,' she whispered from where they were standing at the side of the stage. 'He never forgets the words, and look at them.' She nodded to the audience. 'They love it.'

After that, nobody wanted to listen to Eric and Captain Fortescue – the mood was wrong – and he came off stage to polite applause and in a filthy temper.

'On you go, Catherine,' said Beau urgently. 'Get them back, for God's sake.'

Going over to Tommy, she whispered, 'Let's do something they all recognise,' and when he played the opening bars of 'Blue Moon', there was an instant ripple of applause, which increased tenfold when she got to the end. 'More!' they shouted, and she sang 'Long Ago and Far Away'. When the cheers at the end were so great that she couldn't leave, she beckoned Frances and Della onto the stage and they sang 'Somewhere Over the Rainbow', which they'd been practising hard to get the harmony right and it worked. Oh, it worked so well that the audience of weary soldiers joined in and swayed in time to their singing. When they'd finished, and the camp erupted in shouted 'bravo's and 'hurrah's, the girls looked at each other in delight. What a triumph.

'I don't think we can better this,' panted Frances.

'Oh, wait and see,' Della giggled. 'I'll think of something.'

The sleety rain had stopped by the time the show finished and the heavy clouds had rolled away, but at half past four it was already getting dark.

A couple of planes flew over the camp and disappeared to the east. 'Spotters,' said the colonel. 'I said they'd be along. Now, ladies and gentlemen,' he grinned, 'I insist that you have a drink with us.'

Reluctantly Beau agreed, but looking pointedly at his watch, warned that they could only stay for one because they had to get on to the field hospital for an evening show. The boys needed no further encouragement and led the charge into the officers' hut, followed by Della and Frances. They were keen to get out of the cold.

'Do have a drink,' said the young lieutenant, offering the bottle of schnapps, and Godfrey didn't need to be asked twice. By the time the bottle had done the round, he'd drained his tin cup and was holding it out for more.

'You were wonderful,' said Robert, getting Catherine on his own for five minutes. They stood at the edge of the camp, where the dark trees dripped freezing raindrops onto the muddy ground. He stood close to her so that his hand was touching hers but not actually holding it, and when he gazed down at her, he murmured, 'I'm like a callow boy. D'you know, I wanted to shout out to everyone that the beautiful girl on stage has said she loves me.'

'You could,' Catherine laughed. 'I wouldn't mind. I'm so proud of you.'

Suddenly Robert looked up. In the distance came a sound. Not of the cannon fire, which had continued off and on all afternoon, but something different. It was a low, throbbing noise, like that of an engine, and was slowly moving towards them.

'It's the colonel's bomber,' he said. 'It's on its way. I think we'd better go.'

'Is it dangerous?' asked Catherine, looking over to where Della and Frances were signing autographs and posing for photographs.

'No, not here, if it's been given the right coordinates, but, well, you never know.'

She followed him across to the lorry, where the boys were being encouraged to get on board.

The colonel stopped her. 'Miss Fletcher, you were terrific. I'd love to hear you sing again.'

'Well,' she smiled as she shook his hand, 'if you're in London, try the Criterion, or the Ritz – I'm often singing there. With Bobby Crewe's Melody Men.'

'I certainly will,' he said. And then clinging on to her hand, he asked, 'Are you really "Miss" Fletcher?'

'I'm afraid not,' she smiled, looking over to Robert, who was herding Frances and Della towards the truck while keeping an eye on her. 'I'm married.'

'To someone in show business? Perhaps one of this company?' he asked.

348

'No,' she said. 'My husband is a paratrooper.' The words came out slowly and she wondered how long she would be able to say them. Sometime soon she would make the decision to admit to being a widow.

'Catherine, come on.' Robert strode over to her, and saluting the colonel, he led her away.

'Were you jealous?' she whispered.

'Yes,' he growled, but grinning. 'Wildly.' He left her at the truck, where Frances was urging the Players to get on board, and then hurried round to the Jeep, where Beau and Baxter were waiting for him.

The noise of the bomber was louder. Soon it would be overhead and they all looked up to see if it was visible. It was, a black spot against the western sky, and getting closer.

Trevor started the engine of the truck. The boys were already inside, and Frances and Catherine got in beside them.

'I think we should put on our tin hats,' said Frances.

'Why?' asked Tommy, who was already shuffling the cards.

'Because Beau said we must.'

'Alright,' they all grumbled, but did as they were told.

Catherine and Frances sat by the back flap and called to Della. She was still giggling with the soldiers and blowing kisses. 'If you don't hurry up,' yelled Frances, 'we'll leave you behind and you'll never see Dr Tim.'

Overhead, the bomber was nearly upon them. It was flying quite low and the reverberations from the engines was making the ground shake. 'Bloody hell,' said Della, scrambling onto the truck, 'what a racket.'

'Put your tin hat on,' instructed Frances, and Della,

one leg in and one leg over the back board of the truck, reached over to get it. Suddenly Trevor let in the clutch and the truck lurched into action, sending Della flying out of the back, where she landed with a sickening thump on the muddy ground.

'Stop,' screamed Frances to Trevor, and at that moment the plane let go of its cargo and the bomb whistled down.

It was if the world had exploded.

The pressure wave sent the Players in the truck screaming and tumbling onto the base boards, where they ended up a tangle of arms and legs, their heads bashing against the box used as a card table. Shrapnel and debris peppered the canvas sides like a hail shower, some pieces, sharp as knives, penetrating the fabric.

Frances was the first to move, slowly and painfully dragging herself off the floor of the truck and sitting up. She'd managed to bite a hole her lip and blood was trickling from her mouth, but as far as she could feel, nothing else was damaged. Catherine was moving too, heaving herself upright until she was sitting on the bench against the canvas side. She had a deep cut below her eye where she'd come in contact with the brim of Colin's tin helmet, and she looked dazed.

'What happened?' asked Frances, her voice sounding hollow in her ears. She looked around vaguely inside the truck, where the boys were moving slowly upright, and then outside to the camp, until her eyes fixed on a figure on the ground. 'Oh my God,' she gasped. 'Della!'

By the time Frances and Catherine had scrambled out of the truck, Robert and some of the soldiers had reached her. She was lying in the mud, eyes closed and her arms and legs flung out like a broken doll. A pool of blood was staining the ground beneath her, where a spear of wood, ripped out of the forest in the explosion, had pierced her thigh.

'Is she...?' Frances screamed.

'She's alive,' said Robert, who was kneeling beside her. Then he looked up and yelled, 'Medic! For God's sake, medic!'

Even as he shouted, the medical orderly was on his way. Catherine and Frances stood clutching each other as the medic rapidly strapped a tourniquet round her leg and, biting the cap off a needle, plunged a syringe full of morphine into her arm. He drew a capital 'M' on her forehead with an indelible pencil.

Della's eyes opened and she gazed at the soldier medic, who was gently pulling the shard of wood out of her flesh. 'Hello, darling,' she whispered. 'Who the hell are you?'

Catherine and Frances moved as one to kneel beside her. 'Thank God, you're awake,' said Catherine, tears coming to her eyes, and Frances kissed Della's cheek, then said, 'I told you to bloody well hurry up. Why will you never do as you're told?'

'Stop nagging,' whispered Della, and then looking at her friends, said, 'What happened?'

'You fell out of the lorry and then a bomb dropped,' said Catherine. 'You've hurt your leg.'

'I know.' Della gasped with pain. 'It hurts like hell. So does my chest.'

The medic pushed aside Della's jacket and felt her chest. 'You said she fell out of the lorry first?' he asked, looking up at Catherine.

She nodded.

'Then as well as a compound fracture of her leg, I'm pretty sure she's got broken ribs, and Christ knows what else besides. She has to get to the field hospital, immediately. I'm going to call up the ambulance.'

A group of shocked soldiers had gathered around, staring down at Della, and Frances began to take off her greatcoat to cover her friend, who had now started to shiver. But another orderly ran up with some blankets, and then the colonel arrived.

'Bloody fly boys,' he raged. 'Couldn't read a coordinate if you paid them in gold coin.' He looked down at Della and the colour drained out of his face. 'Will she be alright?' he asked the medic, who shrugged.

'I've called up the meat wagon, sir. Shouldn't take long.'

'What about the rest of you?'

Robert had got to his feet and looked at the cut underneath Catherine's eye and the tear on Frances's lip. The boys, who were standing in a nervous huddle beside the truck, appeared not to have been damaged at all.

'They're not bad, sir. Suffering from shock. What about your men?'

'About the same, Major. Cuts and bruises, and the cook spilt a bucket of boiling soup over his feet, but nothing as bad as this young lady. Fortunately for us, the bomb landed in the trees. If it had hit the camp, it would have been quite a different story.'

The young lieutenant came running up with a bottle of schnapps and some tin cups. 'I thought for the shock, sir,' he said.

'Good idea,' said the colonel, 'and issue a ration to the men.'

Catherine felt as though everything was happening in slow motion. People moved around her, talking and in some cases laughing, the sort of laughter that comes after a fright, but she couldn't join in. She squatted beside Della, holding her hand and listening to Frances, who was whispering soothing words to their friend. She noticed that Della's eyes were closing and looked up to the medic in alarm.

'It's the morphine,' he said. 'Don't worry.'

When the green military ambulance came, the girls stood aside as two Queen Alexandra nurses, in combat uniform, jumped out of the back and efficiently man-oeuvred Della onto a stretcher and then into the ambulance.

'Anyone else?' asked the older nurse. 'What about you two?' she said, looking carefully at Catherine and Frances with their cut faces.

'We're alright,' said Frances. 'We're just concerned about our friend.'

Robert, who'd been standing talking to Beau, stepped forward. 'We'll be following you,' he said. 'We're due at your hospital, anyway, although whether the Players are up to performing, that's another matter.'

'That would be a shame,' said the nurse, getting into the ambulance to join her colleague, who was bending over Della. 'The men have been looking forward to it.'

Night had fallen when they arrived at the field hospital. The weather was bad again, with flakes of snow dancing around, looking erroneously pretty against the arc lamps that lit the duckboards between the long tents. The company was taken into the canteen, where a sergeant cook poured large mugs of tea for them and then proceeded to put plates of fried Spam and eggs in front of them, with a platter of thick pieces of bread and margarine. The boys fell on it as if they hadn't eaten for a week, but Catherine, after drinking a gulp of the dark brown tea, said, 'I don't think I can eat a thing.'

'You can,' said Frances. 'Try.' And to her surprise Catherine found herself gobbling down the Spam and eggs, and even having a go at the bread.

'Shall we go and find Della?' said Frances when they'd finished.

'Yes,' and the two of them got up and went outside into the snowy night.

Robert was walking towards them. 'We're looking for Della,' said Catherine, going up to him. 'D'you know where she is?'

'I do,' he said. And he suddenly put his arms around her. 'Oh God,' he said. 'I've been wanting to do that for hours.' He turned to Frances and put one arm around her too. 'Alright, Fran?' he asked.

'We're alright,' she said, speaking for both of them. 'Shocked but alright. Where's Della? Can we see her?'

'She's in the operating theatre. And I'm told she'll be in there for a while. I'm afraid her injuries are quite serious.'

The girls' faces dropped and Catherine whispered, 'I can't quite believe it. One minute she was blowing kisses, and the next she was...' Her voice choked and Robert tightened his grip on her.

'We're at war, dear girl. This is how it is.' He walked them back to the canteen, and in a moment Beau limped up behind them.

'We've been asked if we can put on some sort of show,'

354

he said. 'They know we've had a terrible shock, but the men were looking forward to it, and it will do them good.' He paused, looking round the weary faces of his company, who wouldn't look him in the eye. 'I shall quite understand if you're not up to it.'

Nobody spoke for a moment, and then Catherine said, 'Of course we're up to it. We are the Bennett Players, wartime entertainers, and if this is what wartime means, then that's what we signed up for. I'm even prepared to change into my performance clothes if you'll give me five minutes.'

The others nodded and started getting out of their seats.

'Thank you,' said Beau. He almost looked as if he was going to burst into tears and, not for the first time, Frances thought that this was a man living on the edge.

'Good girl,' she whispered to Catherine, and saw that Robert was looking at her as though his heart was about to burst.

They put on as good a show as they could manage. Instead of Della opening with her usual upbeat number, Catherine and Frances went on and sang 'Don't Fence Me In', complete with cowboy hats and a lasso that Della had found somewhere at the chateau. The performance missed Della's verve, but the audience didn't notice that and cheered.

The rest of the show went well too; even Baxter with Captain Fortescue was a hit, drawing roars of laughter with his risqué jokes. Catherine did two more numbers, 'As Time Goes By' and finished with 'I'll Be Seeing You'. She called Frances onto the stage to sing the second chorus with her and invited the audience to join in. It worked well, and coming off after the performance, Catherine was satisfied that they hadn't let anyone down.

The nurse who had been on the ambulance came up to the girls when they were changing out of their performance dresses. 'You were fantastic,' she said. 'Now, let me attend to those cuts.' And when she was shaking sulfa powder onto the wounds, she said, 'You'll have bruises in the morning, and you, Miss Fletcher, will probably have a black eye.' She laughed. 'Not enough for Blighty but war wounds, nevertheless.'

'Have you heard how our friend is?' asked Frances.

'She's out of theatre, I believe. Not too good, I'm told.'

'Can we see her?' pleaded Catherine.

'I shouldn't think so,' the nurse said. 'Dr O'Brien likes to keep the recovery tent germ-free.'

After the nurse had gone, Frances said, 'Did you hear that? Della's in the recovery tent. Shall we go and look for it? I noticed that they've all got signs on them.'

Dr Tim found them as they stood outside the tent marked, *Recovery Ward*. 'Well, now,' he smiled. 'If it isn't the two other legs of the tripod. I knew you two wouldn't be far away.'

'Can we see her, please?' begged Catherine.

'Only for a moment,' Frances added.

'Alright,' he said. 'But I warn you, she's still a bit groggy.'

She was lying on a hospital cot, her face, devoid of make-up, was as white as the sheets around her. A blood drip was attached to her arm, and a cage under the covers kept them off her leg. A rubber tube snaked down from her chest into a bottle under the side of the bed.

'*Mon Dieu*,' whispered Catherine.

'Punctured lung,' said Dr Tim, 'among other things.'

'Poor old Della,' said Frances.

'Not so much of the old,' a voice whispered from the bed.

They each kissed her and held her hand for a moment until they were ordered out. 'You can see her tomorrow before you leave,' said Dr Tim.

'How long will she stay here?' Frances asked.

'Oh, we'll get her stable and then fly her home. You can visit her in England.'

As the two girls walked back to the tent they'd been assigned for the night, Frances said, 'I have a feeling that our tour is over. We'll be going home very soon.'

Chapter 24

December 1944

They were back at sea, crossing the Channel in the same landing craft that they'd travelled on before. It was calm, no wind; and the sea was as flat as a mill pond, so different from the tempestuous journey they'd had four months before.

'Della would have loved this,' sighed Frances.

'I don't know.' Catherine shook her head. 'She said that she was sick on the Mersey ferry.'

'Doesn't it seem like a lifetime ago?' They were sitting against the side of the craft on the upper deck with the small crew of sailors. Frances was staring out to sea. It was daytime, and a pale sun was shining in a winter sky. Only she and Catherine were on deck; the others, including Grandmère, were in the bus below them, Grandmère sleeping happily, quite able to ignore the poker school.

'What, since we left England?'

'Yes,' Frances nodded. 'So much has happened.'

It was a week since Della's injury. The two girls had managed to see her, briefly, on the morning they left the field hospital, but it had been an upsetting visit. Della was drifting in and out of consciousness, and when she was awake, she seemed dreadfully confused.

'That bloody doll is staring at me,' she shouted

suddenly, and Catherine held her hand and told her that she was dreaming.

'Oh yes.' Della opened her eyes properly. 'Where am I?'

'In the field hospital,' said Frances gently. 'With Dr Tim.'

That calmed her for a while, and when she looked at her friends, there was recognition in her eyes. 'They're giving me some sort of Mickey Finns,' she croaked, her voice hoarse and weak. 'They're knocking me bandy.'

'Just as well,' Frances grinned. 'Your language is probably worse than the squaddies'.'

Della smiled, but her eyes started closing again, and the Queen Alexandra nursing sister arrived and told them that the visit was over. They met Dr Tim by the door and asked him how Della really was.

'I wouldn't say first class,' he sighed, 'and I think a bit of infection has got in, but she's a fighter. She'll pull through.'

'It'll be a while before she dances again,' said Catherine.

'Ah, well, that's another matter.' Dr Tim shook his head sadly. 'I think her high-kicking days are over.'

'I wouldn't be too sure,' Frances argued. 'This is Della we're talking about.'

He laughed at that, but the girls were sad as they went to board the lorry that was taking them away from the field hospital. Frances's brave words were just those. It was hard to equate the floppy, doll-like figure in the hospital cot with the vibrant, funny Della that they knew and loved.

'How is the dear girl?' asked Godfrey, and when they

explained what they'd seen, the boys looked as miserable as the girls felt.

'We've never asked how you three are,' said Catherine. 'You must have damaged something.'

'Not really,' said Tommy. 'Colin's nose bled for a while, and I hurt my shoulder, but it's alright now, and as for Godfrey, well, he was so full of booze that he didn't feel a thing.'

'Quite right, Thomas. Alcohol has its uses,' Godfrey said, his voice quieter than usual. He ruminated for a moment before saying, 'If only I could persuade Gertrude of that.'

They arrived back at the chateau, relieved to be at a place they knew and felt comfortable in, but telling Guy and Grandmère the sad news about Della dampened their spirits, and when Béatrice exclaimed over the cuts on the girls' faces, tears came into Catherine's eyes.

'Della is so much worse,' she cried. 'My black eye and Frances's lip are nothing compared with her injuries.'

'*Pauvres petites*,' Grandmère crooned. 'Come, eat!' It was as though drinking a bowl of soup was a cure for everything, and strangely, after eating and going up to the big room to flop on the beds, Catherine and Frances did feel better.

Frances was out in the fields with Guy early the next morning when Robert arrived. He'd parked round the back beside the bus and walked through the kitchens before finding Catherine in the salon. He'd brought the mail, but most importantly for her, he'd come to say goodbye.

'I'm flying to England this afternoon,' he told her. 'And I won't be back over here. My mission in France is done.' They had walked out of the house and into the open-sided machinery shed where Guy kept his tractor. It was snowing again, and as she stood there with him, watching the flakes drift slowly down, Catherine realised that nothing would be the same again. The Bennett Players had suffered a blow that seemed almost insurmountable.

'Are we being sent home?' she asked.

'Yes,' he nodded. 'The authorities are scared of the propaganda that might ensue if anyone else gets injured.' He put a finger under her chin and gently lifted her face. 'Oh God,' he said, 'that eye looks terrible. Does it hurt?'

'Not much,' she answered, but she wasn't able to say more because he was kissing her, and she clung to him desperately, as she'd wanted to ever since the bomb.

'I do love you, Catherine,' he said. 'I will love you for the rest of my life. Whatever happens, remember that.'

It was only after he'd driven away that she wondered about those last words. Was it some sort of a warning? But then she dismissed her fears. I love him too, she thought. I can't imagine life without him.

Going back to the house, she found Frances fresh-faced and happily reading a letter from her father. 'He's got some money,' she said, reading through the first page, 'and has started work on the roof.'

'Where did he get it?' asked Catherine absently. She was still thinking about Robert.

'I don't know.' Frances turned the page to look at the scribbled writing on the back and started reading out loud. '*I took a loan from a young man who says he is a close friend of yours. He appears to be a wealthy man, although certainly not of our class. I assume he is one of your show business friends. He's interested in the paintings in the long gallery and thinks he can get a good price for them. I haven't made a decision yet, but I have sold him the Meissen dinner service. It's of no use to us, really, and it paid for repairs to the stable block.'*

She slammed the letter down on the table and looked up, her face working with rage. 'How dare he?' she exploded. 'That dinner service has been in the family for a couple of hundred years. He'll be selling the paintings next, and when Hugo comes home, there'll be nothing left for him.'

'Calm down,' Catherine soothed. 'Who is this man, anyway?'

Frances, still simmering, picked up the letter again and read on. *'Mr Costigan has many contacts, apparently, and can get anything. He even filled the Rolls with petrol, quite legitimately I might add. Although, I'm wary of upsetting Constable Hallowes and haven't put the tyres on again yet.'*

'Jerry Costigan?' Catherine said, puzzled. 'Della's friend?'

'It must be.' Frances glared at the letter. 'And he isn't a friend at all. She loathes him. Don't you remember? She said he was a crook. Oh Christ! The sooner I get back home, the better.'

She stayed angry all day, and when Guy came into the salon, she told him about her father's letter.

'This man, he is someone you know?' asked Guy.

'We have met him, a couple of times,' Frances said. 'He is a person Della has known for years. Her brother works for him.'

'He is discharged from the army?'

The girls shook their heads. 'I don't think he's ever been in the army,' said Frances, looking at Catherine for confirmation. 'He's well off, but Della says that the money comes from the black market or profiteering. Something like that.'

'He does try to help the family, though,' Catherine said. 'Hasn't he paid for Della's sister to see specialists?' Guy looked confused, so she explained, 'The sister, Maria, has something wrong with her spine. She can't walk.'

'So, a good man and a bad one, but Frances' – Guy looked puzzled – 'how has this man got on to your father?'

'I don't know,' she said fiercely. 'But I'm going to find out.'

'Good,' said Guy, getting up. 'So, now you can come and help me decide which would be the best place to put down a few hectares of corn.'

Catherine smiled. 'Surely, Guy, you know more about this estate than Frances does.'

He grinned. 'No. My father spent his time in Deauville, mostly on the gaming tables. He left every decision to his farm manager, and I, then, wasn't interested. I went to college, studied literature and politics, went to lots of parties, drank too much and saw myself as president of France one day.'

'And now?'

'My father is dead. The farm manager is dead. And I've changed.'

'We all change,' said Catherine, with a sad smile. 'The war has taken away all our certainties.'

'But,' Guy said, as he and Frances left the room, 'I might still be president of France one day.'

Beau came to the chateau at the end of the week. 'We're booked on board on Sunday morning, eight o'clock,' he said. 'Sailing from Ouistreham, so, Frances, it means either getting up very early or going Saturday night and parking up on the harbour.'

Frances looked round the group, who'd gathered to hear Beau's news. 'Saturday night,' said Tommy, and they all nodded.

'Alright. You can pick me up at the officers' club on the way. It'll be good to be home, won't it?' he said, looking, for once, positively jaunty.

'Aye,' Colin agreed, 'but, boss, you said "me". Does that mean that effing Baxter will not be travelling with us?'

Beau grinned. 'It does, because he's already gone. He flew home earlier in the week.'

'The jammy bastard,' Tommy growled. 'Trust him to cadge a lift like that while we have to face the raging seas again.'

'I have it on good authority,' Beau smiled, 'that we should expect a good crossing. The weather will be reasonable.' He paused, watching them all chatting to each other, excited and pleased at the prospect of going home. 'Listen,' he said, 'while we are all here together, there is something else I want to tell you. You have been the finest group of people that I've ever worked with, and I can't tell you how much your enthusiasm and commitment have meant to me.'

'Well, thanks, Beau,' said Tommy, 'and speaking on behalf of the Players, you've been a pretty good boss.'

Catherine thought she saw a tear in Beau's eye, but he just grinned and said, 'This isn't the end. In the new year, we'll be travelling on again. We'll do shows all around the country, and if they let us, we'll come abroad again. That is, if you're up for it.'

'By God, we're up for it,' roared Godfrey. 'As soon as you like, sir.'

While Frances stayed with Beau to go over the paperwork, Catherine went to find Grandmère to tell her the plans. She guessed she would be in the kitchen with Madame Farcy, the two of them having become cooking rivals but fast friends, and neither was pleased when Catherine announced their imminent departure.

'You see, *chérie*,' Grandmère said, 'I thought that perhaps I could stay here a little bit longer and then perhaps return to my home. It has been so long and I miss it so very much.'

'But, Grandmère,' Catherine said, 'you can't manage there on your own – you know that. Come back to England with me, and then perhaps next spring or summer, Maman and I will come back with you and see what we can do. Maman might even want to stay – she was talking about it after my father died.'

'Was she?'

Catherine nodded, her fingers crossed behind her back. Maman had never mentioned the idea, but now she came to think about it, maybe she would like to go home.

'Your granddaughter has spoken wisely,' agreed Madame Farcy. 'We have become good friends, yes, but your daughter needs to see you now. I think she has been very worried for years and your presence will comfort her.'

Catherine nodded her thanks to Madame Farcy over Béatrice's head, for it seemed that the housekeeper's words held far more sway than hers.

The day of their departure, Frances bumped into Guy in the bedroom corridor. He was coming out of his room, dressed ready for the fields. He was carrying a shotgun and Frances knew that he was going after rabbits. She longed to go with him.

'We're leaving after lunch,' she said.

'I know,' he answered, and to her delight, he looked rather dejected.

He lingered, awkwardly, the gun crooked over his arm as though trying to decide what to do next; then he turned and opened his bedroom door. 'Frances,' he said, 'come in here. I have something for you.'

'What?' she asked, astonished.

'Come.'

She followed him into his room, half the size of the one she shared with the girls, and spartan to the point of being barely furnished. He propped the shotgun against the wall and opened the top drawer of his cupboard. 'This is for you,' he said, producing a square velvet-covered box. 'To thank you for helping me.'

'I don't need thanks, Guy,' Frances said. 'Honestly, I've loved every minute.'

'But I want you to have it.' He pushed the box into her hands. 'It was my grandmother's. She left everything to me to be handed on to my…' He didn't finish the sentence.

Frances gasped when she opened the box. Even in the poor light, the diamonds on the Edwardian tiered neck-lace sparkled. 'I can't take this,' she whispered. 'It's

366

beautiful but far too much to give away. It must be worth a fortune.'

He shrugged. 'Manon hid it in the well when the German general was here. She hid many things. Farcy is still digging up silver spoons and forks that she buried. But now it is for you. I can't imagine it being worn by anyone better. You have the perfect neck to wear it.'

'Thank you,' she breathed. 'Thank you so much. I don't know what to say.'

'Well, perhaps,' he grinned, 'don't speak. Just kiss me.'

'My God, yes,' she laughed, and allowed herself to be taken in his arms. They kissed until she was breathless, and then he broke away and went to lock the door.

'Shall we?' he said, looking at her and jerking his head towards the bed.

The decision took a split second. Years of abstinence and longing needed to be washed away. 'I'd love to,' Frances giggled, knowing that she sounded like a silly girl, but at that moment, beyond sense.

He was a virile lover, desire making him strong, and she, relieved of her customary persona of complete control, abandoned herself willingly to his touch. It was a joining of two like-minded people, each finding pleasure in the other.

Afterwards, lying satiated in the narrow bed, he said, 'It was not necessary to do that as a thank you. Please don't think that.'

'I'm not,' Frances smiled. 'What I'm thinking is ... well, what I'm thinking is that it's ages since a man made love to me. I'd forgotten how wonderful it felt.'

'You have had lovers before?'

'I have had one lover before,' she corrected him. 'He was someone I adored.'

Guy propped himself up on one elbow. 'He was?' he repeated.

'He was killed at Dunkirk. Four years ago.'

'Oh.' Guy lay back, and Frances thought about Johnny Petersham. God, we were so young, she remembered, but so in love. I thought I'd die when he was killed.

'You are thinking about him,' Guy murmured. 'I hope it brings happy memories as well as sad.'

'It does.' Frances turned her head to look at him and wondered, then thought, What the hell – I might never see him again. 'And I have more than memories,' she said slowly. 'I have a son.'

'But,' Guy frowned, 'you said lover, not husband.'

'I did. We were never married. But he left me a beautiful boy. And so my lover will never be forgotten.'

Guy sat up and gave her a searching look. 'You dedicate your life to his memory?'

Frances laughed. 'No, I don't. I remember him, and how we were together, but that longing I used to have has gone. Other thoughts fill my life now: my son, my house, the Bennett Players. I am not the sort of person who dwells on sad memories; there isn't time for that.'

'Yes,' Guy said. 'Sad memories take up too much time. So, now, I put all that behind me and I will use my gun only to shoot rabbits and pigeons.'

'Then Gautier was the last human?'

He frowned. 'What are you saying?'

'I'm saying that you set him up. Catherine told me that you made a phone call after she asked you to take her to the farm. I think that you were able to contact him. And you meant to kill him.'

He was silent, then said, 'That is quite a charge.'

'It is,' Frances said, knowing that she was treading on dangerous ground but almost not caring. 'And I'm saying it because I know that was what I would have done. The man had to die. The only pity is that you missed.'

He shook his head slowly, and then, when she thought he was going to deny it, he said, '*Mon Dieu*, but you are ruthless. We could have used you in the Resistance.' Then he laughed and said, 'We are very alike, you and I.'

She let out the breath she'd been holding and said, 'Yes, we are. But now I must get up, and so must you.'

He scrambled out of bed, half naked and unembarrassed as he wandered around the room picking up his clothes. 'But, Frances, have you time before you go to shoot a few rabbits?'

'Oh yes,' she grinned, getting out of the tumbled bed and dragging on her pants. 'Now you're talking.'

Later, standing on the swaying landing craft, holding on to the sides while the grey sea raced them home, Frances nodded slowly. So much has happened. And what next?

'Frances!' Beau was calling from the bus and she turned away from looking out to sea. 'What now?' she said to Catherine, and the two of them climbed down the metal stair and got into the bus. Everyone was staring at the locked suitcase that was Captain Fortescue's home.

'Good heavens,' said Frances. 'How the hell did this get in here?'

'I don't know,' said Beau. He looked as bewildered as the rest of the company, including Béatrice, who was obviously wondering why everyone was staring at a suitcase. 'Colin dropped a franc and it rolled behind the wicker baskets. The suitcase was jammed in beside them.'

'Baxter never went anywhere without that bloody doll,' Tommy said, and he fingered the lock.

'You said he flew home earlier in the week,' said Catherine. 'Did you see him go?'

'I didn't. Robert told me. It was on the day he went. The last time I saw Baxter was the night after we came back from the field hospital; he was having a meal in the officers' mess. But that was it.'

Catherine thought back. Robert had arrived at the chateau on that morning and had parked his Jeep beside the bus. Was it possible that he had put the case on board? 'I think we should open it,' she said.

'We can't,' Beau objected. 'It's his private property.'

'I don't think it is any more. D'you know, I'm pretty sure Robert left it for us to find.'

'But why?' said Frances.

'Because I think Baxter went back to England in handcuffs.'

'Handcuffs?' Beau gave a sick little laugh. 'That's a wild accusation, and one I wouldn't expect from you of all people, Catherine.'

'Come off it, Beau.' Frances gave him an irritated look. 'We all knew what he was doing to you. He should have been arrested months ago.'

Beau sat down heavily on one of the seats. 'You all knew?' he asked.

'Sure, boss,' Colin laughed, and Tommy nodded.

'The man was a cad, sir,' roared Godfrey. 'Not fit to draw breath.'

'So,' Frances said. 'We'll open it, and if that horrible doll is still inside, I think we'll bury him at sea.'

'Oh yes,' Catherine laughed. 'What a pity Della isn't here.'

Frances lifted a trapdoor in the floor of the bus where there was a compartment for tools and pulled out a tyre iron. 'Give it here,' growled Colin, and slotting it behind the lock, he gave a heave.

Snap! the lock burst open and Captain Fortescue's painted eyes gazed up at them from his velvet pillow. They stared at it, almost waiting for it to speak, but knowing that of course it couldn't. Nobody really wanted to touch it, but Frances, brave as ever, put her hand inside the case and grabbed it. 'Out you come, you little bastard,' she said, and pulled it away from the pillow. A crackling noise came from beneath the purple velvet and Tommy, curious, lifted it up.

'Wow!' There was a collective intake of breath as the crackling sound was revealed to be that of hundreds of notes: pounds, francs and dollars. The proceeds of Eric Baxter's blackmail and black-market activities during the tour. 'Bloody hell,' said Tommy. 'There's a small fortune here.'

'Yes, well, we'll have that,' said Frances. 'It'll compensate us for all the nastiness that he's put us through.'

'D'you think we should?' said Beau nervously. 'Suppose he comes looking for it?'

'He won't.' Catherine was sure now. Robert had done this deliberately. 'And you, Beau, more than any of us, deserve a reward.'

So while the boys divided the money into seven equal piles, Catherine and Frances took Captain Fortescue and his suitcase on deck. Curious sailors watched as the suitcase went overboard and bobbed away behind the boat. 'Now for you,' said Frances to Captain Fortescue, and held him up over the grey, rippling waves.

'Wait,' said Catherine. 'There's something sticking out of his back. Like the edge of a piece of paper. Can you see?' The two girls squatted down and opened the back of the doll, where all the mechanisms that moved its eyes and ears were housed. Inside, there was a small notebook and an envelope. Catherine opened it. '*Mon Dieu*,' she said, as she withdrew two small black-and-white photographs.

'What are they?' Frances asked. 'Let me see.' She held up the photographs. 'Oh Lord,' she whistled. 'That's Beau,' she whispered, 'and d'you see who he's with? Whom he's kissing?'

Catherine nodded. The two men in the snaps were semi-naked and there was no doubt that they were in a loving embrace. 'There's a signed photo of him at Beau's flat,' Frances whispered. 'You've seen it, along with all the other celebrity pictures. If this got out, he'd be ruined. Even his fame wouldn't save him.'

'That's why Beau kept paying Baxter. Not only to save himself, but' – she pointed to the famous face – 'for him as well. He must really love him.'

'And the notebook? What's in that?'

'It's names, dates and phone numbers,' said Catherine. 'I recognise some of the names.'

'Alright,' said Frances, standing up. 'We'll give the snaps to Beau and the book to Robert, next time we see

372

him. And this creature' – she held up Captain Fortescue – 'is going for a long swim.'

The coast of England was in sight as the girls heaved the wooden doll over the side. It fell into the sea with a satisfying splash and then floated away.

'It's a pity we couldn't chop it up,' sighed Frances. 'Della would have loved that.'

Two days later, they went to see her in St Thomas' Hospital. She was still very ill, but more awake and aware of her surroundings. Ma Flanagan, looking unbelievably smart in a fox-fur coat and a black felt hat, was sitting by her bedside when the girls came into the side room where she was being nursed.

'Oh Jesus and Mary,' cried Ma, 'isn't it grand to see you.' And she fell upon the pair of them with hugs and kisses.

'Get off them, Ma,' said Della. 'They've come to visit me.'

She was ash pale, her eyes huge in her thin face, but she was breathing easier and didn't seem to be in as much pain. 'Tell me everything,' she demanded after they'd kissed her.

'Where to start?' said Frances. 'There's so much.'

'Listen,' said Ma, 'I'm going to find a decent cup of tea. You girls can keep my Delia company for a while. They won't throw you out. This is a private room.' She gave Della a kiss and said, 'See you later, darling.'

It took quite a time to tell Della all that had happened. 'I knew that bloody doll was haunted,' she said, and squealed with laughter. 'Poor Beau, but what a silly bugger.'

'This is for you,' Catherine said, handing her a brown

373

envelope with her share of the money. 'Everyone has had the same. It's quite a lot.'

'Yes,' Frances grinned. 'It'll help at home.' She frowned. 'Della, did you know that your friend Jerry Costigan has been down to Parnell Hall? He's trying to buy some of the paintings, and probably that's not all. My father's already sold him the Meissen tea set.'

'Oh Christ,' Della groaned. 'I think he's after the house. Ma said that he was looking to buy himself a country estate, and he knows that your father is strapped for cash.'

'How the hell does he know that?' said Frances with a scowl.

'It might have been me,' Della said apologetically. 'You told me that you didn't have two pennies to rub together and I told Ma when she asked after you.'

'Well, I have to stop him. I'm going home tomorrow.'

'Oh dear,' said Della. 'I hope you're in time.' She turned her head to Catherine. 'And what about you and the sex god Robert?'

Catherine blushed. 'He's here in London,' she said. 'I'm seeing him the day after tomorrow. We're meeting for lunch at the Savoy.'

'No word on Christopher, I suppose?'

'No, but Robert did say that he had something to tell me. Maybe conformation that my husband is' – she heaved a sigh – 'dead.'

'Fancy you and me both meeting men.' Della gave a weak laugh. 'Who'd have thought it?'

'I would,' Frances smiled. ''Specially you, Dell.'

'You should talk,' said Catherine, leaning across the bed. 'I saw you coming out of Guy's bedroom the other

374

day. The pair of you were quite flushed, and I bet you weren't talking about cows.'

Frances shrugged. 'It was fantastic,' she grinned. 'And that's all I'm prepared to say.'

'What a pair of trollops you two are,' Della giggled. 'Tim and I have only exchanged a couple of chaste kisses. Not even so much as a fumble.' She leant back on her pillows and smiled. 'That's to come.'

Chapter 25

Lord Parnell was waiting in the old car when Frances got off the train. Johnny was on the back seat, with the red setters, who each had a head out of a window.

'Mummy's home,' he cried, as she walked round to sling her bag in the boot, and his grandfather replied, 'Yes, my boy, she is. Now we're in for ructions.'

Frances got in the front seat and, leaning over, gave Johnny a hug and a kiss before pecking her father on the cheek.

'So good to see you, Fran, darling,' said Lord Parnell. There was a hint of nervousness in his voice, which Frances picked up on immediately.

'Hello, Pa,' she said, as he put the car in gear and it rattled way from the station and down the lane. 'Is there anything left in the house, or have you sold it all?'

'Don't be silly, darling,' he said, and looked in the driving mirror to Johnny. 'Mummy is being silly, isn't she?' He glanced quickly at Frances. 'What's that scab on your lip? You look as if you've been in a fight.'

'It's bomb damage,' she answered shortly. 'Remember, there's a war on. And as for being in a fight, well, I think that's to come.'

'Wait till we get home,' he said. 'We don't want to upset the child, do we?'

Frances nodded and leant over to the back again.

376

'Have you been a good boy?' she asked.

'I have been a best boy,' he said eagerly. 'Have you brought me a present? Grandpa said you would.' His little face fell. 'Maggie said those who expects don't get.'

'I think there might be a little something in my bag,' Frances smiled. 'But I'll need lots of hugs and kisses first, when we get home.'

Her father turned the car into the drive and ahead she could see Parnell Hall, dim lights still showing in the downstairs rooms because it was too early for the blackout. She'd always loved the first sighting of her home, its red-brick exterior and the perfectly placed twelve-paned windows. When she was a girl and there was money, the house had glowed. It had been *the* place in the county, and her mother the perfect hostess. That had all gone years ago, and now her mother had gone too. God knows, I don't want her back, thought Frances, but the house? It will come back, she thought fiercely. I'll make it.

Lord Parnell drove round to the rear and parked beside the back offices. As she got out, Frances looked up. Scaffolding had been erected, and there was evidence of building work: stacked roof slates and beams lay about in the yard.

'Where are the builders?' she asked. 'Have they finished for the day?'

'They weren't here today,' her father said. 'But I suppose they'll come tomorrow. They have a lot on, you know.'

'A lot on?' Frances asked. 'Doing what?' Then a thought occurred to her. 'Who are they? Fred Stone's men, from the town?'

'Come on inside.' Her father opened the boot and took out Frances's case. 'The child is getting cold.'

Johnny was clinging on to his mother's hand, jumping up and down and pushing the eager dogs away. 'Naughty dogs,' he shouted, and then in imitation of his grandfather, roared as loud as his little voice could manage, 'Down, sirs.'

Amazingly, the setters obeyed him and bounded away past the stables and into the woodland beyond.

Lord John chuckled. 'My God,' he said, 'that boy's got such a way with the dogs, and you should see him on Achilles – he's fearless.'

'Achilles?'

'Ah yes' – her father ducked his head as they went through into the kitchens – 'you haven't met him. It's the pony. Fine little beast. Just the right size.'

Maggie came bustling through and beamed when she saw Frances. 'Lady Fran,' she said. 'I can't tell you how glad I am to see you. There's been so much going on these last few weeks.'

Lord Parnell cleared his throat. 'Never mind that now, Maggie. I think we could do with a cup of tea. Come on, Frances. We'll go on up.'

Frances raised her eyebrows, and when her father had gone up the stairs to the hall, she whispered, 'I'll see you in a bit, Maggie. You can tell me what's been going on.'

'I will,' the housekeeper said, shaking her head slowly. 'There's a lot to tell.'

It was later, after Frances had handed out the presents she'd brought home: a carton of cigarettes and a bottle of Calvados for her father, a pretty piece of lace to trim her Sunday frock for Maggie, and for Johnny, a collection of pre-war toy cars that Guy had given her just before she left.

'I played with them a lot,' he said, giving her the box of rather battered vehicles. 'But I think your son should have them now.'

Dear Guy, she thought, watching Johnny's little face light up with joy when she put the box on the rug in front of the fire. I do hope I see him again.

'Cars,' the child shouted. 'Grandpa, look!'

Her father grunted as he got down on his hands and knees beside the boy and helped to arrange the cars in a line. 'I'm getting too old for this,' he said.

'Play, Grandpa, please,' Johnny demanded.

'Yes, son. Now, let's put the biggest car at the front. Can you find which one that is?'

Frances watched them. Their friendship was wonderful to see and she never stopped being grateful to her father for accepting Johnny as his grandson. He was a decent man, but now, she had to find out exactly what he and Jerry Costigan had been up to.

She looked around the room, a perfectly square Georgian drawing room, with its dusty full-length damask curtains and the silk-covered sofa, so dreadfully torn on the arms but where the two setters lay, blissfully happy and snoring. All this was in danger of being lost.

'Pa,' she asked, 'who's doing the roof?'

'Oh dear,' he sighed. 'I wondered when you'd get on to that. I'm not sure of their names, but they came here with Mr Costigan. He found them.'

I might have known, she thought. 'And how much have they done?'

'You can see,' her father blustered. 'The scaffolding is

379

up, and they brought in slates and beams. They just haven't had time to be here in the last few days.'

'Few days?'

He picked up a little tin Citroën and ran the wheels round with his fingers. 'I suppose it's about three weeks.'

'My God,' Frances cried. 'Have you given him money?'

'Not exactly. It's a loan, as I said. I'm paying the interest. Don't worry, darling. He's a friend of yours, so everything will be alright.'

'It won't,' said Frances sharply, her face twisted with anger. 'First, Mr Costigan isn't a friend of mine – I've met him briefly twice, but I do know all about him. He is a crook. He is a profiteer, a black-market dealer, a moneylender and loan shark, and he also buys and sells illegal booze. I have heard that he wants to buy a country estate and I think he has his eye on this one. He's going to fleece you first, and then when you're desperate, he'll have it off you, lock, stock and barrel at a knock-down price.'

Her father sat up, his eyes blazing exactly like his daughter's. 'That can't possibly be true. You're exaggerating, surely.'

'No.' Frances shook her head. 'It's all true, every word, and I refuse to let you destroy Hugo's inheritance.'

They glared at each other, but John Parnell knew he'd lost and dropped his head. 'I'm in deep, my dear,' he confessed, 'and I don't know what to do. It's breaking my heart.'

His pathetic confession made her fury melt away and she realised that he was a frightened man. Years of juggling a diminishing income had almost broken him, and added to that had been her own 'disgrace' and then

Hugo's incarceration. Her mother leaving, which should have been in many ways a relief, seemed to have been the last straw. He was exposed and open to predators.

'Alright, Pa,' Frances said with a sigh. 'I'm here now. I'll think of something.'

Rather than being depressed, she was invigorated by solving the problems of the estate, and the next day, she drove to the town to speak to Fred Stone, the builder. She told him some of the events, only saying that her father had been persuaded to call in builders from somewhere else and that they'd let him down. 'I would be grateful if you could come and look as soon as possible,' she said. 'We will pay, of course.'

All the way home, she prayed that her share of the money they'd found in Captain Fortescue's suitcase would be enough.

Going in through the kitchen, she found Maggie plucking a brace of pheasants. 'I can't tell you how glad I am to see you back, m'lady,' she said. 'There were times when I thought you wouldn't have a home to come to. That blasted man, walked around here as though he owned the place. And them builders? They've never built anything in their lives.' She put the birds on the table and, taking a bit of string from her apron pocket, tied them up securely, ready for the oven. Frances, who had poured boiling water into the teapot and put two kitchen cups on the table, sat down opposite Maggie.

'I know that my father has sold the Meissen,' she said, 'and got into some dodgy deal over the roof, but I think he's holding something back. Have you any idea what it can be?'

Maggie got up to singe the last of the feathers from

the birds over the open flame of the gas cooker and then came back to sit down. 'It's not the paintings,' she said. 'I've looked there every day, because I know that Mr Costigan is interested in them, and the Waterford and Royal Worcester are safe in the plate room.' She frowned, sipping at the tea that Frances had poured, then looked up. 'Jethro Western said he saw his lordship walking the grounds with Mr Costigan. They were pointing to Sparrow Wood and all along towards the river. You don't suppose he's sold some land?'

'If he has,' Frances said furiously, her recent compassion for her father curdling in her stomach. 'I'll bloody well kill him.'

At the same time that Frances was threatening to kill her father, Catherine was walking into the Savoy Grill. The maître d' welcomed her with an excited smile. 'Madame Fletcher,' he said, taking her coat. 'Such a long time since you were here. It must be over a year.'

'Two, I think, monsieur, but it's so kind of you to remember me.'

'Who could ever forget that beautiful voice? Now, may I show you to a table?'

'No, thank you,' she smiled, looking round the packed restaurant. 'I'm joining someone...Oh, here he is.'

Robert, looking extraordinarily smart, had come to meet her. He dropped a kiss on her cheek and, taking her hand, led her, followed by the maître d', to the table he'd reserved. 'You look absolutely beautiful,' he said, when they sat down.

'What, with this black eye?' she laughed.

'I would say yellow now, rather than black.' He looked

up to the maître d', who was hovering. 'Miss Fletcher was blown up in France last week,' he said. 'At the front.'

'*Mon Dieu*,' he exclaimed, and then bowing, said, 'In that case, champagne perhaps? On the house, of course.'

'Thank you,' said Robert, and after the man had gone, repeated, 'You really are lovely.'

'It's because I'm not wearing uniform,' she smiled, taking off her calf-leather gloves. 'Actually, I feel quite naked without it.'

'Don't say that,' Robert whispered. 'I might lose control.'

She put her hand across the table so that it was touching his. 'When can we be together again?'

'I don't know. Soon, though.'

The champagne arrived and was poured with an extravagant flourish. Other guests looked on, rather enviously, Catherine thought, and she was embarrassed. An officer at a nearby table got up and came over. 'Excuse me,' he said. 'Miss Fletcher, I saw you sing in France a few weeks ago. I must tell you how much your show was appreciated. It was a real boost.'

'Thank you,' Catherine smiled. 'That is so very kind of you.'

He left then, going back to his companion, while Robert lifted his glass and drained it. 'Is this how my life is to be from now on?' he grinned. 'Champagne and adoring fans following us around.'

'I hope not.' Catherine gave an embarrassed shake of her head, and then she said, 'Robert, you said you had something to tell me. What is it?'

'Should we order first?' His smile had disappeared.

'No. Tell me. Is it about Christopher?'

'Yes, it is, but not conclusive news, I'm afraid. We've confirmed that he was captured by the Gestapo, as I told you months ago. He was taken to the prison in Amiens where they held many Resistance fighters and Allied agents.' He looked down at the stiff white tablecloth. He was drawing lines on it with his fork. 'The prison was bombed.'

'Bombed?' Catherine whispered. 'By the Germans?'

'No.' Robert shook his head. 'We bombed it. It was a special task, precision bombing, to make a breach in the wall so that the prisoners could escape. Many did.'

'Christopher?'

He shook his head. 'I don't think so. Over a hundred prisoners were killed, and many more injured. We have lists of names of the dead and injured and of the escapees, many of whom were recaptured, but your husband's name is not on any of them.'

'Maybe he was in a different prison.'

'No, he was there. Some men who were there confirmed it. We think he may be buried under the rubble.'

Catherine opened her handbag and took out a lace-edged handkerchief. I'm going to cry, she thought, here in the Savoy Grill, in front of everyone. Why did he decide to meet me here to tell me? That was cruel. But the tears didn't come, and instead she stared at him with narrowed, angry eyes.

Robert grabbed her hand. 'Listen to me, Catherine. Whatever happened to your husband happened quickly. Other prisoners endured weeks of torture and he was only there for a couple of days. There was a chance that he and others could escape, and that was why we tried. He was one of the unlucky ones.'

She didn't know what to say. Was Robert trying to explain to her in the kindest way that death had been Christopher's best option? That was too horrible to contemplate and she sat in silence, her stomach churning, while all around her people laughed and clinked glasses and forgot that there was a war on.

When the waiter came, she ordered a fillet of fish, knowing that when it was served, she probably wouldn't be able to eat it. Too many dreadful images were piling into her brain and she needed time to understand them.

Robert ordered the fish too, and while they waited, he looked at her. She was wearing a dark blue woollen dress that had jet beading on the collar, and a small black pillbox hat. Unlike the other women diners, her hair was not rolled and arranged in the current fashion but was left to hang, shoulder length, in soft waves. She looked entirely natural and entirely French, and when she finally spoke, he once again heard the slight accent that had become so dear to him.

'I'm no further on, am I?' she said. 'My husband is still missing in action.'

'If he was alive,' Robert said gently, 'I'm sure we would have heard.'

'You know,' she said, when the fish arrived, two small fillets with a tablespoon of sauce, 'I still have so many questions. First, why were you so keen to get me to France? It was as if I was bait for something.' As the words dropped out of her mouth, she realised that it was exactly that. He'd wanted to see if anyone contacted her. Christopher, perhaps? Her hand went to her mouth as the fish refused to go down and she thought she was going to choke.

She swallowed and then pushed her plate away. 'You believed that Christopher was a traitor,' she whispered. 'That he was the one giving the Germans information.' Robert opened his mouth, but she held up her hand. 'Please, Robert, don't lie to me. I've told you before, I'm not a fool.'

'I won't lie,' he said. 'I'll admit some of us wondered. He was always about when operations were blown, but he was never caught. We sent him to your grandparents' farm to see what would happen. We had someone in place to rescue them if he betrayed them. Sadly, the person we had in place was Gautier, whom we trusted entirely. He did help us and was never implicated in any of the arrests. Always somewhere else.' He looked in his empty glass. 'But then we began to think more widely. He might not have been on the scene, but he had contacts with all of them. Even Guy de Montjoy never suspected him and he was there, in the thick of it. It was later for him. After you showed him that letter.'

'Which you and Larry Best wrote, didn't you?'

Robert blushed. 'I'm sorry, Catherine. We were certain that you'd go after Father Gautier and I encouraged de Montjoy to go with you. I know you thought it was his idea, but I have to think three steps ahead always. Anyway, you flushed him out. You were brave, a perfect agent.'

Catherine frowned. Robert had tricked her, laid trails for her to follow without telling her the truth. Was this what life in the intelligence service was like?

She sighed. 'Gautier allowed my grandfather to be shot. Why not my grandmother?'

Robert shook his head slowly. 'Who knows? Could be

that his original beliefs surfaced and he tried to preserve life, but he was scared and kept her drugged. He is from Alsace, you know, on the eastern border. His father died when he was a boy and he was brought up by his mother, who is very religious. He was a good priest, well liked by his parishioners, but something happened to turn him. We don't know what.'

Catherine thought of him dying in Della's arms and begging her forgiveness. She shuddered at the memory and Robert reached over and put a comforting hand over hers.

They were drinking coffee when Robert asked, 'Did you find Captain Fortescue?'

Catherine smiled. 'Oh yes, and we divided the money we found underneath his pillow.'

'I hoped you would,' Robert said. 'I left him especially for you to find after we arrested Baxter. He'll go to prison for a long time.'

'Poor Beau,' Catherine said. 'He was so glad to get the photographs. He cried, you know.'

'The photographs?' Robert looked amazed. 'Good God, we've been looking everywhere for them. Where did you find them?'

'Some spy you are,' Catherine laughed. 'They were inside the doll, along with this.' She took the notebook out of her bag. 'I don't know if it's any use to you.'

Robert took it from her hands and flicked through the pages. He looked puzzled. 'I'm not sure what this is,' he said. 'I think it's a record of all the money he received from his various criminal activities. Very useful for his prosecution.' He looked at her over his coffee cup. 'He took your letters from my briefcase, you know. Looking for something to blackmail you or me with, maybe. We gave him free range with Beau because Beau was on our watch list. He was so desperately compromised that we were afraid he might be tempted to sell military secrets. I deliberately left my briefcase where he could get hold of it, but it was that bastard Baxter who did the deed. Beau was in the clear.'

'I called Larry Best ruthless,' Catherine said slowly. 'You all are, I think. How could you suspect Beau? He was at school with you.'

'But that's the nature of my job,' Robert shrugged. 'Everyone is suspect.'

'Even me?'

He didn't answer, so she said, frowning, 'And what about Davey Jones? I'm sure he suspected Baxter was up to no good. He told Frances that evening after the show that he wanted to speak to Beau.'

'I know.' Robert curled his hand into a fist. 'He was one of ours, sent in to investigate possible links between Baxter and Beau and the selling of secrets. We think Baxter killed him, but he denies it and we have no proof.'

'Oh God,' Catherine sighed. 'What a tangled web. How will I possibly explain this to the girls?'

'Do you have to tell them?' asked Robert glumly.

'Of course. It can't be top secret, otherwise you wouldn't have told me, and they were part of it. They deserve to know.'

'My role in it all doesn't come out so well. I've made a lot of mistakes. Of course' – he looked round, before bending forward and gently kissing her on the mouth – 'my excuse is that I was terribly distracted by a Mata Hari.'

'Idiot,' she laughed, and looked at her watch. 'Now, I'm afraid I have to go. I promised Maman I'd go to the delicatessen in Soho and buy garlic and olive oil. Grandmère is already grumbling about the English food, and it's the only place I know that sells them. Then I'm popping in to see Della.'

'How is she?'

'Better, I think. Certainly her language has returned to its most colourful. Dr Tim has wangled some leave and is coming home tomorrow.'

They strolled out of the Savoy and stood on the pavement while people hurried up the Strand, walking quickly, as Londoners always do. It was a cold afternoon, but Catherine felt warm and a little dizzy from the champagne.

'We might have to wait a long time,' Robert said, 'but I don't ever want to parted from you. Will you marry me, Catherine?'

A siren started to wail in the distance and Robert took her arm and pulled her to the shelter of the building. 'These bloody rockets,' he swore. 'When will they ever be stopped?'

She stood close to him. 'I do love you,' she whispered, 'and if things were different, I'd marry you tomorrow. But they are as they are. I'm still a married woman. And you're a married man. Until we're free, I can't say yes. And seeing you all the time makes it worse.'

He nodded slowly. 'I don't want to let you go,' he said. 'You're part of me.'

'I know,' she smiled, and kissed him goodbye.

As she walked through Soho, past the door from which Della threw a shoe at Jerry Costigan, Catherine thought of what Robert had told her about Chris. Oh God, she wondered, was he frightened? Did he think of her at the end, or was it quick? Dear Lord, I pray it was quick.

Della was sitting up in bed with her plastered leg in a frame. The tubes had gone from her chest, and although she grimaced with pain when she moved, she was nearly back to her old self.

'D'you like this bedjacket?' she asked, looking down at the bright pink velvet creation complete with a collar of downy feathers. 'Ma bought it in. It's nice, isn't it, but the bloody feathers keep getting up my nose.' She giggled, and then gave a painful cough. 'Oh Christ, unless I keep absolutely still, my bloody chest is agony.'

'Who's paying for this room?' asked Catherine, looking at the vases of flowers and the pile of magazines on the bed table.

'It's Ma, I suppose,' Della sighed. 'She's flush these days. And before you ask, yes, it's got to be the moonshine business.'

'What about Jerry Costigan?'

'What about him?'

'Don't you think it's him? The room, the flowers, everything.' Catherine leant forward. 'Tell me, what's the connection? We know there's something.'

Her friend was silent, scowling. Eventually she looked up. 'Tim will be here this evening. I had a telegram. He's got leave.'

'I know – you told me yesterday.' Catherine sighed. Della had her secrets and was keeping them.

A nurse popped her head round the door. 'I need to attend to Miss Stafford,' she said, 'if you don't mind waiting outside.'

'It's alright – I have to go, anyway.' Catherine leant down and gave Della a kiss on the cheek. 'I'll come in tomorrow.'

Della grabbed her hand and whispered, 'I will tell you, darling, but let me tell Tim first. He has to know.'

Chapter 26

It was snowing as Frances drove the tractor into the back yard. Fred Stone and his boys were packing up for the day, having been working on the roof since early morning. All week they'd turned up faithfully at eight and stayed until five. Maggie had kept them supplied with mugs of tea, and she and Frances had marvelled at how quickly and efficiently they'd gone about their business. Lord Parnell went out regularly to watch their progress but refused to be drawn into a discussion of who the other builders were.

'Them cowboys brung the wrong beams,' grumbled Fred. 'They ain't weathered – you just have to look at them.'

'Something you'd know better than I,' Lord Parnell had conceded, and Fred chewed on his pipe and answered, 'I do that, m'lord. And them buggers have stripped away a lot of the lead, and where is it I'd like to know?' He looked around the yard, where snow was beginning to cover the building materials. 'Because it ain't bloody here.'

As she'd driven up the lane, with bales of hay bouncing along on the trailer behind her, Frances noticed a shiny car turning into the drive up to the house. It wasn't a car she recognised; nobody in the village possessed anything like that, or anyone from the estates around. They were all as strapped or nearly as strapped for cash as her father was. With a sinking heart she realised who it had to be, and after parking the tractor, she went in through the kitchen. Johnny was at the kitchen table with his crayons and a colouring book, and gave her his usual welcoming grin, but Maggie had a face like thunder.

'That bugger's here,' Maggie growled. 'In the library with his lordship. He came round to look at them builders and didn't seem best pleased. I got Johnny here with me, so if there's language, his little ears won't hear it.'

'Good,' said Frances, and went to wash her hands at the sink. 'I'd better go up.'

When Frances walked into the library, Jerry Costigan was sitting in the armchair by the fire nursing a glass of the Calvados she'd brought home from France, while her father stood nervously beside his desk. It was the wrong way round, thought Frances angrily. How dare this man put Pa into such a state.

'Good evening, Mr Costigan,' she said. 'I won't say that it's nice to see you.'

He sprang to his feet and shot out his hand, which she ignored. 'What d'you want?' she asked.

'Come now, Frances... Lady Frances, I should say, don't be like that. We're old friends, aren't we?'

'No,' she said. 'We're not. And I repeat, what d'you want?'

He smiled, showing even teeth in a broad, handsome face. Frances had forgotten how good-looking he was and how he appeared utterly relaxed in any surrounding. 'I have some business with your father,' he said eventually. 'Nothing for you to worry about.'

'I've everything to worry about,' Frances said. 'Those pretend builders you brought here? Who ripped out several portions of the roof and stole the lead? You're a con artist, Mr Costigan, and any business you have with my father is over. So you can go.'

'Whoa,' Jerry Costigan laughed. 'That's a slanderous statement you've just made. I might have to speak to my lawyer about that.'

Lord Parnell coughed anxiously. 'Fran, darling, that was unnecessary. We don't want lawyers involved.'

'But we do,' said Frances boldly, although her heart was beating like a hammer and she was fighting to keep the wobble out of her voice. 'We can have the police here anytime we like to charge you with criminal damage, not to mention usury in the matter of that loan you made to my father.'

'Ah yes, the loan.' Jerry flicked an imaginary piece of fluff from the lapel of his beautifully cut suit. 'I'll expect that repaid in full.'

Lord Parnell groaned and sat down suddenly on the chair behind his desk. He looked a broken man.

'It will be paid,' said Frances. 'After the damage to the roof has been assessed and compensation added on. You'll have to wait. But in the meantime, no interest will be forthcoming.'

For the first time, the smile disappeared from Costigan's face and a mean expression replaced it. 'That's not the way I do business,' he said. 'I have been known to make things quite unpleasant for people who don't pay in full.'

Frances went to stand in front of him and stared up at his face. 'You don't frighten me,' she said. 'I've just returned from France where a man doing the same sort of filthy business as you was flown home in handcuffs. I can get on the phone right now and call up the investigating officer. You may be safe in Liverpool, where you've got people in authority on your books who are too scared to touch you, but you aren't safe here, or in Whitehall.'

His fists curled and for a moment she thought he was going to strike her, and her father obviously thought so too, for he stood up so suddenly that his chair fell backwards. But nothing happened. The fury that had crossed Costigan's face melted and he laughed. 'What a girl,' he grinned, and glancing to her father, he said, 'You've got a real little street fighter here, Lord Parnell.'

He put down his glass on the small wine table. 'I'll be going, then,' he said. 'Don't bother to show me out.' At the door, he stopped. 'I'm staying at the hotel in the town for few days. The best one, of course. Perhaps, Frances, you'd like to have a drink with me.'

'In your dreams,' said Frances, and was cross with herself for grinning. 'Oh, and by the way,' she said, as he was going through the door, 'that land that you're hoping to buy – forget it. It's part of a trust fund my grandfather set up for my brother and me. We'll never sell.'

After he'd gone, her father walked over to the armchair and sat down heavily. 'I've been a fool,' he said. 'I let things slide for far too long. And, Frances, my dear, you've rescued me.' He stared at the fire and then said, 'D'you know, I don't think Hugo could have done that.'

She was still shaking when Maggie and Johnny came in. 'He's gone?' asked the housekeeper.

'Mm,' Frances nodded, 'and he won't be coming back.'

'Grandpa.' The child scrambled onto his grandfather's knee. 'I've drawn you a picture. It's me and Mummy and you. And the dogs and Achilles. Look.'

A few days later, Beau rang. 'Fran, darling,' he said. 'I've got a proposition. How about us doing a show down here? My people are curious about what we've been doing, and there's a military convalescent hospital only five miles away from you.'

'I know it,' said Fran. 'Are you suggesting we put on a show there?'

'Well, no, not exactly. I've spoken to the matron there and she's not keen. Some of their blokes have shell shock and are in a bad way, but she is prepared to organise transport for those who would like to come.'

'But where?'

He cleared his throat. 'What about your big barn? Remember you used to have dances there before the war, harvest suppers and the like? I came to a few of them in the old days. God, we were all there that last time, me and Hugo and Robert, of course. Even Johnny Petersham came. Hadn't he just joined up then?'

'Yes,' she said faintly. 'That was the night that...'

'Are you still there, Fran? Your voice is fading.'

'I'm here.' She took a deep breath. 'I think we can do it, but we're a bit short of the readies.'

'Don't worry about that. I'll sort out food and drink. Now, I can put up the boys here – my parents won't mind – but can you find a room for Catherine? Della, of course, won't be able to join us, which is a great pity, but we can do something like we did the night she was injured. And no Baxter, thank God.' He paused, then asked, 'What d'you think?'

'Well, yes,' she said. 'I think it's a wonderful idea.'

It was three days before Christmas and the barn was looking good.

Beau had been over from his parents' house several times, sorting out a temporary stage, and Fran had begged the piano from the church hall. A big tree had been cut from the estate and placed at the back of the stage. Frances was enchanted when Beau's workers strung lanterns on it, and she added decorations from the boxes in the attics.

The villagers had all been invited and were looking forward to it. 'It's the talk of the village, m'lady,' said Mrs Bertram, who ran the shop, and then she unscrewed the lid from a jar of sweets and offered it to Johnny. 'Take as many as your little hand can hold,' she said kindly, and then smiled at Frances. 'He's put on a spurt. Is he starting at the school?'

'After Christmas,' Frances nodded. 'In the nursery class.'

'It'll do him good,' the shopkeeper said. 'It's nice to have friends.'

'Yes, it is.' She thought about that as she and Johnny walked home and she suddenly realised how much she was missing Catherine and Della. They'd lived in each other's pockets for so many months that it still seemed strange not to have them constantly around.

Catherine was coming down for the show, leaving

Lili in the good care of her grandmother and great-grandmother. 'It'll be a relief to be away from them for a couple of days,' she'd laughed when Frances had phoned her. 'They never stop talking, and our house is always full of refugees who Grandmère collects at the French church and brings home for a meal.'

'Have you seen Della?'

'Yes, I saw her yesterday. She's almost back to her old self, apart from not being able to walk. Dr Tim has got a transfer to a military hospital in London and sees her every day. And Ma Flanagan has gone back to Liverpool. She's buying a house in somewhere called Southport, I think. Can you believe it?'

'Oh, I can,' said Frances, 'and we know where the money is coming from.'

When she got home from the village, her father was waiting for her, waving a letter. 'This is very strange,' he said. 'It's from a Count de Montjoy, and written in very poor English, I have to add. He says he's in London and will be coming down here. He'd be very obliged to talk to me.'

'Oh, it's Guy,' said Frances happily. 'I told you. We stayed in his chateau. When's he coming?'

'Tomorrow. And how difficult of him. We'll be busy with your concert. God knows what he'll think.'

'He'll be alright – he's used to us.'

She picked up Catherine from the station that evening and the two girls fell on each other.

'Oh, I've missed you,' cried Frances. 'I've got so much to tell you.'

'And me you,' laughed Catherine. Then, '*Mon Dieu!*'

she gasped, as Frances turned into the drive. 'No wonder you were so at home at the chateau!'

Frances laughed. 'You sound just like Della. Though probably the language would be worse. Come in and meet my father and my little boy.'

John Parnell was overwhelmed by Catherine. 'What a beauty,' he whispered to Frances, when Catherine had been taken by Johnny to inspect his cars.

'Wait till you hear her sing,' she grinned.

'I've brought Johnny a present,' Catherine called. 'Is it alright?'

'Of course,' Frances said, and they waited while Catherine went into the hall and opened her suitcase. She came back with a toy wooden Spitfire, complete with roundels and a propeller.

'Oh, thank you,' squealed Johnny, and hugged her round the legs.

'That'll keep him quiet for hours,' said Frances. 'Now, let me take you up to your room and you can hang your clothes up. Maggie's lit the fire in there and put hot-water bottles in your bed, and we'll refill them later. This house is freezing, I'm sorry to say, but we'll have a drink down here afterwards to warm us up and a good chat.'

It was late when they finally went to bed. Catherine told her all that Robert had said and how she was still no closer to knowing what had happened to Christopher.

'Have you seen Robert lately?' Frances asked.

Catherine shook her head. 'No, not since that lunch at the Savoy. He's busy, I suppose, but maybe he's angry with me for not accepting that Christopher is dead.'

'I don't think that,' Frances murmured. 'He's so in love with you.'

Catherine gave a very Gallic shrug. 'Perhaps,' she said. 'But tell me, what has happened here, with your father and Jerry Costigan?'

Frances laughed when she told that story. It was much easier in the telling than it had been at the time; she still didn't know where that fierce determination had come from, but had, in retrospect, loved it.

'Oh, I forgot to tell you,' she said, as they were walking up the stairs, each clutching a hot-water bottle. 'Guy is coming here tomorrow.'

'But why?' asked Catherine. 'What does he want?'

'I don't know,' Frances answered. 'We'll find out when he gets here.'

Beau drove the boys over in the morning and they all came into the house. 'Crikey,' said Tommy, looking around. 'I thought Beau's pile was pretty fancy, but this place...'

'Magnificent,' roared Godfrey, 'as fine as a raja's palace I once stayed in. India, you understand, sir,' he confided to Lord Parnell. 'I was there for many years.'

Colin said nothing but walked around with his mouth open. Eventually he said, 'I'd nae like to pay for the coal here. It would take a fair bite out of a man's wages.'

'Time for some rehearsals, I think,' said Beau. 'We'll be a bit rusty, so if you'll follow me, I'll show you the venue.'

They rehearsed all afternoon, slotting in the numbers so that despite the missing acts, it would be a pretty good show. Frances agreed to be Colin's assistant for his magic act, and Tommy rehearsed a montage of popular hits on the piano.

'What if I do a speech from Shakespeare?' Beau asked.

'It might not fit in with the other acts, but it will fill a gap.'

'Yes,' they all agreed, and Beau, pleased, went off to decide which one to do.

At six o'clock, they came back to the house to have a light supper and change. Frances had brought in a girl from the village for the day to help Maggie and they got on so well that Maggie said it was a pity they couldn't keep her.

'I think we might,' said Frances. 'Let me talk it over with my father.'

'Pa,' she started, when she got up to the hall, but the doorbell rang and instead she went to answer it. It was Guy, standing in the snow, the taxi from the town tooting his horn as he went back down the drive.

'Guy!' she breathed, and let him take her in his arms. There was a collective intake of breath from the Players, who were having drinks with Lord Parnell by the roaring hall fire. They were as surprised as Frances's father.

'You are glad to see me, yes?' Guy asked.

'Of course.'

'You have missed me?'

'Have you missed me?' she countered.

'Yes,' he said. 'I have missed you very much. Now, will you introduce me to your father?'

They were a jolly company that evening, excited about the forthcoming show, but loving the idea about performing in a barn.

'I thought singing on boards, loosely balanced on oil drums, was alarming,' bellowed Godfrey, 'but the thought of all that hay flying about does take the biscuit.'

'You'll be fine,' said Tommy. 'Does Gertrude know where you are?'

'No, she doesn't, you dear old thing.' Godfrey looked over his shoulder as though he was scared that his wife was lurking in the corner. 'She thinks I'm still in France. I took up Colin's kind offer and have made my home with him, temporarily.'

Catherine chatted to Guy, while Frances handed round drinks and sandwiches. 'Why have you come?' she asked.

'To see Frances and to speak to her father. Do you know if he speaks French?'

Catherine smiled. 'Probably not.'

'Well, then can you do me a favour?'

Frances was surprised to see her father lead Catherine and Guy into the library and was about to follow them when Johnny came up the kitchen stairs and into the hall. 'Hello, Mummy,' he said. 'There are a lot of people in the house.'

They all came to say hello, and Tommy put a half-crown in the little boy's hand. 'Here you are, son. Buy some sweeties.'

Johnny looked at his mother with shining eyes and Beau, coming up behind them, said, 'That boy is the image of Johnny Petersham. Why didn't you say anything?'

'My mother wouldn't let me.'

He laughed. 'How is the countess? For that matter, where is the countess?'

'I have no idea,' said Frances with a grin, and then turned her head towards the door.

There was the sound of cars coming up the drive and Beau put down his drink. 'I'd better get my coat and direct them, and you lot must get a move on and change.'

It was when they were walking to the barn that Frances asked Catherine what she and Guy were doing earlier with her father.

'You'd be surprised,' said Catherine, with a conspiratorial smile. 'And that's all I'm going to say.'

The barn was full. Not only had the village turned out in force, but several rows of seats were taken up by the military convalescents. Beau's family sat on the front row with Lord Parnell, who looked as nervous as if he was one of the performers. Johnny was sitting on a hay bale, with Maggie beside him. 'Mummy!' he called, pink with excitement, as she stood by the stage, and she gave him a little wave.

Then Beau stepped to the front of the stage. 'Ladies and gentlemen,' he announced, 'some of you may know that I have been running a touring show. We play to factories and dockyards and to the military. Recently we came back from France, where we played to the brave soldiers at the front and to those in the field hospitals. It was an uplifting experience and also had its dangers. Sadly, one of our number was very badly injured and can't be with us tonight, but the rest of us are ready to give you an evening to remember.'

He turned and nodded to Catherine, and as she walked on stage, Tommy struck up with 'Smoke Gets In Your Eyes'. Her voice lilted over the barn, sweetly filling the place with melody, and soon the audience was singing along with her. Frances could see her father staring at Catherine with his mouth open, and Beau's father, Rolly Bennett, goggled at her and yelled, 'Bravo, little lady,' when she'd finished and, 'More!' before getting a fierce look from his wife.

Then Colin did his turn, which went so well that the audience howled with laughter. Frances could see Johnny on his feet jumping up and down and squealing at the fun, until Maggie grabbed him and put him on her knee.

Godfrey sang his favourite, 'On the Road to Mandalay', which everyone knew and loved, before Tommy played his medley.

'It's us next,' Frances said, suddenly nervous at singing in front of people she knew. 'My God, I'm scared.'

'No need to be,' whispered Catherine. 'You know you can do it.'

She could too, and stood beside Catherine as they sang 'Don't Sit Under the Apple Tree'. It missed Della's verve and her high soprano voice, but they sang in harmony and the audience loved it and cheered them to the old rafters. So much so that dust floated down, giving a hazy atmosphere that made the lamps that were strung over the tree and across the beams twinkle more softly.

They had a break then and Beau had arranged for a barrel of beer to be brought in with glasses borrowed from the pub. The men and women in the audience eagerly lined up for that, and some of the nurses who had come with wounded brought glasses back to them.

John Parnell caught up with his daughter at the back of the stage. 'Fran, my darling girl, you were terrific. I would never have guessed.' He bent and kissed her cheek.

'Pa,' she asked, 'what were you and Guy talking about earlier?'

'Oh,' he said, rubbing his hand through his salt-and-pepper hair, 'I think he should tell you that.' He looked beyond her. 'He's on his way now. I'll see you afterwards.'

'Frances.' Guy was standing behind her.

'Hello,' she smiled. 'I haven't had a moment to speak to you. What are you doing in England?'

'I've come to see you,' he said, 'but first I have to tell you that I'm going away for six months.'

'Six months? Where?'

'To the Pacific. To the French colonies.'

'But you can't,' she said. 'The Japs are fighting all over the Pacific.'

'Ah, but, you see, they have never attacked the French colonies. They meant to, but they were stretched too far. My government has asked me to go there to assess what these islands need. I think they have been starved of supplies. So I have agreed.'

'I didn't know you were part of the government,' she said, astonished.

'A very small part,' he smiled. 'But before I go, I have a question to ask you.'

'Yes, what?' She was amazed when he got down on one knee.

'Frances, *ma chérie*,' he said, 'I love you. Will you marry me?'

'What?' she said again, glancing around quickly to see if anyone was watching. Quite a few were, including Catherine, who was smiling like the Cheshire cat.

'Will you marry me? I don't want anyone else to step in while I'm away, because you are the one person I want to spend my life with.'

Frances swallowed and then said quickly, 'Get up, Guy – everyone's looking.'

'But you must answer,' he said.

'Alright,' she laughed, 'I will marry you. Now get up.'

'Good,' he said, and kissed her. 'I have spoken to your father. He has given his permission. Catherine did the translation...I am sorry that she knew before you, but' – he shrugged – 'it was the only way. Also...' He put his hand in his pocket and drew out another velvet-covered box, smaller this time. It contained a diamond engagement ring. 'It was my grandmother's and hidden down the well.'

'I guessed that,' she said, and watched as he slid it on her finger. She looked into his face and felt happiness wash over her. 'I love you,' she said, as Johnny Petersham's image finally faded into the background.

Soon they were surrounded by people coming to congratulate them. 'A fine young man,' said her father. 'Is that a real title, and has he money?'

'Yes, Pa. A hell of a lot more than you.'

Beau came to give her kiss and said, 'We must start the second half,' when there was a commotion by the barn door. 'Oh my God,' he groaned, 'who's this now? It can't be the police, can it? Have we broken some sort of bylaw? The beer, perhaps?'

It wasn't the police; it was Della. She was in a wheelchair with her broken leg stuck out in front of her. Dr Tim was wheeling her to the front and she was laughing with the excitement of it all.

'Della!' Catherine and Frances screamed, and hugged and kissed her. Then the other Players had a go, while the audience watched in astonishment.

'I wanted to come so much,' Della laughed. 'I persuaded Tim to bring me here. In an ambulance!'

Beau got up on the stage and held his hand up for silence. 'This brave young lady is Miss Della Stafford, one of our stars, who was blown up a month ago.' There was respectful applause and Beau held up his hand again. 'And now we'll get on with the show.'

If anything, it was better than the first half. The audience cheered everything, only calming down when Catherine sang '*J'attendrai*', both in French and English.

Frances looked around the barn until she could see Guy, standing at the side next to Maggie, who was holding a sleepy child. She nodded to him, indicating that the words meant something to her. He put his fingers to his lips and blew her a kiss. He'd understood.

Beau came on then and the audience paid respectful attention as he declaimed Henry's speech from the Battle of Agincourt. However, as it went on, they became engrossed, and when he ended on a grand swell with St Crispin's Day, they exploded to the rafters.

After that, Catherine and Frances went on stage to sing again, but Della called, 'Me too.'

'I don't think so,' said Dr Tim, looking concerned.

'I do,' Della replied firmly, and got him to manoeuvre her to the front and waited while the microphone was lowered and chairs brought for the other two girls. 'What have you rehearsed?' she asked.

'"Boogie Woogie Bugle Boy,"' said Catherine. 'Can you manage it?'

'I think so,' Della said. 'My chest is fine. It's the bloody leg that's holding me back. OK, let's do it.'

Frances nodded to Tommy and they sang. It was like old times. Della was fine, posing as well as anyone in a wheelchair could and waving encouragement to the audience. When they'd finished, everybody yelled their appreciation and the girls bowed and blew kisses.

'I'm buggered,' Della whispered, and Tim wheeled her away to recover at the back of the barn.

'You finish, Catherine,' said Beau. 'Send them home happy.'

'Alright.' She stood beside the piano and looked out over the audience as she started to sing 'The Very Thought of You' and heard the groan of contentment that happened when audiences recognised a song they loved. She walked, still singing, off the stage and along the narrow aisle between the chairs and hay bales until she reached the back and came face to face with a man standing in the shadow. It was Robert. Her heart was turning over so fast that she almost missed a beat, but her professionalism kicked in and she carried on singing until she was back on the stage again.

It was a triumph. Congratulations rang out, and the Players had their hands shaken many times.

It was an hour before Catherine was free. They had gone back into the hall, where Maggie had done a buffet of game pie and baked potatoes, which the Players and their guests fell upon with delight.

'I need to talk to you,' said Robert, and opening a door, led Catherine into the empty drawing room and took her in his arms.

He held her so tightly that she felt dizzy and knew something was wrong. She pulled her face away from him and said, 'What is it? You're different.'

It was a long moment while she waited for him to speak. 'I've been in France,' he said finally. 'I've found Christopher.'

'Oh.' Her hand went to her mouth. 'You found his grave?'

He shook his head, his eyes drilling into hers. 'No, my love, I've found him. He is alive.'

Chapter 27

They drove along the same street, where, all those months ago, she'd sat miserably beside Guy, trying to take in the murder of her grandfather and the apparent loss of mind of her grandmother. Past the cafe where she'd been forced by Frances to eat up her omelette, and the market square, nearly empty this cold afternoon, for the citizens of Amiens had hurried away home through the flakes of snow that drifted in on an east wind.

'Are you alright?' asked Robert, looking up at the street name and then turning off the main road into the narrow side street.

'Yes.'

'You sure?'

'Stop asking me,' Catherine muttered. 'You know how I feel.'

'I'm sorry.'

Ahead, she could see the steps leading up to the convent door and thought of Della, cowed at first by the nuns and then, when they were leaving, giving them a rude gesture. Frances hadn't been cowed at all; she'd been determined, solidly brave and resourceful. How very strange it was to be coming back here.

'We've found him,' Robert had said on that night after the show had finished and they were together in the drawing room at Parnell Hall.

'Where?' she asked, her voice dull. She couldn't understand why she wasn't more excited. This is what she'd been yearning for. Christopher alive.

'In Amiens. In the convent where you rescued your grandmother.'

'What?' she breathed, staring at his face, trying to make sense of what he was saying. 'He was there then? And I was so close to him,' she said wildly. 'Oh God, I should have gone from room to room, yelling out his name. I could have brought him home months ago.'

'No. He wasn't there then. Believe me, my love. He was at a hospital miles away being looked after, quite well, it would seem. He was moved to Amiens only a month ago, when they needed the space for acute injuries.'

'But why didn't you know? Didn't anybody ask his name?' She looked at him with exhausted eyes. 'Why didn't he tell them who he was?'

Robert had pulled her down onto the torn sofa and taken her hands in his. 'Darling, Christopher has suffered a head injury. He has lost his speech and, it seems, the ability to write or communicate in any way. We think it happened when the prison was bombed. He must have had a severe blow to his head, for apparently he was unconscious for several weeks. He is conscious now; his eyes are open, but there is nothing...' He stopped, frowning, and she knew he was wondering how to go on.

'Tell me.'

Robert took a deep breath. 'It's as if he was still asleep.'

'I must go to him.'

'Yes, I know. I'll take you.'

And here they were, eight days later, in that cold, uncertain time between Christmas and New Year, pulling up in front of the convent steps, and Catherine could feel her hands shaking.

'Please come in,' said the little porteress nun who had opened the door. 'Reverend Mother is expecting you.'

It was the same walk along the icy corridor, the same timid knock on the door, and when it swung open, it was the same tall, imposing figure who rose from behind her desk.

'Good afternoon, Madame Fletcher,' she said, her voice softer than Catherine remembered. 'And to you, Major.'

'I have come to see my husband,' said Catherine, trying to put some flint into her voice. She found that she was holding her breath. Would Mother Paul object like she had last time?

'Of course.' The nun rose to her feet. 'We have made him ready. Follow me.'

It was a shaky walk up the staircase and Catherine had to reach out for Robert's hand.

'Don't be frightened,' he whispered.

Mother Paul stopped at the door to the day room where Béatrice had been. A nun who was standing against the wall beside the door gave Catherine a brief smile. 'Lieutenant Fletcher is here, madame.' She reached out her hand to touch Catherine's sleeve. 'Please do not expect too much. It is possible that he will not know you.' And she turned the handle and opened the door.

He was sitting on a chair by the window, his shoulders covered by a thin brown blanket. As she walked nervously towards him, Catherine could see a scar on the back of his head, which had scored a line through his straw-coloured hair. For a moment, she thought, I can't do this, and looked back over her shoulder to where Robert was standing by the door, but he nodded his encouragement and she took a deep breath and walked on.

The nuns had put a chair in front of Christopher's and she sat on it and gazed at her husband for the first time in eighteen months.

He looked exactly the same. His strong face, untidy, thick blond hair and intelligent blue eyes were just as she remembered and had dreamt about.

'Hello, Chris, darling,' she said, smiling. 'I've found you at last.'

Her heart thumped in her chest while she waited for him to turn towards her and give her that old familiar grin. He'd wake up from his dream and grab her, holding her in a firm grasp, and kiss her face, her neck, and tell her how much he loved her.

But nothing happened. It was as if she hadn't spoken. He stared ahead, moving his head slightly so that she wasn't in the way of what he was looking at. Catherine turned to see what it was. There was a hook on the door to the cell bedroom on which someone had hung a string of rosary beads, which glinted slightly where the light from a small lamp caught them.

'Chris,' she tried again. 'It's me, Catherine.' And taking his hand in hers, she leant forward to kiss him on the cheek.

He didn't move, didn't acknowledge the kiss and let his hand lie limply in hers.

'Chris, Christopher!' She raised her voice. 'Look at me. I'm Catherine, your wife.'

'Madame.' Mother Paul had come to stand beside her

413

and put her hand on Catherine's shoulder. 'Please don't shout. It will make no difference. He has...turned off, inside.'

'No,' she cried, shrugging off the nun's thin hand. 'He must know me. Look.' She opened her handbag and took out a photograph of Lili. 'This is our daughter,' she said, and held it up in front of Christopher's eyes. 'It's Lili. She can walk now. She says "Mama" and "Papa". You would love her.'

But he looked straight through the picture as though it was invisible to him. 'Christopher,' she wailed, 'please, please look at it.' But it made no difference, and with tears welling into her eyes, her shaking hand dropped to her lap and the photograph slid to the floor.

She was sobbing now and Robert walked in and took her into his arms. 'We'll take him home,' he said. 'With the right treatment, who knows? He might return to you.'

Catherine nodded, but, still sobbing, tore herself away and knelt in front of Christopher and wrapped her arms around him. 'I love you, Chris,' she whispered, burying her head in his neck, and felt dizzy as the remembered clean smell of him filled her nostrils. For a moment, she thought she had got through to him, for he lifted his arm as though to hold her close, but his hand went past her back and onto his face to brush her hair out of his face. She seemed to be only an annoyance to him.

'I think that is enough for now, madame,' said Mother Paul, and her voice softened. 'For both of you.' She raised her finger and the nun who had been hovering in the corridor came forward and, putting her arm under Christopher's elbow, raised him up and walked him towards the bedroom.

'Come on, Catherine,' said Robert quietly. 'Let's go.'

Back in Mother Paul's office, Catherine and Robert filled in the forms that would allow Christopher's transfer to a military hospital in England.

'Do you know how he got to the hospital in Amiens?' Robert asked.

'I believe, Major,' Mother Paul said, 'that he was picked up by a citizen who was clearing the rubble. He was taken to a monastery south of here, where the brothers, bravely assisted by surgeons from the hospital, cared for him. After the liberation, he was transferred to the hospital for further treatment. I think, perhaps, that his condition deteriorated in that time. It was not the brothers' fault. They had little equipment, only love for their fellow man.'

She turned her attention to Catherine. 'And dear Madame Albert. She is well?' she asked.

Catherine nodded. 'She is very well, in England with my mother. They will be coming back to France soon.' She couldn't bring herself to smile at the reverend mother. The memory of Béatrice being force to swallow chloral hydrate was still burning in her mind. 'Why did you drug her?' she asked suddenly, and Robert, who was writing on the form, heard the distress in her voice and looked up.

Mother Paul frowned. 'I was following Father Gautier's instructions. He told me that the memories of what she'd seen were too hard to bear. She should not have to think about them.'

'What had she seen?' Robert's question cut through the sterile atmosphere.

The nun folded her lips and looked down at her empty

desk. Eventually she said, 'Father Gautier was a good man. He was forced to do the things he did. It was one death or fifty deaths. At the end, Monsieur Albert offered to be the one. He saved the village.'

'That's not what my grandmother says,' Catherine spoke hotly.

'She didn't know. Father Gautier told me that she was held inside the house when Monsieur Albert was shot. She didn't see or hear the conversation. Only the shot. She saw her husband when he was already dead and the Germans were taking her to prison.'

Catherine looked at Robert. 'I don't believe that,' she cried. 'What sort of man or priest lies to a bereaved old woman?'

'A frightened man,' said Robert. 'One who knew that his crimes would haunt him for the rest of his life.' He looked at Mother Paul. 'He was the one who shot Monsieur Albert, yes?'

She nodded slowly. 'He had begged for the lives of the villagers, and that was the condition. But, madame, monsieur, believe me' – a passion had come into her voice for the first time – 'he was a good man. A man of faith.'

As they drove away, Catherine leant her head on Robert's shoulder. She felt tired and unable to think clearly any more. Seeing Christopher, the person she'd yearned for, so changed, and so unresponsive to her, had been devastating. She didn't know how to live with it. My husband is alive, she told herself, and I must care for him, but...I love Robert. How can I bear it?

Epilogue

August 1945

'I've been asked to be in a film, starting next year,' said Catherine. The three girls were at Parnell Hall for the weekend. 'But I can't act. At least, I don't think I can.'

'None of them can,' Della had said with a dismissive wave of her hand. 'Not in the sort of films you'll be doing. But you'll look beautiful and sing like an angel.'

'And, of course,' Frances added in her practical way, 'the money will be fantastic.'

Catherine laughed. Frances always worried about money, even now when she had more coming in.

Guy had settled an allowance for Frances, a sort of dowry in reverse, which John Parnell had been too proud, at first, to accept. But Guy had persuaded him and the hall and the farms were much improved. They had a beef herd, which Frances managed, and her father was becoming devoted to his pigs once more.

'He's quite batty about those blessed pigs,' grumbled Frances, as the three girls walked across the parkland back to the hall. 'He talks of nothing else.'

'He's happy,' said Della. 'That's what matters.'

She was walking well now, with a slight limp, but earlier she'd demonstrated her tap-dancing skills on the Minton tiles in the hall, startling Lord Parnell and causing Catherine and Frances to beg her to stop in case she hindered her recovery. 'Don't be mad,' she laughed. 'It's what Tim calls physio…physio…well, physio something. It's good for me. But I don't think I'll ever be able to do the splits again.'

'I don't suppose there'll be much call for it in that place in Ireland,' said Frances. 'What would the mammy think?'

Della scowled. 'She's a right old bitch. When I'm at their place, it takes me all my time not to fetch my hands to her throat. D'you know,' she said reflectively, 'there's something about her that reminds me of Captain Fortescue. It's those bloody black eyebrows jerking up and down every time she opens her mouth to say something nasty.'

That description made the other two burst into laughter and soon Della joined in.

'When's the wedding, then?' asked Frances. 'You know we can't wait to be bridesmaids.'

'Oh Christ,' said Della, 'not until next year. Tim's being posted to the Far East, now that the Jap war is over. It seems that the POWs are in a hellish way and need all the care they can get.' She stopped suddenly and put her hand over her mouth. 'I'm sorry, Frances. I didn't think. Have you heard anything about Hugo?'

Frances shook her head, tears coming into her eyes. 'Nothing, really. The Red Cross had his name on a list at one camp and then he was moved and they're still trying to track him down. But at least he was alive last year, so that's something.'

Her friends gave her a hug and she wiped her eyes and smiled. They are wonderful, she thought. Closer than family.

'And wedding bells for you, Frances?' Catherine asked. 'When will they be?'

'Again, next year,' sighed Frances. 'Guy's mission in the Pacific hasn't finished. I think it's been more difficult than he or his government expected. But he writes all the time. Good letters, full of descriptions. He makes it all come so alive.'

Johnny and Lili came running across the parkland. He was growing by the day and full of energy, and Lili, more delicate, toddled along behind him. She lived at the hall now that Honorine and Béatrice had returned to France. Catherine had paid for a nanny to take care of both children, and in return, Frances had given her an apartment in the house, so that she could make it her base. It suited them all. John Parnell was a loving grandfather to both children, and Maggie and young Thelma, the new maid, spoilt them desperately.

'I wonder if we'll have children. I mean, more children,' said Della. There was a wistful tone to her voice. 'I'd love to have a baby. One that I could bring up.'

She had told them the thing that was the closest secret she'd had, but only after Tim had been told and had accepted it. One day, when they were reminiscing about their time in France, she blurted out, 'You remember me being so scared of the nuns in that place where Béatrice and Christopher was?'

'Yes,' they nodded in unison.

'Well, I was locked in a convent once.'

'What?' They looked at her in astonishment.

Della swallowed. 'I got pregnant and Ma sent me to Ireland to have it so that no one would know. It was the most terrible place; it makes me shudder to even think of it. And when it came time to deliver her, they wouldn't call a doctor but just dragged her out of me. She was barely alive and so badly damaged.'

Catherine and Frances looked at each other. 'You can't be talking about Maria,' Frances said. 'Your sister.'

Della nodded.

'But she must be eleven or twelve now.'

'I was nearly fifteen,' Della whispered. 'Only a kid, really. Ma came to get me, and when she saw Maria, she had a fit. Called the nuns for everything and said we were bringing her home, even though they'd arranged for her to go into a mental hospital. That's what they did for children who were like her.'

'But who was her father?' asked Catherine, bewildered.

'No guesses there,' Frances said. 'Jerry Costigan.'

Della nodded again. 'I was stupid. I'd won some dance competitions and he said he could get me into show business, if I was nice to him. So I was.'

'What did Tim say?' Catherine asked, putting her arm around Della's shoulder.

'Oh, he's fine about it.' Della grinned, returning to her old self. 'It happens all the time, he says, and it doesn't stop him loving me. Isn't he great?' She got up and did a twirl. 'But,' she added, 'we won't tell the mammy.'

Now, in the parkland, Frances thought about that conversation. Poor Della, she thought, having to keep a secret for so long, and then she laughed. Didn't I do the same?

'Have you spoken to Beau?' Catherine asked her. 'He wants us to tour again.'

'Yes,' Frances said. 'That's why I wanted you two here this weekend. He's talking about a four-month tour to the Far East, based in Singapore. He's contacted all the gang. Godfrey and Colin are up for it, but Tommy has cried off. He's not very well, and with his heart condition, the long flights would be murder, literally. But we've got a replacement,' she smiled. 'Someone you know.'

'Who?' asked Catherine. 'Someone from a dance band?'

'No. Felix Strange. He's partially blind, but he can play anything. You should hear him – he's brilliant, and he's in uniform.'

'Wow,' said Della. She turned to Catherine. 'What d'you think?'

'I...don't know,' she said. 'I've got nothing booked that I can't get out of, but...'

'It's up to you, darling,' said Frances.

'But it wouldn't be the same without our star,' Della grinned.

Catherine walked down the drive until she reached the gates. There was a soldier guarding the entrance and he grinned at her, recognising her as the young woman who'd visited every week. His mate said that she was a singer and showed him a cutting from a forces paper that had a photograph of the Bennett Players standing beside their bus.

'Good afternoon, miss,' he said, and she gave him a brief smile as he opened the gate for her.

Robert was standing across the road beside his car. 'Are you alright?' he asked, and didn't mention the tear streaks on her face. 'How is he?'

'You know how he is,' Catherine replied. 'You've seen him. There is nothing there. Nothing. He's a ventriloquist's dummy.' She winced as the thought of Captain Fortescue came to her.

'Did you speak to the doctor?'

'I did,' she sighed. 'He said that one day things might change, but I wasn't to hope. That was exactly what he said last time.'

'You've got him back, Catherine. That's what you wanted.'

'Yes,' she said. 'But I haven't got him, have I? Not really.' I'm still in limbo, she thought. Nothing's changed. She glanced at Robert, who was concentrating on driving through the London traffic back to the flat they shared near Regent's Park. She loved him so much and knew that he felt the same. The fact that they were both trapped seemed to have brought them even closer, and she smiled and put her hand on his leg.

He reached down to take it and drew it up to his mouth for a loving kiss. 'I thought we might go to France for a few days,' he said. 'Would you like that?'

'I'd love it,' Catherine said. 'And then, when we come back, I can get ready.'

'You're going, then?'

She smiled. 'I'm part of the Bennett Players. They can't let them tour without me.'

What Tomorrow Brings

Mary Fitzgerald

August 1937

Seffy Blake falls in love with Amyas Troy the moment she sees him on a Cornish beach. But when he disappears, she is forced to face the aftermath of their affair alone.

In London, Seffy makes a new life for herself working as an assistant to journalist Charlie Bradford, and as Europe hurtles towards war, it is Charlie who sees her through her darkest times.

But when Amyas reappears, Seffy must decide whether to follow her heart, or accept her genuine love for Charlie and keep what remains of her family safe from the terrifying consequences of war.

arrow books

Mist

Mary Fitzgerald

A beautiful romance set in the breathtaking Welsh mountains

When Matthew Williams, a young Canadian, inherits a hill farm in North Wales he leaves his college course and flies to the UK to take up his inheritance. But the farm he has inherited is run down, and with no knowledge of farming, Matthew relies on Lark, a traveller girl he meets in the village, to help him.

For Lark, Matthew's farm is the first steady home she has known for years, and enchanted by the countryside, she throws herself into getting the farm back on its feet.

But when Matthew's father arrives suddenly from Canada, none of their lives will be the same again.

arrow books

When I Was Young

Mary Fitzgerald

'When I was young the war started. When I was young my father was a soldier. When I was young I went to France and fell in love.'

1950

Eleanor is seventeen when she goes to stay on a vineyard in the Loire Valley. But the beauty of her surroundings is at odds with the family who live there. It is a family torn apart by the terrible legacy of war, and poisoned by the secrets they keep.

Despite his forbidding manner, Eleanor is drawn to Etienne, the dark and brooding owner, though his wife's malicious behaviour overshadows everyone's lives. But when death comes to the vineyard, Eleanor finds her faith in her new-found love is tested to the limits.

arrow books

ALSO AVAILABLE IN ARROW

The Love of a Lifetime

Mary Fitzgerald

Sometimes love is not enough

From the moment Elizabeth Nugent arrives to live on his family's farm in Shropshire, Richard Wilde is in love with her. And as they grow up, it seems like nothing can keep them apart.

But as World War II rages, Richard goes to fight in the jungles of Burma, leaving Elizabeth to deal with a terrible secret that could destroy his family.

Despite the distance between them, though, Richard and Elizabeth's love remains constant through war, tragedy and betrayal.

But once the fighting is over, will the secrets and lies that Elizabeth has been hiding keep them apart for ever?

arrow books

THE POWER OF READING

Visit the Random House website and get connected with information on all our books and authors

EXTRACTS from our recently published books and selected backlist titles

COMPETITIONS AND PRIZE DRAWS Win signed books, audiobooks and more

AUTHOR EVENTS Find out which of our authors are on tour and where you can meet them

LATEST NEWS on bestsellers, awards and new publications

MINISITES with exclusive special features dedicated to our authors and their titles

READING GROUPS Reading guides, special features and all the information you need for your reading group

LISTEN to extracts from the latest audiobook publications

WATCH video clips of interviews and readings with our authors

RANDOM HOUSE INFORMATION including advice for writers, job vacancies and all your general queries answered

Come home to Random House

www.randomhouse.co.uk